The Girl On The Quay

Colin Youngman

This is a work of fiction.

All characters and events are products of the author's imagination.

All locations – except one - are real although some liberties have been taken with architectural design, precise geographic features, and timelines.

Cover Image courtesy of

Adam Lang

©Lang Shot Photography

A SprintS Publication

Copyright 2020 © Colin Youngman

All rights reserved.

No part of this publication, paperback or e-book, may be reproduced, stored in a retrieval system, or transmitted, in any form or in any means – by written, electronic, mechanical, photocopying, recording or otherwise – without prior written permission of the author.

ISBN -13: 979-8-65367-018-3

Colin Youngman

DEDICATION

For you.

You know who you are.

Colin Youngman

'Being born is like being kidnapped and then sold into slavery.'

Andy Warhol

'You may choose to look the other way, but you can never say again that you did not know.'

William Wilberforce

CHAPTER ONE

2.05am
MARCH 22nd

The match flared bright in the darkness of Pirate's Cave. The man inhaled deeply as his cigarette accepted the flame. He flicked the match into the waters lapping at his feet and watched it bob and dip with the current.

'How long?' he asked. The echo repeated his question twice.

A reply came from a mouth hidden within the depths of a Hoxton beard. 'Tides turned now. Give it another fifteen minutes or so and we're good to go.'

The smoker lowered himself onto an algae-slicked rock and waited in a silence broken only by the steady breathing of an ebb tide. He ran his eyes over the launch which rocked in the black water alongside them. 'You good to go, Russ?'

A third man busied himself in a Pescador 430, swilling down the deck. 'Aye, boss; we are. How many units are we expecting?'

The boss, Adam Haines, shrugged, ash falling from the tip of his cigarette. 'He said six, but we'll only know for sure when we dock.'

Distracted, the man called Russ caught the back of his hand on a rusty bolt. He cursed. 'Six, you say.' He whistled. 'That's pushing it, man.' He wiped his bleeding hand on an oily rag. 'With the three of us, she'll not take any more. Half a dozen max. Anymore, we leave behind.'

Haines nodded, invisible in the gloom. He tossed away his cigarette. 'Howay. It's close enough. Let's go.'

Russ balled the bloodied rag and threw it onto rocks high above the waterline. He slicked back wet hair, unwound the ropes, and steadied the launch as the other two hopped aboard. Haines and Manville grabbed boat hooks and levered the craft away from the rocks as Russ used the tiller to manoeuvre it through the shallow waters of the cave, out into the restless North Sea.

Once they were beyond the confines of the cave, Russ hauled on the motor. The bow lifted slightly, and the launch set off on an S-shaped trail away from the Durham coast; out towards a fishing vessel anchored less than a mile off Blackhall Rocks.

The three sat in silence, watching the lights of small craft in the distance twinkle like cat's eyes beneath a moonless sky. Further out, the hulks of massive freight carriers traversed between Tyne, Wear, and Tees like lost souls.

Half a mile offshore, Haines grabbed a flashlight and held it against his chest. He flicked the beam twice, then once more, leaving the light on several seconds before he extinguished it.

The three men scanned the ocean. Nothing.

The flashlight repeated the action: flash flash. Flash.

'There. Look!' Russ pointed an arm at a two o'clock angle where the lights of a boat flicked on and off three times. 'That's her.'

Haines smiled. 'We're in business.'

The men resumed their silence as the launch bounced over the rolling sea towards its target. As they approached, the boss spoke again. 'Remember what the Mayan said. He suspects this one might get messy.'

'Any reason why this should be any different to the others?'

'He didn't say. And I know better than to ask. Just be prepared, that's all.'

Russ cut the motor and let the tide drift the launch towards the fishing boat.

Faces appeared over the bows. Arms gestured. Mouths shouted instructions. In the wind and spray, their words drifted away like breath in a frost.

The Pescador bumped against the larger vessel. Began to swing away from it. The three men in the launch grabbed at a cargo net hanging from the trawler and, hand-over-hand, hauled the launch back towards it.

Russ deftly hitched their craft to the fishing boat and swayed out the way as a rope ladder hit the deck.

'Manny, you're with me,' Haines instructed the bearded man. 'Russ - you stay aboard ready to take the goods. And, remember what the Mayan said. Messy, yeah?' Haines grabbed a flare-gun and tucked it behind him into his belt as he clambered up the ladder. John 'Manny' Manville tugged at his beard and followed.

At the top, a man with wild, black hair offered Haines a hand and hauled him aboard. The trawlerman – Jason Momoa in an Arran roll-neck – spoke in perfect English but with guttural Dutch overtones. 'Welcome aboard. I take it you're Haines?'

'Aye, that's me,' the boss said. 'And you are?'

'That's not important. I work for Luuk. That's all you need know.'

Adam Haines shrugged. 'Suit yersel, pal.' He looked around the fishing boat. It was at least four times the size of their own. 'How many crew you got for this thing?'

'The three of us here,' Luuk's man said. 'And two below.'

Haines and Manny exchanged glances. 'What about our consignment?'

'Four.'

'That's not good. We were told six.'

'Luuk said you were getting four. And you're lucky to get that many. He says you defaulted on payment for the last consignment. This is your last chance, he says.'

Adam Haines held up his hands. 'Hey, nothing to do with me, bud. I'm just the carrier.'

The Dutchman nodded. 'Ja. But Luuk says he expects payment, plus interest, within twenty-four hours.'

'Like I say, nothing to do with me. So, are we getting our cargo or not?'

The Dutchman stared at Haines for a while. Almost imperceptibly, he nodded. Stood aside. He motioned for the other two crewmen to move forward.

Haines tensed. He saw Manny do the same. But the deckhands moved past them to a cargo hold. They slid open rusted bolts and heaved at the door. As they did so, Adam and Manny retched. The smell of fish washed over them with the force of a tsunami.

But the hold was empty. At least, empty of fish.

A fourth crew member clambered out the hold. He dragged the first unit behind him: a filthy, bedraggled, and stinking young woman. She looked around wide-eyed and terrified. Another followed, equally filthy, equally frightened. She may have been of Thai or Filipino extract, but it was impossible to tell beneath the grime.

The Dutchman escorted them to the rail of the ship. Helped them onto the rope ladder. Watched them struggle down to where the launch bucked and pitched like an unbroken colt.

Russ took their hands and helped them aboard. The girls immediately made for the stern, as far away from him as possible, and huddled together as if they were conjoined twins.

When Russ looked back up at the trawler, two more women clung to the ladder and made tentative steps towards him. He noticed all four women had something in common, apart from the stench and squalor.

Beneath it all, they were stunningly beautiful.

With the four girls aboard the launch, Haines and Manny prepared to leave. The Dutchman stepped forward, hand outstretched. Haines took it. 'Remember the message,' the Dutchman said. 'Tell the Mayan what Luuk says: he expects to see the money in his account this time tomorrow.'

'And if not? What do I tell him will happen?'

'Luuk says, 'what the lord giveth, the lord taketh away.'

'What the fuck's that supposed to mean?'

The Dutchman raised his shoulders. 'I don't know but let's hope the Mayan does, ja? In the meantime, don't shoot the messenger.'

Haines reached behind him. 'That's exactly what I am going to do.'

He whipped the flare gun from his belt. Held it against the Dutchman's chest. Discharged it at point blank range. An orange ball of flame passed straight through the man's chest and dropped into the broiling sea with a serpentine hiss.

The Dutchman stared down at a sweater singed around the edges of a jagged black hole where his chest had once been.

At the same instant, Manny whipped out an Uzi and sprayed the other trawlermen. Blood spewed as the men kicked and convulsed on the deck. A fourth crew member poked his head through the hold opening; a head which exploded like a ripe tomato. The final crewman emerged through a deck hatch. Hands aloft. Crying. Shaking. Urinating.

Manny ensured it was the last thing his body did.

One-by-one, Haines dragged the fishermen across the deck, their blood decorating it like a Jackson Pollock canvas. He fastened their ankles to fire extinguishers, iceboxes, bilge pumps – any heavy portable device to hand - and let them slip silently into the frigid depths of the North Sea.

Satisfied, he climbed down the rope ladder, jumped onto the launch, and smiled. 'Good evening, ladies. I trust you had a pleasant trip.'

He pulled out a cigarette and lit up.

CHAPTER TWO

2.05am
TWO WEEKS LATER

The undulating mass of the River Tyne slapped against the quay wall. In the dead of night, it beat out the solemn requiem of a funeral march. Only the occasional muffled sound of a lonesome vehicle rattling over the Tyne Bridge disturbed the river's metronomic rhythm.

Rain fell. It riddled the shifting surface like a hail of machine-gun fire. The illuminated arches of the river's bridges sprinkled slivers of light which distorted in puddles formed along the length of the riverside.

In the silence, the heels of the girl walking upriver echoed as loud as a harem of horses. She didn't care. There was no-one to hear. The girl paused for a moment. Leant on the railings and stared into the murky waters of the Tyne.

She raised her head and looked to the opposite bank where the illuminated, post-modern blobitecture of the Sage concert venue cast its peanut-husk reflection over the river. To the woman, it looked for all the world like a used condom. The woman shuddered.

Abruptly, she straightened and lowered her umbrella. She tilted her face skywards and felt the rain wash over her. She stayed that way for several minutes, until her face ran with rainwater and her clothes clung to her slender frame.

Cleansed at last, she set off once more.

Her friends cautioned her against walking alone. Frowned at her for doing so. Warned her of the dangers. But they didn't know what she did for a living. A solo walk along the quayside was a hell of a lot safer than the last few hours she'd spent in an Ouseburn Airbnb apartment with three men she'd never met before.

She trembled again. Lost in thought, she stepped off the kerb as a Premier Inn laundry wagon inched its way down the narrow confines of an alley midway between Lombard and King Streets. The driver touched the brakes, the hiss causing the woman to step back onto the footpath. Embarrassed, the woman beckoned the vehicle through.

Behind the truck, a white transit van trundled forward. Its driver motioned the girl across. She acknowledged the courtesy with a cheery wave.

The van drew to a halt. The driver peered left and right, checking it was safe to pull out. When the rear doors of the van slammed shut, he knew it was.

The driver stamped on the accelerator. In the blink of an eye, the van was gone.

So, too, the girl.

**

Ryan Jarrod picked up a pile of folders from a tray and moved them to a second tray on the other side of his desk. He withdrew another stack of files from inside his drawer and began sorting through them.

'There's got to more to it than this,' he muttered to himself.

For the first time, he began to have serious doubts about the career he'd yearned for years. He let his mind wander. Tried to focus on the benefits of the job. The salary, for one. He'd soon be in a position to upgrade his scruffy Uno to something more appropriate. He really should think about moving out, too. A detective still living with his dad and brother? Nah, that didn't fit.

He knew there was a house waiting for him in his home village, but moving into The Drive didn't seem right, somehow. It held memories. Besides, by rights it still belonged to his grandmother. And they might yet need to sell it to pay her fees.

He sighed. Yawned. Rose from his desk and popped coins into a coffee dispenser.

'Aal reet?' Detective Constable Todd Robson asked from behind.

'Aye. I suppose so.'

'Don't tell me you're disenchanted already. It's only been a couple of months. Wait until you've had years of it like the rest of us poor buggers.'

'I've been here nearly four months, actually. And, to be honest, it's not like it said in the brochure. If I'd wanted to do paperwork all day, I could have stayed in the Civil Service and not work stupid hours.'

Todd Robson laughed, the skin tightening around the scar on his cheek. 'Welcome to the real world, son. It's not all shit and giggles after all, is it?'

Ryan expelled air in a snort and removed the Styrofoam cup, swearing as hot liquid spilled over his tender hands.

'I see they're still giving you gip,' Robson commented.

'Aye. A bit sore today. Some days are better than others.'

Ryan's thoughts drifted back to a time before he'd been accepted into the force; a time when he'd tried in vain to save a girl from the inferno of an office fire. A time when his efforts rewarded him with nothing more than agonising burns and even more painful memories.

He looked at the pink flesh of his skin grafts and shrugged. 'Still, I guess I wouldn't be here today if it weren't for them.'

Todd gave Ryan a playful cuff on the ear. 'So, stop your whingeing, then, and get on with the paperwork. The files won't get to Foreskin by themselves.'

'Indeed, they won't.' The voice came from across the bullpen where DCI Stephen Danskin stood framed in a doorway. 'Can I have a word, Jarrod? In here.'

'Looks like the Golden Boy's in trouble,' Todd smirked. 'Careful or you'll get garrotted by that slipped halo of yours.'

Ryan gave Todd the finger as he slipped into Danskin's office.

Danskin motioned to a chair. 'Sit down, Ryan. And don't look so worried. There's nowt wrong.'

'This isn't my worried look, sir. It's my bored look. It's got to the stage where I'm thinking about ringing some random blokes in India to ask if they've had an accident anytime in the last three years, just for summat to do.'

Stephen Danskin laughed. The minty antiseptic smell of mouthwash, the DCI's alcohol substitute, washed over Ryan. Danskin scratched the stubble on his jaw as he studied the rookie detective opposite him. 'Listen, I'm supposed to have these chats with everybody once a month. Yours has slipped a bit.'

'By about 400%.'

'How, man. Divvent get cheeky.' He said it good-humouredly, but Ryan got the message.

'Sorry, sir. You were saying?'

'I was saying, I'm supposed to have a chat with you all every month. One-to-one, like. Ongoing appraisal and all that shite. I'm not much good at it and nobody's bothered so it doesn't happen often.'

Ryan looked uncomfortable. 'Right. So, you wouldn't be doing this because I'm going out with your stepdaughter, would you? I don't want any special treatment. It's hard enough getting respect from the likes of Todd as it is.'

Danskin maintained both silence and eye contact. Finally, he spoke. 'No, I bloody-well wouldn't. And, remember, only Lyall knows Hannah's me stepdaughter and I'd prefer you kept it that way. I don't want DC Graves to be treated any differently out there,' he wafted a hand in the direction of the bullpen. 'No, I want to know how you're doing. Nip any problems in the bud, so to speak, what with your probation ending next month and all.'

Ryan gave it some thought. The thought lasted all of a second. 'Like I said, I'm bored, if I'm honest. Thought there'd be more to it than this.'

'You were spoilt by the Tyrant case,' Danskin said. 'It's not all shit and giggles, you know.'

'That's the same phrase Todd used.'

'Jeez, take me outside and shoot me if I ever repeat any more of Robson's sayings. I've been working with him for too long.' Danskin considered for a moment. Scratched the back of his head. 'But I meant what I said. The Tyneside Tyrant was a one-off. I've been in the force best part of quarter of a century and never come across a case like that.' He paused. When he continued, it was almost as if he spoke to himself. 'And I hope I never do again.'

The Tyneside Tyrant case still haunted much of the region, and all the City and County force. The reign of terror ended little more than eighteen months ago and would stay fresh in the memory for decades to come. Ryan had been a Special Constable at the time. He'd become embroiled with the case – and DCI Danskin's step-daughter – when he'd uncovered crucial evidence and Danskin had invited him into the investigation.

'Anyway,' Danskin continued, 'How you are getting along with O'Hara?' Danskin had assigned a Detective to mentor Ryan in the early days.

'Gavin's alright. Showing me the ropes, he is. But the ropes aren't long enough. I've nowt meaty to get me teeth into.'

'Son, I can't give you what isn't there. I'm not going out to rob a bank just to give you summat to do.'

Ryan smiled. 'I'm pleased. Not sure Hannah would forgive me when I tracked you down. Because I would. Don't think you'd get away with it.'

Danskin rocked back and forth in his chair. 'I'm sure you would. You're good, Ryan. That's why I encouraged you to apply for the fast-track scheme. I like your confidence.' He stopped rocking. Leant forward. 'But don't mistake confidence for cockiness. That'll get you in a whole load of trouble.'

Ryan felt his face colour. Bugger. He thought he'd overcome the family trait. 'No, sir. Or yes, sir – whatever the correct response is.'

'Ok, then, Detective Constable Jarrod; see what you can do

with this.' The DCI slid a file over the desk. 'Missing person. An adult, so probably not missing at all, really. See what you come up with. It's debateable whether it should be our case or uniform at this stage. I was going to pass it back to them but seeing you're whinging your tits off; you can have it.'

'Thank you, sir. Who do I report to? DS Nairn?'

Danskin shook his head. 'I don't think there's any need to bother Sue yet. No, I'm happy for you fly solo. At least, for now. Any of the lads will give you a bit of advice if you need it. And O'Hara's always there for support.'

'Great. I'll get cracking, then.'

'What is it we have to remember, Ryan?'

'*'Don't see what you expect to see'*. That's your mantra, isn't it?'

'It is. That, and my new one: 'Don't get cocky'. He smiled at Ryan. 'Now, first priority is your paperwork. Get those files to me asap before you take it on. Understand, Detective Constable Jarrod?'

'Yes, sir.'

Ryan left Danskin's office in a lighter mood than when he arrived. He liked being called Detective Constable Jarrod. But he liked the sound of Detective Sergeant Jarrod more.

Or was that being cocky?

CHAPTER THREE

Ryan hurriedly completed the paperwork, cleared his desk, and flipped open the Missing Person file. Three sheets of paper lay inside. Ryan lifted them up, one-by-one.

'Is that it?'

Todd Robson lifted his head. 'What you say?'

'Danskin's given me a MP case to look at. It's only three pages. What am I supposed to do with it?'

'You're a detective. The clue's in the title. You detect things. Investigate them. Comprendez?'

Ryan released a long sigh. He shifted through the pages and discovered diddley-squat. The report was brief, lacked detail, and told him nothing.

The report was signed by a PC Lawrence Gray and contained little except a statement made by a Jack Goodman. According to Goodman's statement, he wasn't related to the missing woman. *'An acquaintance,'* he described her as. The girl was called Jade. Surname? Goodman didn't know. What?

Goodman's report said she hadn't turned up for an appointment. She'd never missed one before. When did she go missing? *Sometime in the last ten days*. Ryan read the line again. It still said, 'Sometime in the last ten days.' Double what? Was she really missing at all?

Goodman claimed he didn't know Jade's address. Her date of birth. Even, her age. *'About mid to late twenties,'* the statement said. Jesus Christ. There was a telephone number, *'but it may not be hers.'*

The only detail came in the woman's description. Piercing jade-green eyes. Like her name. Blonde hair. Around five foot seven. An accent. Definitely not local. A tattoo of a heart tucked beneath her left breast.

The last comment piqued his interest. 'Todd, would you call me a friend?'

Robson chomped on a ham and pease pudding stottie. 'Nah. Can't stand the sight of you.'

'No, seriously. How would you describe me? A friend? Colleague? Acquaintance? And do me a favour, give me a straight answer.'

Todd wrinkled his hooded eyes. 'Somewhere between the last two, I guess. Why?'

Ryan ignored the question. 'Where's me tattoo?'

Robson choked on his sandwich. 'What sort of question's that? You accusing me of spying on you in the shower or summat?'

'So, you don't know.'

'Of course I bloody don't. How the hell would I?'

Ryan scratched his nose. 'I haven't got one, but the fact you didn't know tells me everything.'

Ryan picked up his phone and dialled the number at the foot of Goodman's statement. He was rewarded with a continuous, high-pitched tone. The number was unobtainable. He dialled Jade's number. Nothing.

'Okay, Mr Goodman. I think it's time I paid you a visit.'

He wheeled back his chair, which came to an abrupt halt.

'What's the hurry, Jarrod?' Danskin often called him Jarrod in front of other members of the force. 'You onto something?'

'I don't know yet. I'm about to find out.'

'If you don't know, you needn't follow it up now. Wait until the morning. It's been a long shift.'

'I don't mind, sir. I'd rather get onto it now.'

'But I do mind.' The DCI leant forward and whispered in his ear. 'You've been edgy all day. You need to switch off. Gan and see Hannah for a while. Start on the case tomorrow.' Danskin straightened. Continued in his normal voice. 'Day's over. I'll see you in the morning, Jarrod.'

Ryan flung the file into his drawer and slammed it shut. The contents of the desk jumped from the surface.

After yesterday, seeing Hannah was the last thing he needed.

The thought of seeing Hannah Graves was precisely why he wanted to stay at work.

**

It's odd how little attention the human psyche gives to four of its senses. The girl hadn't realised just how acute they could be until she was deprived of her fifth.

The inside of the van, with its darkened windows and sealed doors, was pitch black. Yet, once she overcame the fear, the confusion, and the shock of her abduction, she began to take things in.

The van didn't run smoothly. It hicked when the driver accelerated through the gears. She'd picked up sufficient trade secrets from her mechanic father to know, when her nostrils picked up the scent of burnt paper, the van had clutch problems.

The route they took wasn't a major one. Too many stop-starts and sharp bends to be a highway. She strained to hear voices but detected nothing over the thrum of the engine. Then, the vehicle lurched to a halt. She estimated they'd been travelling around twenty minutes, though it may have been longer. It was difficult to calculate speed, but she figured they'd covered perhaps eight miles in that time.

With the van stationary, she heard an indistinct electronic noise and the sound of automatic gates swing open. When the van moved again, the tyres crunched over the surface. They were on gravel. Or shale. Not tarmac.

The van swung around. She felt it reverse. Heard a series of beeps become louder, more urgent, before it drew to a stop. It had reversed up against something. The van rocked slightly as someone alighted. The girl heard a metallic scrape.

The rear doors flung open. Rough hands grabbed her and dragged her to the floor. A metal floor. The doors of her prison slammed shut and she was alone in her shadowy world.

Wet, cold, and terrified, she explored the cell with her fingers. It was metal, as far as she could tell, from floor to ceiling. She'd measured eighteen feet in length and progressed four paces along the rear wall when her prison door inched open. She sensed, rather than saw, a figure squeeze through the opening.

Torchlight lit up her face. She recoiled from the brightness. Jumped when a voice spoke.

'Take off your shoes.'

She complied without hesitation.

'Slide them towards me.'

The girl picked them from the floor.

'Put them down! I said slide them. Gently, and slowly, slide them. Don't throw them.'

The man's footfall reverberated in the confined space as he moved towards her. She sensed his eyes roam over her. A shiver ran through her, not from the chill of her damp clothes but from the intensity of his gaze.

A calloused hand feathered her cheek. She whimpered. The hands went to her throat. Her eyes widened. Perversely, she took in the scent of his cologne and found the smell attractive. She despised herself for it.

She backed away from the man, his fingers still around her neck, until she could go no further. She reached behind her and touched rough, rusted steel. The man rotated his fingers around her throat. She heard a click, and she was released from his grip.

She let out the breath she'd been holding as her own hands went to her neck. There was something around it. A collar of some description.

'Who are you?' she asked.

The man shone the beam on his own face. He did so from below his chin. The angle distorted his appearance like a funfair mirror.

'Heeere's Jonny,' he said.

Without warning, he slapped her. Hard. Her head swung to

the right, cheek already reddening. She let out a scream which died instantly. A jolt shot through her. The girl's mouth dropped open and her hands shot to her throat.

'Sorry about that,' the man said. 'Wanted to see if it worked.'

'Dog.' The girl spat directly in the man's face. Spittle hit him straight between the eyes. Ran down the centre of an angular nose. Yet, the man laughed.

'You're close,' the man replied, 'But you're a bitch, not a dog. And you've just found out what happens to bitches when they bark. That thing around your pretty, swan-like neck,' the girl's hands went to it reflexively, 'Is a shock collar. When the bitch barks, it receives a shock. It's not how you're supposed a train a dog but believe me – it works. But, there again, you know that now, don't you?'

The man ran an index finger around her throat. 'So, don't think about screaming for help. I promise you; you won't like it.'

He grabbed the girl's face. Squeezed beneath her cheekbones until her mouth puckered and planted a rough kiss on her tightly closed lips.

'Goodnight, sweetheart.' He left her alone in silent, cold darkness.

The girl slumped to the floor and wept. Stayed that way for what seemed like hours. As her sobs relented, two things struck her.

Firstly, she picked up an odour. Not the man's cologne. It was sweeter. Lighter. It was perfume. Oscar de la Renta, if she wasn't mistaken. Someone else had been held here before her.

It was the second realisation which floored her. Sent her sobbing to the ground once more.

The man had revealed his face.

That's when she knew she wasn't going to make it out alive.

CHAPTER FOUR

An old white Fiat Uno made its way down Fellside Road with Ryan Jarrod at the wheel. Inevitably, he hit the traffic lights at red. Directly ahead of him, the steep descent of Whickham Bank lay like the drop of a roller-coaster track.

Ryan took advantage of the delay to call Gavin O'Hara on his hands-free. 'Gav, I won't be in for the morning briefing. I'm off to interview a bloke in relation to a missing person case the DCI's allocated me. Let DI Parker know for me, will you?'

The lights changed to green. Ryan swung the Fiat right onto Front Street. 'I can't talk at the moment,' he said in response to a question from O'Hara. 'Tell her I'll speak later.'

He caught a flash of lights in his rear-view mirror as the driver behind showed impatience at Ryan's adherence to the twenty-mph limit. He'd love to let the guy past and radio ahead to the local police station not half a mile up the road. He resisted the temptation.

Ryan interrupted O'Hara mid-sentence. 'Sorry, man. Got to go.' He terminated the call and pulled left into a service station more fitted to a motorway than the stone buildings which lined Whickham village's main street.

As he refuelled, he heard his phone beat out The Blaydon Races from inside the Fiat. Ryan glanced through the windscreen at the caller ID. It wasn't O'Hara. It wasn't Lyall Parker, either. Nor even Danskin or Superintendent Connor.

It was worse than any of them.

It was Hannah.

He let the call ring out and made his way inside the service station to pay.

**

In the Forth Street HQ of the City and County Police, Hannah Graves' expletive was lost in the metallic screech of an Intercity 125 on its approach to the adjacent Central Station.

'Trouble at t'mill?' Lyall Parker's derisory attempts at a Yorkshire accent failed to elicit a smile.

'No.'

'To me, that means 'yes', lassie.' He'd reverted to his natural Aberdonian brogue.

'No. It'll be fine. Things will work out.'

'You cannae bring them to work with you, you know. Not in this job. Talk to him. Sort it out.'

'How do you know it's a him?'

Parker smiled. 'I know, Hannah. The pair of you have been like this for a few weeks.'

She sighed. 'You're right. But it will be fine. It's been over a year now. We know each other well enough to get through it.'

He watched her with gentle eyes. 'Want to talk?'

'Only to Ry. But thanks, Lyall.'

'Does Stephen know?'

'Ah howay, man. Let's not make mountains of molehills, yeah?'

Parker prepared to move away from her desk. Hesitated. 'Look, you might think it's none of my business, but if it interferes with your work, it is my business. Sort it. If you can't, keep it civil. I dinnae like pulling rank but I will if I have to. Don't make me, Hannah. That's all I ask.'

Hannah laid a hand on the Parker's shoulder. 'I promise it won't come to that.'

'Good. Now, let's get on with the briefing.'

He moved away from her and corralled the rest of the duty squad into the briefing room.

**

His GPS took him along Darras Road onto Broadway. The speed limit was greater than the twenty mph of his home village, but he travelled even slower, so in awe was he of the palatial homes on Newcastle's most exclusive estate. Footballers, TV personalities, some of the north east's most powerful businessmen; they all owned property here.

From Broadway, he meandered through a few more streets, passed homes circled by high walls and with drives longer than some roads until the electronic voice told him he'd reached his destination.

Ryan took a swift look around and clambered out of his Fiat, conscious it looked as conspicuous as a pebble set amongst a diamond necklace. He was well out of his comfort zone.

He stood in front of a white-walled mansion, took deep breaths the way he had before mounting a pommel in his gymnastic days and, finally, rang the doorbell.

Deep, urgent barks emanated from the rear of the house; barks which turned into rumbling growls. By the sound of it, the garden housed Cerberus with his balls in a vice.

It took an age until Ryan heard a bolt slide and the heavy door open to reveal someone who quite clearly wasn't Jack Goodman.

The woman was tall. He guessed late thirties. Perhaps early forties. Attractive with make-up, possibly quite plain behind it. The woman wore an expensive hairdo and even more expensive perfume.

Behind her, two young girls kicked a ball around in a distant kitchen as big as a football pitch. A third child kicked hard inside the woman's swollen belly.

Ryan put on his official face and held his ID at shoulder height.

Before he could speak, the woman gasped. 'Oh God. What's happened? Has he been in an accident? Is he okay? I always feared one of these nights he wouldn't come home.'

Ryan's new-found composure fled from him. 'Oh, err no. He's fine. At least, as far as I know, he is. Sorry if I alarmed you. I'm Detective Constable Jarrod and I just wanted a word with Mr Goodman. I take it your husband's not home, then?'

A confused look came over the woman's face. 'Mr Goodman's not my husband.'

Ryan missed her emphasis on the second word as his eyes dropped to her bump. 'Sorry, I just assumed you were married.'

The woman appeared more confused than Ryan. 'I am married. But not to a Goodman.'

It was Ryan's turn to bear the puzzled expression. 'So, there's no Jack Goodman lives here? No-one who reported a missing person?'

Slowly, dawn broke in the woman's eyes. 'I think you've been the victim of a silly joke, Detective. I think we both have. My name's not Goodman. It's Bonhomme. It's French for…'

'Good man. Yeah, I know.' He rubbed the side of his face. 'Is your husband's name Jack?'

'No. It's Max.' A clatter emerged from the far end of the hallway. The crash of breaking china. Costly china, no doubt. 'Izzy, Charlotte – what have you done now?' She turned back to Ryan. 'I really must go, Detective. I'm sorry, but someone's been wasting your valuable time. Now, if you'll excuse me…'

Ryan was left with no choice but to excuse her. He was already staring at the outside of a closed and bolted door.

**

Somewhere beneath the beard, Manny Manville's lips smacked together as the first sip of the lunchtime pint hit. Flecks of foam clung to the Hoxton like frogspawn to reeds.

'So, when do you think he'll have them ready?'

Adam Haines dragged the edge of a beer mat across the sodden surface of a round table and flicked ale onto the floor of the Crown Posada. 'Usually takes him a couple of weeks. See no reason why it should be any different with this lot. Why you ask?'

The Girl on the Quay

'The Thai lass, or whatever she was; she was canny cute. Wouldn't mind seeing her in action, that's all.'

'Aye, a bit different to the usual, wasn't she? Fancy checking it out in the next couple of days, Russ?'

'I'm not sure that's a good idea.'

Haines stared across the table. 'Why not? We usually have a gander once the Mayan's cleaned them up.'

The door opened. Street noise entered the bar along with a couple of middle-aged patrons. Russ waited until they were engrossed in a study of the hand-pulls on offer. 'Aye, but it's a bit different this time.'

'How come?' Haines asked.

'Howay man. You wiped out the supply chain, that's why. I don't think we'll be the Mayan's flavour of the month.'

Haines shook his head. 'Russ, man; he half expected it. He thought something was up. He told us it might get messy, didn't he?'

Russ shook his head. 'I don't know. It only got messy because you two got itchy fingers.'

Manville leant forward. 'Listen, pal,' he hissed. 'You weren't on board, right? You don't know what they were going to do. It did start to kick-off. We responded.'

'That's crap, and you know it. You panicked and ballsed up. Nowt more to it.'

Manville balled his fists. Haines rested a hand on the bearded man's wrist. 'Relax, Manny.' He looked directly at Russ, smiling. 'We stick to the story. Luuk's men had knives. Surrounded us. If we hadn't taken them out, we'd be history. And then where would the Mayan be without us? No, we were protecting his interests more than ourselves, that's what we tell him and that's what he'll believe.'

'That's crap, man. The Mayan will go ape-shit if he can't get more girls from Luuk.'

Haines rested his back against the booth wall. 'You're wrong. If he'd been that pissed off, we'd have heard from Chamley or one of his other minions by now. Besides, don't you think he's got plenty lasses already? More than enough to keep him going until he finds another supply line.'

Russ chewed on a nail. 'I'm out,' he said. When he opened his mouth to speak again, Haines filled the maw with the beermat.

'Shut it, Russ the Wuss, okay? Just shut it. Now, mine's a Black Gate, Manny drinking Wanderlust, and get yersel a shandy while you're there.'

**

Ryan spent the afternoon in-and-out of blind alleys. He rang local hospitals checking if they had any unidentified recent admissions. When they asked, 'how recent?' he felt foolish when he couldn't give a date.

The Queen Elizabeth hospital in Gateshead threw up a potential lead. A woman, around late twenties, had been admitted with a minor head injury but acute amnesia. She had no ID on her.

Ryan asked when she'd been brought in and was told four days ago. Ryan pulled at his bottom lip. Probably too recent for it to be Jade. He asked about the tattoo. Yes, the patient had a tattoo. Ryan sat upright. It was on her shoulder. A butterfly. Not Jade.

He left the office and conducted a tour of local hostels and women's refuge centres. Without a photograph or even a description of merit, he'd come up with nothing. On his way back to the station, he took diversions via Gallowgate, Haymarket and Clayton Street, known haunts of the homeless. He shelled out thirty quid in exchange for no information whatsoever.

Back at Forth Street, he searched police records for a Jack Goodman. He didn't expect to find anything and wasn't disappointed. As a last resort, Ryan read through the statement Goodman had made to PC Gray. He needn't have bothered. There was nothing in it to miss.

He felt a presence at his shoulder. 'Todd,' he asked without looking up, 'do you know where I can find Lawrence Gray? I don't know him.'

The voice that came back wasn't Todd's. It belonged to Hannah Graves.

'Shades? He's probably down at the custody desk,' she said. 'Most of his duties are round there.'

'Oh, thanks. Hannah.' Embarrassed, he picked up the file. 'Think I'll go see him. See what he remembers of this missing person report.'

Hannah moved in front of him. 'We need to talk.'

Ryan close his eyes for a second too long.

'Don't look like that, Ryan. We've got to sort this.'

He blew out his cheeks. She was right. They did. 'Okay, Hannah. You're right. But, not now. I really need to see Lawrence, or Shades, or whatever he's called. Are you free tomorrow night?'

'Can't you make it earlier? This is getting awkward, you know. Even Lyall's picked up on it.'

Ryan sighed. 'Tomorrow, Hannah.'

'Alright, then. Bay Horse at seven. Don't be late. I mean it.'

He nodded. Offered a tight-lipped smile. Hannah smiled back. Ryan knew it wasn't genuine. The dimple in her cheek didn't pucker.

'It's a date.'

They both knew it wasn't.

CHAPTER FIVE

A haze of white sunlight filtered into the foyer of the Forth Street station. Officers came and went as shifts changed. A couple of winos made their exit after an overnight stay, a lawyer in a sharp suit left with a bundle of papers beneath his arm, while the Desk Sergeant busied himself with a pile of stationery on the tabletop.

A second constable took down outdated posters from the noticeboard and replaced them with new. He stood back, admired his handiwork, and slipped through a rear door just as the woman in a grey hoodie entered the station.

The woman, rake thin but with pneumatic breasts straining to escape the hoodie, gave a sheepish look round. Clearly uncomfortable, she made to leave.

'Can I help you, miss?' the Desk Sergeant asked.

'No. I was looking for a policeman, that is all.'

The sergeant chuckled. 'Then you're in the right place. You'll find some here, just one or two, mind.'

The woman gave the nervous start of a worried lamb. 'In this moment, I don't see him. I should come back another time.' Her words were accented. Polish, the sergeant guessed.

'Him?'

'Excuse me?'

'You said 'him.' You're looking for someone in particular?'

'Yes. Well, no. Really, it does not matter. I should go.'

'What's the name of the officer you're here to see?'

The woman's shoulders sagged. He wasn't going to let her go; she could tell. 'He's got hands.' She held hers aloft as if the sergeant didn't know what hands were.

'Most of us have, madam.'

'I am sorry. I do not know his name. I just remember he has bad hands.'

Sergeant Milligan studied her from behind his desk. The woman's make-up had been applied with the touch of a professional yet not well enough to completely disguise acne scars beneath. She was attractive in an ethereal way, but an emptiness lurked behind her pale, lifeless eyes. Sergeant Milligan sensed a troubled soul.

'Here. Take a seat,' he motioned to a row of uncomfortable-looking chairs. 'You're in luck. You're our first customer. Someone will be with you in a tick.'

'Will he have bad hands?'

Milligan chortled. 'I can't guarantee that, madam. But we're all here to help.'

The blonde looked less than convinced as she lowered herself onto a chair and buried her head deep in the hood so her dead eyes lay in shadow.

Milligan was true to his word. After only a few minutes, he called her forward with a smile. 'Straight through the door and take second room on the right.'

Milligan pressed a button. The door buzzed as the remote lock released. The woman spotted a red light above the door and kept her head down to avoid the camera as she walked through into the corridor beyond.

In the allotted room, she took one of two seats her side of a pine desk. A door on the wall facing her opened and a policeman entered. Not Milligan. Not the one with bad hands, either.

'Hello, miss. I'm Constable Lawrence Gray. What can I do for you?'

The girl continued to look at the floor.

'Anytime you're ready, madam,' Shades Gray prompted.

'It is my flatmate. I have worries for her.'

'I see. What has she done?'

'No, you are misunderstanding. She has done nothing. She has not come home. I worry something has happened.'

Shades opened his notebook. 'What's her name?'

The woman hesitated. Seemed to wrestle with something

inside her conscience. 'She is Radka. Radka Vosahlo.' She spelt out the name for PC Gray. 'Sometimes, she is called Kayla.'

'Thank you. And your name is?'

The girl stiffened. 'Must you know?'

'That's a strange thing to ask. Any reason why you wouldn't want to tell me?'

The girl shook her head. A strand of blonde hair fell from her hood. She quickly tucked it behind her ear. 'Isla.'

'Do you have a second name, Isla.'

Again, hesitation. 'Pope.'

Gray smiled. 'Can you tell me what Radka, or Kayla…your flatmate, could you describe her to me?'

'She is tall. Perhaps one metre seventy-five. Very pretty. Very high cheekbones. Black hair.'

'Thank you, Miss Pope. Her build?'

'I am sorry?'

'Is she slim, average: you know, her build.'

'She is slim. She has a beautiful body.'

Shades Gray tried to hide it, but an eyebrow arced in curiosity. 'You're doing very well. Does your flatmate have any unusual jewellery, or tattoos? Something that would make her identifiable.'

The girl's hood shook. 'No. Nothing like that.'

'How about piercings?'

Matter-of-factly, Isla Pope answered, 'She has a silver stud. In her labia.'

Shades raised both eyebrows this time. He coughed slightly. 'When did you last see Miss Vosahlo?'

The woman squirmed in her seat. 'Will this take long? I really need to be somewhere.'

'When did you last see Miss Vosahlo?', Shades persisted.

'Two, maybe three days ago, I think.'

'You think?'

Isla Pope fixed the policeman with an icy stare. 'Yes, I think. We work different shifts. We pass in the night like ships, I believe you say, yes?'

'Something like that. Now, did Miss Vosahlo give any indication where she might have gone.'

The girl stood. 'I am sorry. I want to go now, please. I talk to man with bad hands, but I say to you enough.'

Shades sat back. Smiled warmly at her. 'Okay. I tell you what, I'll get you a coffee while I see if my colleague with the bad hands is free. How does that sound?'

The woman sat. 'You promise?'

'I'll do what I can. I won't be long.'

Gray left the interview room and, from his office behind it, he dialled a number. 'Ryan? Shades Gray here. You know the missing persons case you asked me about yesterday? Well, I might have another one. Wouldn't normally bother you, but I get the idea the woman reporting it is hiding something.'

He listened whilst Ryan Jarrod asked him a question. 'No, not quite as vague as Goodman but... I don't know. Just my gut tells me something. Thought you might want to take a look. Can you get down here straight away?' Pause. 'Great.'

Two minutes later, Ryan Jarrod entered Gray's room behind the interview suite. They shook hands. 'Her name's Isla Pope. Missing woman is a Radka Vosahlo. Also known as Kayla. Pope's in here,' he motioned to the door behind him.

'Howay then; let the fox see the rabbit.'

Shades Gray pushed open the interview room door. 'Uh-oh.'

The room was empty.

'Bugger,' Ryan exclaimed. 'So, tell me what she said.'

Gray recounted the interview from memory. Ryan's eyebrows formed the obligatory arch when Shades raised the piercing topic.

'There are some similarities, I give you that,' Ryan said. 'Both reports are distinctly unusual and a bit vague. Did this Pope woman say anything else?'

Shades Gray thought for a moment. 'No, don't think so. Oh, she did say she wanted to talk to a copper with bad hands.'

'What?'

'Bad hands. She said she wanted to speak to a policeman with bad hands.'

Ryan showed Gray his own palms; pink, grafted flesh contrasting with his natural skin tones. 'Like these, you mean?'

Gray's mouth opened and closed like a door in a gale.

'She wanted to talk to me, Shades. Who is she? And, how in the name of buggery did she know about my hands?'

**

Ryan began the afternoon by reviewing CCTV footage. He played, rewound, and played again the moment Isla Pope walked from the reception area through to the corridor beyond.

It was impossible to recognise her. Head down and buried within the grey hood, he could have been standing next to her and wouldn't have known. He cursed the fact Gray hadn't turned on the camera in the interview suite.

'I was just about to when Milligan called me through,' Shades had told him. 'I'd been busy updating the noticeboard in the lobby before I did it. She was the first of the day. You know what it's like.'

Ryan did, but still cursed the uniform cop's negligence. The fact the girl asked for him personally had got under his skin. He needed a break until the personal perspective faded. He vowed to come back to the case fresh and, in the meantime, offered Gavin O'Hara assistance on his investigation.

Ryan didn't get an opportunity to revisit the missing persons cases before his shift ended so, that evening, when he walked down half a dozen steps into The Bay Horse, he had three things on his mind: the mysterious Jack Goodman, the equally-strange Isla Pope – and Hannah Graves.

He checked his watch. Seven-twenty. He was late.

Ryan ducked as he entered the warmth of the bar. The ceiling was low but not that low, and he was tall but not that tall, yet it was something he always did. Inside, the pub was quiet; a typical Wednesday night in the village. Fewer than half a dozen tables occupied, four or five guys gathered at the bar and, sitting quietly in the far corner, Hannah; engrossed in a book.

Ryan took a deep breath and approached the bar. 'Bottle of Becks, Joanne.' He inclined his head in the direction of Hannah. 'What's she having tonight?'

'Just a Coke.'

'And a Coke an aal, please. Ice and lemon.'

'She asked for no ice last time, mind.'

'Should have known. She's cold enough.'

Joanne picked up on his mood. 'Thought she was quiet. You two had a row?'

Ryan snorted a laugh. 'Not really. But I suspect we might be about to.' He collected his bottle and Hannah's Coke from the bar. 'Wish me luck.'

'Anyone sitting here?' he asked as he arrived at Hannah's table, mustering a smile.

'You're late,' Hannah replied, not looking up from her book.

He exhaled through his nose. 'I know. Sorry. Work. You know what it's like.' He could tell she bought it no more than he had when Shades Gray trotted out the same line to him.

He sat next to her. 'What you are reading?'

'A book,' she replied icily. After a pause, her face softened. 'It's a fantasy. Unicorn Alley. By Lexi Aurora.'

'Sounds like a porn star.'

When she laughed, Ryan felt some of the tension ease from his shoulders. He turned towards her. His eyes roamed her face. She'd sprayed a hint of glitter into her brown curls. A lock twisted down her forehead like a tornado. Freckles dappled her cheeks, a single dimple breaking the canvas of sun kisses. She'd eschewed lipstick which only added to her girl-next-door allure.

Their eyes met. 'We've got to sort this, Ry.'

He looked away, spell broken. Ryan stared into the neck of his bottle. Gave the slightest nod.

'I'm nearly twenty-five,' she continued. 'We've been together over a year now and, y'know; well, it's not easy.'

'It isn't for me, either. You don't think I want it to be like this, do you?'

She put a hand beneath his chin. Raised his head so she could look into his eyes. 'Then do something about it.'

He pulled away from her. 'I tried. The other night, I really tried.'

'I know you did. But trying isn't good enough. Not anymore.'

He sniffed. Ran the back of his hand across his eyes. 'It'll get better.'

'Ryan, it won't. Not if you don't do something about it. The doctors told you the burns had healed. There's nothing wrong with your circulation or blood flow. It's in your head,' she tapped her temple with a finger, 'And you need to get it out.'

Ryan crossed his arms. Shuffled away from her. He stared into space. The comfort of the Bay Horse bar slipped from view. He saw nothing. A void. Then, the void was filled by a wall of flame. He wriggled his fingers as he felt the heat against them. Shifted uncomfortably in his seat as the pain moved elsewhere.

In the distance, he was vaguely aware of Hannah's voice 'I've seen the burns. I know you're embarrassed by them. I know you think they're unsightly. But I don't care, Ryan, because they're part of you.'

He wasn't listening. He'd come out of his trance, but he wasn't listening. Instead, he ran his fingers through his strawberry hair. Raised his hand higher and waved towards the bar.

'Barry, ower here, man. Come and join us,' he shouted.

Barry Docherty, Ryan's friend from his Civil Service days, returned the wave. Hannah avoided his gaze. 'You've set this up, haven't you?' she hissed between her teeth. 'You coward.'

'Nah. Well, not really. I told Barry we were going out. Didn't expect him to call in, though.'

'Liar.'

Barry perched himself on a stool. A pretty redhead in a burgundy dress barely long enough for a ten-year old, let alone a grown woman, joined him. 'Hannah, this is Amy. Amy, Hannah.' Hannah afforded the redhead a tight-lipped smile.

The two interlopers exchanged good natured banter while Ryan and Hannah sat quiet as a married couple. After ten minutes, Hannah reached for her jacket. 'I've had enough. I'm off.'

She stood. Her jacket caught Ryan's drink. The contents spilled over Ryan's lap whilst the Becks played a game of spin the bottle on the tabletop.

Ryan shot to his feet. 'How, man. There's nee need for that, man.'

Hannah was already making for the exit. Ryan hurried after her leaving Barry and Amy to exchange 'Ooo's.

Hannah was almost at the bus stop next to the veterinarians by the time Ryan reached her. 'Where are you going?'

'Home. Where do you think?'

'But your car's in the Horse's car park.'

She grabbed her hair with both hands. Stamped her foot. 'Hell.'

Hannah inhaled deeply. Her eyes rippled like a lake's surface. 'Ryan, I'm sorry but this is going nowhere. We both know it, but you won't do anything about it.'

'Let's get you back to your car.' He took her arm. She shrugged him off as she stomped back towards the pub. He set off after her at a trot. 'Okay,' he said. 'You win. I'll do it.'

She shook her head. 'You don't understand, do you? It's not about me winning. It's about helping you get over the fire. You might think you have, but you haven't. You proved that again the other night.'

'I told you I'll do it. And I will. I promise.'

They stood facing each other, either side of her Renault. Neither spoke. Finally, Hannah broke the silence.

'Good,' she said. 'I'm pleased for you. But it's been well over a year now, and I can't wait any longer. I want us to stay friends, Ry. We have to for work's sake anyway, but I really want you in my life. I really do. As a friend.'

Ryan gulped back tears as she lay a card on the car's roof.

'I saw this in my doctors,' she said. 'Thought it might help. It's your call what you do with it.'

Ryan picked the card up. Turned it over in his fingers.

'Bye, Ry. See you at work tomorrow.' She jumped into the Renault and drove off.

Ryan watched until the taillights disappeared from view. He raised his head to the heavens where a crescent moon smirked down at him. He lowered his gaze to the card in his hand:

Dr Hadley Kutz (Ph.D, Bsc, Psy.D, LMFT)
Clinical Psychologist
Relationship Counsellor
Sex Therapist.

CHAPTER SIX

Twenty miles south and eleven miles east of the Bay Horse car park, another cop felt as sick as Ryan.

DI John Craggs of Durham's Prince Bishop force managed to hold onto his stomach contents whilst the coastguard launch cut through the gathering dusk. The moment the skipper cut the motor and let the craft bob and weave like a punch-drunk boxer, Craggs vomited. Explosively.

'Sorry about that,' he apologised as he dragged the back of a hand across his mouth and flicked tendrils of vomit into the sea. 'I'm not much keen on a bath, never mind miles out here.'

'Don't worry, you're not the first. Happens to the best of us. Here, take this.' The skipper tossed Craggs a towel.

The sea's surface rose and fell like the chest of a sleeping beast and, with it, the orange-liveried boat became a rag doll in a terrier's maw. Alongside them, a larger vessel blocked out the horizon.

Craggs looked up at it. 'What we got here?'

'We're moored alongside the Stellendam. She's Dutch. Registered out of Ijmuiden. Come on. Let's board her.'

The skipper took to the cargo net with the dexterity of Tarzan up a vine. Craggs climbed with the surety of an octogenarian on ice. He took the offered hand and levered himself aboard the Stellendam.

'Standard fishing vessel,' the coastguard explained. 'On the small side, but big enough for these waters.'

Craggs spluttered as a wave of spray cascaded over him. He clung to a rusty rail as if his life depended on it. 'What brought it to your attention?'

'She's a 'she'; not an 'it',' the coastguard corrected. 'We had a report from a local trawlerman. He said she'd been fishing this same spot for well over a week. Locals get a bit twitchy over quotas. Especially Dutch ones. Ever since the Bressay Bank filled its boots with a year's quota in a single trip a couple of years ago, the knives have been out.'

Craggs squinted against wind and saline. 'More a matter for HMRC or Ag and Fish than us, though.' He shouted to make himself heard.

'Normally would be. Thing is, when we came aboard, we found her exactly like this. No fish. And no crew.'

DI Craggs flexed the fingers of one hand before reattaching it to the rails. 'A real-life Marie Celeste, eh?' His eyes roamed the deck. 'Shine your touch over here, will you?'

The coastguard swept a beam around the deck.

'Stop. Back a bit. Over there.' Craggs nodded with his head to indicate the spot. He wasn't about to release his grip. The beam came to rest on a series of brownish streaks. 'Is that blood?'

The skipper didn't bat an eye. 'Yup.'

'What? Is that it? 'Yup' is all you can say?'

'Yup. We're on a fishing boat, Detective Inspector. In case you didn't realise, fish bleed when they're gutted.'

Craggs gave an embarrassed shrug. 'S'pose.' After a moment's thought, he continued. 'So, apart from it being a ghost ship, like, why am I here?'

In the darkness, the coastguard made a face. Could have been a grin; might have been a grimace. 'Over here.'

John Craggs prised his fingers from the ship's rail one-by-one, extended both arms for balance, and set off on the trot of a drunken man as the Stellendam rolled with the waves.

The coastguard hauled open a hold door. Rotten fish odours battered Craggs' senses. He swallowed down bile.

'This is why we sent for you, Detective Inspector.'

Craggs stared into a void. 'I don't see anything,' he said.

The Girl on the Quay

The coastguard's torch swept the hold. 'Like I say, no fish. Very unusual. Especially after a week or two. But still not quite as unusual as this.' The beam settled on a pile of stained rags in one corner. The torch swung the length of the hold. 'Or this.'

Craggs screwed up his eyes. Peered intently. Couldn't make out what he was looking at. 'What are they?'

'In the blue corner,' the coastguard mimicked David Diamante announcing a WBC heavyweight bout, 'Introducing, all the way from the Netherlands …Designer Brassiere.' The torch swung back in the opposite direction. 'And, in the red, please welcome…a pile of used sanitary products.'

He flicked the beam into DI Craggs' face. 'Pretty unusual for a crew of hairy-arsed fishermen, don't you think?'

**

Lana Del Ray's 'West Coast' filled the air. On stage, lit so she appeared in silhouette like a Bond movie intro, a girl straddled a silver pole. Behind her, the ornate swirls of the words *'Whipped Cream – the Club for Gentlemen'* were projected against a lavish gold curtain.

The girl slid down the pole. Gripped it between her thighs. Arched her back until long black hair touched the stage. A strobe flashed offering the audience a tantalising view of the naked girl.

'Scrubs up well, doesn't she?' Adam Haines shouted over the music.

Manny Manville sipped a brandy. 'Told you the Thai lass was the best of 'em. I can always tell.'

'Oh aye; like the one you pulled in Berlin. Remember? Turned out to be a ladyboy?'

'How could I forget,' he laughed. He inclined his head towards the stage. 'She's definitely all woman that one, though.'

The strobe hit again. Lingered longer this time. The girl planted one foot on the ground. Raised the other until it rested against the pole at head-height.

Manville's glass stopped half-way to his lips. 'Jeez, will you look at that.'

Abruptly, the stage flooded with red and burgundy light, the girl curtsied coquettishly, the music stopped, and the lights went out.

A smattering of half-hearted applause from the small audience signalled the end of her routine.

'Quiet tonight,' Manville commented.

'It's early, man. Give it another hour until the girls start coming to the tables. It'll soon fill up. Another two hours,' he signalled to a chrome spiralled staircase blocked by a cut-out of a topless woman, 'The private booths upstairs will open. That's when the stag parties, and the rich old blokes who can't get any at home, come.' Haines laughed at his unintentional pun. He looked at his empty glass. 'Your shout. I'll have a Glenlivet.'

Manny pulled a face as he rose from the leather sofa. 'Hope I'm good for a mortgage.'

Manville made his way back from the bar in darkness to the accompaniment of Billy Idol. Another woman occupied the stage. Taller than the Thai. Curvier. When she performed her gymnastics on the pole, her breasts didn't move with her.

To the right of the stage, a bulky security guard surveyed the audience. Shaven head and a neck so thick the back of it formed the shape of a Big Mac, his appearance ensured the Whipped Cream Club remained trouble-free.

A wire coiled upwards, from a black radio transmitter fixed to his lapel, to his ear. A finger like a black pudding touched the earpiece. His head moved left and right as he searched for something.

'Shit. We've got trouble.' Adam Haines pointed towards the heavy walking towards them.

'Shit,' Manville echoed.

The monster tapped Haines on the shoulder. 'This way.' He carried on walking safe in the knowledge the men would follow. 'The Mayan wants a word.'

'The Mayan? He's here? Not one of his gofers?'

'No. The Mayan.'

Haines's 'Shit' promoted itself to a 'Fuck.'

The door closed behind them with a satisfied click, the sound muffled by a thick pile gold-and-black carpet. The walls of the room were gold, the blinds black. A gold and black crystal chandelier hung low from a ceiling decorated like a wedding cake.

Haines and Manville faced a gold-coloured desk behind which sat a man dressed in black.

The Mayan.

Jet black hair, black suit, coal-black eyes. He smiled to reveal a gold tooth. Another man stood alongside him. Chinless, bald, and bespectacled, with Freddie Mercury-like gnashers, Lou Chamley was the Mayan's accountant, lawyer, and fall-guy. He was also a champion arse-licker. When the Mayan indicated the door, Chamley exited without question.

'Take a seat, please.' An order, not a request, delivered in a colonial-British accent.

Haines and Manville lowered themselves into plush black leather chairs. The heavy took his place beside the door, whilst his white twin slipped outside to replace him in the auditorium.

'I see we only have two of our Wise Monkeys. Such a shame. Never mind. How are you, gentlemen?'

'Good, thanks.' Haines lied for both of them.

The Mayan didn't respond. Short in stature but broad of shoulder and forehead, he watched them from beneath thick eyebrows. He waited until he saw the men squirm in their seats before continuing.

'A little over two weeks ago, I ordered a consignment of goods. Six, in total. You brought back four. Why?'

'It's all Luuk's man had. We thought it better to bring back four than none.'

'I see.' A long pause. 'Tell me what happened that night.'

Manny let Haines do the talking. He recounted the mission, leaving out the slaughter at the end.

The Mayan steepled his fingers. 'Did you have any trouble?'

Haines and Manville exchanged glances. 'It got messy, like you said it would.'

The man across the desk leant forward. 'I know it did. And, my friends, that leaves me with a problem. Luuk has cut off all contact. He's demanding more money than we agreed...'

'Luuk's man said you owed him from the last trip...'

'Shut your poisonous mouth.' The words came out as a serpentine hiss.

After a lengthy pause, the Mayan spoke again. 'My problem is, Luuk wants paying for his crew and his boat, as well. And I don't think I should do that, do you?'

Manville spoke for the first time. 'Look, you need to know. All was going smoothly until Russ lost it. We didn't know he had a gun with him. When Luuk's man started to get arsey, he peppered the whole crew. Adam and me, we had nowt to do with it.'

The silences frightened Haines the most. This one stretched to infinity and beyond, all the while the Mayan's eyes drilled into the two men on the opposite side of the desk.

'So, that brings me to my other little problem,' the Mayan said at last. 'Well, more than a little one, actually. You see, not only am I unable to get any new girls, but the ones I already have are disappearing. Not just any of my girls, but the best ones. Now, how do you account for that?'

Haines eyelids slid shut. He exhaled. Luuk's man's words came back to him. *'What the lord giveth, the lord taketh away.'* It all made sense now.

'Of course,' the swarthy man continued, 'I wouldn't meet his demands for their return. Why would I pay him twice for the same product? No; that wouldn't do. It wouldn't do at all.'

The Mayan clapped his hands. Haines and Manville's arses nearly inverted at the sound. He smiled, the gold tooth glinting in the light. 'Anyway, too late for all that. What's done is done. Thank you, gentlemen. You may go.'

Haines and Manville rose from their seats like greyhounds out the trap. They exchanged a brief smile of relief. As they approached the door, the Mayan spoke again.

'Oh dear. How remiss of me; I almost forgot. Before my girls began disappearing, I gave Luuk my word on something. I promised him I'd replace his crew. After all, I haven't much need for seamen now, have I?'

He gave them a dazzling smile. 'My friends, I'm certain Luuk will afford you the warmest of welcomes.'

Haines and Manville turned the colour of snow.

'Titus, be so good as to escort the gentlemen to the ferry terminal.'

CHAPTER SEVEN

After a night devoid of sleep, Ryan lay amidst a tangle of sheet and duvet. The resonant snores of Spud, his faithful pet pug, rose from the foot of the bed.

'At least someone got some sleep.'

The dog lifted his ears and fluttered open his eyes. He yawned. Within seconds, the snorts and grunts resumed.

'Come on, Spuddy-boy. Time you got up.'

Within ten minutes, Ryan was washed, dressed, and had snapped Spud's collar around his neck.

Ryan closed the door quietly behind him. He dragged Spud away from the heavenly odours of the gatepost and set off for the early morning walk, even though a walk was the last thing Ryan wanted. He really needed to talk. He knew his father would either clam up with embarrassment or spout some well-intentioned but inappropriate wisecrack. His brother, James, was growing up fast but not fast enough. He was still a kid at heart.

That left one person; the one person who would neither judge nor criticise. The one person who would do nothing but listen and let him talk.

Soon, with Spud's leader securely fastened to a handrail, Ryan approached a building oddly out of place with its environs; one which dwarfed nearby homes with the exception of a half-built shell of a structure further downhill.

The building was plush to the point of ostentatious, yet it put Ryan in mind of the Addams Family mansion every time he set foot inside. He entered a glass-fronted hallway, pressed a button on the interior door, and waited for the buzz.

'I'm here to see Doris Jarrod,' he said into the intercom.

Through the interior window, Ryan saw a face appear from a room down a corridor and vanish just as quickly.

'Hello Ryan. Hang on for a couple of minutes, please. I'll see if your gran's ready.'

He'd visited his grandmother at least four times a week ever since his father finally admitted she needed round the clock care. Ryan had sweet-hearted Angela, the manager, into allowing him access at odd hours, given the shifts he worked. This morning was one such occasion.

While he waited, he gazed around the lobby. On the windows hung framed Care Quality Commission certificates, a montage of headshots of the home's staff, a centrepiece photograph of the official opening ceremony by a minor local TV celebrity, and a few shots of the residents engaged in activities.

The intercom buzzed again. 'Sorry. She's not ready. Your gran had a bit of a restless night. Is it important?'

'Nah, not really. I just needed to talk to her, that's all. Can't be helped. Thanks anyway.'

Ryan stuffed his hands deep in his pockets. He took a final look at the opening ceremony picture; the standard shot of a figure cutting a ribbon flanked by other dignitaries. An engraved brass plate on the frame read:

'Our grand opening, performed by Paul Mooney (centre) with our manager, Ms Angela C Doyle (right), and, left, Mr Max Bonhomme.'

Ryan hit the intercom. 'Angela - who's Max Bonhomme?'

**

Ryan ran all the way home, Spud's little legs a blur as he tried to keep up. Once inside, he rang the station.

'Gavin, can I run something by you? It's about me missing person case.'

'Ah man, can't it wait? I'm due to give evidence in court this morning and haven't even started my prep.'

'No bother. How about DS Nairn?'

'No can do, I'm afraid. Sue's just been called away.'

Ryan sucked air between his teeth. 'Patch me through to Danskin, then.'

Gavin O'Hara chuckled. 'It's not your day, mate. He's on late shift. Still at home.'

'Okay. Probably something or nothing. It'll wait.'

He hung up. Went to make a coffee. Changed his mind and pulled out his phone again.

'It's Ryan. Can I pop round?'

In less than fifteen minutes, his Fiat Uno was parked up outside an apartment block on the fringe of the Great Park estate. He was buzzed up but stood outside the door for a moment, gathering himself. He didn't know what reception awaited him.

He needn't have worried. From the feelgood music swirling through the apartment, DCI Stephen Danskin obviously hadn't been told of Ryan and Hannah's break-up.

Ryan stood in the kitchen door and watched his DCI flip an omelette while swaying to the rhythm of Brown-Eyed Girl.

'Want one?' he asked, shoving a bottle of Corsodyl out of sight. Before Ryan could answer, Stephen plucked an egg from the box, tossed it in the air, flexed a bicep and let the egg bounce off it. He caught and cracked it into a mug in one movement. Repeated it with a second while singing 'Sha la la la la la la la la la la te da.'

Despite his downbeat mood, Ryan found himself smiling. 'Anthony Bourdain says you can tell a lot about a man's character by the way he makes an omelette.'

Danskin dropped a fistful of grated cheese on top of the eggs sizzling in the pan. 'You can tell a lot about a man by how much shit he knows. For a young bloke, you know a helluva lot.'

'Aye, but give us an Ikea flatpack and I wouldn't have a clue.'

Danskin scooped the omelette from the pan and plated it for Ryan. 'So, I take it you didn't come here to talk cookery.'

The Girl on the Quay

'No. I came to ask what you know about a bloke called Max Bonhomme.'

Stephen's fork poised on its way to his mouth while he thought. 'Doesn't ring any bells. Should it?'

'I don't know. It's that missing person case you assigned me. The report came in from a Jack Goodman. Turns out he doesn't exist. I went to the address Goodman gave and spoke to the woman who lives there. She'd never heard of him. Turns out her husband's Max Bonhomme. Bonhomme's French for...

'Goodman. See, I didn't get where I am today by not knowing stuff, an' aal. Anyway, carry on.'

'I thought nowt of it really until today. I went to see me gran at her care home. Found out the home, and a dozen others, is owned by a Max Bonhomme.'

Danskin motioned Ryan into the small lounge. Between a mouthful of omelette, Danskin asked, 'Unless any of the residents have gone missing, I think it's just a coincidence. You've no reason to suspect Bonhomme, have you?'

'No, it just seemed odd, that's all. And, you do know a second girl's been reported missing, don't you?'

'It's my job to know, son. Do you think they're connected?'

Ryan shrugged. 'Only to the extent both reports are weirdly vague, and the person who reported it did a runner.'

'Any idea who?'

'That's where it's really odd. The second report was made by someone called Isla Pope. I've never heard of her, but she asked for me specifically. When she thought I couldn't be found, she disappeared.'

'She asked for you by name?'

'Not exactly. But she knew about my burns. She asked for the officer with damaged hands, or words to that effect.'

Danskin nodded. 'Does seem peculiar, I admit. So, if you're after my advice, either find whoever this Jack Goodman bloke is, or leave yourself out to dry and hope Isla

What's-her-face turns up again. Reet, I'm off duty so give it a rest, will you? How's things between you and my lovely stepdaughter?'

Ryan's eyes narrowed. Was the DCI trying to catch him out? Had Hannah already told him? He caught sight of a photograph behind Danskin; a photograph of the DCI with his ex and a freckle-faced child. Ryan forced himself to look away.

'We're having a break, sir.'

Danskin looked genuinely shocked. He clearly hadn't known. 'Sorry to hear that, son. You need to know, though, it doesn't change the way I treat you, either at work or out of it. Unless, you two can't work together. Then, I'll have to ship one of you out.'

'It's too early to tell if I'm honest. I don't think either of us wants to move to DCI Kinnear's watch so I'm sure we'll do our best to make it work.'

Without looking up from his plate, Danskin asked, 'Was it working together, or was it the burns?'

Ryan fixed Stephen with a cold stare. 'What?'

'The burns. Must make it hard for you.'

'How the hell do you know about that? I've only ever told you about my hands. Not the others. Jesus, don't say Hannah's been talking about them.'

It was Danskin's turn to dish out the cold stare. 'Hannah would never do such a thing.'

'Then, how?'

Danskin clasped his hands together as if in prayer. Raised them so his fingertips rested against his lips. 'Getting accepted onto the detective fast-track scheme is hard, you know.'

Puzzled, Ryan asked, 'What's that got to do with the price of fish?' Then, 'Wait, no. You promised me you wouldn't use any influence to get me through the recruitment. Don't tell me I only got taken on because of you. You've seen my application file. You were involved in the recruitment process, weren't you? That's how you know about the burns.'

'Whoa, whoa. Slow down. You warned me not to put a word in for you. And I told you I hadn't done that for Hannah. If I hadn't done it for wor kid I wouldn't for you. No, you got here under your own steam, trust me.'

Ryan's face turned crimson. Flushed with embarrassment that the DCI knew of his damaged groin, and red in the angry belief he'd manipulated Ryan's recruitment. 'I've had enough of this. I'm putting in for Kinnear's team. I can't believe you did this to me.'

Stephen blocked the door. 'Howay, man. Calm down, sunshine. I didn't influence your recruitment. If you must know, your scores were the third best the recruitment team's ever seen.'

Ryan's brow wrinkled. 'I get it now. You were snooping at my file to see if I was suitable for Hannah, is that it?'

'For Christ's sake, Jarrod; no. Listen. Your scores were the best. You did it all yourself.' He hesitated.

'Except?'

'The medical, Ryan. You failed the medical. And I went out on a limb for you and said you'd be ok. That's the only part I played. That's how I know about your other injuries, and that's why you're on my team. If it goes belly-up, it's all on my plate.' He took a last mouthful of his brunch. 'Now, get out of here, get your head in the right place, and go find Goodman or Pope. Preferably both.'

Ryan stood, tried to process what Danskin had told him. Tried to determine if he felt angry or grateful. He made for the door.

'Oh, DC Jarrod? A couple of things: firstly, think very seriously about whether you still wish to work with Rick Kinnear. Give me an answer tomorrow. Secondly, I'd appreciate my plate back if you don't mind. I've only got four of them.'

Ryan looked down at the object in his hand. Now, he felt plain foolish.

CHAPTER EIGHT

Back at the station, Ryan wiped clean a whiteboard. He hadn't authority to set up a crime board - hell, he didn't even know if there was a crime – but he needed to map what he knew.

He drew a circle, inserted a question mark inside it where a photograph would normally sit. Beneath it he wrote *Jade* between quotation marks and *Disappeared:* followed by a set of dates. A three-week window. Too broad for it to be meaningful.

Next, he jotted down her approximate age and the fact her accent wasn't local. He stepped back from the board. Tapped the marker pen against the palm of his hand. Moved back to the board and added *Tattoo. Heart. Beneath left breast.*

Ryan drew a line under the data, beneath which he wrote *Jack Goodman.* As an afterthought, he added: *(Max Bonhomme?).*

Alongside it, he began another entry. It followed the same structure.

Radka Vosahlo / Kayla

Jotted down a window of three days.

Late twenties? Eastern European?

Piercing. Stud. He glanced towards where Todd Robson sat, smiled, and refrained from committing the body part to public scrutiny.

He wrote down the name of the informant. *Isla Pope.*

Finally, he added, *Known to DC Jarrod?*

Deep in thought, Ryan strolled to the floor-to-ceiling window riverside of the station's third floor. He rested one hand against the glass and looked out over the Tyne until his breath fogged the window like a kid at a sweetshop.

Ryan's gaze took him from the Redheugh Bridge to the west downriver to where the chrome arch of the Millennium

Bridge straddled the Tyne. Between them, five more bridges traversed the two-mile stretch of water which flashed like a silver scimitar in the low sun.

Two miles, seven bridges; bridges linking the city of Newcastle to the town of Gateshead. Ryan turned and rested his back against the glass. He looked towards the board on the opposite side of the bullpen. Two missing people, how many links?

Somewhere, there lay at least one link: something which connected him to Isla Pope and, quite possibly, another between Jade and Kayla - whoever they may be.

If only finding it was as easy as crossing a bridge.

**

Bony fingers of light parted a thin line of bushes. The fingers scrabbled over a shale surface until their tips touched metal. Slowly, they inched their way upwards and wriggled around the frame of the container door.

Radka Vosahlo knew it was daytime.

She could have been inside her metal box for weeks but she knew it was only days. She knew because she counted the bottles. Each day, a small grate at the foot of her prison opened for a few seconds and someone rolled a fresh bottle inside. It was all she ever got. One bottle. No food. No soap. No toiletries. Someone wanted her alive, for the time being at least, but only just.

When she'd arrived, her prison contained the lingering essence of expensive perfume. Now, it hummed of her sweat, urine, and faeces. All of which told her, for whatever reason, she'd been held captive longer than the previous occupant.

The sound of an engine brought an end to her thoughts. The sliver of light around the edge of her prison darkened. A vehicle had drawn up outside. Her daily water delivery.

Sure enough, she heard the squeal of a metal bolt drag from its clasp. The door inched open. Not the letter-box sized grate at the foot of the door, but the door itself. For the first time since her incarceration began, she wasn't alone.

'Time for you to checkout, petal,' a voice said. 'I need to clean your room for the next guest.' Radka heard the man sniff the air. 'You've left the place in quite a state. I wouldn't count on getting your deposit back if I were you.'

The man's footsteps echoed in the confined space as he moved towards her. Radka's eyes darted to the exit. Backed up against it, the rear doors of a familiar van stood open. She looked at the man approaching her. Tall. Muscular. She knew she stood no chance against him yet hope flared within her as brightly as the daylight outside.

Until she saw the hypodermic in the man's grip.

A hand reached out to her. She flinched, but the extended hand didn't contain the needle. It reached behind her neck. She felt the collar loosen as the needle in his other hand approached her throat.

The instant the collar came off, Radka opened her mouth to scream. But the scream wasn't hers. It came from the man behind her as she grabbed his testicles and twisted. Hard.

Her captor dropped both hands to his groin. She swivelled and kicked at the man's scrotum with a bare foot. She swore loudly as his hands deflected the blow. She'd played her ace and he'd trumped it.

His eyes widened. He raised his hands. Radka closed her eyes and cowered from the blow.

It was a blow which never came. When she opened her eyes, her assailant lay on the floor; a hypodermic needle stuck deep in his balls.

Radka laughed and cried at the same time. She dashed towards the exit, bent double, and flung herself into the transit. She cursed. It was a sealed unit. No way into the cab.

The wooden boards laid across the van's floor trembled as she retraced her steps. She glanced at the man in the rear of the shipping container. He remained unconscious, or worse.

Radka Vosahlo squeezed between the van and her prison door into blissful sunlight.

She took a moment to bask in it. Felt the rays warm her flesh. Breathed clean, fresh, air. Felt alive. She giggled to herself as she slid open the passenger door and glided towards the driver's seat.

'Going somewhere?' the man in the seat asked.

**

Ryan tapped the edge of the business card on his wooden tray. He looked at the phone lying on the table. He toyed with it. Put it back down. Raised the card and read it. The card, too, returned to the tray.

Mind made up; he tapped the number into his phone.

A chair screeched next to him and someone sat down. Ryan disconnected the call without speaking.

'Sorry, did I interrupt you?' Nigel Trebilcock. Nigel, or 'Treblecock' as those in the squad called him no matter how often he told them it was pronounced 'Bilko, as in Sergeant Bilko', was on long-term secondment from Cornwall. Ryan like him but, right now, he swore at the interruption.

'I was just finishing.' He pretended to drain dregs from his already empty coffee cup. 'Break over.'

Trebilcock tore at the wrapper of his Gingsters. Took a bite. 'No worries. I was just going to let you know Foreskin likes your mock-up crime board, I was.'

'Yeah, well, it hasn't got me very far. I've nee idea whether either of the lasses are really missing, never mind if they're connected.'

Trebilcock dabbed a crumb from his lips. 'Foreskin reckons they could be.'

'What? Missing or connected?'

'Who knows? He was talking to himself, like he does. Guess what else he said?'

'I'll name that tune in one. Wouldn't be 'don't see what you expect to see,' would it?'

Trebilcock laughed. 'The DCI's so predictable, isn't he?'

'Aye. Todd's given him a new nickname on top of the Foreskin one.'

'Come on then, you know you want to.'

'He calls him Inspector Cliché.'

Trebilcock sprayed pasty in Ryan's direction. 'That's quite clever for Todd. Don't tell him I said that, though.'

Ryan picked up his phone and stood to leave. 'I need to get back. If Foreskin's sniffing around the board, he'll want an update.'

'Ok. See you later.' Trebilcock picked something off the table. 'Do you need this?'

Dr Kutz' card.

Ryan snatched it from Trebilcock's fingers. Tried to establish if the young Cornishman knew what it was. By his deadpan look, he hadn't. Either that, or he was an expert poker player. Ryan decided to play it cool. 'Nah, not really but I'll take it just in case.'

Trebilcock glanced over Ryan's shoulder. 'Looks like you're leaving just in time. I think Gav's after you.'

Sure enough, Gavin O'Hara bustled towards them with his short-stride gait; a walk which always reminded Ryan of Spud the pug.

'There you are,' O'Hara said. 'Howay, you're wanted.'

'It'll be Inspector Cliché, no doubt.' He winked at Trebilcock over his shoulder.

'No, someone at front desk.'

Ryan pulled a face. 'Do you know who?'

Gavin raised his eyebrows. 'Would you believe, it's Jack Goodman.'

**

Jack Goodman fidgeted with his hands while he sat waiting. Ryan watched the image on a monitor in the adjacent room. Saw the man tap his foot so swiftly his knee bounced as if he had Parkinson's.

After a couple more minutes observation, Ryan opened the interview door. 'What can I help you with, Mr Bonhomme?' He emphasised the name.

Bonhomme sprang from the seat. 'What do you think you're doing, coming around to my house? Talking to my wife? Keep away. Just…keep away.'

Ryan took a step back and pointed to a red light above the door. 'Calm down, Mr Bonhomme. You're on camera. I'd much rather you helped our enquiries rather than arrest you.'

Max Bonhomme retook his seat. His brow furrowed. 'Just a minute, how were you certain my name was Bonhomme? You said that before I mentioned my wife. How'd you make the connection? My name could've been Goodman for all you knew.'

'Let's just say, I've seen your face.' Ryan sat down opposite. 'Now, are you here to threaten me or tell me about Jade?' He opened the file he'd brought down with him.

'Both.' He saw Ryan's eyebrows rise. 'I mean, I'm here about Jade.'

'Good.' Ryan waited. The man said nothing. 'Ready when you are.'

Bonhomme cast his eyes downwards. 'I've been having an affair. That's why you mustn't come to my house. Cassie can't know.'

'Mr Bonhomme, you shouldn't have given us your address if that's the case.'

'I realise that now. The Constable I spoke with caught me on the hop. I didn't think it through. I realised what I'd done by the time he asked for my phone number. Made one up.'

'I know you did. If you'd given the right number, you'd have taken my call. I wouldn't have needed to involve your wife at all.'

Bonhomme shifted nervously. 'I've been stupid, haven't I?'

Ryan didn't reply. 'Anyway, I'm more interested in finding Jade. That's if she's missing at all.'

The Girl on the Quay

'Of course, she's bloody well missing. Why else would I be here?'

'Mr Bonhomme, let me ask you the questions, ok? That's how this tends to work.'

The man slumped in his chair. 'Ok. I'm just worried about her, that's all.'

Ryan softened his face. 'I'm sure you are. So,' he opened his notebook, 'What's Jade's full name and address.' Bonhomme looked somewhere over Ryan's right shoulder. 'Mr Bonhomme? The name and address, please.'

Bonhomme's face collapsed in on itself. 'I don't know.'

Ryan took a deep breath. Refrained from stating the obvious. Instead, he asked, 'How long have you been involved with Jade?'

'About four years.'

Ryan sat back. Looked long and hard at the man opposite him. 'I'm sorry, Mr Bonhomme, I'm struggling here. Help me out, man. You've been having an affair with a woman for four years and you don't know her name or where she lives. I'm sure you'll understand why I find it hard to believe.'

Max Bonhomme shrugged. 'She wouldn't tell me.'

Ryan shook his head. Ran a hand around the back of his neck. 'I'm sorry, but this isn't helping me at all. Why wouldn't she tell you?'

'Because that's not how it works.'

Ryan tried a different tactic. He remained silent. Waited. And waited.

Finally, Bonhomme's head dropped to his chest. 'Because Jade's an escort, that's why.'

Ryan's eyes widened. It began to make sense now. 'A prostitute.'

Bonhomme was off his seat in an instant, the chair scuttling over the floor like a cockroach in light. 'Jade is not a prostitute.' He spat out the last word. 'Don't you ever, EVER, call her that.' He pointed an accusatory finger at Ryan.

'The camera,' Ryan reminded.

Bonhomme retrieved the chair and sat as if he'd been sent to the naughty step.

Now the genie was out the bottle, the words flowed from him. 'It started when Cassie was pregnant with the twins. It was a difficult pregnancy. She was in-and-out of hospital. It coincided with my business taking off. I already owned a couple of care homes but around that time I set out to build new ones from scratch. Aimed for the top end of the market.'

Ryan thought of the grandeur of Doris Jarrod's home and motioned for Bonhomme to continue.

'I was away from home a lot overseeing the site work. It was difficult for Cass. For both of us. By the time the twins were born, I had new facilities opening. I was invited to functions, did a few publicity interviews, showed the press around. I even shot a couple of TV ads, that sort of thing. Then there were the grand openings. I opened the first three alone. In Dawdon, Low Fell, and Whickham.'

Ryan remembered the photograph in the Whickham care home lobby: some bloke from TV, the manager, and Max Bonhomme. Alone.

'My PR team suggested I should bring Cassie to events with me. Said it would make me look a family man. Prospective clients prefer that, they said.'

His voice dropped to a whisper. Ryan leant forward to hear.

'Cassie was struggling with the girls at the time and her body was still recovering. So, when I went to open my residence in Windermere, it was impossible for Cassie to come along. Trevor – my PR guru – found someone else.' Max Bonhomme looked up wistfully. 'He found Jade.'

The interview suite had fallen silent. Bonhomme turned white. Gripped the edge of the desk as if it were about to run away. At length, he continued.

'She was the perfect escort. Polite. Warm. Friendly.' He paused again. 'Beautiful. So beautiful.'

'And she slept with you.'

Bonhomme shook his head. 'No. Not that time. But, as I attended more events, Trevor said it made sense to have the same woman with me. So, I did. Naturally, Jade and I grew closer. The third time, that's when it happened.'

Ryan interrupted. 'Did you pay her?'

The man closed his eyes. 'Yes.'

'And since then?'

'Every two weeks or so.'

'Do you still pay?'

Bonhomme inclined his head. It was barely perceptible, but he did.

'Then, I'm sorry but you're not having an affair. You're using a prostitute.'

'Detective, we love each other.'

'I hate to say this, but it doesn't sound like love to me.'

'It is. On my part, anyway. As for Jade, I'm sure she feels something for me, too. Love?' he shrugged. 'I'd like to think so. She always kept our dates.' He saw Ryan look at him. 'Our appointments,' he conceded. 'That's how I know she's missing. No matter what you think, I KNOW something's happened. And I want you to find her.'

Ryan rubbed his top lip. 'You do realise she'll have other clients? I'll have to trace them.' He saw Bonhomme shudder. He clearly didn't like to think there were others. 'Where do you pick her up? Where's her patch?'

Anger flared in Bonhomme again. 'Jade isn't a common whore. She doesn't have a 'patch,' as you call it. She has an Agency'.

'I need the name and the number.'

Max Bonhomme shook his head. 'There's no number. It's all on-line. It's called Orchid Petals,' he said.

Ryan remained in the interview room long after Bonhomme had left. He rewrote his notes. Considered where the case went from here. This was fresh territory for him. The world of vice? Escorts? Prostitution? He had a lot to learn about life.

Which reminded him: it was about time his learning started.

He dialled the number of Dr Kutz.

CHAPTER NINE

'Good work, Jarrod. Looks like you do have a case after all. Well done, kidda.'

Stephen Danskin stood next to Ryan by the makeshift crime board. He put two fingers in his mouth and whistled. The hubbub around them died. 'Lyall, Todd – get yersel ower here. Ravi, you an' aal.' He beckoned the men towards him.

Once they were gathered around the board, Danskin asked Ryan to run through the details on it. Soon, he was adding the new stuff.

'We now know that Jade is a prostitute. 'Escort,' Bonhomme calls her.' He wrote her profession alongside her name. 'We know one of her regulars is Max Bonhomme.' He picked up a cloth and erased the name Jack Goodman from the board. 'And, crucially, we know she works for an agency called Orchid Petals.'

Todd Robson chortled. 'Subtle as a fart in a lift.'

'Do we know anything about the agency?'

'Only that it's an on-line thing,' Ryan answered DI Parker's question. 'I presume this means it's fronted-up as a kosher business. Not sure what category it'll be listed under at Companies House, mind.'

'Ravi; see what you get,' Danskin ordered.

'On it, sir.' Ravi Sangar levered himself from his perch on the end of a desk and made for a PC.

'Have you a photo of the lassie?' DI Parker asked.

'Shit. No.' I didn't ask.'

'Jarrod, man,' Danskin chastised.

'I know. But it should be easy to get one. Bonhomme said she went with him to PR events. There's bound to be photos of her with him.'

Danskin agreed. He glanced around the bullpen. 'Treblecock, drop what you're doing. Get on to The Mercury. See if they've got any library photos of a Max Bonhomme opening a care home. We're looking for him with a blonde lass in her twenties. Video footage preferably. Get as much of it as you can.'

'What do I tell them it's for? They're not exactly on the best of terms with us, sir.'

'Tell them the Bishop of Durham wants to hire her. I don't know, man; use your bloody imagination. There'll be plenty in their on-line archives so if they get shirty, find it yersel.'

Danskin rubbed a hand over the bristles on his head. 'Does this tell us anything about the other lass on here? This Radka Vosahlo?'

'Not directly, sir, no. I've made no progress with that case yet.'

'There mightn't be a connection,' Lyall Parker suggested.

The DCI agreed. 'There mightn't even be a second missing person. We don't know for sure.'

'No, sir. We don't. Do I leave it for now?'

Danskin considered it. A diamond-shaped prism of sunlight projected itself onto the makeshift board. Seemed to arrow in on the name 'Jade.' The DCI scratched his jaw. 'For now, aye. Let's see what we can find out about this Jade.' He twisted his head to the right. Raised his voice. 'Ravi, you come up with anything yet?'

'I've found the site, sir. Professionally produced. Classy. Like an upmarket magazine cover. Glossy looking. Expensive looking, an aal.'

'Find the girls. See what you can come up with on Jade. Her second name would help. Even better, get her photograph. It'll save Treblecock some effort.'

'No can do, sir. Members only. I can hack in, but it'll take time. Can it wait?'

Danskin blew out his cheeks. Looked at Parker. 'What d'ya think? Is it really that urgent?'

'We dinnae know enough about the case yet. She might have gone away with a John for all we know. She might even just be pissed off with Bonhomme and keeping away from him. Och, we've nothing to corroborate his story.'

Ryan disagreed. 'My gut tells me there's something in it, sir.'

The DCI took time to consider his response. 'Superintendent Connor would chuck a wobbler if we were caught hacking in. But I trust your instinct, Jarrod.'

'One of us could always register with the agency,' Lyall Parker suggested. 'We could get access that way.'

Todd Robson grinned like a Cheshire cat. 'I'm your man.'

'Robson; I'm sure you're registered with dozens of dodgy sites but Sangar said this one was 'classy.' 'Expensive,' remember? Doesn't exactly fit your profile, does it?'

Todd removed a finger from his nose. 'Probably not,' he conceded.

'I'll do it, Stephen,' Lyall Parker volunteered. 'I'm older. A bit more urbane. Might get under the radar more than Todd would.'

Robson raised the offending finger in Lyall's direction.

'Ok. Lyall sets up a profile; all agreed?' Danskin's question was rhetorical. 'Find out as much as you can. Right, lads. We've all got other work to do. Get on with it.'

The small group began to disperse. 'Jarrod?'

'Sir?'

'There's a crime board waiting over there for you. Go and set your stuff on it, proper, like. You're leading on this.'

'Thank you, sir.'

Danskin lowered his voice. 'It'll keep you from moping about Hannah. Remember, I'm watching how you deal with things.'

Hannah. For fifteen precious minutes, he'd forgotten about her. He'd also forgotten Dr Kutz's secretary had told him that there'd been a cancelled appointment which she'd happily offer Ryan.

He checked his watch. It'd be a struggle to make it.

With a bit of luck, Ryan thought, he wouldn't.

**

Ryan's mind was so focused on the case, he was on Kells Lane before he realised he'd driven straight by Kutz's surgery, or practice, or whatever the technical name for it was. He settled on 'surgery'. 'Practice' made him uneasy. He'd prefer it if Kutz didn't need any practice.

His Fiat undertook a quick lap of The Victoria and, after finding itself back at the Durham Road traffic lights, wriggled its way onto Chowdene Bank. Ryan almost missed the turn into the surgery on the way down. Like a slalom skier, he swung the car between stone gateposts, one bearing a nondescript brass plaque with the inscription *Dr Hadley Kutz,* onto a long driveway. Ryan was relieved the plaque hadn't also screamed *Sex Therapist* to all and sundry.

He'd visualised a typical low-rise, prefabricated NHS building. How wrong he'd been. Dr Kutz worked out of a grand, three-story Victorian house. Stone-built and set amidst mature gardens, Ryan presumed this was also Kutz' home.

As he approached the front door, the butterflies in his stomach metamorphosised into a squabble in a pigeon coup. What the hell was he doing? By the time he had an answer, it was too late. He was inside being greeted by a matronly woman in her late fifties as if he were an old friend.

He caught the woman's name – Olivia – but switched off after that. She could open the talking for England. All Ryan wanted was to get the box ticked for Hannah and get the hell out of there.

Mid-sentence, Olivia said, 'Dr Kutz is ready for you now.' She motioned towards a wood-panelled wall. 'Centre door.'

Ryan couldn't prevent an 'Oh shit' escape his lips.

The surgery's interior wasn't what Ryan expected. There was no wall-to-ceiling bookshelf, no collection of dusty leather-bound tomes, no Angel fish circling in an aquarium,

The Girl on the Quay

Dr Kutz wasn't seated behind an ancient wooden desk; hell – there wasn't even a leather couch.

Instead, the room was contemporary. Simply furnished, calming décor. A two-seater sofa sat alongside a low-level coffee table. At one end, a man occupied another chair. Dr Kutz seemed, well, 'normal'. Not austere or professor-looking at all.

He welcomed Ryan forward with an informal 'Hi, Mr Jarrod. May I call you Ryan? Please, take a seat. Can I offer you a drink? I'm afraid it's only water or orange-juice.'

'I'm fine, thanks.' Contrary to his expectations, Ryan felt at ease with Hadley Kutz. Perhaps this wouldn't be too painful after all.

The therapist opened with small talk, general chit-chat, gleaning background information on his age, domestic circumstances, career. Kutz went on to explain what the session entailed.

Before Ryan realised it, the subject matter had moved on. He found himself talking about his previous sexual experiences. It took him all of three minutes. Soon, he was discussing Hannah. The fire. The psychological effects it had on him. Ryan flushed as he teared up.

Kutz interrupted him. 'Sorry to intrude but, please, don't hold back on the tears. Let it all out. It's perfectly normal to become emotional,' he reached into a box and handed Ryan a tissue, 'Trust me, I'm used to it.'

Ryan took the tissue and blew his nose. 'Thank you. I wondered what they were there for. Quite a relief to find out.' He gave an embarrassed laugh as he reached for another.

'Don't feel the need to hide your emotions behind humour. Please continue when you're ready. But, just talk about your feelings. Try not to jump to conclusions about the causes behind the issues you're experiencing.'

'Sorry. Don't see what I expect to see, you mean?' Ryan couldn't believe he'd actually used Danskin's motto.

'Exactly.'

There was something about Dr Kutz. Ryan warmed to the man. Soon, Kutz was probing him about his attitude to women. Touched on, and dismissed, the Oedipus complex. Before he knew it, Kutz was winding up the session.

'Is that it? Am I done?' Ryan asked.

'For now. Olivia will explain the next steps to you when you leave.'

Ryan blinked at Kutz. 'You mean there's more?'

'We've only just begun, Ryan. Normally, the second and subsequent sessions I like to see couples together. Help them work through their issues. I'm just a catalyst. So, book a time when both you and your partner are free to attend.'

Ryan was taken aback. 'I thought I'd explained. Hannah's not my partner any longer.'

'You did explain. But it appears to me she doesn't want your relationship to end. Why else would she refer you to me? Ask her, then make the appointment. I'm sure you'll find Hannah will agree.' Dr Kutz glanced up at the wall clock behind Ryan. 'Now, we have five minutes. Is there anything you'd like to ask me?'

He shook his strawberry blond hair.

'Take your time. I find my clients often rush away then think of something they wished they'd asked.'

From somewhere, an idea came to Ryan. Kutz may be able to help in Jade's case. He'd have to phrase it carefully, but it was worth a shot.

'What about if I go to a professional about my problem?'

Kutz gave Ryan a puzzled stare. 'That's what you are doing.'

'No, sorry. I didn't make mesel clear. I mean, like...God, this is embarrassing, Another woman.'

Kutz sat back in his chair. 'I thought you understood. This is counselling. Therapy. You might find a rare therapist in the States would offer surrogacy, but you certainly won't get that from me.'

Ryan apologised once more. 'I didn't mean it like that. I just wondered what your thoughts were on prostitution. Whether it might help me.'

'I wouldn't suggest you went down that road. I'm here to help you rebuild your relationship, not end it irrevocably. I'd never recommend that to you.'

Ryan had opened Pandora's Box so he ploughed on regardless. 'But you must know of some clients who've used them.'

'I can't discuss other clients, even in a generic way.'

'What about the girls? What sort of woman gets herself involved in that sort of thing? I mean, I don't intend going down that route, but I'm curious.'

'I would suggest it would be a fairly desperate woman who trod that road. Another reason to avoid it.'

Ryan had his foot in the door. He was asking the questions now, eliciting information from Hadley Kutz on a subject so alien to him it could have come from Mars. But he didn't want to overdo it. He was sure having Kutz on board would benefit the enquiry.

Ryan quit while he was ahead. There'd be other opportunities. All he had to do was persuade Hannah to attend the next session.

'All I have to do,' he said aloud. 'Simple as.'

CHAPTER TEN

Ryan gave the door a tentative knock. Waited for the invitation. When it came, he and Lyall Parker entered Danskin's office.

'We've got a bit of a problem, sir,' Ryan began. 'DI Parker will explain.'

'Aye. It's the missing lassie. I've set up a profile for the Orchid Petals agency. Two-hundred quid just to register, I'll have you know. Daylight robbery. And I've nae idea what I'll chalk it down as on ma expenses claim.'

'Bloody hell. If I'd known that I'd have waited for Treblecock to get the photograph from The Mercury.'

'You still need it.'

'You mean the agency's a scam? A rip-off?'

'Not exactly. Problem is, it's a two-stage registration and verification process. Now I've registered, they want a skype interview before they send me a password to access the girls' profiles.'

Danskin sat back in his chair. 'Not taking any chances, are they? What do you make of it – is security tight because it's a pukka business, or because they've something to hide.'

'Got to be the latter, sir,' Ryan said. 'We know it's a cover for prostitution.'

'If Max Bonhomme's to be believed, it is. What happens if what he's said is a load of cock and bull?'

'Unlikely. I mean, he's got a lot to lose. Why would he invent something like that?''

Stephen nodded. 'True.'

'What I'm after is a steer,' Parker said. 'If I do the interview, we need to set a space up so it looks like ma hoose and not a polis station. And, we'll need Ravi to do some wizardry on the server so it can't be traced back here. It'll take a bit of time.'

Danskin considered Lyall's words. He picked up the phone. 'Treblecock, have you got any images of the missing hooker yet?' He raised his eyes to meet Ryan and Lyall's. Nodded. 'Great. Get them in here.'

'There's your answer, lads. Don't sign up for the skype-thing yet. Let's wait for more evidence first. I'm sure they'll have lots of clients getting cold feet. They won't smell a rat, even if we go back in a couple of days.'

Treblecock arrived with a fistful of photographs. Dished them out to the men.

Danskin let out a low whistle. 'Bloody hell.'

'Aye, she's a bonny wee lassie,' Parker agreed.

The images had been blown up to erase the background and cut out everyone bar Bonhomme and Jade. Even allowing for the distortion, Jade was a beautiful woman.

Danskin placed her photograph on his desk. Plonked his elbows either side of it and rested his chin on balled fists. 'Now, where have you gone, Jade?' he asked the girl in the picture.

He raised his eyes to Ryan. 'Anything on the other woman yet?'

'Radka Vosahlo? Or Kayla? Nowt yet, sir.'

'Ok.' He handed the picture to Ryan. 'Lyall, park the skype call for now. Jarrod, before we allow Lyall to shell out any more of our not-so-petty cash, you see what you can dig up on the agency. It's got to have a shady past. Check our files. Let me know what you come up with. Treblecock, you stick Jade's images on the board.'

'And,' he added, 'For Christ's sake don't let Robson get his grubby mitts on them. God knows what he'll make of her.'

**

In contrast to the state-of-the-art City and County police station in Newcastle, the Prince Bishop force operated from an old whitewashed terraced building which opened straight onto the New Elvet thoroughfare in Durham city.

In a room deprived of any natural light, DI John Craggs picked up the telephone on its fourth ring. 'Craggs.'

'Detective Inspector, how are you?'

'I'll be better when I know who's calling me.'

The voice at the other end chuckled. 'Of course. My apologies. It's Henrik Kramer all the way from rainy Ijmuiden. We spoke about the Stellendam.'

Craggs pulled at an ear lobe. 'Ah, Henrik. Of course. The old fishing boat. Did you manage to get the rust bucket back home safely?'

Although there'd been a custody battle at Superintendent level over who had rights to the trawler, Craggs was relieved the Dutch won. Despite the strange circumstances of its discovery and the mysterious contents of her cargo hold, Craggs' Super finally conceded there was no hard evidence of a crime, let alone any British involvement. Superintendent Wallace released the Stellendam back to the Dutch. 'One less thing for me to worry about,' had been Craggs's reaction.

'I thought I'd bring you up to speed,' DI Henrik Kramer said, the 'speed' coming out as 'schpeed.'

Craggs wrinkled his brow. 'That's good of you, but not sure I need to know.'

There was a pause on the other end of the line. 'There's been some developments,' Kramer said.

John Craggs set down his pen. Why did he think he was going to regret saying, 'Go on'?

'Nothing for you to worry about. Yet.'

Craggs groaned. His Dutch counterpart continued. 'We've done some analysis on the Stellendam. Thought you should know we found dried blood on the deck. A lot of it.'

'I know. Fish bleed when they're gutted,' he repeated the line the coastguard had fed him.

'Ja, indeed. But some of it – in fact, most of it – was human blood.'

Craggs closed his eyes. This was coming back at him; he just knew it. 'And?'

'Like I said to you, in this moment it's not of your concern. Our forensics matched it to a Remi Theijs. He is known to us. He has one conviction for bodily harm after a drunken brawl in Amsterdam, and two more relating to football violence in Alkmaar.'

There was a pause. 'Am I expected to say something here?' Craggs asked.

'Not at all, John. I just presumed you were taking notes.'

Craggs picked up his pen and a sheet of paper. 'I am. So, carry on.'

'Remi Theijs was the skipper of the Stellendam. But there is also the blood of at least four other individuals who we have not yet traced. I hope they are not British, but I wanted you to know in case we need to contact your Superintendent.'

John Craggs digested the information. Thought through the implications. He'd mentioned the blood in his report, thank heavens, so there'd be no comeback.

He breathed out his relief. 'Yes, I appreciate the call, Henrik.'

'One more thing, John. We found some bullet holes mid-way up a mast and five more in the deck. The Stellendam is now part of a homicide investigation.'

Bullets most definitely didn't feature in Craggs report. Fuckity-fuck-fuck.

**

As the sun dipped below the horizon, its crimson essence lingered in a Turkish flag of a sky.

Leila Kinamasi, tall, lithe, and graceful, lay her hands on the stone wall of the Free Trade Inn's beer garden and took in the unparalleled view of the Tyne as it cut a swathe through Newcastle and on towards Blaydon.

She checked her Raymond Weil watch. Drew in air. Downed the last few drops of her gin. It was time for Leila to become Ebony.

She reapplied her make-up until her lips glistened wet and scarlet. After smoothing down her close-cropped black hair, Ebony set her well-practiced hip sway into action as she walked downhill towards the quayside.

She reached the Ouseburn barrage, planted like a whale's jawbone in a narrow canal-like tributary just a few yards from the Tyne, deep in thought. Perhaps tonight wouldn't be too bad. Her client had requested a companion to show off to his business contacts. Perhaps the Ed Sheeran concert at the Arena was the worst she'd suffer tonight.

Or, perhaps it wouldn't.

The man was there already, waiting for her outside the apartment. He was early. Not a good start. The Mayan liked the girls to greet their clients inside the apartment. 'Never on the street,' he told them. 'You might be a common whore but never act like one.'

Ebony withdrew a red-and-white capsule from her bag, popped it into her mouth, and tossed back her head. She was prepared for a long night.

She studied her companion as she approached. Casual but expensive clothes, clean shaven, much smaller than her. Attractive but a bit too pretty for her taste. Could be worse, though, she concluded.

'Ebony?' The man sounded shy. Again, not her type.

She lowered her voice an octave. 'Hi.' She grabbed him around the waist and pulled her to him so he caught her scent. She pecked him on the cheek, then tenderly wiped the lip-stick smudge from it.

'I'm not used to this sort of thing,' the man said, eyes cast to the pavement. 'What do we do now?'

'Well, a drink would be nice. We've got time before the concert. Unless, you want to meet up with your associates first.'

'Who? Oh, no. Drink would be good.'

They set off for the Pitcher and Piano in an uncomfortable silence.

'What's your name?' Ebony asked.

'Malcolm.'

'What do you do for a living?'

'I'm in IT. Look, do you mind if I pop to the cash machine? It's just round here.'

'Do I look that expensive?' she teased. When Malcolm didn't reply, she tried hard not to roll her eyes and settled for an, 'Of course not.'

They ducked into a lane beyond the Law Courts.

Malcolm began patting down his pockets. 'My wallets here somewhere. Bear with me.'

A van trundled towards them.

'Ah, here it is.'

He removed his hand from his pocket. He didn't hold a wallet. Between his fingers, the blade from a Stanley knife glinted under a streetlight. Ebony's eyes widened.

'Keep your mouth shut and you won't get hurt. Otherwise, you'll have no tongue.'

The van crawled to a halt. Another man leapt from it, opened the doors, and in seconds Ebony found herself sprawled on the floor of the van as it sped away.

The transit weaved its way along a Quayside increasingly busy with revellers. The girl in the back began pounding on the van doors. Loud, staccato bangs.

'Shit, man. Listen to her. You should've shut her up,' the driver shouted.

'Didn't have time, did I? Anyone could have seen us if I'd arsed about.'

The walls of the van reverberated with Ebony's frantic efforts. She hammered against the wooden boards covering the floor. The driver veered onto the Swing Bridge. 'She's drawing too much attention. You'll have to shut her up.'

'How am I supposed to do that from here?'

'Look, I'll pull in somewhere up Bottle Bank. Bound to be quiet up there. You make sure the bitch shuts up. Tie her up.

Sit on her if you have to. Just, shut her up.' All the while, Ebony continued to hammer against the van walls.

'Now,' the driver said. 'I'm pulling in here.'

The van had barely stopped before the man who called himself Malcolm was out the door and at the rear of the transit. He readied the blade, hauled open the doors, and stopped in his tracks.

Ebony wasn't banging on the walls. At least, not with her hands she wasn't. The girl was in the throes of a seizure; five foot eleven inches of legs, arms, torso, and head crashed against any surface they came into contact with. Abruptly, it stopped.

Malcolm returned to the driver's cab. He clambered in, ashen-faced.

'That's better,' the driver said.

'Better? You know fuck all, man. The girl had some kind of fit. She's not quiet because I shut her up.' He turned towards the driver.

'She's quiet because she's dead.'

CHAPTER ELEVEN

Lou Chamley gnawed on the quick of a finger as he broke the news.

'I wouldn't normally call you this early, but I think we've lost another one.' He slurped back the saliva pooled around his protruding teeth. 'Ebony didn't turn up for her date last night. The client isn't happy.'

He heard a soft whistle down the line.

'Who is it?'

'Richard Callaghan. He'd taken out a corporate booking for the Sheeran gig. Everyone had partners. Except him. He says we embarrassed him and potentially cost him a shitload of contracts. He'd spun them a yarn about his exotic younger girlfriend, built her up, then had to contrive some feeble excuse for her non-appearance. Callaghan claims we made him look like a loser.'

'Probably because he is.'

'He's also a good client, sir. Or, was. He says he'll never use us again.'

The silence down the line was palpable. Eventually, the Mayan broke it.

'I don't care about Callaghan. There's plenty more where he came from. What we don't have is another girl like Ebony.'

Chamley looked at the walls of his office in the Whipped Cream venue. Glossy posters of a host of dancers. There seemed no shortage of potential replacements. 'We could always promote another of the dancers,' he offered.

'Don't be a tit all your life, Chamley: of course we'll promote one of the dancers. But she won't be an Ebony. Or a Jade. Or any of the others Luuk's taken. I gave him Haines and the other piss-artist on a silver platter but he's not going to stop, is he?'

'Doesn't look like it,' Chamley agreed. When he heard a hiss at the other end of the phone, he continued. 'It's always possible Ebony's sick. Luuk mightn't have taken her.'

'Have you not checked?'

'Yes, sir. I called her immediately before dialling you. Her phone's dead.'

'In that case, you retard, Luuk's taken her.'

'If he has, we'll hear from him. Do we pay this time?'

Chamley had to hold the receiver away from his ear. 'No, we don't. I'm not being blackmailed by that Dutchman,' the Mayan screamed. 'He can do with her what he pleases. As you say, Ebony can be replaced. The Thai girl who came in on his last shipment; the one we named Mai Tai. She shows promise.'

Lou Chamley feared crossing the Mayan but felt he should remind him. 'She's very new. Doesn't even speak English.'

The phone moved from his ear again when the Mayan bellowed back. 'Chamley, I don't give a flying fuck. And neither will the clients. They won't hire her to discuss the state of the economy, will they?'

'You're right, as always sir. I'll get onto it straight away.'

'I know you will. And you'll do a couple more things, too. You'll beef up security. We need more than Titus and that other bonehead.'

'Okay. The other thing you want me to do?'

'If you hear from Luuk before I do, you'll tell the Dutchman he can stick the ransom up his cheese market.'

**

The squad arrived to find Danskin's office transformed.

Strips of wallpaper had been fastened to the wall by drawing pins. A photograph of some random guy's graduation hung in a frame against it. The DCI's desk had been pulled away from the window, covered in a tablecloth borrowed from hospitality, with a comfortable chair from the station's break-out area wheeled behind it. Danskin had even set a bottle of Corsodyl mouthwash – his go-to vodka substitute – on the desk for added authenticity.

'I've changed my mind,' he said by way of explanation. 'I want Lyall to register with Orchid Petals after all.'

'Aye, and Mrs Parker wasnae impressed at the four o'clock call, either.'

'That says something, Lyall: that she's more bothered about an early-morning wake-up call than she is about her husband registering with an escort agency.'

Ryan and Ravi Sangar laughed. 'So,' Sangar asked, 'You want me to mask the mainframe?'

'No need. Lyall's got a spanking new i-pad he'll be using. What I do want, is for you to somehow patch it into a PC in the bullpen so we can watch the action. I want to see whoever's behind the agency.'

Gavin O'Hara was curious. 'Have you new evidence, sir? Yesterday, you didn't think this was urgent.'

'It might be something or nothing, but the agency's bound to have some background on this Jade character. Seems to me it's the best way we have of finding more about her.'

Forty minutes later, Lyall Parker sat behind a table in his faux residence, i-pad in front of him, false ID at the ready in case it was required. Outside, in the bullpen, Danskin and Sangar sat by one PC with Ryan, Gavin and Sue Nairn huddled around another.

Ravi gave Danskin the nod. The DCI signalled to Lyall through the office window and, like a film director, counted down 'three, two, one, and – silence, everyone.'

Ravi scribbled on a notepad. *'We're seeing what Lyall sees,'* it said.

What Lyall saw was the soft-focus cover shot of the Orchid Petals website, not a person. Danskin pulled a face. Not a good start.

The second surprise was that the voice which spoke to Parker was female. Smokey, but not overtly sexual. The voice asked Lyall to confirm his name. 'Angus Watson,' he replied.

'Do you have any photographic ID, Mr Watson?' the voice asked.

'Och, that I do,' he said, making a play of rummaging in his wallet for the fake driving license.

'Please, hold it up to the camera.'

Lyall Parker obliged.

'Splendid. Thank you, Mr Watson. We can't be too careful,' the voice said. 'We're a reputable organisation and we like to take care of our girls.'

Ryan and Sue Nairn rolled eyes at one another, while Danskin struggled to contain a tisk.

'We have all the details we need from you, Mr Watson. I can confirm you are now registered. Welcome to Orchid Petals.' The image on screen changed and a shifting gallery of beautiful women smiled their welcome to Parker. 'Your password will be e-mailed to you presently. Please change it to a password of your choosing before entering our site.'

Danskin made an ok sign with his hands. That's what he needed to run his checks on Jade.

Lyall had rehearsed his next lines. 'I'd prefer to have brunettes, and I need them to be able to accompany me to prestigious events. I'm captain of the golf club and also treasurer of a charity. I'd need a girl with poise, confidence, and glamour who could represent me.'

'Mr Watson,' the female voice said, 'All our girls fit your requirements to a tee, if you excuse the pun.'

Lyall hesitated. Looked down at the desk, as he and Danskin had discussed. 'What about after the events? I presume I can enjoy my escort's company?'

The detectives in the room held their breath. Ryan crossed his fingers. This was the moment Orchid Petals revealed their true colours.

'Our fee covers you for the duration of your event, and no more. As I said earlier, we are an agency of repute.'

The Girl on the Quay

Bollocks. No confirmation of Orchid Petals involvement in vice. Still, the main purpose – the only purpose – of Lyall's audition was to gain access to the missing woman's background. With the password pinging its way to Lyall's i-pad, it was mission accomplished; anything else, a bonus.

'Of course,' the voice concluded, 'Whatever you and your companion choose to do afterwards is entirely in your hands. All and any private arrangements you make are nothing to do with Orchid Petals.'

Danskin mouthed, 'It's not enough.'

Until the voice added, 'I do make sure our girls know how accommodating to be, though.'

Ryan and Gavin exchanged high-fives as the woman ended the skype session.

**

'Are you sure?'

'Yes, sir,' Ravi replied. 'There's no-one called Jade on the agency's books.'

'Right.' Danskin plucked at an eyebrow. 'Could she have another alias?'

'Negative,' Ryan said. 'I've gone through every girl's image. There's around thirty of them. None are the girl photographed with Bonhomme.'

'So, we're no further forward. Jarrod, this is your case – what do you suggest?'

Ryan paused for thought. 'We could park it. Write Bonhomme off as a saddo fantasist. Possibly charge him with wasting police time.'

'Or?'

'Or, I have one more crack at him first. Unless he's in the middle of some sort of breakdown, I can't see why he'd make something like that up. He's got a wife. Kids. Another on the way. Aye, and, I've seen his home, an aal. It makes Buck House look like a favela. Why risk it all?'

'Get onto it, then. But gan canny. I don't want Superintendent Connor kicking off if Bonhomme lodges a complaint.'

The group broke up. Ryan took a sip from a glass of water. Pondered his next move: telephone Bonhomme or turn up at his house? The latter was a risk. Get it wrong, a complaint would surely follow.

His thoughts were interrupted by a voice.

'How's tricks?' Hannah stood by his shoulder, a file in one hand, evidence bags in the other.

'Full of busy. You?'

She held up the bags. 'You know; busy.'

The conversation was awkward. Stilted.

'Look, just so you know. I've been to,' he hesitated, 'My appointment.'

Hannah offered a pursed-lip smile. 'And?'

'He was okay. IT was okay.'

'Good. I'm pleased for you, Ry.' She began to move off.

'Hannah?'

'Yeah?'

'He wants you to come with me to the next appointment.'

She looked around. Lowered her voice. 'Didn't you tell him it was over?'

'I did. But Dr Kutz says it's usual to attend together. Besides, and I know this sounds crass – I don't mean it to – I think he can help with my case.'

She straightened. 'Really? You expect me to believe that? It wouldn't be a ruse to get back with me again, would it?'

'Honest, guv,' he held his arms aloft, 'No. In fact, I told him I didn't want you there.'

Hannah bristled. 'What the actual fuck? You mean you're giving up on us? Just like that?

'Ah, man; howay. You just accused me of using it as a way to get back with you; now, you're saying I don't want you. I don't understand you anymore; I really don't.'

A figure approached. Put an arm around each of them. 'Keep it civil, guys. I warned you, didnae I?'

'Sorry, Lyall,' they said together.

'You will be. Now, take a break. A walk into town. Anything. Just sort it out.' He relieved Hannah of her items.

'That's what I'm trying to do,' Ryan protested. 'It's her.'

Lyall Parker tightened his hold. Walked them to the elevator as if they were under arrest. 'Go. Now. The pair of ye take half an hour. An hour if you have to.'

He pushed them into the lift, bent an arm inside, and pressed the 'G' button. Parker left them to it as the door slid shut.

**

Ryan and Hannah left the station in silence and turned right down Forth Street. At the same time, a figure prised itself off the adjacent wall and fell into step behind them.

A chill wind whipped up, scattering litter along the footpath. The skies darkened as grey clouds gathered and obscured the sun like a drawn curtain. Hannah zipped up her leather jacket and thrust her hands deep within its pockets.

Still without speaking, they walked onto Orchard Street and through the railway arches. Their stalker followed at a safe distance and continued to do so when they veered left on Neville Street.

The pursuer saw their frames sag as the tension between them eased. The stalker was close enough to hear them when they eventually spoke, both at the same time. They gave an embarrassed laugh.

'You first,' the figure heard Ryan say.

'I was just going to say I'm sorry. I was out of order back there.'

'Aye, you were but it's alright as long as we can stay civil. I don't want us to fall out, Hannah.'

She smiled. 'Me neither. And, about the appointment? I'll think about it.'

'You will? Cheers. It means a lot. I wasn't joking when I said Dr Kutz could help with the case, you know. He told me a couple of things I didn't know; that I'd never considered.'

'Don't get ahead of yourself, Ry. I haven't said 'yes' yet. But I promise I'll think about it.' They walked past the Split Chimp pub heading towards the Central Station. 'Anyway,' she said, 'I'm intrigued how you think Dr Kutz contributed to the investigation. What did he say, like?'

Rain began falling. Big, fat, bird-drop splats. They quickened their pace but still the gap between the stalker and them narrowed to touching distance.

'Well, for starters…'

Ryan felt a hand on his shoulder. Instantly, he spun one-hundred and eighty degrees and was behind his assailant, ready to put him into restraint.

Except it wasn't a him.

'I have been looking for you,' a voice from within a grey hood said.

Ryan found himself looking into a pair of pale, lifeless eyes. Something in them stirred a memory deep within him.

'Do I know you?'

The girl indicated towards a building opposite. 'You saw me in there. And, later, you were at the hospital. You had bad hands.'

Ryan looked at the woman. Glanced across the road towards the building she'd indicated. Flicked his eyes to Hannah, and back to the woman.

'I am Ilona,' she said. 'Ilona Popescu. Do you not remember?'

Remember? How could he forget?

CHAPTER TWELVE

Memories of Teddy McGuffie's battered face still haunted Ryan's nightmares. Ryan was a Special Constable at the time. He'd stumbled across McGuffie's beaten body on the same day the Tyneside Tyrant unleashed his crusade of terror on the region. With McGuffie's case lost amidst the maelstrom which followed, Ryan vowed to investigate it.

McGuffie, a cab driver, worked for Charlton's Cabs, a shady company operating out of premises in an office block opposite the Split Chimp. Ryan remembered a young woman working the radio behind a grill-protected front desk. The woman had lank greasy hair, acne-scarred face, and lifeless eyes.

The woman – Ilona Popescu – disappeared before the case was solved. The only other time Ryan set eyes on her was at a hospital pharmacy while awaiting discharge after his burns treatment. She was in the waiting area, watching him with bruised and blackened eyes.

It was a vastly different Ilona Popescu sat opposite him in Pink Lane Coffee parlour. Her hair, still blonde but without coloured roots, shone. Her make-up disguised her pockmarked complexion. Yet, her eyes remained cold and dull.

'What do you want?' Ryan asked her.

'In you, I think I can trust.' Ilona eyed Hannah suspiciously. 'But you, I am not sure.'

'She's fine. She's my… I work with her. Honestly, you can trust her.'

Ilona remained slumped in her seat. Finally, she decided she had no choice but to trust her. 'I am wanting your help. I have lost my friend. She is called Radka. I think she come to harm.'

Ryan and Hannah exchanged glances. 'I know you came to the station. Why ask for me?'

'It is as I say. I can trust you.'

'You can trust any of us, Ilona. Detectives, uniformed police; we're all here to help you. And, why the false name?'

She stifled a snort. 'I cannot tell anyone but you. I am, how you say, illegal. We both are, Radka and me. That is why.'

The coffee shop began to fill up as passers-by took refuge from the downpour. Ilona's head danced from side-to-side, watching them.

'No-one's listening, Ilona.'

'I would not be so sure.' Finally, she continued. 'I come from Romania. Radka from Slovakia. We do not belong.'

Ryan reached forward and took her hand in his. 'If you want me to find Radka, I have to know everything.'

Ilona Popescu let out the sigh of a wounded deer. She remained silent for a long time. When she did speak, it was as if she addressed her coffee cup.

'I come in lorry. There were twelve of us. Six were to go in one truck, the rest in a second. There was a false floor. The man led six into the first truck. Only, he miscounted. He put seven in. I was the last. We were made to lie down. The floor covered us like the lid of a coffin. We only felt fresh air again when we got to Dover.'

She stared into the swirls of a latte. 'We waited for the second truck. The one I should have been in. When they lifted the floor, all were dead. The truck, it let in fumes from its, its…'

'Exhaust.'

'Yes. Its exhaust. They all poisoned. I should have been poisoned, too.'

Hannah's palm settled atop hand mountain. 'And Radka? She was with you?'

Ilona shook her head vigorously. 'No. I meet Radka much later. I sleep rough after Mr Charlton – the man who ran the cab firm, yes? – threw me out. He beat me for talking more to the police. Radka was kind to me. She often dropped me some coins as she passed. Soon, the coins became notes. We talked. She, like me, could not speak to others. I think she felt we were comrades. To me, she talked about all things.'

Ryan noticed Ilona spoke about Radka in the past tense. Did she know something, or just feared the worst? He said nothing.

'Then, she asked if I wanted to stay with her. She was so kind. She even told me there was a job where she worked. It was only a job in a bar. But it was a job. I got it. It helped pay for these,' she cupped breasts too large for her frame, and fell silent.

'Where do you think Radka is now?' Ryan asked.

Tears welled. 'I think she is hurt.'

'What makes you say that?'

Her gaze shifted to the coffee shop window where rain streaked its surface like tears down a cheek. She watched folk hurry by; folk doing the things normal people do.

'Where I work. It is not normal. It is a place only for men.'

Ryan began to join the dots but asked the question all the same. 'I thought you said it was a bar?'

'It is a club. Radka danced there. Do you not understand?'

'I think I do. What's the club called?'

'It is Whipped Cream.'

Ryan glanced towards Hannah.

'Worswick Street,' she said in answer to the unasked question.

Ryan hesitated before diving in with his next query. 'Why did you say 'danced'?'

'I am sorry? I am not understanding.'

'You said 'she danced there', not 'she dances'.'

'Ah. I see. Because she does not dance anymore. She earns more money. Much money.'

For the first time since they sat down, Ilona looked Ryan dead in the eye. 'Radka has sex with men.'

Ryan noticed Hannah wince. He removed his hand from Ilona's and lay it on Hannah's knee. He felt her tense, then relax.

'Have you heard of something called the Orchid Petals agency?'

Ilona's eyes opened like sinkholes. 'You know of it?'

'Sort of.'

'They take some of our dancers. Then they bring in more dancers. And then they take some more. It goes on and on.'

The girl finally lost her composure. 'Please find Radka for me. We are more than just friends, yes?'

Ryan felt his heartrate accelerate as he prepared the next question.

'Ilona, do you know someone called Jade?'

**

The door to the bullpen burst open with the force of a wrecking-ball. Ryan Jarrod bustled in, red-faced with excitement. Hannah trailed behind him, breathless.

He clapped his hands. 'Gather round, lads. We've got a breakthrough. Ravi, Gav, Todd – to the board, please. You too, Treblecock.'

'Who the fuck does he think he is?' Todd muttered.

'Never mind that. Get your arse ower here.' Todd's eyes widened but he followed Ryan's order.

DI Parker signalled to Danskin who emerged from his office, prepared to lead on whatever it was. When he saw the way Ryan took charge, he hung in the background.

'Okay, this is what we got,' Ryan was saying. 'We have a definite link between Jade and Kayla. They're both prostitutes, and they both work for Orchid Petals.'

'I thought we'd rubbished that link,' Gavin O'Hara said.

'Well, we need to think about it again. And there's more. They were both dancers at a club. Whipped Cream, it's called. Anyone know it?'

'Why's everybody looking at me?' Todd Robson asked when heads turned in his direction.

'It's down Worswick Street,' Ryan continued.

'I know,' Todd said amidst laughter.

'This is serious, Robson,' Ryan chided. Stephen Danskin put his head down and smiled in admiration.

Ryan picked up a marker pen and added the words 'Whipped Cream' to the crime board alongside Orchid Petals. 'Now, the girls at both Orchid Petals and the club all go by aliases. First names only. Hence, Radka Vosahlo became Kayla.' He wrote another name on the board. 'And we now know Jade is a Sobena Crzwyswski.'

'Christ, can I have a vowel please, Carol,' Todd said aloud.

This time, even Ryan smiled. 'I'll pronounce it once more: it's Cruz-isky, apparently.'

'And you thought Trebilcock was bad,' Treblecock said.

'I'll get onto it straight away,' Todd offered. 'See what I can find on.., on…,' He struggled with the name. Settled for 'Jade.'

'No rush, Todd. Don't think you'll find anything. They're illegal. I guess that's one of the reasons they use aliases.'

Superintendent Connor had joined the crowd. He stood next to Danskin. 'The kid's good,' Connor whispered. Danskin inclined his head and beamed paternally.

'Do we have a photograph for this Radka / Kayla girl?' Ravi Sangar asked.

'No, not yet. My informant's going to WhatsApp me one later.'

Danskin asked the next question. 'Who's your source, Jarrod?'

Ryan looked at him as if he'd just asked whether ET was a true story. 'I can't reveal that, sir. Let's just say it's someone close to both the club and Radka Vosahlo.'

'Right answer, Jarrod,' Superintendent Connor smiled. Ryan flushed. He hadn't noticed the Super amongst the crowd. 'Do you have anything else for us?'

'Not directly, no. My source is understandably frightened of reprisals. I'm sure I'll get more from her, but it'll take time. There is something else, though; something I got from another source. And, it's given me a theory.'

'Had your horses a minute, Jarrod,' Danskin interrupted. 'You know my views on theories, especially this early in the investigation. We don't want to see what we expect to see,' Todd Robson disguised a laugh as a cough as the DCI continued. 'It's good work, Jarrod, but we need more evidence before we get to the theory stage.'

Superintendent Connor intervened. 'The boy's on a roll here, Stephen. I don't think there's any harm in hearing what he has to say. Proceed, Detective Constable Jarrod.'

'Yes, sir. Thank you, sir.' Ryan tore off a chunk of blue-tac and affixed a flip-chart sheet to the wall. He drew a rough triangle on it.

'This triangle,' he said, 'Represents all female sex workers. And this,' he shaded the very tip of the sketch, 'Indicates the portion who go into the business willingly. They do so because they enjoy the risk, the danger. They do it because they like sex.'

Todd Robson rubbed his hands together. 'Bring it on.'

Ryan ignored him. 'That's about two-percent of all those in the industry. Think about it for a moment. Only two-percent do it out of choice.'

He drew another line in the centre of the triangle. Shaded the portion above it with hash-markings.

'Fifty-one percent are on the game because they have to. They've rent to pay. Kids to feed. They're riddled with debt or they need to pay their dealer for their next fix. They feel they've no other option.'

Ryan wrote '47%' in the lower portion of the triangle.

A phone rang in the office. 'I'll get it,' Nigel Trebilcock said.

'Now, this leaves the bottom part of the triangle.' Ryan tapped the tip of his marker pen against the number 47.

'This segment alone represents almost fifty-thousand women who offer sexual services in the UK. And, you know what? All of these are forced into...'

'Sir,' Nigel Trebilcock shouted over Ryan's voice. 'I think we need to leave what Ryan's got to say for now. This is urgent.'

'I hope it is, Trebilcock,' Connor warned.

'Trust me, it is. Someone's calling in a suspected homicide. We've a corpse on our hands.'

Trebilcock looked at Ryan.

'It's the body of a young woman.'

CHAPTER THIRTEEN

Ryan sat in the rear of the car, Nigel Trebilcock alongside him; up front, Danskin with Hannah at the wheel. They travelled in silence, leaving Lyall back at the station to oversee Ravi, Todd, and Sue Nairn's efforts to uncover anything on Orchid Petals, Whipped Cream, or either of the missing women.

Ryan watched the streets of Tyneside pass in a grey blur of mediocrity. The world had taken on the appearance of a grim 1960's docu-drama. Rain fell continuously. Traffic splashed through pools of water. People walked hunched beneath umbrellas or buried deep in drab raincoats.

Through the mist, a skeletal framework loomed like the ribcage of a long-dead beast. Trebilcock wiped at the window and pressed his face against the glass. 'Where the hell are we?'

'Dunston staiths, mate,' Ryan explained.

'Oh-kay. I'll rephrase the question. What the hell is it? Apart from something out of a Mad Max movie, that is.'

'These days, it's not much. It's Grade II listed but that doesn't stop bastards setting it on fire every few years. According to me dad, it's the largest timber structure in Europe.'

Trebilcock tried to push his face through the glass to get a better view. He almost broke his nose when the car lurched onto a pot-holed approach road.

'What's the point of it? It looks like it's built in the middle of the river.'

'Probably because it is. In the olden days, coal wagons would line the deck of the structure. Ships queued all the way from here back down to where the Redheugh Bridge

The Girl on the Quay

stands waiting to be loaded with coal. You see, from the top platform, the wagons could tip their cargo directly into the ship's hold. Much quicker than shovelling it aboard.'

The Cornishman shook his head. 'Bugger me. Is that where the phrase 'coals to Newcastle' comes from?'

'Ah divvent knaa. Sir, do you?'

Danskin didn't reply. He was fixated on a convoy of vehicles gathered around a tented village. He zipped up his coat. 'We're here.' He was out the car before Hannah applied the handbrake.

Vehicles stood parked at odd-angles, blue lights flashing. A ribbon of blue-and-white tape rippled in the breeze. Danskin showed his ID and shared words with a couple of uniformed officers guarding the only entry point.

Hannah remained in the car while Ryan and Trebilcock made their way towards Danskin. When they joined him, the DCI provided an update. 'The officers tell me they're still securing the scene. Pathologist's here already. It's Aaron Elliott, unfortunately.' The name meant nothing to either Ryan or Nigel Trebilcock. 'He's in charge of the SOC until he says otherwise. Forensics are almost done but they're not ready for us yet,'Danskin said, impatience tangible in his voice.

Ryan surveyed the scene with a sense of remoteness, as if he were watching an episode of CSI. It was his way of preparing himself for whatever horrors awaited him inside the cordon.

Within the inner cordon, he watched a trail of white-suited and hooded figures scurry back and forth along a single route as if they were worker ants. In their hands, they carried sealed plastic bags.

Behind, on the balcony of riverside apartments, rubberneckers gathered and made up their own version of events. Some filmed the activity, eager to be the first to download events to social media.

Ryan's gaze took in sparse greenery on the riverbank. Carrier bags, ripped and torn, fluttered like flags where they'd snagged on shrubbery. Beyond, the tidal basin was a sea of oozing, foul-smelling mud.

Further out, the monstrous spectre of the staiths stood mournfully over two stooped figures kneeling in quicksand-like sludge. Through the mist and gloom, a light flared bright. Three, four, five times. Satisfied, the photographer stood and made his way gingerly along a trail of railway sleepers laid over the mud.

'Christ, this place gives me the creeps,' Trebilcock's Cornish burr brought Ryan back to reality.

Ryan shrugged and flicked raindrops off his hair. 'Never thought of it that way. I live up there somewhere,' he pointed in a vague upwards direction towards a village draped in impenetrable fog. 'Second nature to me.'

'It stinks like hell, on top of everything else. No, sorry, Ryan - I'll take a cider orchard on a sunny day over this every time.'

'It's home to me, man. Even the stink of the river doesn't bother me. When the tide's in, it's not half as bad.'

The photographer, drenched and muddied, exchanged words with Danskin before heading off to disrobe. The DCI signalled Ryan and Trebilcock through the outer cordon. 'Elliott says we can go in now. Only two of us, though. Treblecock, you see if you can find out anything from Forensics. Probably too early to tell but give it a go anyway.'

Trebilcock somehow stopped himself from punching air as Danskin addressed Ryan.

'Jarrod, you're with me. Let's get wor fancy dress on.'

**

The 'fancy dress', as Danskin called it, was more awkward than Ryan imagined. The overshoes bit was fine, but the cloaking, the double-gloving and other paraphernalia were trickier.

'Bloody hell, sir, all Vera does is pull on a pair of marigolds and gets stuck in.'

Stephen Danskin chuckled. 'I forgot it's your first time. I'll try to make sure Dr Elliott is gentle with you. It's not all an assurance against contaminating the scene. Some of it's for your own protection.' He looked across the seething mud bath. 'I reckon it'll be pretty toxic out there.'

'Great,' Ryan muttered as he stepped onto the designated route. The wooden plank wobbled as it took his weight. 'Jesus.'

'Take your time. Just divvent fall off or you'll sink like a brick.'

'You're not helping much, sir,' Ryan said as he tottered awkwardly along the plank.

The wind hit them as soon as they left the shade of the riverbank. Slime oozed over the boards making their journey even more hazardous. The plastic shoe coverings offered no grip. Twice Ryan had to grab at Danskin's arm to prevent falling from the makeshift pathway. At least it kept Ryan's mind off what waited at its end.

Aaron Elliott saw them coming and rose from his squatted position. 'Sorcerer's brought his apprentice with him, I see.'

Dr Elliott was younger than Ryan had expected. At least, he seemed younger. It was hard to tell under all the garb. Ryan thought the pathologist had an oddly shaped skull until he got close enough to realise the plastic bonnet was distended because of a mass of hair tucked beneath it, not a deformity.

'DC Ryan Jarrod, meet Dr Aaron Elliott: a man who enjoys his work far too much.'

Elliott laughed. 'I'd shake hands but, you know…' He showed Ryan gloves blackened with mud and God-knows-what-else. 'You're not a shredder, are you?'

'A what?'

'A shredder. You haven't got eczema or psoriasis?'

'No.'

'That's good. I know you're all gowned up but you'd be surprised what can escape. I don't want your skin flakes all over the scene.'

Danskin interrupted the exchange. 'Howay, then. What you got for us?'

Aaron Elliott motioned towards a blackened hillock protruding from the mud. 'Thar she blows,' he said.

'What can you tell us?' Danskin said as he inched towards the body.

'She's dead.'

'Remind me again, how much do we pay for your expertise?'

Danskin and Elliott stood at the edge of the platform, staring down at the corpse.

'Female. Perhaps thirty, at most. Hard to tell given the viscosity of the surface, but I'd guess she either fell or was pushed or thrown from up there.'

All three of them looked up at the gigantic timber structure hiding in shame amongst low-slung cloud.

Danskin crouched close to the body. He gagged. Reached into his pocket and rubbed Olbas oil beneath his face-covering. 'She smells rank but looks fresh. Any idea how long she's been here?'

'Appearances can be deceptive, Detective Chief Inspector. I wouldn't like to hazard a guess.'

'Humour me, Dr Elliott. Hazard one.'

Ryan dared to edge closer as Elliott stared down the length of the staiths where the wooden structure narrowed the Tyne in a pincer effect.

'See down there? The staiths cut across the river in a way that restricts current. Which means all this,' the pathologist waved an arm to indicate the acres of sludge all around them, 'Is saltmarsh. Or what remains of one.'

Danskin waited for Elliott to continue. When he didn't, he prompted him with a 'So?'

The Girl on the Quay

The pathologist looked at him as if he were the village idiot.

'In a saltmarsh, bacterial and fungal assemblages associate. In this particular saltmarsh, an amplicon abundance indicates the saprophyte communities have established correlations with dominant fungal and bacterial taxa. Which, in turn, lends itself to possible ecological interactions between decomposer organisms.'

'Oh, of course,' Danskin agreed. 'Now, tell me again. In fucking English, this time.'

Aaron Elliott gave a resigned sigh. 'Saltmarshes trap carbon in the layers of mud. Not only the mud. It means they're more efficient at storing the carbon dioxide in any organic matter found within them. Now, coupled with the fact the surface is waterlogged, the marsh contains precious little oxygen. Are you with me so far?'

'I think so, but it tells me nowt about how long the lass has been lying in that mess.'

'Bear with me. I'm getting there. So, decomposition requires oxygen. As I've said, there's much, much less oxygen in a saturated bog like this so a body won't decompose at the normal rate.' He gave Danskin a condescending smile. 'Like I said, I wouldn't like to hazard a guess how long she's been here. I'll know more when I get her back to the lab.'

Danskin and Ryan felt the platform shake beneath their feet. They looked over their shoulders to see four stretcher bearers, dressed like astronauts, wheel a gurney towards them. Ryan's stomach lurched when he noticed a body bag draped over it in readiness.

'And, right on cue, here's her burnished throne,' the pathologist said.

Ryan and Danskin stood aside as the suited figures squeezed by them. Dr Elliott took charge of proceedings. 'Okay, gentlemen. She'll be stuck fast in there. Brace yourself; I don't want to lose anyone overboard.' The stretcher bearers positioned themselves. 'On my count. One, two, three and…HEAVE.'

The bog sucked obscenely as it fought to keep its grip on the girl. Slowly, messily, the team dragged the woman onto the platform. Slime and filth trailed from her and splattered the platform.

Ryan recoiled from the mess. The woman was unrecognisable, mummified within foul-smelling coagulant. The girl remained coated in black goo, almost as if she were charred, as they lifted her onto the stretcher.

Charred.

Ryan's stomach heaved at a memory, as much as the sight. His cheeks bloated. He retched.

'Don't you dare spray vomit over my scene,' Dr Elliott warned.

Ryan swallowed down the sweet thickness in his throat. He watched the crew zip up the body bag and teeter back towards the shore. He spoke to Dr Elliott for the first time.

'I need to ask you something. We're working on a theory the woman may be Eastern European. Is it possible to give us an indication of the girl's ethnicity at this stage?'

'No, of course not. Not without further testing.'

'Thought as much,' Ryan said.

'But I can tell you I think it's highly unlikely she's from east Europe. In fact, I'd go as far as to say the odds are close to a hundred to one against.'

The Detectives made eye-contact. 'Really? What makes you say that?'

'Well, beneath all the black slime and mud lies a woman who is also black. If I remember correctly, ethnic Africans make up little more than one percent of the Eastern European community.'

**

Ryan took an age to change and dispose of the PPE. He emerged from the tent, ashen-faced, where Stephen Danskin waited.

'Bad as that, yeah?'

'Pretty much.'

'You'll get used to it.' Stephen draped an arm around Ryan's shoulder. 'Come on, let's get you back.'

Ryan shook his head. 'It's not that, sir. I saw worse things when the Tyrant was at large.' He stilled as he remembered a human-torch of a girl he'd failed to save. Thought back to the muddied corpse they'd only just hauled out of the Tyne's mudflats. Ryan banished the memories to the recesses of his mind.

'No, sir. It's more disappointment than anything. It hasn't helped the case. I'd have put money on it being Jade or Kayla.'

'That's the way the cookie crumbles, son.' The DCI led Ryan back to the car. 'Treblecock can have this case. I want you focused on the missing lasses.'

Danskin opened the car door. 'Howay, Ryan,' he said. 'Me and Treblecock will hitch a ride back to the station with one of the uniforms. Hannah, you drop Ryan home.'

'Sir?'

'Oh shit. I forgot. Sorry. Look, we'll all go back that way. Whatever happens, we need to get you home, Ryan.'

Five minutes of silence followed as the vehicle and its occupants crawled through late rush-hour traffic. When they drove by Whickham police station, Danskin gave a mock salute. Seconds later, Ryan ordered Hannah to stop.

She pulled into a bus stop at the foot of Broom Lane. Across the road, the Bay Horse beckoned. 'It's a bit early for that, Ryan. Especially by yourself.'

Ryan was already out the car. 'I'm not going for a bloody pint, man.'

He bent double and emptied his stomach contents into the gutter.

CHAPTER FOURTEEN

A sour-and-sweet fug hung over the man at the window table. Alongside him, a woman nursed a cup of coffee in both hands and blew across the top of its steaming contents. She stared into the darkness outside, looked through her own reflection, and saw the twinkle of lights glitter-sprinkled in the inky waters below.

These weren't the waters of the Tyne: they belonged to the OZ Achterburgwal; the lights, red and blue, to the windows of Amsterdam's infamous De Wallen.

It was the windows, not the canal, which attracted the attention of Luuk Van Eyck. He took a drag on a joint and handed it to the woman, who inhaled deeply. Van Eyck's gaze never left the activity on the opposite bank.

Across the canal, the narrow street was a throng of men, women, and some in-between. They sang, shouted, pointed to the girls in the red windows and looked on inquisitively at those backlit by lilac blue neon.

Luuk Van Eyck took a slug of Amstel and retrieved his joint. He stared at the women lined up in their windows as if they were carcasses on an abattoir's hooks. Most wore lingerie barely sufficient to cover themselves. Others dressed as nurses, policewomen; even a nun beckoned to passers-by.

Luuk watched the women flirt with everyone on the cobbled street. They'd tap on the glass, wink, or open their window and make ribald offers to men who acted as if this were entirely normal. Probably because, here, it was.

'Fools,' he said, taking the aromatic herb deep into his lungs. 'How do they expect to make a living like that? Look at the competition all around them. It's like a barrow-boy attracting trade from Coster Diamonds.'

The woman took a sip from her coffee cup. Giggled. 'Shine bright like a diamond,' she sang.

Luuk Van Eyck, an overweight Jason Statham lookalike, extinguished the joint in her coffee. 'Shut your mouth. There's so many of them ripe for a better life.'

'You mean, a different life. It's no better.'

Luuk shrugged. 'It is better. They would earn more. They don't have to display themselves like window dressing. But who cares about them, anyway? It would be a better life for me, for sure. Have you any idea how much the Mayan pays for each consignment?'

'Luuk, the Mayan wasn't paying anything, remember?'

The Dutchman dug his nails into his companion's wrist. 'Don't question me.' He released her hand. A drop of blood oozed from the wound. 'And the Mayan fool thinks he can placate me by betraying the cronies who took my business from me.'

Across the canal, a pimp dragged a woman along behind him, a new product to sample. He offered her to a man in denim shorts and a ZZ Top t-shirt. They negotiated a price and the couple disappeared into an alleyway, hand-in-hand.

Luuk crushed the Amstel can in his fist. 'I want you to go back to England.'

The woman shook her head. 'No. No, I can't. It's too dangerous. What if he sees me?'

Luuk turned towards her. 'Then, I guess I'll have to find myself another woman.'

His companion grabbed his hand. 'You wouldn't.'

'Care to bet?'

The woman seemed to consider it. 'How long would I be there?'

'As long as it takes. I want to know what the Mayan's up to, if he's still getting new girls, and where he's getting them from. Most importantly, I want my fucking money.'

The woman exhaled. 'When must I go?'

Luuk smiled. 'Tomorrow.' He checked his watch. Tomorrow had become today. 'In seven hours, to be precise.'

He reached inside his puffer jacket and handed her the ferry ticket.

**

Stephen Danskin sat propped against a desk, pen tapping against his teeth, as Ryan arrived for duty.

'You're sharp, sir.'

'Aye. Couldn't sleep.' He pointed his pen towards the crime board. 'There's some good stuff on there, Ryan. Well done.'

'Thanks, sir. I didn't really get to finish my brief yesterday before the body was called in.'

'Oh aye. Your theory.' He said the words as if they were contained within speech marks.

'With respect, Superintendent Connor seemed keen to hear it.'

Danskin expelled air. 'Okay. When the rest of the team get here, finish what you had to say then you can get on with finding hard evidence, not fly-by-night theories.'

Lyall Parker arrived with Sue Nairn, followed by Gavin O'Hara. 'Bit of a wild goose chase yesterday,' Parker said. 'We didn't find much on either Orchid Petals or the Whipped Cream club.'

'Bugger,' Danskin exclaimed. 'Tell me. In fact, no. Save it 'til the others arrive. No point going over it twice.'

Ten minutes later, Danskin's team were huddled around the crime board with Ryan in front of his flipchart.

'Yesterday,' he began, 'I explained about the profiles of those involved in the vice trade. This is where I got up to,' he indicated his roughly-drawn triangle, 'Forty-seven percent. This represents the proportion of women who are forced into the sex industry by a third party. They are controlled by pimps, abusive partners, or hounded by gang members.

They do it under the threat of violence or, more often than not, actual acts of violence.'

Danskin yawned and checked his watch. 'And your point is?'

'My point is, sir, that on the balance of probabilities, it's highly likely Sobena Crzwyswski and Radka Vosahlo – Jade and Kayla – are either pimp-controlled or gang-controlled. Find the pimp or the gang, and we are halfway to finding them.' He hesitated. 'Or, whatever happened to them.'

Gavin O'Hara interjected. 'Sorry, Ryan, I don't want to knock any of this but aren't we getting ahead of ourselves here? We've no evidence to support…'

Ryan held up a hand. 'Let me finish, Gav. My source told me that the IMO reckon over one-hundred and fifty thousand women in Eastern Europe alone are ferried out of the area under deception, to be forced into prostitution elsewhere.'

He paused. Made eye contact with everyone in the room. 'And, there are three things we know about Jade and Kayla.' He counted down on his fingers, from three to one. 'We know they are sex workers. We know they are Eastern European. And, we know they were transported here illegally.'

'What are you implying, Jarrod?' the DCI asked.

'Sir, I'm asking us to consider whether Orchid Petals and the Whipped Cream club are centres for sex trafficking.'

Silence fell over the bullpen as they considered the possibility.

'That's a helluva theory without anything to back it up,' Danskin said.

'I agree, sir. So, why don't we start finding something to back it up?'

'Don't you ever listen to anything I say, lad? We don't do it because we'd lead ourselves in one direction. We'd be looking to see what we expected to see.'

Todd Robson didn't laugh this time. He didn't laugh because he agreed with the DCI. 'When you were out and about on a jolly yesterday,' Todd began, 'Lyall, Ravi, Sue and me did some digging. Nothing we found supports your theory. In fact, it kicks it in the nuts.'

'Hadawayandshite, man. How do you know?'

'Seriously, you've been spouting bollocks for the last ten minutes, man.'

Ryan flushed, angry and embarrassed that his work was being rubbished by his colleagues. 'You got any better ideas? We've got the lives of two young lasses on wor hands here. We've got to work on something.'

Todd moved towards Ryan, straightened himself. 'Listen, sonny Jim,' he said, finger jabbing in Ryan's chest, 'If you shut your gob for five minutes and listen to what Lyall and Ravi have to say for themselves, you might find you'll want to get off your pedestal and crawl back under your stone.'

Ryan launched himself at Robson. Grabbed him by the shirt collar. Todd smiled. Turned his head away, then jerked it back and caught Ryan flush between the eyes with his forehead.

Danskin and Parker were on them in an instant. 'My office. Now.' To the rest of them, 'Show's over. Get on with your work.'

The walls of Danskin's office shook as he slammed the door and let rip with an expletive-ridden rant. Finally, he calmed sufficient to ask Ryan and Todd what they had to say for themselves. He was surprised when Todd spoke first.

'I'm sorry. I was out of order but, man, he gets on me tits sometimes with his Mr Know-it-All attitude. The kid's only been here five minutes and needs to learn. But, as I say, I apologise.'

He offered Ryan his hand. Danskin was relieved to see it taken with grace.

'You two want your heads knocking together, do you know that?'

'Bit late for that, sir,' Ryan said, massaging a bump on his forehead already the size of a marble.'

The DCI couldn't quite hide a smile before adding, 'You should both be on a charge. There's only two reasons why this time – and this time only – I'll let you off with a warning. Reason number one: I need you both on the case. Number two: you're still on probation, Jarrod. A charge would be enough for you to be thrown out on your ear. I don't want that because, God knows why, I think there's a lot inside that head of yours.'

'Thank you, sir.'

'Anything remotely resembling that behaviour again, you'll be finished. Understand?'

'Yes, sir.'

'Good. Now, I don't intend taking this sideshow back out there. Robson, get DI Parker and Sangar in here. I want to hear what they found yesterday.'

When Todd left the room, Danskin spoke to Ryan, slowly, deliberately. 'Watch your step, Ryan; watch your step. Give that heed of yours a wobble, get it back on the job and away from Hannah, and you'll be okay. I want no more slip-ups.'

'There won't be any, sir.'

'I know there won't.'

Once Lyall and Ravi stepped into the office, and the latter stopped looking around like someone who feared he'd entered a warzone, Danskin asked Parker for the update.

'Whoever's behind the agency is either very smart or it's all above aboard. If you ask me, I'd put my mortgage on the former. As a canny Scotsman, that's as safe a bet as you'll ever get.'

'Evidence?'

'There isnae a shred of it, sir.'

'I find that hard to believe, Lyall,' Ryan objected.

'Aye, I'd have said the same if I hadn't checked it with ma own eyes.'

Danskin produced a notepad. 'Okay. Fire away.'

'Well, the agency hasn't attracted any interest from the vice squad. None at all. No reports of illicit activity. No complaints. No nothing. Their fees are totally transparent. You pay an initial members fee – don't I know it – then the agency lists each girl separately. Each has her own rate displayed on her profile page, alongside her skills.' He ignored Todd Robson's guffaw. 'The profiles show the type of occasion the lass is best suited for; business convention, theatre accompaniment, sports event, after-dinner engagement and such like. Everything's open and above board.'

Stephen interrupted. 'They're hardly going to advertise 'shags for sale', though, are they?'

Ravi Sangar piped up for the first time. 'I agree but you'd expect to see a hidden menu somewhere. Not exactly the dark web, but an avenue for clients to understand exactly what they get for their money. From my preliminary assessment of the site, there's nowt like that.'

'And this is where it gets more intriguing,' Lyall continued. 'DS Nairn tapped into their Companies House info. She's also been onto HMRC. It's early days, but so far Orchid Petals accounts tally precisely. Their incomings match the number of bookings exactly and they match up with the rate each girl charges. Yet, they have nae staff costs. They havnae any registered employees. Every penny of the engagement fee goes straight to Orchid Petals' coffers.'

Danskin shook his head. 'So, what do the girls get out of it?'

'To all intents and purposes, they get nothing. In short, the lassies are all volunteers.'

'Nee way. I'm not having that,' Ryan interjected. 'They're sex slaves. Must be, man.'

'Unless they all fall into your two percent who are goers,' Todd offered.

'Na. The odds are too great. Besides, my source would know.'

'Och, I'm sure you're right, Ryan. But, as far as Orchid Petals are concerned, anything the girls earn from their clients is nowt to do with them. Legally-speaking, if they get nothing from it, Orchid Petals in the clear and there's sod-all we can do.'

Danskin strolled to a window. Opened it. Traffic noise and muffled passenger announcements from the Central Station joined their conversation. 'What about the club?'

'Much the same thing. It's been subjected to a couple of random raids but nothing illegal discovered. There's been a few reports of drug use but, ironically, club staff reported them. If anything, it puts them in a better light.'

'Did you discover owt that helps us?' Danskin asked.

'The name above the door of both operations is a Mr Louis Chamley. He hasn't got a record. Ma next suggestion is we have a wee chat with him.'

Stephen Danskin smacked his lips in thought. 'Do we have a reason? I mean, a quantifiable one?'

'Of course we do, man, sir,' Ryan said. 'We've got Jade and Kayla missing. We know they worked for the agency. We know Kayla used to dance at the club. That's a good enough reason, surely?'

Ravi Sangar spoke again. 'I'm not sure it is. There's no trace of Jade on the agency's books, remember.'

The squeal of brakes from a passing Trans-Pennine Express, like the theme from Psycho's shower scene, filtered into the room.

'And there isn't a Kayla, either.'

Ryan gave the look of a child who'd just heard the truth about Santa Claus.

'Jarrod, I strongly suggest you have a word with your sources. We all know there's something in this, but we need everything to line up. At the minute, the line's about as straight as a dog's hind leg.'

Danskin showed Ryan the door.

CHAPTER FIFTEEN

Ryan slumped in his chair, round-shouldered as a chimp, forlorn as an abandoned puppy. He remained motionless for several minutes.

Slowly, he gathered himself. Glanced around. The others watched him. As in all moments of embarrassment, communication became non-verbal.

Todd Robson mouthed, 'You alright?' Ryan made the ok signal in response. Todd replied with a thumbs-up, to which Ryan smiled his appreciation.

Sue Nairn pointed at the centre of her forehead. Ryan lip-synced 'It's fine.' Nigel Trebilcock put two fingers to his temple and gave a Yankee salute. Ryan winked back in response.

Buoyed by his colleagues' support, his thought-processes sharpened. Time to let the others get on with their work. And, time for him to chase up Ilona Popescu.

He picked up his phone and headed towards the lift lobby to make the call. Across the bullpen, all alone, Hannah Graves stared at Ryan's crime board. She motioned with her head for him to join her.

It was the last thing he wanted.

'This triangle thing,' she said. 'Are you confident these facts are correct?'

'Aye, I am.'

She sighed. 'It's shocking.'

'It is.'

'The other stuff you said. What was it, a hundred-and-fifty thousand women forced into prostitution? Is that right, as well?'

'Yep. But that's only the number from eastern Europe. There'll be other hotspots. Far East, parts of Africa, I guess.'

Hannah looked at the triangular diagram. After a long while, she asked almost to herself, 'It's so sad. Where do they all go?'

Ryan shrugged. 'Amsterdam. Berlin. Spain, I believe. Who knows for sure?'

'But not Newcastle. It doesn't make sense.'

He had no answer. Silence settled over them like a cloud.

At length, Ryan spoke. 'I've got to go. I need to find Ilona. I haven't got the full story out of her yet.'

As he moved away, Hannah said, 'You didn't get all this from Ilona.'

'No. I got the basics from Dr Kutz. Researched the rest of it.'

She looked at him. 'So, you weren't lying to me when you said Kutz might be able to help with the case?'

'No, Hannah. I wasn't.'

'In that case, I've made my mind up. Book an appointment. I'm coming with you. Do it now.'

Ryan pulled up the contact list on his phone.

'And once you've done that,' Hannah said, 'Put some ice on your head. You've got one of Katy Perry's boobs growing on it.'

**

The illuminated 'No Spaces' sign shone brightly through the morning gloom yet, like someone compelled to touch a 'Wet Paint' notice, traffic still queued at the NCP entrance.

Across the narrow road, the grey and crumbling façade of the Worswick Chambers building overlooked the activity with the disapproval of family elders watching an errant grandchild.

Heaven knows what they made of the newest kid on the block.

The doors to the Whipped Cream club stood open as a Kuehne-Nagel truck poured its kegs and bottles into the darkened maw. Music, heavy of bass, vomited back out into Worswick Street. The occasional flash of light, red, violet, sometimes white, lit up the street like lightning.

Inside, a sweaty Lou Chamley dashed between supervising the sound and light check, and overseeing the brewery delivery. In the end, the phone call ensured he achieved neither.

'I know. I'm sorry. I've just seen your missed calls. It's a bit busy.'

'I pay you to be busy, Chamley.'

'Yes, sir.' He made a noise like Hannibal Lecter as he sucked back saliva.

'Any developments?'

'We didn't lose any more if that's what you mean. We didn't get a demand, either. Perhaps Luuk's given up.' He hoped he sounded convincing.

'I'm not convinced,' the Mayan said.

'I agree. I don't think he'll give up, either.'

'You sycophantic imbecile. You've just contradicted yourself. I want you to tell me the truth. Has there been any developments? Answer honestly, or I swear I'll spear your balls on your teeth.'

A reflex sent Chamley's hand to his groin. 'We've heard nothing from Luuk. We've lost no more girls. We've had no more demands.'

Chamley heard the Mayan breath down the phone. 'Have you strengthened security yet?'

'Sir, it was only yest…'

'I take that as a no. Get it done. Today.'

He heard the engineer shout for him. The brewery guy waved a chitty and mimed a signature. Chamley help up two fingers; '*two minutes,*' they indicated.

'I'll make sure Dominic gets onto the security.'

'No, not Dominic. Nor Titus. Nor any of the bartenders and certainly none of the girls. YOU, Chamley. You'll get onto it and, by lunchtime, I want you to call me. You'll confirm you've found three more chaperones, another for the door, and at least one for the floor to supplement Dominic and Titus. They can't do it all.'

The sound engineer gesticulated in Chamley's face. The brewery guy threatened to restock the dray. A photographer arrived for promo shots.

'By lunchtime, sir. I understand.'

'And before all that, get Mai Tai prepared. I know she's been screened but I see she's still not on Orchid Petals menu.'

For once, Chamley bit back. 'I can't do everything.'

'Your balls, Chamley. Think of your balls.'

'Yes, sir. I'll do it straight away.'

The Mayan knew he would. That's why he'd already disconnected the call.

**

If anywhere merits a place on a list of the coldest places in the UK, the Royal Quays Outlet Centre is it. Positioned on open land less than a mile from the Port of Tyne International Ferry terminal, exposed to winds whipping along the river direct from the North Sea, even in summer it's rarely better than frigid.

The woman fresh off the DFDS ferry emerged from a Trespass store with the cheapest fleece she could find. She ripped off the tag with her teeth and pulled it on over last night's clothes. She ordered a pastry and black coffee from an adjacent patisserie, took a window seat, and reported her arrival to Luuk Van Eyck via the WhatsApp messenger service.

She shivered, yawned, stretched, and wondered what the hell she was doing back in Newcastle. She had nowhere to stay, little cash to play with, and nothing to wear but the clothes she was dressed in.

'Go fuck yourself, Luuk,' she muttered to her coffee cup. Yet, she knew she'd do exactly as he'd asked. She, and everyone else, always did.

She stared out the window. A young couple passed hand-in-hand, a street cleaner brushed up litter and shook his head as a gust of wind ripped his spoils from him. A handful of folk scuttled by, most of them window-shopping. A young girl hitched a ride with Peppa Pig on a mechanical fairground attraction. At the other end of the spectrum, an old man slumped on a bench and bit into a Greggs.

The woman in the patisserie pulled out her phone. Scrolled through it idly. Her gaze alternated between the virtual world of Facebook and real life outside.

Suddenly, she sat up; alert and fearful. A familiar, shaven-headed black man made his way towards her. The woman looked left and right. She daren't leave her seat in case her motion alerted the man to her presence, like the T Rex in Jurassic Park. But, if she stayed still, he was heading straight for her. She picked up a menu and covered her face.

When she plucked up the courage to peer over the top, Titus was no more.

The woman dashed out the café, furtively watching out for her stalker. Next to the patisserie, along a narrow passageway, she saw a washrooms sign. Safe refuge. She took a step into the alley. Just as Titus emerged from the gents.

He had his eyes cast down at his phone. He hadn't seen her. Not yet. Panic-stricken, she pirouetted and re-entered the patisserie. Stood with her back to the door.

'Have you left something, dear?' the lady behind the counter asked.

'No. I thought I had, but I remember now.' She remained stock-still.

'Well, can I get you anything else?'

The woman didn't move, didn't speak.

'Are you ok, pet?'

Still nothing.

'Hello?'

The Girl on the Quay

The Dutch woman closed her eyes. 'Is there a man outside? A black man? I think I am being followed.'

The proprietor hurried past her to the window. Looked in all directions. 'I can't see anyone.'

The woman sagged like an old armchair. 'Good. Thank you. I shall leave now.'

She hurried out the café. Made for the outdoor mall's exit. She passed the young girl who wanted back on Peppa Pig. Her sister occupied the seat and refused to budge. The girls were arguing. Playing one parent off against the other.

'Daddy: mummy said it was my turn.'

'No, she didn't.'

'Yes, she did. Didn't you, mummy?'

The Dutch woman was alongside them, showing even less interest than the mother.

The father emerged from the shop. 'For heaven's sake, girls. Play nicely.' He looked to his wife for support. But he didn't see his wife.

Instead, he saw a face from his past.

Max Bonhomme dived back into the store as the Dutch woman hurried by.

**

Fifteen miles south, a breakfast plate was pushed to one side. In the Homer Hill Farm shop restaurant, John Craggs unfurled a newspaper while his full English settled.

He'd earmarked today for paperwork. He had no reason to hurry into Durham this morning. He'd convinced himself he deserved a lunchtime start. Until, that is, his phone vibrated on the table and performed a honeybee's waggle dance across the surface.

'Craggs.'

'Detective Inspector, my friend: how are things across the sea?'

'I hope you're not about to give me indigestion, Henrik.'

Henrik Kramer laughed heartily. 'In this moment, I don't think so.'

'Okay. Then if not this moment, which moment is it, because I sense it's coming sooner or later?'

'You are a wise man, John.'

'Howay man, get crackin'.'

There was a puzzled silence. 'I'm sorry?'

It was Craggs turn to laugh. 'My fault, Henrik. It's a local term. Sorry. What I meant to say was, hurry up and tell me what you've got to say because I've stuff to do.'

'Ah I see. I understand. I am bringing you up to date on the Stellendam.'

Craggs felt his eye-lids close in preparation for a blow. 'And?'

'We have made little progress on our homicide investigation, but we are fairly sure we know why the Stellendam was in your waters.'

'For fuck's sake, Kramer. You should write thrillers; do you know that? Stop dragging it out and tell me.'

The insufferably cheery chuckle came over the airwaves again. 'Let's just say we were wrong. She had been fishing, after all.'

'*Champion,*' Craggs thought. '*Nowt for me to get involved with.*' He opened his eyes just as the blow landed.

'Fishing for mermaids,' Henrik Kramer said.

CHAPTER SIXTEEN

Ryan pried himself off the post box on Oakfield Road, wandered to the junction of Warwick Avenue and, like an expectant father, strolled back again. He checked his watch. Scratched his nose. Checked his watch again.

Eventually, a familiar mustard-colour Renault came into view and slowed to a halt in the pull-in by a row of three shops.

'Cheers,' he said, climbing in.

'Hi.'

He raised his rear from the seat and removed the object he'd sat on. 'Still not finished with Lexi?' he asked as he tossed the copy of Unicorn Alley into the footwell.

'Never read any more of it.'

They sat in silence broken only by Ryan's GPS-like directions, until Hannah finally asked, 'What's our tactics?'

The question threw him. 'You know, I haven't the foggiest. I guess we'll just play it by ear. I mean, I want the conversation to fit around the therapy. I'm not sure Dr Kutz would appreciate us wasting his time if he knew he was being used.'

'What's he like?'

'He's okay. I think you'll like him. Dead easy to talk to. Take the next left.'

Hannah hauled the Renault onto Chowdene Bank.

'I'll let you take the lead, then.'

'Doesn't work like that. He sets the agenda. I thought, maybe, we could let this run as a normal session? When we go to the next one, we'll have more case details and have a better idea how we can use Dr Kutz's expertise to help us. Turn in here. This one; with the gateposts.'

Hannah Graves brought the Renault to a halt in a wake of shale. 'You just said: *'When we go the next one.'* Take it easy, Ry. I might be here to support you but I'm also here to help those girls. If what Dr Kutz has to say gets me under the skin of the case, then that's my real goal. Don't read any more into it, and don't assume I'll attend any more appointments.'

Ryan led Hannah inside and introduced her to Hadley Kutz's garrulous receptionist. He managed to get in his half-truth, 'I'm not,' before they were submerged in Olivia's chatter.

**

The sun shines on the righteous, and Superintendent Len Wallace. One of the few afforded the luxury of an office with windows in the New Elvet station, Wallace was lit up like the Angel Gabriel when John Craggs entered the room.

Craggs hoped it was a good omen. He was convinced Wallace was bi-polar, and never knew which persona would confront him.

'Ah, Craggsy; how the devil are you, old boy? You couldn't have timed it better. Sun's just come out to greet you.'

He was in one of his jovial moods. DI Craggs genuinely believed his luck was in.

'DCI Harrison isn't around so I wondered if you had a minute?'

'Lucy's up ay Aykley Heads for a few days. Didn't she tell you? How remiss.' He fumbled in a draw. 'Care for a slice of cake?'

Craggs shook his head, more in astonishment at Wallace's apparent transformation into a Test Match Special commentator than as a signal of refusal.

'The Stellendam, sir. Got a bit of an update.'

Wallace rummaged through a draw in search of a fork. He came out with a plastic, tea-stained spoon instead. 'Yes. Don't tell me we should have hung onto the old girl.'

'Not exactly, sir. There's still no direct evidence of British involvement, and DI Kramer from Ijmuiden says they've made precious little headway on the murder investigation.'

'Mm mm. Carrot cake's good. Sure you don't want a slice?'

'No thank you.'

'So, you have an update on nothing, is that what you've come here to tell me on this beautiful morning when the clouds have lifted, and the birds are settling on the outfield?'

Jesus, I prefer him when he's grumpy. 'The Dutch do have a theory. I haven't much information to go off, but they seem to think the Stellendam's a front for ferrying illegals across the North Sea.'

Wallace wiped a crumb from the side of his mouth. 'That's a Border Force issue. Immigration. Customs; that sort of little-boy stuff.'

'Not exactly, sir. This isn't routine immigration stuff. Kramer thinks the trawler's involved in people-trafficking.' He watched Wallace for a reaction. When there was none, he continued. 'Sex-trafficking, to be exact.'

Len Wallace coughed and choked on his cake. 'Sex trafficking?' He spluttered. Reached for a glass of water. Coughed once more. 'Remind me: where was she anchored, again?'

'A mile or so off Blackhall Rocks.'

'Hardly the Soho of the north. Is this Kramer fellow reliable? Seems to me he's just bowled you a long-hop.'

John Craggs shielded his eyes from the sun. He squinted at his Super. 'Don't really know him, sir.'

'Well, as far as I'm concerned, his lot fought tooth-and-nail to get the damn skiff back. They're welcome to it. Unless this Kramer chap comes up with hard evidence, ignore it. My advice to you is, stay clear. You've enough on your plate. Speaking of which, I think I'll have another slice.'

John Craggs left Superintendent Wallace to the caricature he'd become.

He knew he should be relieved the case was no longer his, yet he couldn't shake off the strange feeling that he wasn't.

Not in the slightest.

**

'I could do with a stiff drink.'

'We're on duty, remember.'

Hannah rolled her eyes. 'I know. It's a turn of phrase.' She started the engine and pulled away from Hadley Kutz's practice.

Ryan's stomach gurgled. 'I'm starving. There's a Porky's restaurant further up Kells Lane. Or Rosa's on Durham Road if you fancy an Italian.'

She took her eyes off the road and fixed them on Ryan. 'We're not on a date.'

'For God's sake, Hannah. Stop trying to read something into everything I say, will you?' He flipped the sun visor down and threw himself back in his seat.

Hannah drummed the palm of her hand on the steering wheel. 'Okay, Ry. Fair enough. And, you know what, I could do with something to eat. But not a meal, right? Chips or something, yeah?'

Ryan's face softened. 'Chips are good.' After a while, he added, 'You remembered I'm seeing Ilona at one?'

'Yep. And I'll come with you if you like.'

He smiled. 'I'd like that.' She looked at him. He held up his hands. 'Colleagues, I know. Don't get the wrong idea.'

They agreed to head up to Whickham. On route, Ryan asked Hannah what she thought of Hadley Kutz. Of Kutz; not the session. 'I know,' he'd said. 'You just came today for me and the case, not us.'

Hannah ran her hand through her curls as she drove. 'Yeah. He's okay, actually. Wasn't quite as invasive as I thought he'd be. He doesn't smile much, but he's fine.'

Traffic slowed to a crawl as they neared the Metrocentre, so Ryan told her to veer off the Western By-Pass and up Lobley Hill.

The Girl on the Quay

'He knows his stuff,' she continued. 'I can see how you think all his knowledge could help get into the minds of those behind the club and the agency. Listen, if I do agree to see him again with you, do you promise we'll talk about the case?'

Ryan fought against the hope welling deep inside him. 'Sure.'

'Then, I'll do it.' They turned right at traffic lights atop Lobley Hill onto Whickham Highway. 'I'm not talking about my exes again, though. No way Jose. God, how embarrassing was that? I don't even talk to myself about them, never mind Hadley Kutz. Or you, for that matter.'

Ryan smirked openly. 'How old did you say you were when you did that with Danny Smith at school?'

She slapped him on the thigh. 'Stop it.' But the dimple was back in her cheek.

Hannah found a place far too small for the Renault somewhere behind the Bridle Path. On the third attempt, she squeezed in. 'Right, Lance's here we come. It's your shout, Ryan.'

'It is, but Lance's isn't Lance's anymore, remember?'

'Oh aye. Can we get something else, then? It's a lovely day. Maybe take a sandwich into the park?'

'Sounds like a plan.'

They picked up their lunch from the Yellow Teapot and wandered up into the park on a diagonal route, skirting the playground and onto freshly mown grass.

Nature looked down kindly upon Ryan and Hannah as they wound their way uphill. Bees flirted with flower beds, birds sang in the trees, and butterflies shamelessly flaunted themselves. Ryan fought the compulsion to take Hannah's hand. Instead, he satisfied himself with a bite of his panini.

Hannah picked at a Greek salad. 'Listening to the birds reminds me. What was Kutz on about when he mentioned pigeons, swans, and people?'

Ryan laughed. 'It was something he mentioned at the last session. I was teasing out facts about the type of blokes who use the likes of Jade and Kayla.'

'Prostitutes, Ryan. You can say the word, you know.'

'Okay, then. Prostitutes.'

They settled at the foot of the remnants of an old windmill at the south-west tip of the park. Sat on cool grass and felt the mill's colder stone against their backs. Ryan wiped greasy palms on his jeans and continued.

'Kutz made a comparison with swans and pigeons. He said swans make a conscious decision to mate for life. If they lose their partner, they remain celibate for the rest of their days. Pigeons make the same commitment. But, when a partner dies, they are free to find another as long as the bird has nee other partner. Man, on the other hand, makes a similar promise to his partner, 'til death us do us part', and all that, but consciously chooses to renege on his vow. 'That', Kutz told me, 'Is why prostitutes always thrive.' And, you know, he's right, Hannah. We'll never stop it because the demand's always there.'

Hannah set down her salad tray. Brought her knees to her chin. 'Men are bastards.'

They sat in silence while birdsong lightened up the trees of Millfield Road behind them. To their left, a line of beech and sycamore trees shielded them from the rest of the park. To their right, manicured land sloped away, down towards Broom Lane and Front Street. Ahead, across the valley, the buildings of Newcastle craned their necks to look in on them.

They both jumped when Ryan's phone beat out its strident message tone. He glanced at the screen. 'Shit.'

'Bad news?'

'Ilona can't make it. Something's up at work.'

Hannah straightened, at once alert. 'The club?'

'Yeah. Nowt urgent. They've all been called in. Some discussion about security.' His thumb typed out a reply.

'What about it?'

'Hannah, man. I'm not a mind-reader.'

She sucked at the dregs of her Diet Coke. Ryan's phone pinged again.

'She says she can do it tomorrow. Same time. You still up for it?'

Perversely, Hannah replied with another question. 'What's this park called?'

'Eh? Where'd that come from? Chase Park.'

She plucked a daisy by her feet. 'Odd name.'

'Aye. Me dad reckons it goes back to the Jacobite rebellion. Apparently, the folk round here were great supporters of King George. It's why we're called Geordies, he reckons. Anyway, the Jacobite lot, whoever they were, weren't best pleased with the locals. They harried the King's supporters over the fields, including this one. Technically, where we are is named King George's Field. Anyway, because the Jacobites chased wor lot through here and down towards the river, they named the park Chase Park.'

'Wow. I never knew.'

Ryan stood. Brushed himself down. ''Course, like most stuff me dad says, it's utter bollocks. Got nowt to do with that at all. Howay,' he said, 'Let's go.'

Hannah remained seated.

'That's what's wrong with the case, Ryan. We're chasing shadows. We need the traffickers to come to us.'

Ryan narrowed his eyes. 'What're you thinking?'

Hannah pulled at her curls as she rose. 'I'm not sure yet. Let me work on it. I might come up with a cunning plan.'

CHAPTER SEVENTEEN

He pulled back the sheet. Allowed his eyes to roam over the naked woman lying in the darkness. He took in every inch of her, every contour, every blemish. The man took particular interest in her blemishes. And the scars. Despite them, she was beautiful; truly, beautiful. Even in death.

Aaron Elliott flicked a switch. A fluorescent light buzzed to life like a wasp at a windowpane. Stark white lighting flooded the room, the subtlety of the scene ruined.

He beckoned towards the window. Outside, Sue Nairn and Nigel Trebilcock glanced at each other, faces tight and drawn. DS Nairn nodded. They pulled up their facemasks to cover nose and mouth and entered Dr Frankenstein's laboratory.

'Is this one not interesting enough for the Detective Chief Inspector, Susan?'

'Not at all, Aaron. He can't lead on every case.'

'True, but I thought he'd have the courtesy to see her at her best. She's looking lovely today. Not like the last time Foreskin saw her.'

Sue Nairn wrinkled a face of disgust. 'I've brought Detective Constable Trebilcock with me. He's been assigned the case.'

'Splendid. Come, please: take a look.'

Trebilcock and Nairn took a step closer to the slab. Trebilcock thought the woman had a look of David Bowie's wife about her. He swallowed hard.

Sue Nairn averted her eyes. 'Do you think you could cover her up? Give her some dignity?'

Elliott's eyebrows rose to meet the hair bunched under his plastic head-dress, but he pulled the sheet over her. At least, enough to cover the bits that offended DS Nairn.

'How did she die? I mean, do we have a case here or not?'

Aaron Elliott didn't answer. Not directly. He picked up the woman's right arm by the wrist. 'We have here at least six contusions. I say 'at least' because they were formed close to mortem. Had she lived a little longer, more may have emerged. And see here,' he moved around the table and raised the other arm. The sheet slipped to expose a breast. 'The left arm shows similar wounds, all the way up and onto the shoulder. There are similar contusions on her lower back.'

Trebilcock moved for a closer look. 'So, she put up a fight? There was a struggle?'

Elliott moved to a bench. Sorted through a number of Ziplock bags. Found the labelled bag he was after. 'You may think so, but this is interesting. In here, we have several flecks of paint removed from around the follicles on her arm and her lower legs.'

'From a weapon?'

'Possibly, but unlikely. Most assailants use bare-metal implements, not painted ones.' Elliott stood back. Raised his arms. 'But, hey; what do I know? That's your territory, guys.'

'These wounds wouldn't have killed her, though, surely?'

'Definitely not. But, this could.' Again, Elliott rummaged through items on the bench. He produced two A4-sized photographs. 'This is the back of m'lady's cranium.' He pointed a gloved finger at three separate wounds. 'Three early-stage, post-traumatic haematoma. Sufficient to cause a minor skull fracture.'

Trebilcock glanced at the girl on the table. In a matter of moments, her flawless beauty had been pulled apart. 'She was attacked from behind,' he said to Sue. 'Defenceless.'

Aaron Elliott smiled. 'Aha. Let me finish. You see, around the wounds, we found splinters of wood. I have the bag over there somewhere,' he indicated his inventory.

Trebilcock scratched his wrist, deep in thought. 'We found her beneath the staiths. Could she have got the splinters from there?'

Elliott eyed Trebilcock like a victorious gladiator waiting for the Emperor to deliver his verdict. 'Okay. Shall I put you all out your misery?'

'Please do,' Sue Nairn groaned.

'The splinters around her wounds come from chipboard. Nothing to do with where we found her. Nothing at all. And, here's another conundrum. I found remarkably little material from the marsh in her trachea, oesophagus, lungs, or stomach. Only minute quantities of soil, mud, or water. All of which indicates she entered the saltmarsh post-mortem.'

'She was already dead?'

Dr Elliott gave it the jazz hands. 'Eureka.'

'Right. So, whoever killed her dumped her here. We do have a murder on our hands.'

Aaron Elliott smirked. 'Except for one thing. Well, two things, actually. One: there was something in her throat and lungs, but it wasn't debris from the marsh. It was gastric juices and partially digested food, along with a not insignificant volume of alcohol. Secondly: the toxicology report shows she'd recently taken lamotrigine.'

Sue and Nigel shrugged blankly.

'Oh, come on, detectives. Do I have to do all your work for you? Our beautiful friend here is epileptic. She received injuries to her arms, legs and skull whilst fitting. The seizure, coupled with or perhaps precipitated by, alcoholic intake caused her to choke on her own vomit. The cause of death was pulmonary aspiration. Put simply, natural causes.'

Nigel didn't know whether he was pleased or disappointed. 'Natural causes? So, I don't have a case?'

'I do love this job,' Aaron Elliott laughed. 'Yes, natural causes. But, before you get carried away, I don't think your job's quite over yet.'

'How come?'

'Put the evidence together, detectives. She had a seizure. The tonic-clonic phases caused her to obtain multiple injuries. The girl vomited and, without the ability to control the function, inhaled the material and suffocated on it.'

'Exactly. Your point is?'

'She died before she hit the water. I would guess around thirty minutes before. Your job is to work out how the splinters she received in her headwound don't originate from the staiths.'

The detectives dipped their heads sagely. But Elliott wasn't finished.

'More importantly, you need to work out how she got from the top of Dunston Staiths to the Tyne saltmarsh under her own steam. Pretty difficult when she was already dead, don't you think?'

**

'She's not going to turn up, is she?'

Ryan checked his watch. 'She's only ten minutes late. Give her time.'

Hannah Graves took the last bite from her cheese scone. 'I'll give her another ten. We've got a case to solve. Can't waste time drinking coffee and eating scones, man.'

'It's my case, not 'ours'. And you're drinking green tea, not coffee.'

Hannah prepared to shoot Ryan down, only for Ilona Popescu to enter the Costa outlet at that very moment. She'd scraped her hair back and hid it beneath an Amish-like scarf. Make-up free, she looked pale and insipid.

Ryan placed her order at the counter while Ilona shuffled to the table, head bowed.

Once seated, Ilona told them she hadn't long. They'd changed her shifts and put her on early evening. It would take her ages to get her make-up on, she said.

'You could have put it on before you came here,' a frustrated Ryan commented.

'Someone may see me. I cannot be recognised. No-one knows me like this. I say again: I have not got long. What do you want from me?'

'Answers, Ilona. I want answers. If I'm to find Radka, you need to be straight with me. Now, do you know where she'd been before she went missing?'

Ilona glanced around the coffee shop like Fagin. She lowered her voice to a whisper. 'For sure, I do not know. I would think she met someone by the Quayside. I know Radka met many clients by the river, but she would not tell even me where.'

Hannah took notes while Ryan raced through his questions, keen to extract as much as he could before Ilona disappeared again. 'What about Jade? The same?'

'I cannot say.'

'Have you heard of a Louis Chamley?'

'Of course. He runs the club and the agency. Or, he is pretending.'

'What do you mean by that?'

'Everyone knows it is the Mayan. Mr Chamley is not really in charge.'

Ryan and Hannah made eye contact. 'Who is the Mayan?'

Ilona shrugged. 'Bad man. I do not know his name. No-one does. All the girls are afraid of him.'

'Do you know where I could find him?'

Ilona shifted in her seat. 'I do not. People do not find him. It is he who finds them. Even if I could tell, I would not. He would kill me.'

Hannah stretched her fingers until they met Ilona's. 'Could this Mayan have done something to Radka? To Jade?'

Ilona barked a laugh. Short, sharp. 'Yes. He could harm anyone. But I do not think it is him. The girls are – how you say?' She squinted into sunlight streaming through the glass window. Looked out over the shops of the Silverlink. In time, she found the right word. 'Valuable, yes? They are too valuable.'

The Girl on the Quay

Ryan paused for thought. Subliminally checked his watch. 'This Lou Chamley, is that his real name?'

Ilona considered the question. The thought had clearly never crossed her mind. 'No-one else has a second name. We must always use one name and one name only. It must not be our real name. Mr Chamley has two names. It may be his name, yes.'

Hannah posed the follow-up question. 'You say everyone only has one name. What's that all about?'

'Yes. In the club, I am Isla. When Radka was there, she was Kayla. Sobena was Jade. The Mayan must approve our name.'

'Why?'

'For me, I do not know. For the dancers, the names must be sexy. Because after dancing, they are going to the men.' She laughed. 'Radka argued with the Mayan over her name. *I am Radka Vosahlo,*' Radka had told him. The Mayan said, '*you cannot be*'. So, she became Kayla. The Mayan did not know the name Radka Vosahlo means 'to reach great heights of joy' in Radka's language.'

She looked at Ryan, a faint smile in otherwise cold eyes. 'It is a very good name for her, is it not?'

Ryan's mind sifted through the information Hadley Kutz had given him. He thought of the tip of the triangle. The two percent. 'Ilona, this is important. Would Radka sleep with men voluntarily?' He saw the perplexed look on her face. 'Without being forced?' he clarified.

Ilona laughed again. This time, a genuine, hearty giggle. 'Radka does not like men. I thought you knew. Radka and I are lovers.'

Ryan felt himself blush. He brought his mind back to his questions. 'So, she was forced?'

He was surprised to see Ilona shake her head. 'I do not think so. None of the girls talk about what happened before they come here. I do not know if they are afraid, shy, or the memories are too bad, but they do not speak. I know Radka was pleased to come. To dance was better than what she had, no?'

Hannah asked the next question. 'Why did she stop dancing?'

'Because the Mayan said to her, *'you must go with men'*. No-one argues with the Mayan. Also, he looks after girls. He knows the men are rich. They treat the girls better than if they were street girls.' She paused for thought. 'Perhaps, it is still a better life than if they had not been brought to England.'

Hannah spoke to Ryan. 'We need to find out more about Whipped Cream. It's where it all starts from.'

Ryan nodded his agreement. 'Does Lou Chamley run the club by himself?'

'I think he does what the Mayan tells. He hires staff, like me, and security, and DJs and people like that. But not the girls. The Mayan chooses the girls.'

Ryan's phone rang. 'It's Lyall. I'll have to take it.' He moved away from the table.

'I too must go,' Ilona said.

A light had come on behind Hannah's eyes. She clasped the waif's wrist. 'You said Chamley had changed your shifts. Why?'

'He does it much in the last few weeks. He has not enough staff. They frightened by what happens. They leave. I am only one to stay long time.'

Ryan hurried back to the table. 'We're needed back urgently.'

'That's fine,' Hannah said. 'I've got what I needed.'

Her smile was as enigmatic as the Mona Lisa.

CHAPTER EIGHTEEN

Ryan and Hannah arrived to find the rest of the squad already huddled like circled wagons, Lyall Parker in the centre clutching a handful of documents.

Gavin O'Hara stood alongside Todd Robson. Sue Nairn rested against a desk with Trebilcock seated behind it. Ravi Sangar's fingers lay on a keyboard as he stared at a blue screen above their heads. Stephen Danskin took a back seat, observant as ever, as Parker opened the briefing.

'Good timing, Hannah, Ryan. I want a wee update on where we all are. First, Sue and Treblecock. I gather you've got news on the lassie found at the staiths.'

Trebilcock deferred to his DS. 'Yeah. It's a curious one,' Sue began. 'The girl's an epileptic. Anti-convulsant found in her bloods, mixed with alcohol. She had a seizure. Choked on her vomit. Cause of death: natural, according to the pathologist.'

She noted Danskin's furrowed brow and continued. 'I agree it seems odd, sir. What's more, so does Elliott. He's sure she didn't die at the scene. Indications are, she was moved there after death, then someone threw her body off the staiths into the crap below. We don't have a murder on our hands, but we have a case of some description.'

Gavin let out a low whistle. 'Any idea why somebody would do that?'

'We're working on it, Gav. Early days. I've got Dr Elliott checking dental records. If we can find out who she is, that'll be our starter for ten.'

Nigel Trebilcock piped up. 'I'm looking into what might have triggered the fit. If she was on meds, unless she's recently diagnosed and on an unstable dose, something must have brought it on. Could have been the alcohol but may just as easily have been flashing lights, contra-indication with other drugs, extreme stress; all are potential triggers. It may give us a clue as to what she was up to immediately prior to her seizure.'

'Good thinking, Treblecock. Thanks. Sue: anything else to add?'

She shook her head.

Parker continued in his soft brogue. 'Me next. I've been looking into this Lou Chamley character.' An officer wheeled in Ryan's crime board and positioned it alongside Parker. 'There's still nae evidence against him. He's no' got a record. Not even a parking ticket or speeding conviction. He lives alone, near The Ravensworth in Lamesley. I've had uniform out scouting but there's no suspicious activity. Still, it's worth keeping tabs on him.'

He unfolded a glossy picture of Chamley and attached it to the board with a magnetic tile.

'Christ, he's an ugly bugger,' Robson said.

The others looked at Todd. With his hooded eyes, off-centre nose, and scarred cheek, he looked every-inch the comic book villain.

'Oh, aa knaa, man,' he said, 'But howay – look at him. He could eat a bunch of grapes through a tennis racket with teeth like that.'

When the hoots of laughter died down, Parker turned to Ryan. 'What you got for us?'

'For starters, we no longer think Chamley's the hub of the operation. He's a stool pigeon for someone called the Mayan. I've precious little information on him as yet, but my source insists he's the main man behind both the Whipped Cream club and Orchid Petals. He picks the girls. He even names them. Everyone kow-tows to him. And, my source tells me, he puts the fear of God into everybody.'

'We need more on him,' Parker said, stating the obvious. 'Anything else?'

'Aye. Radka, or Kayla, went missing from the quayside area, we think. It's possible Jade did, too.'

'Good work, you two. Any more?'

Ryan walked away from the group. Ripped the flipchart off the wall, returned and pinned it over the crime board.

'Here we go again,' Todd groaned, but with a wink in his eye and a smile in his voice.

Ryan circled the bottom third of the triangle. 'Remember what this represents? Women forced into the game. Many from abroad. From the far east, Africa, and eastern Europe. Eastern Europe - where Jade and Kayla originate. Now, remember what my second source said: some are coerced into the vice industry by force, real or threatened. Others, by deceit.'

Danskin watched the young detective present his case to the group. Both convincing and authoritative, he had the respect of his audience. The more he watched Ryan Jarrod, the more of himself he saw.

'What if,' Ryan continued, 'Jade and Kayla were common whores in another life? What if they were lured here under the pretence of a better life? A life as a dancer. Then, once here, what if they were then ordered back into prostitution, but in the guise of an agency? There'd be no street-hawking, no parading in windows, or back-street brothels. Whatever their background, and whatever the Mayan wanted them for, it'd be better than what they left behind. What if that's how the Mayan keeps the girls?'

The others considered his words. 'The trouble with your line of thought,' Gavin said, 'Is that he's not keeping them. They're disappearing. That's why we're here.'

Ryan had no answer. He could only shrug. Mutter, 'True.'

Just as the silence became intolerable, Lyall Parker rode to the rescue. 'Hannah – you got anything to add?'

She opened her mouth to speak. Glanced at Ryan, then at Stephen Danskin. 'Not yet, Lyall. Not for this forum, anyway.'

Only Ryan thought her choice of words curious.

**

Ilona Popescu ended the call as she hurried down Pilgrim Street. She turned into Worswick Street and collided head-on with a woman travelling the other way. Her phone slipped from her hand.

'Excuse me,' Ilona apologised, but the woman turned her face away and was already on the other side of the road. Ilona bent and retrieved her phone, checked it still worked, and popped it into her bag.

The call had worried her. Terrified her, even. Yet, at the same time, she was excited by it. Excited because, for the first time in over a week, she had hope.

She rushed past the dilapidated and abandoned bus station. Ahead, beneath a black and gold awning, the familiar figure of Benny Hay awaited her.

Benny, head doorman to the Whipped Cream club, was the only constant presence throughout Ilona's time there. If she ever questioned her sexuality, a man like Benny would be the one to cast the doubts. Tall, strong, and square-jawed, he aroused her curiosity.

Benny greeted her with a, 'Hi, gorgeous.'

'Hi, Benny. I am sorry. I am late. I have no time to talk tonight.'

'You needn't spend so long in front of the mirror, darling. You're beautiful just as you are.'

'Thank you. You come inside for drink when you off duty, yes?'

'Can't tonight, love. I'm on all night.' Another man, dressed identically to Benny, moved out of the shadows. 'This is Paul. I'm teaching him the tricks of the trade. You'll find Chamley's bringing a few new starters in. Paul's one of 'em.' He turned to the man. 'Paul, we call this one Isla.'

The man called Paul raised an eyebrow.

'She works the bar,' Benny Hay explained.

'Ah, right. Thought she wasn't sexy enough to be one of the girls.'

It wasn't the words that upset Ilona. It was the fact Benny didn't come to her defence. The thought shocked her. Head bowed, she squeezed between the men into the club.

'Word to the wise,' Benny whispered to her. 'He's here tonight.'

'The Mayan? He here again?'

'Aye. Becoming regular, isn't it? Keep your nose clean, Isla. He's in a pig of a mood, an' aal.'

Ilona had more important things to worry about. Her feelings for Benny, for one; her recent telephone call for another.

**

After a brief comfort break, Hannah returned to the briefing room in time for Lyall Parker to request Ravi Sangar's update.

'I thought you'd never ask,' he said. Ravi's fingers flew across the keyboard. Orchid Petals homepage appeared on the wall-mounted screen. He typed in Lyall's password and the agency's inner menu displayed itself.

'We have three new recruits to the Orchid Petals catalogue.' The images of three girls appeared on a split-window. 'We have Roxette,' he homed in on a statuesque redhead, 'Dee-Dee', a brunette with the eyes of a cat and improbably full lips, 'And Mai Tai.'

Todd scowled. 'Whoa. That looks a bit dodgy. How old's she?'

'Don't know,' Ravi said, 'But I doubt they'd risk everything with an underage girl.'

'She certainly looks it.'

'But, that's not what's interesting. I wondered why three girls had appeared so recently. So, I did a bit of techno-magic and accessed Orchid Petals cached data.'

Ravi's fingers glided over his keyboard. The images of the three girls slid to the side of the screen. His eyes settled momentarily on Ryan. He offered him the faintest of smiles.

'If we had any doubt about the work Ryan's done, I think I can safely dispel them. What I'm about to show is Orchid Petals catalogue as it stood three weeks ago.'

Ravi hit a key. Thumbnail portraits flooded the screen, too small to identify. He moved the mouse over one image. Hit 'enter'. The image of the girl known to them as Jade filled the screen.

'The information Ryan obtained from Max Bonhomme is spot-on. Jade was on the books of Orchid Petals. Not only that,' he shifted the mouse again. Hit enter. Another beautiful face illuminated the screen. A familiar face.

'So, too, was Kayla. What we have is incontrovertible proof that both Jade and Kayla are not only missing, but also offered their services on behalf of the Orchid Petals agency.'

The rest of the crowd nodded, satisfied the case was real, live, and accelerating.

'Hang on,' Ravi urged, 'I'm not finished yet. We've two missing women. Thanks to Ryan, we know who they are. They seem to have been replaced by two of,' he referred to a notepad next to him, 'Roxette, Dee-Dee and Mai Tai. I wondered why three new girls to replace two. I delved a bit deeper. Guess what? Jade and Kayla aren't the only changes from Orchid Petals register of three weeks ago.'

Danskin moved forward. He sensed Ravi had stumbled on something crucial.

Another click. Another image.

'Three weeks ago, this girl was on the books, too. Her name is Madonna. She's not listed anymore. Has she gone the same way as Jade and Kayla?'

'O'Hara,' Danskin's voice. 'Get onto front desk. Find out if they've had any more reports.'

Ravi's mouse hovered over another image. 'While you're on,' he said, 'here's another for you to consider. Another one who's no longer with Orchid Petals. See if they've any idea who this is, as well.'

Ravi hit enter. The fourth girl's face appeared.

Nigel Trebilcock interrupted the activity. 'No need, Gav. This one's not missing.'

Heads swivelled towards him.

'I've just seen her on a slab in Aaron Elliott's mortuary. It's the girl we hauled out of the mudflats.'

CHAPTER NINETEEN

Inside the Whipped Cream club, preparations were well-underway for its opening.

A cleaner coiled the lead of an industrial-sized Dyson around her arm and hoisted it into a storage cupboard. Another woman in coveralls walked down the spiral staircase. She held two spray-guns of cleaning fluid between the fingers of one hand, a chamois cloth, and a bag bursting with soiled tissues in the other.

Ilona shuddered. She slipped off her coat to reveal a low cut, skin-tight top, breasts peeking above it like a pair of curious meerkats. She nodded a greeting to a girl already at her station behind the bar. The colleague wore a transparent blouse with only Betty Boop stickers to disguise her nipples.

In front of the bar, three girls wrapped in gowns perched on stools. Two had their hair piled high above their heads; one in curlers, the other pinned in place beneath a light scarf. The third had no need for a head adornment. Her style was strictly Sinead O'Connor. All three sucked lurid coloured cocktails through gold and black straws.

'That's enough, girls. Backstage and costumes, please. Doors open in fifteen minutes.'

Lou Chamley's request went unheeded. He wiped errant saliva from his chin and tried again. 'Hey: Lola, Monique,' he searched for the third girl's name. Settled for, 'And you, get ready. Now.'

The shaven-headed girl reluctantly prised herself off her stool and made her way backstage. Her gown flopped open. She saw no point in readjusting it. A light engineer high up in the rigging almost toppled from his position at the freebie she'd afforded him.

The other two girls ignored the command and remained at the bar. Behind it, Ilona busied herself. She checked and refilled optics, polished spotlessly clean glasses, and generally did everything she could to tumble out her top.

Out the corner of her eye, she noticed an office door open. A squat, dark haired man appeared in the gap. Lola and Monique instantly left their drinks and followed the other dancer backstage.

'A word, Chamley.'

Lou Chamley jumped to the Mayan's order and hurried into the office.

'What's this?' The Mayan pointed at a littered desktop.

'I'll tidy it. I've been so tied up hiring extra security I haven't had time to get organised. You're right. It's unprofessional. I'll do it now.'

'Stop your waffle. I'm not bothered about the shit on the desk. But I am bothered about this.' The Mayan waved a single sheet of paper in his hand.

'What is it?'

The Mayan slammed the paper onto the table. He spoke between clenched teeth and lips which moved less than a ventriloquist's. The words came out as a hiss. 'It's from Luuk. The demand you told me we didn't have.'

Chamley's jaw opened. 'We've got another one? For Ebony?'

'No, for Princess-fucking-Anne. Yes, it's for Ebony.'

'I had no idea. I've never seen it before.' He walked to the Mayan's side. 'Jesus Christ. Luuk's doubled his demands.'

'Double of nothing is still nothing, and that's what the Dutchman's getting. You, on the other hand, will get a sharpened tent-pole up your arse if he gets his hands on another.'

Lou Chamley swallowed hard. 'I've done all you asked. You've seen the new guy on the door. I've got more floor security starting tomorrow.'

The Mayan stood with his face inches from Chamley's. 'What about the chaperones? The girls aren't disappearing from here. Luuk's targeting the agency bitches. Prioritise, you idiot. How many times have I told you?'

Chamley blinked several times. Slowly moved his head away from the Mayan. 'I've done what you asked, and more. You wanted three new chaperones: I've managed four. Brings our total to ten.'

The Mayan nodded. 'That's better.'

'Sir, can I suggest something? We've got thirty girls with the agency. Even now, with the new recruits, we can only ever chaperone ten. Why don't we limit the number of girls booked out each night? Ten girls plus ten chaperones equal no easy targets. I doubt even Luuk would want to risk a public street-brawl.'

The Mayan stared, open-mouthed. 'You've a mollusc for a brain, you really have. Money, that's why we won't limit bookings. I'll be losing two-hundred percent a night. I'd rather take the risk.'

He poured a tequila. Smiled to himself. More of a leer than a smile. A gold-tooth gleamed under the light. 'There again, the risk's all yours, isn't it?'

The Mayan raised his glass in toast. 'Tent poles, Chamley; tent poles.'

**

'Sir, with respect, this is my case and I'm asking you to trust me with it.'

'Jarrod, we've two missing women, an unknown third dead, and another who probably falls into one of those two categories. The common denominator is this damn strip club and the glorified brothel. It would be a dereliction of duty if I didn't order us in right now.'

'The guvnor's right, Ryan,' Lyall Parker agreed. 'Think o' the consequences if we lose another one.'

Ryan prowled the briefing room. 'Not tonight. Leave it 'til tomorrow, and you have my consent to go in.'

Danskin's eyes narrowed. 'That's mighty big of you, Jarrod. I hate to remind you but it's not your consent to give.'

The rookie detective and Stephen Danskin faced each other like gunslingers at dawn. Lyall stood alongside Danskin, the others adopted a neutral position.

'Please. Twelve hours. That's all I ask.'

'I divvent get it. What difference does it make? No; it's not worth the risk. The Super will want me knackers in a sling if another one goes walkabout. I want you and O'Hara knocking on the door of that club in the next fifteen minutes. Talk to Chamley. Find out about this Mayan character.'

Ryan rolled his dice one last time. 'Sir, I believe we'd endanger a woman if we go in tonight, not the other way round.'

'You need to explain. And, quickly. You've now got fourteen minutes and counting to get to the club.'

Ryan sucked air between his teeth. 'My primary source is on duty at the club tonight. I don't want her position compromised.'

Danskin slapped his palms against his thighs. 'Fuck it,' he said, finally. 'Okay, but if anything goes wrong, it'll be your knackers in the sling, Jarrod.' He saw Ryan's face drop. Realised what he'd said. *Shit, me and my big mouth.*

His tone softened. 'You've done well so far, son. I'm happy to go with your gut. Tomorrow it is.'

**

In the bar known to all as The Monkey Bar, an attractive lone woman sipping a pint of lager was always going to draw attention. She didn't mind the looks. Men ogling her was second nature. It was the fact one of them might recognise her which worried her.

She slipped out onto Pilgrim Street before making the call. 'There's a new doorman. I think I can get in without being recognised. That's not the problem. Once I'm inside, people will know me. I can't do what you ask, Luuk.'

Luuk told her she could, and she would.

The woman demanded money. 'I need make up. Hair-dye. New clothes. I can't look as I do. Even if they don't recognise me straight away, I am a woman. A woman would not go to a place like that. They'd pay close attention to me. I would be identified.'

'Not if you worked there. You wouldn't draw a second glance. You'll get the money, but your disguise will be cheap. You'll dress as a cleaner, or pretend you've come to fix a leak. Or restock the condom machines. Wear anything as long as it gets your ass inside and the information out.'

He terminated the call.

It had been a long day. An exceptionally long one. The girl stretched. Time to find a cheap hotel. She rubbed her shoulder.

The barmaid she knew as Isla had given her a helluva whack.

**

While Ravi Sangar remained behind with a crew poring over three weeks-worth of quayside CCTV footage in the vague hope they'd spot a needle in the haystack, Stephen Danskin dismissed the rest of the squad.

Parker and O'Hara bid their goodnights. Trebilcock offered Ravi an extra pair of eyes, while Sue Nairn caught up with paperwork at a distant desk.

Hannah Graves asked Danskin for a word. Ryan hung about. He wanted Hadley Kutz advice and, for that, he needed Hannah with him.

'Olivia. Hi. Ryan Jarrod here. Remember?'

He waited until the receptionist paused for breath then dove in before she had a chance to resume her soliloquy. 'Sorry,' he interjected, 'I haven't long. I'm checking Dr Kutz's availability in the next week or so.'

The Girl on the Quay

'Let me see.' Ryan craved silence while she checked the diary. He didn't get it. Olivia filled the gap with endless waffle. Finally, he heard her say, 'When were you thinking of?'

'As soon as possible.' Hannah would have to fit in with whatever Olivia could offer.

'Well, there's no availability this week. Then, Dr Kutz is on holiday for a week. He's going back home to spend some time with his family. His mother's not well, you know, poor old soul. I hear she's not long left. Dr Kutz was saying only the other day...'

'Listen. Just leave it. I'll be in touch.' He ended the call. Shit. It was all on Ilona now.

Ryan empathised with Hadley Kutz. He remembered how he'd felt when his own mother's condition worsened.

Her last few days had been unbearable. For him and the family, more than for her; she was in the arms of morphine. The hard part was watching his father shuffle through life like a zombie. His younger brother wondering why his mum didn't tuck him into bed anymore.

Ryan hadn't been much more than a kid himself, but he guessed it wouldn't get any easier the older you got. Yep, he knew what Dr Kutz was going through. He rubbed his forehead to dismiss the melancholia and decided to wait for Hannah anyway.

He could see her in Danskin's office. She seemed animated. He watched her pace up and down. She gesticulated towards Danskin. For his part, the DCI was on his feet, finger pointed into Hannah's face.

Her body language changed. She raised her shoulders. Spread her arms, palms open, in a pleading gesture. Danskin shook his head. Made a chopping motion with his hand. It screamed, 'End of.'

Ryan saw Hannah fling open her stepfather's door. Watched her storm out. She stomped straight past Ryan, left the bullpen, and took the stairs.

Colin Youngman

'What the hell was all that about?' he wondered.

CHAPTER TWENTY

A flame-haired teenager slouched in an uncomfortable straight-backed chair. Next to him, an old woman sat with her chin resting on her chest. She snored quietly. On her left-hand side, Ryan Jarrod drummed his fingers on the wooden arms of his seat.

'How man, Ryan. Stop the drumming. It's getting on me tits.'

'Sssh. Watch the language, man.' Ryan needn't have worried. Apart from his grandmother, the only other occupants of God's waiting room were either asleep or staring at a TV with its volume set at space-shuttle launch level.

'Wish she'd wake up,' James Jarrod said. 'I feel a bit of a pri …wally sat here.'

'Aye. I know what you mean.' The finger-drum tempo picked up a notch. Ryan checked his watch. Clicked his tongue. 'Right, I'm gannin,' he said.

'You can't, man. She hasn't seen you yet.'

'I can't hang around all day. I've got work to do. People are depending on me.'

'And what about gran? Doesn't she depend on you?'

Ryan sat back down. James was right, of course.

At the back of the room, Angela Doyle watched on as a trainee carer helped an old codger park his Zimmer as if it were a Boris Bike. With the help of his carer and the furniture, the resident walked his way to a card table and dealt himself a hand of Patience. Something Ryan had precious little of these days.

His brother wasn't about to let it lie. 'You haven't seen her for nearly a week. I know he won't tell you himself, but dad's upset by it. He's disappointed in you.'

'Dad's upset by it? That's rich coming from him. When was he last here? I don't see him bothering his arse much.'

His brother leant across Doris Jarrod as he spoke. 'You're not being fair on him. You know it brings back memories of mum, and how useless he felt. He's probably fighting his own battle right now. Be kind. Cut him some slack, man.'

Ryan closed his eyes. When, exactly, had his teenage brother become possessed by the ghost of Plato?

'Aye, you're right. Listen, James; I really do have to go. When she wakes, tell her I'm sorry. Tell her I promise I'll be back soon, yeah?'

James flung himself back in his seat, arms folded. 'Whatever.'

Pleased his young brother had been successfully exorcised, Ryan left the care home. On his way out, his eyes sought the photograph in the hallway. He knew the sight of Max Bonhomme would bring his mind back to case mode.

**

'It went really well. I'll tell you all about it when I get back. Love you.'

Max Bonhomme ended the call just as a hand came to rest on his naked inner thigh. He felt its fingers probe upward. A whimper escaped his throat. He raised his head from the pillow and watched her sleek black hair leave a trail over his stomach. He lay both hands on the crown of her head, felt her hair between his fingers, and scrunched it tightly.

Fifteen minutes later, Max Bonhomme noted the name 'Mai Tai' in his diary and left the apartment.

Outside, the quayside had sprung to life.

**

The Dutch woman shared her room with street noise and an off-duty desk clerk, but it meant the room came free. Even better, he was spent out and spent up by midnight, so she'd grabbed a few hours' sleep. She felt better for it.

Her mind was sufficiently clear to form a plan. She decided she'd get her clothes from a charity shop. She remembered a store called Wilkos or something; the props she needed would come from there.

In her head, she pictured herself hanging onto the tails of the cleaning team as they entered the club. She doubted there'd be door security at that time. If there was, she'd just have to hope the new guy was on duty. She ticked an imaginary box on her plan.

Once inside, she was aware of the CCTV positions. She would wear no make-up, dye her hair, and keep her head down. Another tick.

She knew the office door security codes. They changed monthly but Chamley only ever used three different code sets. The lock allowed three attempts before triggering the alarm. She'd get in, no matter which cycle the lock was on. Tick.

Staff churn in the club was high. With a bit of luck, she wouldn't see anyone who knew her. All she had to do was pick a time when Chamley was pre-occupied and hope to hell the Mayan wasn't around. Tick.

Anything else? Oh, yes. That barmaid, Isla. She was still there. That might turn out to be a problem.

In her mind's eye, she drew a big, fat cross.

**

The bed was empty without her. Everything in the apartment belonged to Radka, yet she was nowhere. It was as if her very being had vanished along with her physical presence.

Ilona Popescu hadn't slept but that had been no escape from the nightmares or her memories. She saw herself huddled in the shadow of Castle Keep. Pictured the beautiful girl walk by her, turn, and drop a few coins in the red, yellow, and blue bobble hat on the pavement. Then, two nights later, the same. She recalled the first time Radka had spoken to her. The smile they shared.

And, she remembered the last time they'd spoken. Or, more accurately, argued. How she'd finally admitted it: she was jealous of the men. How Radka had goaded her. Told her it wasn't just men. That, sometimes, it was women. Women like Jade.

Ilona cried herself to sleep and dreamt of Radka, Jade, and the one they call the Mayan.

**

He'd asked Titus to join him. It was early for the big man. Too early. He rubbed sleep from his eyes with one hand and scratched an unshaven jaw with the other.

'You were on duty last night, were you not?' the Mayan asked.

'Uh-huh.'

'Anything different?'

'How?'

'As in, was anything different? Any unfamiliar faces?'

Titus waited for the question to make sense. 'A new guy on the door.'

'Were you on the floor alone?'

'Dominic was on duty with me.'

The Mayan's eyes narrowed. 'Just Dominic? No-one else?'

'Just Dominic.'

'Who's on tonight?'

'Dominic again.' A light came on. 'And a new guy. Forget his name.'

The Mayan raised an eyebrow. So far, so good. One on the door. At least one on the floor. 'Did you see anyone here with Chamley? Either yesterday or the day before?'

Titus blinked several times. 'It's a club. There were lots of people around.'

The Mayan rubbed his temple. 'I'll put it in Janet and John terms for you. Apart from the new pairs of hands you've mentioned, did you see Chamley interview people? Just to be clear, an interview means talking to people. Asking them questions. See if they're suitable for a job. If you need another clue, they'd probably be muscle.'

The big man looked to the ceiling in thought. His mouth opened several times. Finally, he spoke. 'Dunno.'

The Mayan exhaled through his nose. Started to speak.

'Oh yeah,' Titus interrupted. 'I did see him with four blokes. Didn't think of it as an interview.'

'What were they doing?'

'I thought they were clients. They were looking at the Orchid Petals girls.'

The Mayan smiled. 'Thank you, Titus. I can put my tent poles away again. Chamley won't be needing them.'

'Huh?'

'Never mind.' He gave Titus a dismissive wave. 'That's all. You can get yourself back to bed now. Your brain must need a rest after all that thinking.'

**

DI John Craggs knew to tread warily. Superintendent Wallace had morphed from cricket commentator to snarling prop forward overnight. The last thing Craggs needed was a scrotum squeeze, eye-gouge, or ear nibble.

It was a head down arse up sort of day.

The rest of his crew were out-and-about. Craggs had the office to himself. He planned an easy day, well out of reach of the prop forward. He chased up a couple of leads, approved a press release, did a bit of paperwork. He took a gulp of coffee and screwed his face at its sour coldness.

In the corridor, he fed the vending machine. While he waited for his fresh drink to dispense, he multi-tasked and dropped a coin into the adjacent machine and tapped in the code for a packet of crisps.

Coffee in one hand, change in the other, he clumsily ripped open the bag with his teeth. The crisps were Seabrooks; the flavour, sea salt and vinegar. That's when he realised what troubled him.

That damn ghost ship bobbing away in the North Sea just off Blackhall Rocks was going to haunt him until he got to the bottom of it.

So much for a quiet day.

**

DCI Danskin's team arrived in dribs and drabs. Sue Nairn was first. She used the time to rubber-stamp a backlog of reports on her desk.

Ravi Sangar was next in. He disappeared into the tech room and summoned a couple of uniforms in with him.

Danskin himself turned up, round-shouldered as if he carried the weight of the world. Sue raised both eyebrows towards him. He waved her concerns away.

Next up: Hannah. She didn't look much better, although she at least bid her colleagues good morning. '*Her colleagues,*' Sue noted; *not the DCI.*

O'Hara, Trebilcock and Lyall Parker arrived almost together.

With Todd Robson downstairs chatting to surveillance, it meant Ryan was last in. 'Been visiting gran,' he explained, though no-one had asked.

'Foreskin's in a bit of a fettle, by all accounts,' Gavin O'Hara warned. 'Just so you know.'

'Thanks for the warning, Gav. He was last night, an aal. Him and Hannah were going at it hammer and tongs.'

'What's the plans for today?'

'Waddya mean?'

'It's your case, Ry. We're waiting for direction.'

'I thought I'd been giving it. I mean, I've stood back when Lyall and the DCI have had their say, obviously, but other than that…' his voice trailed off as he wondered what could have been done differently.

'Don't lose sleep over it, mate. Don't get me wrong: you've done okay with it. Well, more than okay, actually, but if you want to show your mettle, why don't you kick off the daily briefing, rather than wait for Lyall?'

'Do you think?'

'Aye, I do,' O'Hara encouraged.

Ryan cleared his throat in preparation. It's as far as he got. His thunder was about to be stolen.

Ravi Sangar entered. 'Where's Foreskin?' Without waiting for a reply, he burst into Danskin's office. 'Sir, you gotta see this.'

Sangar turned to the assembled squad. 'Someone hook the screens up for me. The Kayla lass: we've got her on CCTV.'

CHAPTER TWENTY-ONE

'We first pick her up here,' Ravi explained. 'Picture quality's not great. It's pissing down.'

Stephen Danskin leant towards the screen. Screwed up his eyes. 'You sure it's her?'

'Yes, sir. It becomes obvious later on.'

'Okay. I'm trying to visualise where we are.'

'It's the camera on the side of the lawcourts, looking east along the quayside.'

'Got it. So, she's come down City Road, do we think?'

'Or all the way along from the Ouseburn, perhaps,' Sue Nairn offered.

'Ravi? Got owt from Ouseburn way?'

'Sorry, sir. We got a CCTV failure anywhere east of this one.

'That's a bummer. Bloody typical.'

Ryan noted *City Road?* and *Ouseburn?* on the crime board while the on-screen footage showed the girl walk towards the camera, her movements jerky, her features hidden beneath a large umbrella. She disappeared beneath the camera and out of shot.

'Where does she go from here?'

The image changed. The footage revealed an amorphous mass which gradually came into focus. The shape was an odd-looking statue, the head and torso of a creature with Mongolian features and a mace protruding from its midriff.

'We're looking at the River God statue.' Ravi read the digital display at the foot of the screen. 'And, any second now, here comes our girl.' Right on cue, Radka Vosahlo appeared in shot.

'She's crossed the road. Why would she do that?'

The Girl on the Quay

Seconds later, Stephen had his answer. Another camera picked her up further along the quayside. She had her back to shot, her front tight up against the railings on the edge of the Tyne.

'Don't tell me she's a jumper, after all the work we've put into this.'

The room fell silent, the air heavy with electricity like the moment before a storm.

The woman didn't jump. Instead, she lowered her umbrella.

'What the hell's she doing?'

'Getting rained on, sir.'

'I can see that, man, but it's almost as if she's having a shower, the way she's tipped her head up like that.'

The girl turned and exposed her face to the camera for the first time. Ryan's heart raced. He felt himself become light-headed. Realised he'd been holding his breath. Ryan knew it was her. It had to be. But he needed confirmation. 'Zoom in, Ravi. I want to see for myself.' The image blurred. Became pixelated. 'Is that the best you can do?'

'Afraid so but divvent worry; it's her.'

'How do you know?' Lyall Parker asked.

Ravi grimaced. 'I know.'

A phone rang in the office. 'Someone get that. We'll freezeframe.'

Nigel Trebilcock was the one to answer it. 'It's Todd. He's got nothing new on Chamley's movements, but says a car's been spotted parked nearby on a couple of occasions. He's checking it out.'

A nerve twitched above Danskin's jaw. 'Let's roll on, Ravi.'

Sangar pressed play. Radka, or Kayla, crossed the road without looking. Why would she? The streets were deserted. She walked out of shot leaving the camera to stare at nothing but the façade of Trinity Chambers.

The next shot came from a different angle. The camera pointed along the length of the river's frontage. It revealed a clear stretch of road disturbed by nothing but sheeting rain.

'Christ, where are we now? I'm getting dizzy here.'

'We're almost at the Tyne Bridge.'

Another phone rang. Gavin O'Hara went to answer. Ravi paused the video.

'Just let it play, Sangar.'

'No, sir. I think we all need to see this.'

Everyone moved closer. This was it. They sensed it.

Gavin re-joined the group. 'Nowt important. It'll wait,' he said.

Ravi restarted the video. 'Right, here we go. The first opening we see between the buildings there, that's Lombard Street.'

The woman holding the umbrella jerked into frame.

'She's just crossed the entrance to King Street. There's a courtyard tucked behind the buildings she's about to walk past. Access to it is via a narrow alleyway. Now, watch.'

Shielded by her umbrella, Radka stepped off the kerb, then recoiled. A truck emerged a nanosecond later.

'Bloody hell, that was close,' Gavin said.

They saw the nose of another vehicle edge forward. Radka stepped out. A hand appeared outside the umbrella and gave a brief wave. She crossed the alley. They saw her freeze. Turn as if responding to something. Radka took a single step into the alley, out of camera shot.

Almost immediately, the van gave a momentary wheel-spin before it shot away in a wake of spray.

The quayside streets stood deserted.

**

The Prince Bishop HQ in New Elvet was almost as quiet as the streets of the quayside the night Radka Vosahlo disappeared.

A couple of Detective Constables lurked around, but John Craggs was pretty much left to his own devices. Thoughts of the Stellendam, its crew and its cargo nagged away like toothache. Sooner or later, he knew, something rotten would end up on his desk and stink the place out.

He decided he'd get his equalizer in before Superintendent Wallace scored first. He'd find out what the hell happened that night.

Craggs typed in co-ordinates covering a three-mile radius from Blackhall Rocks. Next, he typed in a three-week timeframe, ending with the night the coastguard alerted him to the trawler's presence.

A list of reports of criminal behaviour or suspicious activity populated the screen. Craggs began scrolling through each and every one. After half of an hour wading through ASBO-type incidents around Horden, he realised he'd be there forever.

He filtered the list by location, rather than volume. Blackhall Colliery appeared first. It revealed nothing of note. Certainly, nothing to indicate the presence of an organised people-trafficking ring. Most of the regular suspects couldn't organise a shopping list never mind an international vice mob.

He extended the circle as far south as Crimdon and north to Seaham. Any further south, he'd hit Hartlepool; north, it'd be Sunderland. There'd be all manner of crap lying under stones there. Far too many for one man to cover.

Ninety minutes of fruitless activity later, he'd reached Seaham, his northern-most boundary. Craggs yawned. Rubbed his eyes. And, a miracle happened. Right at the top of the list, he noticed the name Jackie Duggan.

Duggan was a petty criminal who honestly believed he was going straight. Craggs had arrested him so many times, he saw more of him than his brother. In fact, he knew him so well he'd become one of Craggs's most dependable informants.

Jackie Duggan's name glowed out from Craggs's monitor because he'd failed to show up at Seaham police station *'In breach of bail conditions,'* the report said.

The breach itself came as no surprise. It was the excuse Duggan gave which caught Craggs's attention. He made a note to self: *'Catch up with Jackie Duggan before brown stuff hits fan.'*

Duggan alleged he missed the appointment because of an accident at sea.

**

Danskin's crew stared at a screen devoid of life. No matter how hard or how often they looked, the Kayla / Radka woman had disappeared as if she were Dynamo.

Time stood still. Nobody moved, nobody spoke; the whir of Ravi Sangar's kit the only sound.

After an eternity, Ryan heard a voice say, 'Play that again.' It was his own voice though he had no recollection of speaking.

Ravi obliged. Every member of the squad extended their neck forward like tortoises. They saw the truck. A van behind it. Radka's hand emerge from beneath the umbrella. She crossed the street. Turned.

'There. Stop. Play that again, Ravi,' Ryan said.

Radka crossed the street once more. Turned. A shadow briefly crossed her. 'Someone's jumped out the van. See the shadow, there? Any chance of a clearer shot?'

Sangar zoomed in. The image became even more indistinct. 'Negative, Ryan. That's all we've got.'

'Shit.'

They watched the moment twice over. It got no clearer with repetition.

'The van. Surely we've got the reg. on camera?'

On screen, the van fishtailed right. Its rear plate glistened wet beneath a streetlight. Ravi enlarged the image. Same thing happened. The image blurred.

'Bollocks.'

The Girl on the Quay

'Where does the van go? Can we follow it?' Lyall Parker proposed.

'Let's see, shall we? Anything from hereon in is new to me,' Ravi said as the footage began to play.

A camera at the foot of Sandhill caught a brief flash of white as a vehicle slewed onto the Close and was gone in the blink of an eye.

'Double bollocks.'

Then, the van reappeared on the Swing Bridge.

'Stop. The plate. Can we get anything now?' Ryan moved forward, face inches from the wall-mounted monitor. Danskin and Lyall Parker joined him.

'It's no' much better,' was Lyall's verdict.

'Not local. Could be EG,' Danskin offered. 'Where's that?'

'I think it's FG. Nottingham, isn't it?'

Sue Nairn was already on Google. 'If it's FG, it's Nottingham. EG is Essex.'

'That's a start. Keep with the van if we can. We might get a clearer shot. Where's it go next?'

A camera mid-way up Bottle Bank offered a side-on view. Nothing conclusive. Several minutes of nothing followed while Ravi searched other cameras in the area.

'We've lost it.'

'Looks that way, Jarrod. Right, let's regroup. Consider what we've just witnessed.'

'Sir. Here – on the Tyne Bridge.'

They turned back to the screen. It displayed the clearest image yet of a white van on the northbound carriageway. The transit zipped beneath the green arch of the famous bridge.

'Is that the same van?'

'Hard to tell. It's got no markings and neither did the other one, so it could be.'

Gavin O'Hara put in his tuppence worth. 'There's thousands of white vans out there, man.'

Ryan disagreed. 'Not at that time of night, there's not. Run it back a few frames, Ravi. If we get the plate, we should be able to read it this time.'

Sangar went back too far. The sound of breath between clenched teeth was palpable as he rolled the film forward, frame-by-frame, until the white vehicle appeared. He hit pause a fraction late. Rewound another couple of frames.

'It is a different van,' Gavin said without a hint of triumph. 'It's a Y plate. York. Shit.'

They slumped back in their chairs. Danskin rubbed the back of his neck. Parker pinched his lower lip. Sue Nairn stared at the screen. Ryan spoke. 'How long was our van out of sight?'

Ravi checked the digital read-outs. 'There's three minutes and two seconds between losing our guy and picking up this one. That confirms it. It's definitely not our man. Wouldn't take that long to get up Bottle Bank and whiz round here.'

'I disagree. That's precisely why I think it is the kidnappers. I reckon they stopped to switch plates. It would only take a minute or two at most if they stuck magnetic plate over the old one.'

'We'll soon find out.' Ravi fast-forwarded the reel. The van appeared to travel at lightning speed until a camera picked it up again on the Swan House roundabout, and another at the fourth exit.

'That's the last of the City Centre footage. I'll have to commission more to follow it further,' Ravi said.

'Do it,' Danskin commanded. After a pause, 'Where do we think he's headed?'

'Well, he's on Melbourne Street, out towards Walker,' Ryan said.

'Or City Road. Or Ouseburn. We're back where we started.' Danskin slammed his fist on the desk. 'Shit-a-brick: what if he's looping back onto the quayside? What if he's gone back for another one?'

The thought hit them like a blow from a heavyweight. Stunned them into silence.

A silence broken by the shrill of a telephone. They jumped.

Hannah Graves's turn to answer it. Ryan had forgotten she was there. She'd remained sullenly quiet throughout the entire briefing.

The rest of the crew mulled over the footage. Tried to make sense of what they'd witnessed. Posed endless questions no-one could answer.

Until Hannah brought proceedings to a halt.

She addressed the room but reserved her glacial stare for Stephen Danskin.

'We've got another body.'

CHAPTER TWENTY-TWO

The naked woman lay in repose, her hair fanned around her head like a halo. She had her knees slightly drawn up. Her left arm rested by her hip; the fingers of her right hand pointed towards a shallow lake.

Stephen Danskin, Nigel Trebilcock and Ryan Jarrod stood atop her right breast and followed the trail of her finger to where Aaron Elliott prodded and poked the bloated corpse far beneath their feet.

They were at Northumberlandia, the 'Lady of the North', the world's largest freeform land sculpture of the female form. Covering fifty acres with five miles of footpaths winding around her voluptuous curves, she was both nature reserve and artwork, and a tourist attraction to boot. But not today. Today, she belonged solely to the City and County Police.

A police constable read from his notebook. 'A local man found her. Andy Simpson. He was out walking his dog and photographing birds. He was standing right here when he spotted a flock going mental down by the lake.'

The three detectives looked down to the site where Elliott knelt, just as he had done at Dunston staiths, while the constable continued.

'Simpson thought it unusual because it was a mixed flock. He says he used his camera zoom like binoculars and closed in for a better view. Through the lens, he said he saw the outline of something in the lake. He wasn't sure what it was at first because the sun had come up and the reflection off the water blinded him.'

'Is Simpson still here?' Danskin interrupted.

'Yes, sir. He's in the café with a cup of tea. We've got somebody with him. He's a bit shook up.'

'I bet he is. Don't let him go 'til I've had a word. You were saying, constable?'

'Aye, anyway, it took him about five to ten minutes to wind his way down from here. As he got closer, his dog started going ballistic. Nearly pulled him over. So, he unleashed it. When it got to the lakeside, it started whining and whimpering. Pawing the ground. Tail between its legs, sort of thing, but it wouldn't come back when Simpson called it. When he got nearer, he realised why.'

They stood in silence, the idyllic views an oxymoron to the scene beneath them. To the east, they saw the distant coastline of the North Sea, white horses cresting its surface. Westward, the sun caught the fuselage of a Boeing jet aircraft as it rose from the tarmac of Newcastle International Airport. The rolling contours of the Cheviots to the north mirrored Northumberlandia's own curves while, just visible to the south, the Angel of the North stood protecting the region from evil. Judging by what lay in the lake, it had failed in its obligations.

Danskin hoped Aaron Elliott was having better luck with his responsibilities down below them. 'Howay, let's get off this tit and see what the other one doon there's got for us.'

The constable headed one way to sit with Andy Simpson while the three detectives wound their way towards Elliott, all with a distinct sense of déjà vu.

The pathologist spoke without raising his head. 'Ah, the three wise men. Or is it the three wise monkeys? I'm never sure which is more appropriate.' Elliott rose from his squat, knees cracking as he did so. 'My joints never get used to soaking themselves in freezing water.' He lowered his mask once he had his back to the scene. 'What can I do for you?'

Danskin inclined his head towards the body tangled in weeds three feet below the surface. 'What the bloody hell do you think you can do for us; sell us an ice-cream?'

'Fair enough. Here, you can come closer if you want. She won't bite.'

They shuffled their feet in pretence but had no desire to get any nearer the corpse.

'First thing I need to know is,' the DCI asked Elliott, 'Is there a connection between this one and the lass we found at the staiths? We think there is, but we need a positive ID first.'

'Well, we'll never know as long as she stays in the water, will we?' the pathologist replied.

Ryan recoiled as Aaron Elliott prodded the bloated body and thanked God it wasn't his job to fish her out.

'I could do with a hand here,' Elliott said.

It wasn't his job, was it?

'Jarrod,' Danskin said.

Hell, it was.

'Don't I need to be suited up?'

Elliott laughed. 'You're a quick learner. You passed the test.' He rummaged in one of three backpacks. Brought out a sealed bag. Tossed it to Ryan. 'One-size-fits-all. You know the score. Be quick about it.'

Nigel Trebilcock helped Ryan don the PPE. The Cornishman grimaced through clenched teeth. 'Congratulations. For once, I'm pleased I didn't have the winning ticket, I am.'

Ryan gave a short, sarcastic-ridden laugh and waded into the lake alongside Elliott.

The body felt swollen to the touch, blown up like an overfull water balloon. Even from beneath the surface and behind his mask, Ryan detected a ripe, sweet smell. He shut his eyes, held his breath, and turned his head aside as, on Dr Elliott's count of three, they hauled her onto the bankside. When they lowered her, she rippled for a second as if she were jelly from a mould.

Elliott waited for his attendants to arrive and bag the body. 'Not long now, darling,' the pathologist said. 'We've got a date in the lab. I promise I'll be gentle with you.'

The Girl on the Quay

Before they zipped her up, Ryan forced himself to look at the corpse's face for the first time. He expected to see Jade or Kayla; Sobena or Radka.

What he saw was a mummified waxwork that could have been anyone.

**

A patrol car and an unmarked vehicle entered Worswick Street's one-way system travelling in the wrong direction.

They drew to a halt beneath the Whipped Cream awning. DI Parker and Gavin O'Hara leapt out of the unmarked car. Danskin had instructed Sue and Hannah to remain at the station with Sangar and Todd Robson. 'Not a place I want my women officers to witness,' had been his reasoning. Privately, he had a different motive but not one he could divulge.

Parker flashed his badge at Benny Hay, who remained unmoved. 'We're not open yet,' Benny said.

'We're no' here for the show, laddie. Step aside.'

'You got a warrant?'

Gavin O'Hara laughed. 'You've been watching too much TV, pal.'

Benny drew himself up even taller in the face of Gavin's challenge. 'You still need a warrant to search the place.'

Lyall Parker stood down O'Hara. 'Och, you're right. How silly of us. Except, who said we were here to search?'

Benny Hay looked down on the Scotsman. ''Cos we're not open yet. We've no customers inside. If you're looking for drugs, you'll need to search. No warrant, no search.'

Parker shook his head. 'Good answer, but it's not right. Is Chamley here?'

Benny didn't utter a word, but the Mr Spock-style raised eyebrow spoke volumes.

'I'll take that as a yes. Move over, sonny. We'd like a word with him.'

He let them pass but only after radioing inside, where Titus answered the call by meeting them in the darkened corridor.

Parker flashed his badge again. 'Take me to your leader,' he said.

Titus glowered down at them, the whites of his eyes the only part of him visible in the gloom. 'He's not here.'

'Sorry, big man, but we think otherwise. Now, where can we find Chamley?'

'Ah, you want Mr Chamley.' They missed the inflection in his words. 'He's in his office. I'll show you.'

Titus escorted Lyall and Gavin into the empty and unlit auditorium. It still retained the smell of last night's sweat and alcohol. Gavin made a face. There was something deeply unpleasant about it. They turned right as they reached the bar and waited outside a closed door. Titus knocked and held back for Chamley's reply.

Lyall and Gavin didn't.

They marched in on Titus's knock to find Chamley engrossed in paperwork festooned across a cluttered desk strangely at odds with the otherwise pristine room.

The chinless man looked over the top of his spectacles, sat down his pen, turned off his monitor screen. 'Yes?'

'I'm Detective Inspector Lyall Parker. This is DC Gavin O'Hara. City and County police.'

Chamley's eyes darted between the two of them. He stood. Offered them his hand. 'What can I do you for?'

'We'd like a word. I think it would be better if we did this at the station.'

The club owner's smile disappeared. His teeth gnawed at his lower lip. 'Well, I'm sorry but I don't. I've got a club to run,' he checked his watch, 'and I've a lot to do.'

'We're here to talk about Jade, Kayla, and Ebony.'

Chamley played it deadpan but Parker noticed he tried too hard not to blink.

'You can leave us now, Titus,' Chamley instructed. As the guard left the room, he added, 'Come back and lock the office in a few minutes, please.'

Titus stared out Lyall and Gavin and, satisfied they'd blinked first, he left them alone.

'Okay, gents. I'll come with you,' Lou Chamley consented. 'You have precisely one hour. If I'm not back by then, I'll sue the backside off you.'

He stepped towards the exit. 'By the way, you forgot Madonna. You'll want to talk about her, too.'

**

The Dutch woman couldn't believe her luck. Not only had she just witnessed Lou Chamley disappear into a police car, the events had distracted Titus and Benny who were deep in conversation as the cleaning company's minibus pulled into the spot the police vehicles vacated.

She stepped out the shadows of the disused bus station and joined the cleaning team as they entered the club unchallenged.

Once inside, she assumed the gait of an older woman, her new greyish hair colouring a perfect fit for the role and kept her head down for the benefit of the CCTV. Whilst the others unlocked storage rooms and handed out equipment, she already had hers: a rag-headed mop and red plastic bucket.

She made a play of sweeping the floor behind the bar, gradually edging her way towards the office corridor. On her way, she collected a bar towel and pretended to flick dust from the fittings.

Ensuring her head stayed down, she raised her eyes and checked out the surroundings. She saw only the cleaning team; three domestics polished away at table-tops, a couple plugged in vacuum cleaners, another on stage improvised a pole dance with her mop to the screeches and cackles of her workmates.

Quickly, she backed around the corner into the corridor so that the camera above the office door wouldn't capture her face. She raised her mop above her head. Mimed flicking at cobwebs where wall and ceiling met. She worked her way along the wall until she was beneath the camera and felt her mop rest against the camera mountings. The woman gave a quick push on the broom handle, turning the mop head through ninety degrees as she did so.

With the camera lens pointing flush against the wall, the woman began her work on the security code. She needn't have bothered. As soon as she touched the keypad, the door swung open.

She was inside, the Mayan's secrets at her disposal.

Luuk would be delighted with her.

CHAPTER TWENTY-THREE

'It's my case, sir. I should be in there.'

'Sorry, Jarrod; this thing's grewed and grewed like the Lambton Worm. I'll make sure you get the kudos when it's all over, but I need to lead on this now.'

'Howay, man. I'm up to the job.'

Stephen Danskin looked directly at him. 'I'm not sure you are.' He held up a hand to quell the protests. 'It's no reflection on you, son. I'm not sure you are, because I'm not sure I am.'

They continued their discussion as they negotiated the stairs down to the interview suite. 'Sir, the body. What was all that stuff around it? She didn't even look real.'

'I can't remember the fancy name for it but for some reason it happens sometimes in drownings. Something to do with the effect of water temperatures and algae and currents, or lack of, on decomposition. I'm sure Dr Elliott would be delighted to fill you in on the detail.'

Ryan grimaced. 'And to think I complained about being bored.'

Danskin laughed. 'I told you it wasn't all…'

'Shit and giggles,' Ryan finished the sentence for him. 'See, I do remember stuff.'

Stephen pushed open a door and let Ryan through first. They were in a small, dark room with a large window overlooking the interview suite. The glass had a slight tint. As long as the light stayed off in their room, they remained invisible to the occupants of the other.

They watched Lyall Parker use his teeth to rip off the cellophane packaging around a tape. Danskin pressed a button and the conversation became audible.

'...really necessary?' they heard Lou Chamley ask.

'Standard procedure, I'm afraid,' Parker replied. 'Nothing to worry about, I assure you.'

Ryan didn't think Chamley looked assured at all.

'As you know, I'm Detective Inspector Lyall Parker. With me is Detective Constable Gavin O'Hara. For the purpose of the tape, can you confirm your name, sir?'

'Louis Chamley. Look, I've a legal qualification myself but, to be clear, do I need representation here?'

'I don't know. Do you?' Lyall softened the tone. Smiled. 'Och no, you're not under arrest, if that's what you mean. We just need to know a little more about some of your companies, and the people who work for you.'

Chamley dried errant spittle with a finger. 'Go ahead. I'll tell you all I can.'

'Thank you. Now, I understand you run an organisation called the Whipped Cream club. It has links to an escort agency; Orchid Petals.'

'You already know that.'

'I do. What I don't know, is where you get your employees.'

'They aren't employees. They're volunteers. They come and go as they please.'

Gavin O'Hara jotted something down.

'We'll get onto where they go in a moment. For now, where do they come from?'

'They hear about us. We've a good reputation. They come to us. Simple as.'

'And, you don't think to ask where they come from?'

'Does the British Heart Foundation ask where their volunteers come from? Or the PDSA? Or any other charity? No, I don't ask where they come from. All I need to know is that they are fit, healthy and attractive. They have to be, in my line of business.'

Gavin O'Hara spoke next. 'You're not seriously comparing what you do to a charity, are you?'

The Girl on the Quay

Chamley shifted in his seat. 'You know, I didn't think of it in that way until you mentioned it just now. But, in a way, it is. I provide a service to people in need.'

O'Hara tried to keep the contempt out of his voice. 'In need of what? A fumble in a darkened corner of your club? A BJ after a night out? Sex your customers wouldn't otherwise get?'

'I should warn you that we do not condone, support, or have anything to do with any such activities. My club is beyond reproach. You lot know that. You've visited it enough. Have you found anything? No, of course you haven't. Because there's nothing in the club for you to find.'

Lyall Parker sat back in his chair. Stared at the man opposite him. After a few moments silence, he asked, 'And what about the agency?'

'Same as. Everything is perfectly above board.'

'Except,' Parker said, 'It's not, is it? We have reliable information that at least two of your 'volunteers' have sex with your clients.'

Chamley feigned surprise. 'Not on the agency's time, they don't. If you have proof, I'll most certainly ensure they do not get any more appointments. Of course, if it happens outside of any hours the agency charges for, and we take no remuneration from it, I can't possibly be responsible. They are grown women, after all. I can't be held accountable for how they choose to boost their tips, surely?'

In the adjacent room, Danskin wrote *'Smart bugger, isn't he?'* on a sheet of paper. Ryan nodded in agreement.

Lou Chamley took a sip of water. As he did so, O'Hara said, 'Tell us about Jade, Kayla and Ebony.' O'Hara noticed the level of water in the glass shift slightly. Chamley set the glass back down.

'And Madonna. You keep forgetting Madonna.' He'd recovered his composure. 'The four of them started dancing in the club, as most do. They were extremely popular. Punters lapped them up, so to speak. They quickly outgrew the club. Moved to the agency. Again, they were booked most nights. Probably the most popular girls we've ever had.'

Parker smirked. 'We'll need access to your client list, of course.'

'Out of the question. Absolutely not. Our clients have a right to confidentiality. We pride ourselves on our discretion.'

'Och, I can be discrete as well, don't you know.'

'No. You will need a court order. And, unless you have some trumped-up charge with any half-decent solicitor would see through from a distance of fifty miles, no court in the land will grant you one.'

Parker knew he was right. He changed the angle of attack. 'You talk of the girls in the past tense. Why?'

Chamley chastised himself. Remembered he needed to choose his words with greater care. Thoughts of sharpened tent poles filled his mind.

He took his time answering. He'd get off the hook if he revealed the ransom demands but, it would only serve to put the spotlight firmly on the club and the agency. And, by default, on the Mayan.

He wiggled in his seat. The sharpened tent pole had moved from his mind to his anus.

'I use the past tense because they're no longer with the agency. They moved on, I guess.'

'You guess?'

'Yes. I guess. Like I say, the girls come and go as they please. Madonna was first. Made herself unavailable. A couple of weeks later, Jade, then Kayla, turned down engagements. Ebony was the last to do so.'

Lyall Parker leant forward. 'Mr Chamley, you dinnae seem surprised.'

'Look, if the girls were up to the sort of thing you suggest, they've probably earnt enough. Or, they got fed up working nights.' He shrugged. 'Money isn't everything, you know. Perhaps they just wanted to return home.'

'Aye, Jade and Kayla might. Not forgetting Madonna,' he said with sarcasm. 'But Ebony, for one, didn't.'

The man opposite blinked three times. 'You know where she is?'

'That I do.'

Silence. The bald-headed man removed his spectacles. Cleaned them on a tissue. Replaced them.

'Don't you want to know where she is?' Parker persisted.

Silence.

'Ebony's dead, Mr Chamley.'

Chamley's Adam's apple bounced like a tennis ball. Saliva dribbled down his chin. Eventually, he managed a 'Poor girl.'

Lyall and Gavin let him stew in silence. Watched him closely. Gauged his reactions. What they got wasn't what they expected.

'Shame. But, hey-ho. Can I go now, please? My club awaits.'

Parker and O'Hara looked at one another, open-mouthed. In the other room, Danskin and Ryan did the same. Yet, last time they checked; indifference wasn't a crime.

Parker had no choice. 'Aye, that you can. For now.'

Chamley stood, composure regained. He turned his back. Smiled to himself. Took a step towards the door. 'If there's anything else I can do for you, detective inspector; anything at all, just ask.'

Danskin scribbled *'Wrong thing to say'* on his notepad. Ryan noticed the DCI's grin.

'If you put it that way,' Parker concluded, 'You can answer one more question for me.'

'Of course.'

'Who's the Mayan?'

**

Aaron Elliott hummed a little tune to himself as he wriggled his fingers until the glove was a snug fit. He turned to the table, folded down the sheet in a series of precise pleats so it lay over her pubic bone, and stood back to admire her.

He looked the girl in her eyes, or where her eyes had once been, and winked.

Elliott clipped the portable recorder to his gown, pulled on a headset, and unmuted its mic via a toggle half-way up the lead.

'Unknown female. Height, one metre seventy-eight; age range twenty-five to thirty-three. The body was found in shallow water, fresh - as in non-saline - but stagnant. Maximum depth of lake circa six foot. When discovered, the body lay face-down in less than three foot of water. The water was tepid as a result of sun warmth. Substantial algae and bacterial presence.'

He muted his mic while he gave a slight cough.

'Precise post-mortem period not known. Body partly coated in adipocere. Given the conditions in the lake and the results of water samples taken therefrom, best estimate of death is approximately ten days from discovery, and within the range seven to fourteen days.'

Adipocere is a wax-like substance which oozes from internal body fat and coagulates on the surface of the skin, mummifying the corpse. It delays, but doesn't entirely prevent, the process of decomposition.

'Close visual inspection confirms initial on-site impression of no significant perimortem injuries. There are a number of small contusions and abrasions – note to self: confirm numbers and precise locations separately – around body but nothing to indicate the causes are anything outside of daily living activities.'

He raised the woman's chin. 'Slight swelling to lower jaw.' He looked at bluish-grey markings around her throat. 'Haematoma around trachea. Query: attempted strangulation?'

He peered in closer. Shone a pen torch on the bruising. Magnified the site. Satisfied, he concluded, 'No sign of petechial haemorrhage. Manual asphyxiation ruled out as cause of death.'

Next, he ran his fingers over the woman's head. 'No cranial damage. Skull intact. Facial features significantly affected by organic activity whilst in water rendering further inspection futile. Chances of a visual identification extremely unlikely.'

Elliott's eyes caressed the nude form on the table. 'No signs of localised bleeding on torso. Visual inspection complete.'

He paused the tape and hummed his way a table. He lowered his mask, sipped water, and picked up a scalpel. Dr Elliott took one final look at the complete body. 'Sorry, my darling, but it has to be done.'

He turned the tape back on as he pressed down hard and began to make a Y-shaped incision which would expose the girl's innards.

Elliott fished around inside the cavity, snipped through, and removed internal organs, and popped them on scales. He typed the results into a computer which provided comparisons with historical autopsies going back decades.

As expected, the lungs provided Elliott with the answer he needed.

'Lung weight discrepancy typical of emphysema aquosum. Some evidence of Paltauf's spots in the pulmonary pleura of left lung.'

Elliott straightened. Rotated his neck until it clicked.

'Cause of death: drowning.'

He switched off the mic. Thought for a moment. 'Strange place to drown.' He looked at the woman. 'I wonder, did you fall, or were you pushed?'

Elliott depressed the button on the toggle and spoke again. '…without prejudice to pending toxicology report.'

The pathologist took another gulp of water. 'Now,' he said to the corpse, 'I guess that nice Detective Chief Inspector will want to know a bit more about you, whether you've had any fun recently. Sorry, my dear, but I need to get up close and personal. I do apologise if my hands are cold.'

He pulled back the lowermost fold of the sheet, so her genitals were exposed. His eyebrows arched above his facemask.

'Well, look what we have here.'

The wall-mounted phone rang. He tisked. 'I'm sorry, my love. I'll just get that. Be right back.'

He lowered his face mask. Wiped away sweat pooled beneath it as he whistled his way to the phone. 'Dr Crippen here. How may I help you?'

'Hello, Dr Elliott. I just thought I'd warn you; the girl in room two?'

'I'm attending to her right now.' His voice came out hoarse. Elliott cleared his throat and moistened dry lips with his tongue. 'If it's Foreskin that's asking, tell him I'm just about finished.'

'No, sir. That's not it.'

'Come on, then. Spit it out.'

'I just thought you should know. We've got her bloods back. She's HIV positive.'

Elliott looked at the blood smeared on the telephone handset, on his gloves, his gown. He felt it smeared over his face where he'd wiped his hands.

He tasted it on his tongue.

Elliott's eyelids slid shut.

'Thank you,' he said. 'Be a good girl and ready me a course of post-exposure prophylaxis, would you?'

Aaron Elliott replaced the receiver. Spoke to the butchered carcass lying on his table.

'Here's another fine mess you've gotten me into, Stanley.'

CHAPTER TWENTY-FOUR

Those party to Chamley's interview gathered in a huddle in one corner of the bullpen. Hannah Graves and Todd Robson joined on the periphery.

Danskin spoke first. 'What did you make of all that?'

'He's as shifty as a poker player's bluff,' Parker concluded. 'Wouldn't trust him at all. But, fair play to him, he no' tripped himself up. Everything he said was plausible, even if we know it's crap.'

'Aye,' O'Hara agreed, 'He had an answer for everything.'

Danskin breathed out until his lips vibrated like a horse. He dragged a hand across his eyes. 'Observations, Jarrod?'

'I hate to say it, but the lads are right. He's in it up to his neck but there's not enough to detain him.'

Stephen Danskin began patrolling the floor like an expectant father. His hand drummed against his thigh as he paced back and forth. 'What did you make of his reaction when you mentioned the Mayan?'

'I could smell his shit,' O'Hara said. 'He recovered well but you could see him tense. I just wish he hadn't had his back to us. The eyes would've told us everything. By the time he turned, he'd composed himself.'

'What did he say about him?' Robson enquired.

'Played a dead bat,' Danskin said. 'Actually, played and missed, more like. Pretended he didn't know what we were talking about. Denied all knowledge. Said he was in sole control and there was nobody above him in the food chain.'

Robson snorted. 'Snivelling gets like that are never top of the food chain. He's lying.'

'We all know that, Todd,' Ryan said. 'But, we can't prove it. As far as I can see, we can't touch him with a barge pole.'

'I agree, Jarrod. But, I'd add the word 'yet' to that. We can't touch him yet. What we need is a positive ID on the lass at Northumberlandia. He can put Ebony down as a coincidence, what with her death being natural causes, and all. If we can prove the lass in the lake is either Jade or Kayla, and that she was murdered, it'll be enough to get him back in. I'll squeeze him 'til his balls pop.'

Ryan thought of Ilona. 'Heaven forbid it is one of them.' They all looked at him. 'I know, I know; it almost certainly is. And, if so, and it's murder, the Super would authorise access to the agency's client list. There'd be all sorts of slugs in that garden, I bet.'

'Anything from Elliott yet? We really could do with a bit of clarity here.'

'We no' heard anything, sir. I've got Sue chasing it up.'

They sat in silence, ruminating on what they had so far. 'You know,' Ryan continued, 'The club's where it all starts. If we could only find where Chamley, or the Mayan, get the girls from, I bet a pound to a penny that'll give us enough to get Chamley back in. Even better, if we can follow a lass's progression from dancefloor to agency, we'd surely find something about the Mayan that way.'

'The second option's out the question, Jarrod. If another one moves up the pecking order, it's probably cos another girl's disappeared. Four's quite enough, thank you very much.'

Hannah entered the fray. 'I've been saying we need to know what's going on in that club for days now. Haven't I?' she added curtly.

Sue Nairn rode to Danskin's rescue. 'Sir,' she said as she strode into the office waving a sheet of A4. 'Elliott's report on the girl in Northumberlandia.'

'Give us the highlights, man.'

'Death by drowning, it says. Elliott adds he's not a coroner though he says he wouldn't lay money on it being accidental or misadventure. But, he says, there's insufficient evidence to support murder, either.'

'Shit.'

'He says he's waiting for toxicology reports before submitting final conclusions.'

'Do we have an ID, man? We need an ID.'

'Negative, sir.'

'More shit.'

'But there is one positive in his report,' Nairn continued. 'And it's not a pleasant one. It's HIV. She's HIV positive.'

The squad fell silent. Tried to understand what this brought to the table. Ryan and Hannah knew. They exchanged glances. Danskin grabbed the report out of Sue Nairn's hands.

'Fits with the job,' Robson assumed.

'I don't know, Robson. Does it? I mean, whatever we think of it, the agency prides itself on the girls being classy. I bet they'll be screened. Won't they?'

He got no answer. They all wondered, but none knew.

'Sir. Can I have a word? In private?' Ryan asked.

'Better be quick.'

Ryan pulled the DCI into a corner. Hannah knew what they'd be discussing. She joined them.

'Sir, do you agree the chances of this being Jade or Kayla is high?'

'Higher than high. we can't be certain.'

'I need your permission for something. My source from the club?'

Danskin's eyes narrowed. 'Yes?'

'Well, she needs to know. She's in a relationship with Radka Vosahlo. A sexual one.'

'Christ.' He lowered his head. 'Hang on, though: can it be transmitted woman-to-woman?'

That was something none of them knew. Ryan bet Hadley Kutz would. Until he'd spoken with him, all he could say was, 'I'd rather not take the chance, sir.'

'I can't run the risk of prejudicing the case. Until we know whether it's Jade or Kayla, or either of them, we keep schtum.'

Ryan jumped straight in with it. 'Check Elliott's report. If our girl had a piercing in her labia, it's Radka Vosahlo.'

'What?'

'Just check, will you?'

He scanned through the report. Came to the final few paragraphs.

'Wheeyabugger.'

'So, we know who she is. We know she's from the club. We know that's two out of four dead. At least two.'

Danskin's eyes shifted to Hannah's. She raised an eyebrow. Almost imperceptibly, he inclined his head. Hannah dipped hers in acknowledgement.

'Sir,' Ryan said. 'Now we know, do I have permission to inform my source?'

'In the circumstances, Jarrod; you do.'

'I'll do it, sir,' Hannah offered. 'It might come better from a woman.'

Ryan began to object. 'What? Hadawayandshite, you're even elbowing your way into me case, now.'

'Oh, for heaven's sake, Ryan. Grow up, man.'

The DCI stepped in. Prevented the row escalating. 'Good thinking, Graves. Besides, Ryan, I've a job for you. The best way to get to the Mayan is through Chamley, and the best way to do that is to prove the lasses were murdered or, even better, find something that backs up your people-trafficking theory. Let's get back to the others.'

Contented, Ryan joined Danskin and made towards the rest of the crew.

'Go warn your informant, Hannah.' Danskin glanced over his shoulder. 'You know the score.

'Thank you, sir,' Hannah said to his back.

'Be careful, Detective Constable Graves; be careful.'

**

A sunbeam blazed its way between a gap in the curtains, illuminating the figures on the bed as if they were players on a stage.

From the street below, the sound of trams, bicycle bells, laughter and voices mingled like the discordant tuning of an orchestra until it drowned out the giggles and squeals in the room.

When the phone rang for the third time, Luuk Van Eyck rolled to the edge of the bed. 'Ja?'

'I've been to the club.'

'You.' He reached for a side table and threw a wad of euros onto the bed. He covered the mouthpiece. 'Carry on,' he said. The two girls on the bed grabbed the notes, tossed them into the air, then entwined themselves on the mattress as notes rained down on them.

Turning back to the phone, he spat out a question. 'What do you want?'

'I got into the club for you, Luuk. I did it.'

He wiggled his backside into a pair of jeans. 'And?'

'There's ransom notes. I saw two. Just lying on his desk.'

'Never mind that. Did you get the money?'

'There was no money'

'Then, you didn't look hard enough.'

'I did find out what you wanted. About the girls. The office was a pigsty, but I searched through it all. There was nothing to show the Mayan has another source for his women. He is worried, though. The files show he's recruited more men. Muscle. But no new girls.'

A shriek rose from the bed. A girl with dusky skin had her teeth clamped around the nipples of a blonde.

'What was that?' the woman on the phone asked.

'It's outside. A catfight,' Luuk explained, winking at the girls.

'Oh. Right. So, I would say the Mayan and Chamley have brought in extra protection for the girls already here rather than import more.'

'I don't give a shit about the security. Or the women. I just want what I'm owed.'

The Dutch woman suggested the club's takings must be in the safe.

'Then, you must make it unsafe. Open it.'

The woman protested. 'I cannot. I cannot go back.'

The blonde levered herself off the bed. Wrapped her arms around Luuk. Nuzzled his neck as he spoke. 'Yes. You will go back. You will get every euro, every penny, every dime the Mayan has.'

'Luuk, I can't…'

'Enough!'

The second girl joined Luuk and the blonde. She wheedled tapered fingers down the front of Luuk's unzipped trousers.

'You will do as I ask.' He terminated the call.

The dark-skinned girl dropped to her knees. Leered up at him. 'Yes, master. I shall do as you ask.'

**

Ryan pinched the bridge of his nose. 'Have you got any paracetamol I could have?'

The woman pushing the meds trolley shook her head. 'Can't do that. Sorry. I can stretch to a glass of water if it'll help.'

'Gan on, then.'

The carer poured three fingers-worth into a plastic cup so flimsy it collapsed in on itself as soon as he took it from her.

'What's your day been like, gran?'

'I've been to the coast with me mam,' Doris Jarrod said, beaming.

'That's nice.'

'The candy floss had dragonflies in it.'

'Oh dear.'

'Then, I played on the sand. Sadie Micklethorpe and me made sandcastles. Sadie's in my class. A right little tinker, she is.' She stared into space. A car horn tooted outside. 'Is that the air-raid siren?'

Ryan closed his eyes. 'Are you sure you can't give me any paracetamol?'

The carer smiled. 'She's not having one of her better days, is she?'

Ryan turned back to his gran. 'It's okay, gran. It's the all-clear.'

Doris Jarrod was already asleep.

Angela Doyle caught him on the way out. She had a load of papers in her hand. 'Did any of the staff tell you?'

'Tell me what?'

Angela rolled her eyes. 'Sorry, someone should have warned you.'

'About?'

'Your gran. We think she might have a water infection.'

Ryan nodded. It made sense.

'And about the fees,' Angela continued. 'I'm afraid we're going to have to increase them. I'm spoke before about assisted funding. The local authority will contribute. Of course, you may have to sell your grandmother's house.'

There goes my bolt hole in The Drive, Ryan thought.

'I'm really sorry. Financial review, new tax year and all that. Costs have spiralled like you've no idea. It's not my decision, you realise, but the owners really have to pass those costs on. Seems we're barely breaking even.'

'Okay. Look, I'll have a word with me dad. Let him know, like. It'll be a wrench for him to let it go, I know that much.'

'Of course. I understand and, please, don't think I'm telling you that's what you should do. You need to think about it. Take advice if needs be.' Angela offered him a sympathetic smile. 'I'm sorry. I probably shouldn't have said anything.'

Ryan headed for the exit. Such was the day, he didn't even cast his customary glance at Paul Mooney, Angela Doyle, and Max Bonhomme.

It had been a long day. And, the days were about to get longer.

Much longer.

CHAPTER TWENTY-FIVE

Beneath a ripened peach of a sun, the centrepiece of Whickham village was chocolate-box perfect.

The stained glass of St Mary's church twinkled in the sun's rays like lights on a Christmas tree. A rainbow shimmered deep within the spray of sprinklers tending the lush village green. On the gentle slopes of its lawns, flower beds stacked within dry-stone walls sprouted fresh tufts of plants which, in a few weeks, would glorify the landscape with vibrant yellows, reds, and purples.

Above it all, the sky glowed with the purity of spring; a crisp powder blue speckled with cotton bud clouds. The only grey hung above the head of the young man slumped on a bench in the middle of the splendour.

A pug sat on the man's lap, idly licking itself clean. His master let out a groan. The dog looked up, cocked its head to one side, then returned to its ablutions. Ryan Jarrod sighed once more.

He'd overcome the loss of his mother but, right now, he felt the loss all over again. The grandmother he adored was a shell of the proud woman she once was. His friends had drifted away. With the exception of Barry Docherty, they'd tired of his constant refusals of nights out. It was the job, not him, but they didn't understand. How could they?

Now, even the job had escaped him, his investigation in the hands of others. Danskin, Parker and, even, Hannah Graves, were ahead of him.

Hannah. He'd lost her, too.

Ryan felt rain on his face. Looked skywards. The sky above his head was crystal clear. It wasn't rain. The splashes he felt were his own tears.

Suddenly, he gave in to his pent-up emotions. His shoulders quivered with the hurt of it all. Great, heaving sobs escaped him. Spud rested his paws on his master's chest and licked away the tears. Ryan tickled him behind the ears with both hands, drawing comfort from the weight and warmth of the dog.

He needed Hannah. Knew he should apologise for the way he'd snapped at her. She had been right: she was better placed to tell Ilona Popescu about Radka. To warn her of the infection. To encourage her to get tested.

He dialled Hannah's number for the third time that morning. And, for the third time, his call went straight to voicemail. She didn't want to know.

Ryan stretched and yawned. He was exhausted, and drained. He'd reviewed the abduction footage of the woman known as Kayla until the wee small hours. He played it over and over again. Ravi Sangar sat alongside him. Together, they traced the Y-plates shown on the transit. The plate was registered to a Vauxhall Astra belonging to a Margaret Orange. 'Pronounced O'Range,' she'd explained. She had also confirmed she could see the Astra sat on her drive in Aysgarth.

Another dead end, so Ryan set Ravi the task of sifting through reports of stolen vehicles nationwide. Specifically, stolen white transit vans. An impossible task. Again, he got nowhere.

It was almost three a.m. before Ryan rolled into bed. He awoke to a message from Stephen Danskin ordering him to get some rest. Report in after lunch, Danskin had told him. An order.

Right now, lunch seemed a long way away.

With Spud secured in a back-seat harness, he drove his Fiat out of the Harry Clasper car park on autopilot. Fifteen minutes later, he found himself meandering through the maze of narrow streets behind the former Alexander Fleming maternity hospital.

He was in the leafy and eclectic suburb of Jesmond; home to the up-and-coming and the wannabes. Home to students, doctors, artists, and entrepreneurs. And, home to Hannah Graves.

With the window of his car wound down a few inches to give Spud some air, Ryan strode up to the row of Victorian houses which contained Hannah's ground-floor apartment. Her name was one of six above a panel of doorbells alongside the building's entrance. She didn't answer his ring. Was she on duty? Ryan couldn't remember.

Ryan strolled to her window. He didn't know why, but his heart raced. Something felt wrong. He cupped both hands above his eyes and pressed his face against her window.

There was no sign of her inside. No sign of anything. It was tidy, clean. Not like he'd seen it before.

A window above slid open. 'You looking' for something?' a voice called down.

Ryan stepped back so he could see the woman as he looked up. He shielded his eyes from the sun. 'Just wondering if Hannah was about. Hannah Graves.'

'Yes, I know who Hannah is. You missed her.'

'Okay. I'll call back later. Just checking she's aal reet. She's not answering her phone. I'll see her later.'

'I doubt you will. You've misunderstood. When I say, 'missed her', I mean she's gone. Moved out.'

Ryan's heart missed a beat. 'I divven't think so. I think we're talking about a different person.'

'No. Hannah. Pretty lass. Curly hair. Lots of freckles.'

Ryan swallowed.

'I saw her last night,' the woman continued. 'She was packing three or four suitcases into a car.'

'What?' was all he could say.

'Looked like they were off somewhere.'

'They?'

'Yeah. Her and her fella.'

The Girl on the Quay

Ryan's mouth opened like the Tyne Tunnel. 'Her fella?' It took him two attempts to say the words.

'Aye. Tall bloke. They seemed happy enough. Lots of laughter and banter. You know the score. All smiles they were, far as I could tell.'

'What did he look like?'

'Didn't take much notice.'

Like hell, you didn't, Ryan thought. Nosey cow. 'You must have some idea.'

He saw the woman shrug. 'It was dark. I heard him, though. Wasn't from around these parts. Student, I guess.'

Ryan felt himself sway. His stomach lined itself with cement. 'How do you mean?'

'Well, his accent. It was queer. He sounded like a cross between a farmer and a pirate.'

Ryan grabbed at a wrought-iron fence to prevent himself from collapse.

He knew who she was with. She was with the only person who had an accent like that.

She was with Nigel Trebilcock.

**

John Craggs licked grease from his fingers one-by-one. The useless plastic fork snapped the first time he dug into the tray of haddock and chips, so he'd resorted to spooning up the white flesh with his fingers. He made a sibilant sound as he ladled more hot fish between his lips.

Across the road from Downey's fish restaurant, the rusty red patina of Tommy - a nine-foot high statue of a first world war infantryman hewn out of Corten steel – sat shrouded in a sea fret so dense it defeated the sun's best efforts to break through.

Hidden deep within the miasma, a man with prematurely greying hair leaned against a blue rail, staring out to sea. The North Sea was as calm as it ever was around these parts but, although he couldn't see it, the man heard the waves pound against the black-and-white lighthouse perched at the tip of Seaham's curved and elongated north breakwater pier.

'You're a hard man to find, Jackie Duggan,' Craggs commented as he sidled up alongside him.

'Aye, well. Keeping a low profile these days, aren't I?'

Craggs held his tray in front of Duggan. 'Chip?'

Duggan took a handful.

Craggs looked into the tray and shook his head. 'Not low enough not to break bail, though, I hear.'

'Not my fault. I could've drowned, I could.'

'What happened?'

Duggan thought for a moment. 'I take it you're asking for a reason.'

'Just taking an interest in your welfare, Jackie, lad.'

The man with salt-and-pepper hair barked out a short laugh. 'Aye, that'll be reet. Tell you what, you put a word in for me with the probation lot, get the bail thing out the way, and I'll tell you.'

Craggs thrust the empty carton into an overfull trash can. 'I'll see what I can do. Can't say fairer than that.'

'I was out in me boat. Dropping off me lobster creels.'

Craggs looked at him. 'Really?'

'Aye. I told you, I'm on the straight and narrow, now.'

'You got your Limited Shellfish Permit?'

'Piss off.'

Craggs laughed. 'Not that straight then, Jackie, eh?'

'Look, do you want to know, or what?'

Craggs shut up and let the man continue. 'I'm living up top of Church Street way, one of the roads behind St John's. It's not much more than a five-minute walk down to the harbour where I keep me boat. I was feeling good about myself, you know?' He choked back a laugh. 'That didn't last long once I set off.'

'What happened?'

'I sailed her down the coast past Horden, Blackhall Rocks way. I'd heard there's a good spot in the shelter of the headland. I'd just got there. Started getting me traps ready when I heard a motor start up. Thought nowt of it at first. The motor sounded canny close, but I couldn't see anything. It wasn't showing any lights.'

'Were you lit up, Jackie?'

Duggan replied without looking at the DI. 'Course not. I'm not going to draw attention to myself, am I? Not without a permit.'

Craggs turned so his back lay against the railings. Out of the mist, Tommy sat on his ammunition box, eyes downcast, rifle grounded. Kramer's words came back to Craggs. *We found some bullet holes mid-way up a mast and five more in the deck.*

'Carry on,' he said to Duggan.

'Aye, well, anyway. Like I say, the boat sounded nearby. Then, the motor picked up, really kicked up a gear as if it had somewhere to be in a hurry. That's when the wake hit me. It must've been virtually on top of us cos me little skiff got chucked aboot aal ower the place. I tried to steady her, but it was no good. Next thing I know, I'm arse ower tit in the water. Freezing, it was. Miracle I wasn't hypodermic.'

Craggs chuckled. 'Hypothermic. The word's hypothermic.'

'Whatever, it's a miracle either way. So, there I am splashing around. I managed to cling onto me boat like that fella in Titanic. Luckily, a bloke out sea fishing heard me shout and got me and the boat back to shore. I was in nee condition to meet bail next day, though.'

John Craggs couldn't disagree. 'I'll put a word in for you, Jackie. I promise. Now, where exactly was this?'

'I told you. Down Blackhall Rocks way.' He looked at the detective. 'I can take you there if you like.'

**

There was no way Ryan was going to wait until lunchtime to report into Forth Street. No way at all. For a man whose proud boast was that he never got angry, Ryan Jarrod was losing his shit with an all-too-frequent regularity.

He no longer cared. All that mattered to him was the urgent need to beat the hell out of Nigel Trebilcock.

The white Fiat screeched to a halt on double-yellows outside the station. Ryan grabbed Spud in his arms, the bemused dog panting like a steam train. Ryan charged at the revolving doors. They spun with the speed of a corncrake. He raced through the foyer like Forrest Gump, leaving Shades Gray and Sergeant Milligan open-mouthed.

Ryan jabbed the elevator's call button four, five, six times. When the doors eventually slid open, he elbowed his way in before DCI Rick Kinnear's mob had a chance to exit.

He shouted at the elevator to get a move on. When it halted at the third floor, he forced his way through the doors as soon as they started opening. Ryan flew along the corridor. Flung open the bullpen door with such force it rammed against the office wall with the sound of a thunderclap. He dropped the wriggling dog to the floor.

'Where's Treblecock? Where is he? I'm gonna kill him.'

Lyall Parker, Sue Nairn and Gavin O'Hara looked up at Ryan, his face puce, eyes bloodshot. Spittle sprayed from his lips. 'Come on. Where is he? Treblecock – get your arse out here. Now!'

Todd Robson tried to catch him as he raced by. 'Howay, Ryan man. What the hell's going on?'

'Got sod all to do with you, mate. It's between me and Treblecock.'

'Calm doon, Ryan. He's not here. He's out on a job.'

Ryan noticed Hannah was missing, too. He smashed his fist into a wall, the plasterboard shattered around it like an eggshell. 'Bollocks.'

He threw himself into a chair. Grabbed a fistful of hair and kneaded it between his fingers. Tears ran down his cheeks in a torrent.

'Get him some water, Gav,' Lyall said. 'Och, laddie. Come on noo. What's up?'

Ryan couldn't form any words. Nothing recognisable. Just guttural moans between his sobs. Gavin O'Hara offered him the water. Ryan slapped the mug out of his hands. 'Whisky. I need whisky.'

'You're on duty,' Lyall said, softly. 'And, I've never seen you drink Scotch all the time I've known you.'

Slowly, with deliberate deep breaths, Ryan brought himself under control. 'He's gone off with Hannah, Lyall. Treblecock and Hannah. God, I feel sick.' He screwed his eyes so tight his head ached.

'Look, I need you to focus on the job. We've had some developments. Kinnear's crew have gone back over some old files. They found a report from a bloke on his way back from shift work. He said he'd seen a vehicle being driven erratically down near North Shields fish quay. He reckons it was doing a canny lick round a tight bend. Took off the wing mirrors of a couple of parked cars, apparently. I guess you're ahead of me in thinking it was a white transit.'

Ryan took deep breaths. Tried to focus. 'Our white transit?'

Parker hunched his shoulders. 'Don't know yet. But it was the night Kayla was taken. And, the timings just about fit with the CCTV footage we got from the bridges. What's more, the guy who reported it believes he's seen it down there a couple of times, always at odd hours.'

Ryan shook his head. 'I can't do this, Lyall. Not right now.'

'Listen. You can. Whatever you think's going on, get it out o' that wee heed o' yours. You go making threats like that against Treblecock, you'll find yourself out the force. You're on your ninth life, remember, and probations up any minute. Stick with it. I dinnae want to lose you.'

Ryan's riposte was lost amid someone clapping their hands.

'Listen up,' DCI Danskin said. Parker, O'Hara, Todd Robson, Sue Nairn, and Ravi Sangar stopped what they were doing.

Ryan noted only Nigel Trebilcock and Hannah were missing. He tried to put the thoughts of what they might be doing together out of his head.

'We're making progress with the case. Excellent work, everyone, but it's all too slow.' Ryan thought the DCI sounded subdued, a note of worry in his voice. 'We know Jarrod's right about the ties with Whipped Cream and Orchid Petals. Chances are, he could be right about the other stuff, an' aal but I can't let us see what we expect to see.'

Ryan saw Todd Robson put his head down and watched his shoulders shake.

'We need to move and move fast. Girls are dying. I'm not losing another on my watch. We need to infiltrate the organisation.'

Gavin O'Hara let out a low whistle. 'Undercover, like?'

'Yes. I've discussed it with Superintendent Connor and he's agreed I can have an extra pair of hands.'

Danskin's door began to open.

'Meet our new recruit.'

Todd Robson's eyes bulged like a cartoon character. Gavin's jaw hung loose as if it were broken. Ravi blinked rapidly.

The new recruit stood before them. She wore knee length boots. Ripped and torn bondage trousers, significantly more rip than fabric, fastened by a heavy studded belt. Above it, the officer's midriff was bare.

A jewel hung from her navel. Wrapped around it, a flamboyant tattoo of a Chinese dragon, red, blue, and gold. Its tongue licked up between the upward swell of breasts barely concealed beneath the briefest of crop tops.

Even Ryan wasn't sure. Not entirely. Not until Stephen Danskin introduced the new recruit by name.

'Guys, say hello to Lexi.'

CHAPTER TWENTY-SIX

Hannah's alter-ego sported jet-black hair swept across the crown of her head in a Kirsten Stewart sideways wave. The style disguised her natural curls which were further masked by waist-length extensions.

Her freckles lay behind make-up as white as a clown's. Coloured contact lenses made her brown eyes blue. From the corner of her right eye, a lightning bolt of blue and black mascara zig-zagged to her temple.

She wore lipstick the colour of a bruise.

Hannah - or Lexi - appeared to Ryan in ultra HD. Everything else in the room he viewed as through a steamed-up bathroom mirror. He knew Danskin continued to speak yet all he heard was white noise. A hum of discordant static.

As the mirror began to clear, he saw his colleagues resume their duties. Danskin turned his back on them. Made his way towards his office. The Lexi woman followed him.

Ryan snapped out of his trance. 'I need a word.' He chased after them into the DCI's room. Slammed the door behind him.

'Well?'

Is that the best I can do, his subconscious screamed, *'Well?'*

'I know, Jarrod. I know.' Danskin sounded forlorn. Defeated.

'I'm mighty pleased you know, sir. Because I sure as hell don't.'

'Sit down,' Danskin ordered, 'Both of you.'

They sat.

'Listen, I'm no more in favour of this idea than you are. It's Hannah's plan. All of it. She suggested we put someone inside.'

'Actually,' she said, 'It wasn't my idea. It was Ryan's.'

'Huh?'

She smiled. 'That day in Chase Park, after we'd been to see Dr. Kutz? You explained how the park got its name, remember? And I said that's what was wrong with the case. We were chasing it. And getting nowhere. I told you we needed to let them come to us.'

'This is madness, man. How do you expect to get in there? Just walk in and ask a lass for a table dance? That'll work, I don't think.'

'Ryan, it's all sorted. I've been planning it ever since that moment. I'm not going in there as a customer. I've got a job there.'

Ryan's mouth worked, but no words came. His eyes flitted between Hannah and Danskin, pleading for an explanation; for something that made sense.

'I start tonight. Hence,' she moved her hand down her body, 'all this. I'm Lexi now. Remember Isla said they were short staffed? Well, I applied for a job. I'm the new barmaid at the Whipped Cream club. Oh, yes: I'm also Isla's new house-mate.'

Ryan slumped back in his chair. His senses reeled like a carousel. He ran his fingers through his hair.

'I need to ask: is that what you and Treblecock were up to?'

Beneath her eyeliner, she squinted. 'How do you know about that? You been spying on me?'

'I'm a detective, man. I know you've moved out. So, tell me: are you with Treblecock or Isla?'

She regarded him coldly. 'You're a right one, you are. I'm with Isla, of course. Treblecock helped me move, that's all. I mean, I couldn't trust you to help, could I? You'd have gone off on one. You've just proved it.'

He knew he shouldn't, but he laughed. Laughed in relief, and at his stupidity. 'When did you and Ilona hatch this up?' he asked once he'd gathered his composure.

The Girl on the Quay

It was Danskin's turn to pay attention. Ryan realised his mistake.

'Aye, sir. My contact's name is Ilona, not Isla. Ilona Popescu. You might as well know my other source is a Hadley Kutz. The doctor Hannah mentioned. He's a…behaviourist.'

Danskin arched one eyebrow.

'It's a long story. Anyway, Ilona and Isla are one-and-the-same. She's known as Isla at the club.' He turned his attention back to Hannah, his tone colder. 'Come on, then. When?'

She chose her words carefully. 'A while. Really, since that day at the Silverlink when you left us to take a call from Lyall, remember? I started working on her then.'

'Hannah, she's my informant. You shouldn't interfere.'

Danskin interjected. 'Leave it, Jarrod. It's done now.'

'Ilona didn't want to go along with it, not at first,' Hannah explained. 'It was only when I broke the news of Radka's death she finally agreed. She'll do owt to catch the kidnapper. Oh, by the way, Ilona knew about the HIV. She'd been giving the Mayan's medics her blood whenever Radka was screened. That's how Radka continued to work.'

It made sense to Danskin. It would to Ryan, too, once he calmed down.

'And another thing,' Hannah added. 'Ilona knew Radka was dead.'

'How'd she know that? Is she involved?'

Hannah shook her head. 'Almost certainly not. Intuition, I reckon.'

Ryan raised his head. Stared at the ceiling. 'Sir, this is madness. What if Ilona is involved? You're putting Hannah's life in danger, even before she steps foot in that place. Even before she faces the Mayan. God, man, what will he do to her if he finds out she's a cop?'

'Ryan, I've thought of all those things. I've argued with Hannah until I'm blue in the face.'

Ryan remembered the looks between her and Danskin, the argument he'd witnessed in the very room they were seated in.

'I even took the idea to Connor,' the DCI continued, 'Fully expecting him to knock the plan into touch. He didn't. The Super thought the plan was... super.'

Hannah put her hand on Ryan's knee. 'It's the only way, Ry.'

He looked into her eyes. Blue eyes, not brown. He didn't recognise her anymore. Not only in looks, but in her behaviour. He hadn't really known her for weeks when he thought about it. This wasn't Hannah Graves. This was Lexi. And, he didn't think he liked her.

He made one final attempt at getting Danskin to see sense. 'She's your daughter, for God's sake.'

To his surprise, he saw tears glisten in Danskin's eyes. 'What else can I do? We need someone inside.'

'But why Hannah? Why not one of the others?'

'Which others, man? Sue Nairn? Hardly. Robson in a frock? No, decision made. Hannah's going in. Tonight.'

Ryan knew he'd lost the argument as well as the girl. 'Okay. But, on condition that I go to the club tonight as well. Scout it out. Make sure for myself – and for you – that's she's okay.'

Danskin rose. Peered out into the bullpen. 'Great idea.'

'Good. I'll take Ravi with me. They'll know Gav from his interview with Chamley. Less suspicious if there's two of us, so Ravi it is.'

'I agree, but not Sangar. I think we need someone who seriously knows how to look after themselves. Take Robson. I'm sure he won't need much persuasion.'

'Thanks, sir.'

'But, I've another job for you first.'

'Sir?'

'Yeah. Just something I need cleaned up.'

'What is it?'

'Your bloody dog's just cocked it's leg aal ower your crime board. Sort it out, will you?'

**

Deep within a haze of mist and drizzle, the putt-putt of the two-stroke outboard motor sounded as muffled as a fart beneath a blanket.

'I really hoped you might show me by road, Jackie,' Craggs said as he clung to the bow of the tiny craft. 'I'm not liking this.'

'Nah. Where we're going's inaccessible by road.'

Duggan had piloted the craft out of Seaham marina, zig-zagging its way through a flotilla of vessels and around the concrete breakwaters as if it were a ball-bearing in a maze puzzle. Once out in open water, it chugged its way southbound.

Everything – sky, mist, and sea – was the same battle-ship grey; the coastline hidden beneath an invisibility cloak.

Craggs flicked water off his sodden hair. 'It's blazing sunshine in Durham, you know that?'

'Should've listened to the shipping forecast.'

'I didn't know I needed to.'

The strident blast of a foghorn, like the roar of a predator, caused Craggs to jump, the boat's nose tilting down into the waves with the shift of weight. Water flooded the deck of the vessel.

'Jeez. Where's the lifejackets, Jackie?'

Duggan shrugged. 'Dunno.'

'Howay, man. You got to have them somewhere.'

'Dunno.'

'What do you mean, you don't know?'

'Not my boat. Mine's in dock for repairs, still.'

Craggs mouth opened until a stream of saline closed it for him. 'Who's boat is it, then?'

'Dunno.'

'What?'

'I said I don't know.'

'I know what you said. Will you stop saying you don't know and tell me who this belongs to?'

'Dunno.'

'For Christ's sake.'

'You said you wanted me to show you where the launch that dunked me came from, so I'm taking you. What's the problem?'

The stolen vessel lurched as a wave hit it. Its nose tilted skyward as if snuffling a scent. Craggs cheeks billowed. 'Just hurry up and get me on dry land.'

Out of the fret, the hulking shape of precipitous cliffs loomed. 'Not far now. Just around the headland, here, and you'll be back on dry land.' Jackie Duggan leant on the tiller. 'If the tides right. Otherwise, we're going to get wet.'

Craggs pulled at his waterlogged clothing. 'Don't think I can get any more wet than I already am, Jackie, mate.'

Duggan cackled. 'Trust me, you might.'

He slowed the motor. 'Right. So, the bugger came at me from just round here.'

The cliffs were closer now, less than a hundred metres away, stretching into the distance as far as the eye could see. Not that that was far.

The keel of the craft scraped along rocks. 'Holy Mary, mother of God,' Craggs cursed.

'You're aal reet, man.' Duggan pointed to the south. 'About two miles that way is Crimdon. Rocks all the way. Virtually impossible to walk it. And, unless you fancy a spot of abseiling, the only other way down to the beach is by boat.'

'I get your point, Jackie. No need to rub it in.'

'Okay. Out you get.'

'Eh?'

'This is as close as this thing will get us. Get out.'

Craggs gaped at him. 'We're in the middle of the bloody sea, man. You've got to be joking me.'

'It's only about eighteen inches deep. We'll be okay.'

With a laboured effort, the DI swung his legs over the bow. Pushed himself into the icy North Sea. In up to his waist.

'Bloody hell, man.'

'Oops. Looks like I miscalculated. Sorry 'bout that.'

Jackie Duggan tossed a rope around a pointed rock jutting above the surface and followed Craggs overboard. He breathed fast and shallow at the first hit of the frigid waters. 'Right. Pound to a penny the bastard came at me from out there.'

Craggs eyes followed the outstretched arm of Jackie Duggan to a yawning chasm in a rocky promontory thirty yards ahead. 'Pirate's Cave, that is. The upper cave, anyway. There's a smaller, lower cave an' aal. Let's go. Do you want to hold my hand, John?'

'Hadawayandshite. Just get on with it.'

The unlikely twosome stumbled over the rocky seabed, inching towards Pirate's Cave. Gradually, they began to rise from the waves. Thigh-high at first, then knee level.

Craggs slipped as a rock gave way underfoot. He reached out for stability. Another stone gave way. He put his left arm beneath the waters to prevent himself tumbling.

When he withdrew his arm, he glanced at his wrist. Blood dripped from a wound. 'Fuck's sake.' The salt stung like hell. Worse, his SAFC wristwatch had been rendered as useless as his team. 'Aw man. Hell's teeth.'

'Shut your gob. We're here now.'

Duggan was right. They were inside Pirate's Cave, its roof twelve foot above them. 'What do you want to do now?'

Craggs realised he didn't have a clue. 'Have a look around, I suppose.'

So, that's what they did. For ten minutes, Craggs and Duggan explored the cavern, neither knowing what they were looking for.

'I'm bloody freezing, Jackie, man.' He shivered so much the words barely made it out his mouth. He sat down on rocks high above the waterline. Rubbed his arms vigorously.

Looked down into the waters below. The sea had a slickness to it, blues, and greens like a starling's plumage.

Oily.

Craggs stood, a cascade of pebbles rolling into the sea. 'Jackie, y'know what, I think there's oil in the water, just there. See?' He moved closer. 'It is. It's oil. From an engine, you think?'

'Aye. Could be.'

Craggs looked around. 'I need to get higher. Get a better look.'

He clambered onto a plateau. 'Hey, will you look at this?'

The remains of a fire - nothing more than charred sticks, but a definite campfire – lay at his feet. Behind it, an empty pack of cigarettes. A pizza box. A discarded Stella can.

'Somebody's been here.'

'Aye. I bet it's the bastard who turned me over,' Duggan agreed.

'Look at the tide mark. It's way above the embers; almost to the roof. You can't start a fire underwater. Whoever it is, they've been here since the last high tide.'

Another mini avalanche tumbled into the murky water as Craggs explored further. 'Jackie, son. You've just given me a breakthrough.'

'Pleased to hear it. Now, my bail?'

Craggs made his way to the back of the cave. 'What? Oh, aye. Divvent worry about that. I'll sort it.' He unwound something hanging from a stalactite. Held the object up between pinched fingers. It was a rag, stained black by oil - and reddish-brown by blood.

'Bingo. There'll be DNA all over this little beauty. We'll soon know who ran you out the water.'

More rocks slithered.

'I'll save you the bother, should I?'

Craggs turned. In the cave's maw, a ghostly figure stood cloaked in mist. He had his arm wrapped tight around Jackie's neck, a hand over his mouth.

The Girl on the Quay

The other hand pressed a Beretta against Duggan's temple.

CHAPTER TWENTY-SEVEN

The man with the Beretta had wild eyes. They flicked from side to side as he twitched nervously. Unkempt hair hung over his brow, stood in tufts behind his ears. His clothes were damp and dishevelled.

Crack cocaine, Craggs decided. The man would be edgy, unpredictable, and dangerous. Even without the pistol.

'Let him go, pal.'

The man shook his head so rapidly Craggs thought he could hear his brains rattle.

'We've done you no harm. We're not here for you.'

The man tightened his grip around Duggan's neck. 'You think I'm stupid? Course you're here for me. I knew it'd be a matter of time. Thought I might have held out here a bit longer, though.'

'Listen, let my friend go and we'll leave you alone. Our boat's just outside. Let him be and we'll head back where we came from.'

The head shook again. A trace of a smile appeared, then was gone. 'You haven't got a boat.'

'I promise you; we have. Jackie here tethered it to a rock out there. Have a look if you don't believe me.'

'Don't need to. I know you haven't got a boat. I know because I've just holed it. Given the tide, it'll be eight feet under in less than half an hour.'

Craggs hoped the sound of Duggan's muffled cries for help behind the man's hand disguised his own expletive. 'Look, let Jackie go. He's done nowt.'

The man barked out a laugh. 'Not yet, he hasn't; but as soon as I let him go, he will. So, not a chance.'

Craggs changed tact. 'I'm John Craggs, I'm a...'

'I don't care who you say you are. And I already know what you are. D'ya think I'm stupid or summat? I know the Mayan sent you.'

'The Mayan?' Craggs repeated, puzzlement rather than fear on his face. He took a couple of steps forward. Stopped before it became too obvious.

'Don't come that game with me. Was it you who got rid of Manny? And Haines?' Russ Morton pierced Craggs with his bug-eyed stare.

'Sorry, pal. I've nee idea what you're talking about.' Another step.

The man was shaking. Was it just the cold and wet? Or was it something else? Like, fear?

'I know the Mayan's done for them. I'm not stupid. I've tried contacting them. Why do you think I'm hid out in this shit-hole?'

Craggs slid his foot forward another few inches. The other followed. Like a kid on ice for the first time, he skated forward another foot. 'I've heard enough. You're off your heed, bonny lad. Time to show you who I am.' He reached for his ID in the rear pocket of his trousers.

Until he heard a metallic click; the sound of a safety being released.

'Get your hands in front of you. Where I can see them!'

Craggs raised his hands. 'Okay, okay. I was just going to prove to you I'm not who you think I am. Look, I'm going to turn around so you can see I'm not hiding anything. Are you alright with that?'

The man didn't reply.

'Is it okay?' Craggs repeated, hands still aloft.

Slowly, the man nodded. 'I'll kill him, mind.'

Duggan's eyes yawned impossibly wide.

'It's okay,' Craggs reassured. 'Everything's okay.'

He turned his back. 'See, there's nothing in my belt. I'm just going into my pocket here. I'll only use two fingers.'

Craggs waited for a response. It didn't come.

'Are you cool with what I'm doing? Let me know if I'm spooking you.'

'I'll blow his fucking brains out if you're up to summat.'

Gently, Craggs slid two fingers into his back pocket. Wrong pocket. It was empty.

'Right. My mistake. I'm going into the other one, now.'

He repeated the action. His fingers scrabbled around inside the pocket. He closed his eyes. Let out a groan. Empty. His ID must have floated out when he jumped ship.

'Well?' the man holding the Beretta said.

'It's gone. Me ID. It's gone.'

'Ha. Told you, didn't I? You're the Mayan's goons. Both of you. Thought you could fool Russ Morton, did you? Thought I'd fall for it like a village idiot? Like Manville? Like Haines? Well, you're wrong. You are so wrong.'

He released his grip on Jackie Duggan. Put his foot against Duggan's arse and pushed him into Craggs. They both crumpled to the slick surface, Duggan atop Craggs.

'Bloody brilliant,' Duggan whispered. 'Our only chance and you've ballsed it up. Why couldn't you keep your badge in your jacket like any other cop? Tosser.'

Russ Morton moved forward. Towered over them. The barrel of his gun shook in his trembling hand. He released the safety again.

Craggs and Duggan closed their eyes. Waited for oblivion.

It didn't come.

Craggs opened one eye. Morton no longer stood over them. 'Jackie, he's gone. He's only bloody well gone,' he laughed.

'Thank Christ. I couldn't miss another bail hearing.'

They both laughed uproariously.

Until they heard Morton's voice.

'I'm back,' he said. 'Didn't think I'd leave you all alone, did you.'

They looked towards the entrance to Pirate's Cave. A sixteen-footer, retrieved from its sanctuary within the lower

The Girl on the Quay

cave, lay across it. On board, Russ Morton with his pistol trained on them.

'I decided you weren't worth a bullet. I'll save them for the next lot the Mayan sends. And, the ones after that.'

Craggs watched the craft rock gently in the waves. 'You'll let us go, yeah?'

'I wouldn't go that far,' Morton said. 'No, I'll let the sea do the dirty work. Tide's coming in pretty fast. Couple of hours at most and it'll be up to the roof of the cave. I'll just bide my time out here, watching and waiting. Like I've done every high tide since I came here.'

He slapped a palm against his craft's hull. 'If this girl weren't running on fumes, I'd have been long gone. As it is, she's enough fuel to get me a few hundred yards offshore then, when tide's gone out, she'll be bringing me back. By that time, I'll have my home all to myself again.'

He still aimed the Beretta at Craggs at Duggan.

'You two, you'll be swimming with Davy Jones. And, I don't mean him out The Monkees.'

**

Todd Robson relaxed into the comfort of a luxurious wrap-around chair. Ryan Jarrod looked like someone in a dentist's waiting room.

While one smacked his lips at the taste of the complementary pint, the other fidgeted and picked at his fingers.

'Relax and enjoy the show, man.'

'How can I? This feels so awkward.'

'You mean you've never seen a naked woman before? I didn't think your lass was so coy.'

'She's not 'my lass'. Not anymore. Doesn't make it any less embarrassing.'

Todd glanced at his watch. 'It'll start heating up soon.'

'Have to say, it's been pretty tame so far. I've seen more in an Ibizan nightclub than this.'

Robson smirked. 'Tell me if you still think the same by the end of the night.'

From their table towards the left wing of the club, Ryan turned to face the bar. Isla tended one side. Dressed in a silver bikini top and matching micro-shorts, she resembled a human glitterball. Very 70's, Ryan thought.

Along from her, a shorter girl laughed and joked with a punter. When they'd picked up the drink that came with the entry fee, Ryan heard one of the regulars call her Champagne. She was blonde, bubbly, and as full of life as her pseudonym suggested.

Todd described her differently. 'All tits and arse.'

Ryan had barely given Isla or Champagne a second glance. He was transfixed by Lexi. Still in her post-punk, quasi Goth garb, she chatted to an older guy. As he took his drink from her, Ryan noticed he took her hand, ran his finger up the inside of her wrist. She winked at him and stroked his cheek before moving to the next punter.

Ryan clenched the fist of one hand and nibbled a fingernail of the other.

'Look, she's playing a part,' Todd reassured him.

Ryan exhaled through his nose. 'Aye, that's what porn stars say, isn't it?'

'Look, stop it. We're not here to babysit. Don't do owt that'll blow her cover. And,' Todd said pointedly, 'Stop watching her. We're here for the show, as far as anybody's concerned. Make it look like we are.'

Ryan dragged his eyes away from Lexi and onto the stage. A long-legged blonde wore a short, tight T-shirt above a white thong. The music changed. Rihanna's 'Umbrella' beat out.

From above, a sprinkler released a torrential shower. Water rained down on the girl as she gyrated. Her hair clung to her face in long strands. Not that anyone noticed. They were too focused on her transparent T-shirt.

'Looks like it's cold,' Todd smirked. Ryan gulped his beer.

The Girl on the Quay

As the song drifted towards its conclusion, two rope swings, like trapeze, descended either side of the dancer. The girls sitting on them were soon as exposed as their colleague.

The moment their feet hit the stage, the track changed. 'Some techno-trance shit,' Todd described it as. Lights flashed in a seizure-inducing frenzy, picking out one girl after the other, then back again. The girls peeled off their sodden T-shirts and tossed them to the front row of tables.

Surreally, a Vengaboys track played. The girls raised their hands above their heads. Clapped to the beat. The audience joined in, some banged on the tables, others stamped their feet.

'Here we go,' Todd said.

The lights went out. So, too, the music. Apart from dimmed lighting behind the bar, the auditorium was in total darkness, the only sound provided by the customers' rhythmic applause.

A low bass rumbled from the sound system. It grew in intensity, until Ryan felt the beat throb deep within his chest, like a thunderous heartbeat.

A spotlight flared. Picked out a girl to the right of the theatre. She had leapt from the stage. She put her hand to her waist and ripped apart the Velcro fastening of her thong. She was totally naked. And inches from the eager faces of a stag party sat around it.

The second spotlight homed in on the lead dancer, similarly naked, just as close to a group of clients. Ryan's mouth dropped open when he saw the table hosted both men and women.

Ryan pointed it out to Todd Robson. He wasn't listening. He was staring over Ryan's right shoulder. Ryan followed Robson's line of sight. Spun his head around. And found himself nose-to-nipple as the third spotlight flared on their table.

'Hi sweetheart,' she said. 'My name's Brooke. What's yours?'

Todd kicked Ryan beneath the table. 'Ryan,' Ryan said.

She removed her thong. Draped it over Ryan's shoulder. 'You are sweet, honey.' The girl's fake American accent couldn't hide its Soviet influence. 'Can I dance for you?'

Ryan felt the heat of his face. Tried to stem the blush. The more he tried, the more he coloured.

'Or,' the girl whispered, her lips feathering his ear, 'I could show you in private. Upstairs.' Her tongue slipped from between her lips and licked Ryan's earlobe.

Todd came to his rescue. 'Tell you what, petal. It's a bit early. Give him a couple more pints and come back, yeah?'

The girl sneered. 'It'll cost you double next time.' She snatched her thong and threw herself at another table.

'You could've scored there, man.'

'Look, can we go? There's nowt here for us. This is a bloody nightmare.'

'You on the turn or summat? It's class, man. Anyway, I thought you wanted to make sure Han…Lexi was okay?'

At the bar, Ryan saw Lexi flirt with a group of lads. One of them leant over the bar. Ran his fingers up the dragon tattoo. Up towards her breasts.

Ryan stood. Todd Robson dragged him back to his seat. 'Sit doon, man. Don't be ridiculous.'

'Look at him. He can't get away with that.'

'He's not. Look.'

Todd moved his head to one side. Ryan followed the gesture. A monster of a man in a black tuxedo marched towards the bar. His pecs and biceps were so huge he walked as if he had a plank of wood beneath each arm.

Just as the punter's finger wormed its way beneath Lexi's crop-top, one massive arm looped around the guy's neck. Seconds later, he was face down in Worswick Street.

The Girl on the Quay

Satisfied Lexi, or Hannah, was in safe hands, Ryan told Todd they'd seen enough. Todd hadn't, not by half. But, he relented.

'Okay. Nee sign of Chamley, let alone the Mayan,' Todd thought aloud. 'Nobody's touched the dancers. And, judging by the Hulk there, they're not going to, either.' He swallowed down his beer. 'Shame, but if you insist. I might come back later.' Ryan glared at him. He held up his hands. 'Joking.'

A man two tables behind watched until Ryan and Todd left the theatre. He let out the breath he'd been holding since they'd stood. Now they had gone, he could enjoy himself.

He thrust his hands deep into his pockets and wandered to the bar. He liked the look of the new girl; the one with the tattoo and the flash on her forehead. He liked her a lot.

The man timed his approach so the new girl would be free to serve him. As he prepared to speak, a young lad dived in front of him. He'd come from the booths upstairs, where a stag party waited for a more personal service. The lad unfurled a drinks order as long as a toilet roll in front of Lexi.

'Can I get you something, sir?' Champagne asked.

'What? Oh, yeah. Jack Daniels, please.' He spoke to Champagne but stared at Lexi. As she continued to take the young man's order, the older man shrugged and turned his attention to Champagne. 'Have one yourself, will you?'

'Thank you very much. I'll have a Bacardi. I'm Champagne, by the way.' She extended a hand in mock chivalry.

The man followed her lead. He took it. Kissed it.

'Hi, Champagne. Delighted to meet you,' the man said. 'My name's Jack. Jack Goodman.'

CHAPTER TWENTY-EIGHT

For almost quarter of an hour, John Craggs thought it was going to be okay. The water level within Pirate's Cave hardly rose.

Then, by stealth, it inched higher.

The lowermost layer of rock appeared little more than slick at first. Next time he looked, seawater lapped over it. Moments later, it had disappeared beneath a rippling flow.

And, thus it began.

The brooding, grey waters of the North Sea gurgled and slurped at their feet. Craggs and Duggan stepped higher. The tide searched them out, caught up with them, and gnawed their ankles once more.

At the cave's maw, Russ Morton looped a rope around a stalactite as the water's motion threatened to drift his vessel away from his captives.

Not that they were going anywhere, other than higher ground.

In seconds, Craggs and Duggan were knee-deep again. They levered themselves up another layer. Moments later, they were in it up to their calves. The ocean's thunder had invaded the silence of the cavern. It resonated against the walls of Pirate's Cave. Pounded the two men against the cave's rocky face.

The sea licked higher. Tasted them. Threatened to devour them.

'I'm not a bad person, you know,' Morton shouted. 'Not really. If I knew what the Mayan was up to, what he made the girls do, I'd never have got into it. Haines and Manville? They're different, they are. Or, they were until the Mayan saw to them. But not me. I'm okay; I really am. And, as you've discovered, you lot won't find me an easy touch.'

The Girl on the Quay

John grabbed Jackie Duggan's wrist and hauled him up another tier as Morton's monologue droned on.

'Like Luuk's man said, *what the lord giveth, the lord taketh away*. He brought you to me and, now, He's taking you away.'

Duggan turned to Craggs. 'He's off his rocker.'

'I'm not sure. Some of it sort of links to a case I'm looking into.' A wave thundered against his hips. He stumbled forward. 'Not that I'll be working it much longer.'

They could go no higher. All they could do was wait.

Five minutes later, the water was up to their chests, each wave heavier than the last. The current pulled at their legs. Tried to drag them into its depths. Craggs lost his shoes in the backward surge. His socks, too. By the time the water reached his throat, his trousers were round his ankles.

Pebbles and shale and shells covered the rock beneath his feet. He curled his toes into the debris, digging for purchase. The voracity of the undercurrent ripped off his toenails. There was no pain. All he felt was the cold. Icy, mind-numbing cold.

And fear.

A wave crashed over their heads. Craggs turned his face upwards. Lifted nose and mouth clear of the water. With every tidal surge, brine flowed over his face. Filled his mouth. Flooded his nostrils. Stung his eyes. As each wave ebbed, he spluttered and spat it out. Took in a lungful of air before the next surge washed over him. Rinse and repeat.

Alongside him, Jackie Duggan had managed to turn himself onto his back. He floated with his face inches from the cave's roof. As still more of the North Sea washed in, his head crashed against the razor-sharp wall of Pirate's Cave. Blood matted his hair. A thick redness ran down his face, was washed away, then painted again.

'Jackie. Listen up.' Craggs spat out water. 'Take my hand.' Spluttered again. Shook his head to clear his eyes. 'We're swimming for it.'

Duggan wiped away blood. 'Now you tell us. We could've done it an hour ago.'

'Pfffst,' Craggs spat. Coughed. Took in a lungful of North Sea. Coughed again. 'No, we couldn't. He'd have seen us. If we go now,' he retched as saltwater hit his stomach, 'If we do it now, he'll think we've gone under. Now, give me your hand.'

John sensed Jackie's fingers around his own. It felt like the grasp of icicles. 'When I say, take as much air as you can. And, I mean as much.'

He waited for the next wave to recede.

'Now!'

They sucked in air and plunged into frigid, silent, blackness.

Craggs kicked. He hoped Duggan did the same. They moved, but Craggs couldn't tell whether it was forward or if the tide had carried them backwards.

He kicked again. And again. His chest tightened. Lungs burnt. He had the overwhelming desire to breathe. Fought it back. The need welled within him once more. If he didn't breathe, he'd suffocate. If he did inhale, he'd take in water.

'H2O', Craggs's brain told him, over-and-over again. 'H2O.' The O means oxygen. There's oxygen in water. Oxygen means air.

Craggs did what his brain told him. He opened his mouth.

Panic hit. Gurgling, shouting, and screaming underwater, he kicked for the surface. Something held him back. Jackie Duggan. Duggan was drowning him.

Craggs lashed out, caught Duggan a glancing blow with his foot. Pain from his ripped toenails shot through him, but he was free from Duggan's grasp. He kicked upwards.

He broke the surface. He didn't recognise it at first. He still held his breath, kept the water in his lungs. It was only when he heard the ocean's power he realised he was free. Craggs sucked in more air than his lungs could take. Water

The Girl on the Quay

exploded from his mouth like a whale's blowhole. Vomit curdled around him.

He didn't care. He was alive. More, Morton's boat was cave-side of him, the skipper staring intently into the blackness.

Craggs rolled onto his back, stared into a sky now sprinkled with stars, and kicked his way around the headland. Once out of Morton's sight, he skirted a smooth black rock which rose from the seas like a bathing elephant. He snuggled against it. Caught his breath.

'So, about me bail, then?'

Craggs jumped. Sat atop the rock, a bloodied Jackie Duggan looked down on him.

'I'll get back to you on that,' Craggs spluttered. He laughed. Coughed up another lungful of seawater.

Duggan held out a hand. Hauled Craggs onto the rock. They lay there like basking sea-lions.

'It's a canny hike to Crimdon in your shreddies, mind,' Duggan said.

'I think I'll manage it, even with me toes done in.'

'You're ok, John, yeah?'

'I think so.' He said it through chattering teeth. He gave the question more thought.

'No, actually; I'm bloody hypodermic,' he said.

They lay back and howled their laughter at the moon.

**

An old black-and-white Western movie played on the TV. It sprinkled patterns of light and shade over Ryan's face as he sat in darkness.

He wasn't watching it, but he knew sleep was futile. His mind and thoughts were still in the Whipped Cream club. He shouldn't have gone. He should have sent one of the other lads. Seeing Hannah there, what the place was like, how the punters behaved; it had affected him more than watching Aaron Elliott haul the cadavers from their resting places.

Ryan thought back to something his old mentor, Frank Musgrave, had told him in his days as a Special. 'It changes you, lad. Don't think you'll be any different because you won't. This job changes us all.'

He rummaged at his feet for the glass. Held it up so the golden liquid reflected in the luminescence of the TV. Sipped the whisky he never drank.

He looked up to the ceiling and raised his glass Heavenwards. 'Cheers, Frank. You tried to warn me, God bless you.'

Ryan linked fingers across his stomach and closed his eyes.

The Blaydon Races had never sounded so loud. Ryan jumped at the ringtone. Didn't know where he was. He rubbed his eyes.

'It's half-past two in the bloody morning,' he yawned into the mic.

'It's ten past three actually, and I've been waiting.'

'Sir?' Ryan levered himself up, savouring the wonders of a forty-minute nap.

'Well, man. I thought you'd have reported in. What's the crack?'

'Didn't want to trouble you. Thought I'd report in in the morning.'

'Didn't want to trouble me? She's me stepdaughter, man, as you took great pride in telling me. I've been worried sick.'

'Yes, sir. Sorry, sir.' He put a hand to his chest as the whisky rifted on him. 'She's okay.'

He heard Danskin let out a long sigh. 'Thank God.'

After a moment's reflection, the DCI asked, 'Find anything?'

'Nah. No sign of Chamley. No hint of the Mayan being there.' He decided to spare Danskin some of the more lurid details. 'Security's pretty tight. I think Hannah's going to be okay.' Was he trying to convince himself?

'Look, I'm at the station...'

'It's ten past three in the morning, sir.'

'I know. I was waiting for your bloody report, wasn't I? By the time I realised I wasn't getting one, there was no point going home. Wouldn't sleep, anyway.'

'I get that, sir. So, you were saying?'

'Listen, does this Isla-stroke-Ilona woman have a drug habit?'

Ryan's brow wrinkled in thought. 'Not that I know of, sir. I know she was on the streets for a while, but she gave me nothing to think she might be a user.'

'And Radka Vosahlo? What about her?'

'Never been mentioned.' Ryan almost heard Danskin's brain ticking. 'You onto something, sir?'

'Possibly. I'm not sure. I've spent the last half hour catching up on e-mails. There's a one there from the lab. I didn't pick up on it straight away cos it wasn't from Elliott. Seems he's quarantined himself after learning he'd been fiddling around inside an HIV carrier.'

Ryan put two-and-two together. 'You're thinking she may have got HIV from a needle rather than sex?'

Danskin breathed down the line again. 'Yeah. You see, if she had a habit, that explains it.'

'Explains what?'

'The e-mail. It was the tox report. It showed traces of a substance in Vosahlo's bloods. Fentanyl. It's what killed Prince. And Tom Petty, apparently.'

Ryan remained silent. 'I suppose it might be something which helps her cope with…well, what she does.'

'That's what I thought. But, thanks to the wonders of Google, I've discovered several things about Fentanyl.' He ticked them off on his fingers. 'It's the most potent opioid licensed for medical use. It's one hundred times more powerful than morphine. Fifty times more potent than heroin. And, guess what? Fentanyl doesn't show up in routine tox samples. It has to be specifically tested for. For once, Elliott's done something I appreciate.'

Ryan was wide awake now. Alert. 'Just the sort of drug you'd use if you wanted to kill someone.'

'Precisely. If she didn't self-administer, we've proof there's not only a vice-ring operating, we've also got a murderer on the loose.'

Ryan was on his feet. 'I'm coming in, sir.'

He kicked over something at his feet. Sat down again.

'Once me dad's whisky's worn off.'

CHAPTER TWENTY-NINE

Ryan called a cab rather than wait for the Grouse to clear his system. The journey gave him time to think. Not that the journey took long. The streets were deserted, which made it easier for him to understand how Jade and Kayla and Ebony could all disappear unnoticed.

Apart from a couple of bloodied and incapable drunks and a handful of uniformed officers waiting for a call, the station was nigh on as abandoned as the streets. Even the third-floor bullpen was spookily dark. Except for Danskin's office. It was lit up like a Polish church.

'Morning Jarrod.' Danskin was unshaven, pallid-skinned, with eyes like a bloodhound.

'You could do with a rest, sir, the state of you.'

'Cheers. You're not looking so chipper yersel.'

Ryan caught sight of his reflection against the pre-dawn blackness outside. The DCI wasn't wrong.

'It's been a difficult night,' he said simply.

Danskin offered his sympathy, but added, 'Better get used to it. We'll have a few more of them before she's back with us.'

Ryan ruffled his hair. 'I'll call her as soon as the others get in. See what I can discover about Radka's habit, if she had one. Assuming she'll take my call this time. I presume we'll get Chamley straight in if we get evidence it's murder?'

'Wish I could say yes, but it's not looking good.'

'You discovered something already?'

Danskin breathed in through his nose. 'I've had word from Hannah.'

'Already?'

'Actually, I called her.'

'In the middle of the night?'

Danskin managed a laugh. 'Remember where she's working, man. Doesn't close 'til gone two. Anyway, she's had a chat with Ilona. Jury's still out on Radka. Seems she was a user, but not an abuser. Occasional only, but enough to cast sufficient doubt to keep Chamley out of our hands for now. I've asked the pair of them to see if there's any indication what Radka might've been partial to.'

Ryan noticed Danskin had wheeled the crime board into his office and added a note about Radka's habit. He'd posted a similar question next to Jade's profile.

And, the DCI had flagged up the lamotrigine discovered in Ebony's system.

'Sir, are you wondering whether the epilepsy drug might have been taken recreationally rather than for a medical condition?'

'Well spotted. You're more awake than you look. It's an angle we've not considered before. We're hung up on the sex industry position. I don't want us to close off other possibilities.'

It didn't sit right with Ryan, and he made his views known. 'I think drugs might be a side issue to the real one. I'm sure, from what I learned off Hadley Kutz and what I know of the case, we're on the right track.'

An unfamiliar ringtone chirruped from Danskin's pocket. He took the call. Muttered a few 'a-has' and 'yeps' and tutted a couple of times before hanging up.

'That was Hannah. No sign of any Fentanyl. But, no sign of any other drug, either, and we know she took them, so it proves nowt.' He shook his head. 'Never thought I'd say this, but we could do with Elliott back on the job. Think what you like about him, he knows his stuff.'

They sat in silence, both ready for sleep to take them but neither surrendering. Just to keep them focussed, Ryan asked, 'See you got yourself a new phone, sir.'

'You haven't seen it, okay?' He saw the bemusement on the young DCs face. 'It's only for Hannah. Can't compromise her position. If the Mayan, or whoever, ran a check on her phone and found she had the entire City and County police in her contacts list. Well,…' He left Ryan to work out the consequences.

Oddly, he saw Ryan smile. 'That's why I can't reach her, isn't it? She's got a burner phone, just in case.'

Stephen slid open his drawer and withdrew a familiar zebra-patterned mobile cover. 'Got it in one. I'm keeping her's safe.'

'I need her number, sir.'

'You don't. I've got it and so has Lyall, and we both use unregistered devices to contact her. Not our personal ones. The number goes to no-one else.'

'Howay, man. I'm not going to give the game away, am I?'

Danskin stared at Ryan. 'Are you not?'

'What do you mean by that?'

'Hannah told me about your attitude at the club. The way you reacted when the punters came on to her.'

'Oh hell. I hoped she hadn't noticed.'

'Well, she had. And, if Hannah had, so could anyone else. Chamley, the Mayan, someone acting for the Mayan.'

Ryan remembered how observant the heavy had been in riding to Hannah's rescue. Folk did notice things. 'Hell,' he said again.

'No harm done this time, but you need to calm doon. Take a step back. Don't get personally involved.'

'You're not, sir.'

Danskin sagged. Looked as if he'd aged fifteen years in one night. A nerve pulsed above his clenched jaw. 'She's all I've got, Ryan. All I've got.'

What was Ryan supposed to do? Pass him a tissue? Give his DCI a cuddle? Instead, he did nothing.

In time, Danskin looked up from the spot he'd been inspecting on his desk. 'Anyway, Hannah did ask me to pass on a message.'

'She did?'

'Aye. She asked if you'd enjoyed the little show Brooke gave you.'

Ryan felt his face colour. He looked down at the floor.

Stephen Danskin chuckled. 'And divvent worry. I'll keep you in the loop. I can see you're worried, despite all that's happened between you.'

'Thank you, sir. I appreciate it.'

'And in case you're wondering, you're still on the case. I need you. Only you and I know what's at stake.'

The thought sobered Ryan more than any hair of the dog.

Even more so when Danskin added, 'Trust me, if you're worried now, it's going to get a helluva lot worse.'

**

Craggs and Duggan never made it to Crimdon. They set off for it, for sure, once they were certain Morton had sailed offshore until the tide turned, but they'd staggered less than half a mile over stones, boulders and rocks before Craggs collapsed face-down in a rock pool.

Jackie Duggan dragged him out. Slapped his cheeks. Shouted in his ear. The only response he got was the ramblings of delirium.

Craggs's feet were coagulated husks, but it was the cold which did for him. He shivered convulsively, flesh deathly white, lips blue, eyes rolling in their sockets. Duggan stayed with him. The crook covered him with what little warmth remained in his own body and closed his eyes. Moments later, a sea-angler stumbled upon them.

Craggs awoke in an A&E bay in Stockton's North Tees Hospital, wrapped in tinfoil like a Christmas turkey. He stared, fascinated, at a hemodialyzer as it sucked blood from him, warmed it, and returned it to his body.

The Girl on the Quay

Only then did the pain from his feet hit him. He raised his head and looked down. His feet lay outside the covers. Someone at the end of the bed prod and poked at them with a needle and withdrew fluid.

The sight of his feet hurt John Craggs more than the activity. They were black as a leper's and so swollen the instep folded over his toes like a beer belly over a belt. The hike from Crimdon had shredded the soles of his feet. Blood seeped from beds where toenails once lay, acute paronychia already established.

Without looking up, the doctor tending to them said, 'You won't be playing footie for a while. Welcome back, by the way.'

The doctor said his name but Craggs was in too much pain to take it in.

'Now you're back with us, we'll get you up to a ward. Might be a bit of a wait 'til we find a bed, I'm afraid.'

'It's okay. Doesn't matter about that. I'll just get myself' off home once you're finished.'

'No sir-ee. You'll be with us for a night or two yet. Make sure these two black beauties aren't going to drop off first.' He saw Craggs face. 'That was a joke, by the way.'

'Not funny. Look, I'm a Detective Inspector of police. I've got to report in a case I was out working on.'

The doctor left the feet alone. 'You can report it in, but you won't be working it. Not for a while, anyway. I'd say it'll be a week, possibly ten days, before you're back pounding the beat.'

'I don't pound the beat. I'm a detective, man.'

A nurse arrived. She checked Craggs's pulse and stuck a thermometer in Craggs's ear. 'Thirty-six point eight,' she declared. 'Heart rate sixty-two.'

'Good. You were thirty-four point four when you arrived, and your heart was up and down like Jordan's knickers.'

'Does that mean I was hypodermic?'

'The term's hypothermic.'

'Private joke.'

'Okay. But, yes; you were. Another reason for you not to rush back.'

A thought struck Craggs. 'Where's Jackie? The bloke I was with?'

'At home, I hope. Discharged him half an hour ago. He's fine. And stop changing the subject. No work for at least ten days, do you hear me?'

Craggs sighed. 'If you insist.' He jumped as the doctor hit a tender spot with his probe. 'I need to call someone, though. Can you give me ten minutes? In private?'

The doctor stood. 'Very well. But make it brief. And just the one call.'

Craggs gave a rueful smile. 'That's what I normally say to the blokes I arrest. Don't suppose I can borrow a phone, can I? Mine's probably somewhere off the Dutch coast now.'

Left alone, Craggs checked in with the station, obtained the number he needed, and dialled.

A sleepy voice answered. 'Ja?'

'Wakey-wakey, Henrik. John Craggs here from the Prince Bishop force in England. Looks like I'll be taking an enforced break. I thought I might as well get away for a few days. Are there any hotels you recommend in Ijmuiden? Preferably one close to your station? I shall bring news with me.'

**

Max Bonhomme lay both hands against the back of the door and gently pushed it shut without a sound. A massive hound padded along the hallway to greet him. Bonhomme tickled the dog's ears. The dog gave a single wag of its docked tail and, satisfied, returned to its bed.

Bonhomme carried his laptop into the lounge. The greenish glow from the screen lit up his face. He typed in a password. His finger moved over the touchpad until the cursor hovered over his banking app, moved on, and settled on another favourite.

He opened the website. Typed in another password.

The Girl on the Quay

It was a pity about Jade. Still, there were plenty of other girls. It was time to find another.

Preferably, one who looked similar to the new girl.

The one with long hair and tattooed midriff.

CHAPTER THIRTY

Coffee was supposed to be a universal panacea. Ryan had read all the Jack Reacher novels and it always worked for him. Why, he wondered, did it not have the same effect on Ryan Jarrod?

Three cups stood on his desk, each drained of their contents, yet he still felt like a parcel of shite. The rest of Danskin's squad had arrived, all busy taking calls and following up leads, yet Ryan sat paralyzed by fatigue.

His body craved sleep. His mind wanted action. They reached a compromise of impasse. His head drooped to his chest, woke him with a start, then fell again. Ryan felt hands on his arms. When he opened his eyes this time, Gavin O'Hara stood in front of him.

'Ryan. Ryan; wake up, man. Foreskin wants you. Says it's urgent.'

Ryan gulped down a lungful of office air and, alert once more, joined the DCI and Lyall Parker in Danskin's room.

'Just a minute, Hannah. Ryan's here. I'm gonna put you on speaker phone. Go over what you've just told me.' Danskin swilled Corsodyl round his mouth. Swallowed it.

'Okay. So far, I've found nothing of substance. I think what Chamley told us is correct. I can't speak for lasses with the Agency, but as far as Whipped Cream goes, none of the girls are paid a wage. He doesn't employ them in the traditional sense.'

'Hannah, it's Ryan here. I wasn't at the club for long, but I didn't see any of the punters tip the lasses.' He thought for a moment. 'In fact, even if they did, they had nowhere to put it. They were stark bollock naked. If he doesn't pay them, how do they make their living?'

'You must've been too busy watching the show,' she chided. 'Each table has a card reader attached to it. It's all electronic. Contactless payment. Didn't you notice?'

Ryan settled for a sheepish, 'No.'

Danskin scratched his jaw. 'What about the likes of Ilona? We know she hasn't got papers either, just like the dancers, so how come he employs her?'

'He doesn't. The same goes for her. And me, for that matter. Even we aren't salaried. Every drink has a service charge added. That's how we get paid. And, I tell you what – it's good money. If we get that much, lord knows what the dancers must rake in.'

While Ryan and the DCI digested the information, Lyall asked the next question. 'Apart from the fact the lassies from the club move onto the whoring, anything else to link the club to Orchid Petals?'

'It's early days for me, Lyall, but no direct links yet.'

Ryan spoke again. 'You got a job there canny easily. I mean, if he doesn't vet those who work there, could the Mayan or Chamley have recruited somebody who's behind it all? Or, what about somebody who's left recently? Somebody with a grudge?'

Silence.

'Hannah?'

Nothing.

'You still there?'

The three detectives looked at one another.

'Is everything okay there, Hannah?'

They held their breath.

'Yeah, sorry.' They exhaled as one. 'I'm in the kitchen. Ilona came in. I want to keep her out of it as much as I can. Don't want her position compromised in case anything…well, you know what I mean.'

They did but didn't want to think about it.

'I'll see if I can have more of a scout round when I go back later today. I do know they've beefed up security at the club.'

Danskin spoke next. 'If that's true, it would make it unlikely Chamley or the Mayan's behind it. Why would they do that?'

'Possibly to make it look like they're not behind anything?' Ryan offered.

'Nah, not buying it. I think we're looking at a third party here,' Danskin countered. He opened the window wide. Both he and Ryan took in air and rubbed sleep from their eyes.

'Tell us what you know about the security.'

'I've only done one shift, sir. Give us a chance. But, some of the punters were talking about a new doorman. He's only been there a day or two so he can't be behind the disappearances. I gather there's a few more bouncers inside the club as well. They all seem efficient enough to me.'

Ryan pictured the guy riding to Hannah's rescue. 'It's not the club we're having issues with, though. Why wasn't there any security for the likes of Radka? Or Sobena? Or Ebony, whatever her real name is?'

'Was,' Danskin countered. 'Whatever her real name was. Remember what the endgame is here.'

'That's my next task, Ry; to find out more about how the Agency works. Like I say, I'll see what I can do later. But, for now, all I know is what's happening at the club. There was a new guy on last night called Hugo and there's another tonight. No name for him yet.'

'Who recruits them? The Mayan?'

'No. Chamley, from what I can gather. The Mayan finds the girls; Chamley the rest.'

'So, these new guys,' Lyall Parker said, 'Are they replacements or additions?'

'They're additions, by all accounts. The two head security guys have been there since the club opened. Names are Titus and Dominic.'

'Sounds like a Shakespeare play,' Ryan joked. No-one laughed.

'Sir, I have to go. I'll check in again later.'

'Okay. Good work, Hannah.'

'Thanks, sir.'

'And, be bloody careful,' he added.

'I will. Bye, all.'

'Bye, Hannah,' the DCI said.

'See you,' Parker concluded.

Ryan next. 'Love you.'

His mouth opened wide, face beetroot red. WTF had he just said?

**

'Are you ever going to get off that thing? I'd appreciate a hand with the twins here.'

Max Bonhomme looked up from his laptop. 'This is business, honey.'

'And these two and me, we're family. Which comes first?'

Slowly, Bonhomme closed the laptop lid. 'Girls, come here a moment.'

Charlotte limped towards her father, one shoe on, the other in her hand. Izzy remained on the bottom stair brushing the hair of her Little Mix doll.

'Izzy, you as well.'

'But Daddy; Jade needs her hair brushed.'

Max Bonhomme's eyes flicked towards his wife at the mention of the doll's name. He cleared his throat. 'Leave Jade for now. She's fine where she is.'

Izzy threw the toy at her mother and stomped across the kitchen.

'Listen, girls. I want you to be good girls for Mummy. Daddy has to go away for a day or two…'

'Oh, for Heaven's sake, Max. Again? You drop it on me just like that?'

'Cassie, not now. I'm talking to the girls. Charlotte, Izzy – you know Daddy's got to earn more pennies so I can buy you some new toys, don't you?' He finished tying Charlotte's shoelaces and smiled at Izzy. 'You must be tired of Jade by now. Who do you want next? Should I get Jesse for you?'

'No. I like Jade.'

'I like Jade, too, but sometimes it's good to have a change.' He moved his laptop closer to him. 'So, be good girls and Daddy will be back soon, yeah?'

'Oh-kay,' they sighed in unison and skipped off to their rooms.

'Same goes for you, Cass. I need to earn pennies to keep all this.' He gestured around the house. Stood. Walked up close to his wife. 'You be a good girl, too. Understand?'

Cassie Bonhomme understood well enough.

**

Ilona Popescu, in her Isla persona, unzipped her light jacket. Beneath it, she wore skin-tight leather shorts and black leather bra. And nothing else. The cab driver's face told her there was no need for any other tip.

Lexi, for her part, again exposed her flat stomach and the tattoo and jewel which seemed to go down so well with the punters on her first shift. Not that there would be any punters for an hour or two. The club wasn't open yet.

The new guy on the door let them in with a leer.

'If he's like that with us, what's he like with the dancers?' Lexi/Hannah asked.

'They look the same way. That is the way men look at girls.'

'Not all men, Isla.'

'Yes. All men. I am sure even your Ryan.'

'Pretty sure you're wrong about that.' Only as an afterthought did she add, 'He's not my Ryan.'

The Girl on the Quay

Once inside, Isla and Lexi set to work behind the bar. They made an inventory, stocked up on bottles and spirits, opened money bags and poured change into the till.

'I need to get in the club's office today,' Lexi whispered.

'You know there are cameras, yes?'

'Will they be on already?'

Isla shrugged. 'I do not know. Perhaps not.'

More staff arrived and busied themselves. Floors were cleaned, lights checked, 'one-two's' said into microphones.

'When will Chamley get here?'

Isla spat out a laugh. 'Get here? I am thinking he never leaves. He will be here already, for sure.'

Two dancers, one with a shaven head, practiced moves on stage. Fully clothed and without make up, it made for an incongruous sight.

Another girl sat at a table, drink in hand. Lexi raised an eyebrow.

'They help themselves, sometimes,' Isla explained.

Lexi stared at the girl. Wondered where she came from. Ryan's triangle came into her mind. Lexi wondered WHAT she'd come from. She tore her eyes away.

'She's dressed soon.'

'Ah yes. That is Dionne. She always ready. How do you say, she like to be in character, yes? The others, they not disturb her.'

Isla carried on with her duties while Lexi pondered her next move. 'What does Chamley drink?'

The Romanian girl laughed. 'He drinks Perrier water. That is all. Not like the Mayan. He drinks spirit. Any spirit.'

Lexi reached for a tray. Placed an ice-bucket on top along with four glasses, two bottles of water and a cognac.

'I need you to do something for me. I want you to make our friend Dionne a drink. A cocktail. Something that will stain. Then, I want you to take it over. You'll slip, or trip, or anything that makes sure the drink ends up on her.'

Isla's eyes widened. 'No. She will go like a tiger.'

'Exactly,' Lexi smiled. 'Do it now.'

Isla did exactly as asked. Dionne reacted as predicted. She screamed at Isla. Roared at her. Climbed over a table to get at her. Chairs spilled. Everyone looked.

And Chamley tore out of his office to see what hell had erupted.

Lexi picked up her tray and walked into the office of the Whipped Cream club.

The décor reminded her of a Tutankhamen exhibition she'd visited in the O2, but she wasn't there for the vista. Besides, the esoterics were ruined by the pyramid of paperwork festooned across the desk.

In one corner of the room, Lexi spotted a safe. That would have to wait for another day. Today, she'd focus on what was close to hand. She began by clearing a space for the drinks tray; her cover story should she be disturbed.

She flicked through the papers. Bills, invoices, stocklists. Nothing significant, she thought, but she whipped out her phone and took images anyway.

A spreadsheet lay at the top of the second pile. A list of names and times. Clients, perhaps? Midway down, Lexi spotted the name Hugo Fray. Hugo. The bouncer. These weren't clients. They were staff. Possibly, the date and time indicated an interview schedule. She snapped an image.

The next pile revealed nothing of interest. She moved on. Beneath a book lay more names. Judging by the cliched monikers, it was the names of the girls. Another photograph taken.

She moved towards another stack of papers. Stopped. Froze.

A noise.

There was someone outside the door.

Her heart raced. She tried to compose herself. 'I'm delivering drinks,' she rehearsed the line in her head. It didn't sound convincing.

Lexi strained to hear.

The Girl on the Quay

It was her imagination.

Three sheets down on the next heap of papers lay ransom notes for Jade, Kayla, and Ebony. She never got to see them.

This time, there was someone outside the door.

This time, the door began to open.

CHAPTER THIRTY-ONE

The instant Lexi threw herself to the floor and crawled beneath the desk, Hannah realised her mistake. If she hadn't been in character, it's something Hannah would never have done herself. She knew, as soon as she hit the deck, she'd blown her cover story. The drinks waitress routine was dead in the water.

Only the modesty panel of the desk hid her from open view. She made herself impossibly small, like a cornered mouse, beneath the table. She curled herself into a tight ball against a metal wastepaper bin.

Hannah heard the door close. Chamley was in there with her.

In her mind's eye, she pictured him looking around the office. Had she left any tell-tale signs? The drinks tray was okay - its presence could be explained away – but disturbed or missing papers couldn't.

She felt her heart pound so loudly she was sure he must hear it. She slowed her breathing right down. It was dusty beneath the desk. Her nose twitched. Pray God she didn't sneeze. Not now.

A thought came to her. Perhaps it wasn't Chamley in the room. Perhaps it was the Mayan. Hannah stopped breathing altogether.

She closed her eyes as papers rustled atop the desk as the man looked through them. A knuckle tapped against the surface. She jumped. Somehow, she avoided hitting her head on the underside.

Hannah listened to his breathing, tried to gauge where he was. He was right above her. She sensed him take a stride. He was coming around the desk. Any moment now, he would slide back the chair, sit on it, and find her.

Sweat beaded her brow. She felt it trickle down her nose, hang to its tip like a dewdrop, then fall into the waste-bin. To her, it sounded like a cannon ball tossed into a bucket.

A foot kicked the desk. Hannah stifled a whimper. He moved again. Two more steps and she'd be exposed.

She heard one step. Waited for the second.

Instead, Hannah heard something else. It sounded like the winding of an old-fashioned alarm clock.

There it was again. Hannah recognised the noise. It wasn't a clock. It was the cogs of a combination lock rotating. He was opening the office safe.

She unfolded her arms from around her head. Risked a peek. Sure enough, she could see the toe of an old trainer shoe tap impatiently against the safe.

Suddenly, the noise stopped. The safe door hadn't opened, but the noise stopped. And the scuffed white shoe was no longer visible.

When she heard the door click shut, Hannah thought she would cry with relief. She didn't. What she did do, was get the hell out of the office.

**

Hannah was grateful for Lexi's blanched make-up. It disguised the absence of colour in her own face. Safe behind the bar, she picked up a glass and began polishing it until she noticed it shake in her hand. She sat it on the bar top and waited for the adrenalin rush to fade.

Chamley was back in the auditorium, spraying spittle in the direction of Isla and the dancer known as Dionne as he argued with them. Hannah watched until the two girls embraced. Neither smiled. As Dionne flounced to the dressing room, she threw out her arms in a flamboyant gesture.

Chamley waited until she was out of sight, then followed Isla to the bar.

'Watch and learn, Lexi,' he said. 'Don't ever make the same mistake as your friend here. She was inches away from losing her job. And, the Mayan doesn't like losing anyone; trust me.'

'I'm sure Isla didn't mean it.' She gave Chamley a disarming smile. 'By the way, I've taken the liberty of delivering some refreshments to your room for you. I hope that's okay.'

'It is. Thank you, Lexi. I'd rather you do it than your friend. She'd have thrown it all over the carpet.'

As soon as he was out of sight, Ilona turned on Hannah. 'Do not make me do that again. I cannot do without this job. I am wanting to find out why Radka died and to stop horrible things happening to any other girls. I want it more than you and your friends do, but I must not lose this job. I have rent to pay. I am not going homeless. Not again.'

'I can't promise you anything, Ilona, other than we will catch whoever is doing this.'

'Do not call me by that name. I must always be Isla here, and you Lexi.'

'Listen, I will have questions for you later. I'll do my best to keep you out of it from now on, but I can't promise.'

'So, you got what you needed, yes?'

'I have for now. I'll check in with the DCI later. And, thanks Isla. I mean it. I thought Chamley was bound to get me when he came back to his room, but you bought me enough time.'

Isla scowled. 'Mr Chamley did not go back to…' The girl froze mid-sentence, lips parted ready to deliver the next words. She stared across the theatre.

'Isla? Are you okay?'

Isla's head followed a group of women cleaners marching towards the exit, duties done for the day.

'You look like you've seen a ghost.'

'I think, perhaps I have.'

'What do you mean?'

'You see the lady with the grey hair?'

Lexi squinted across the darkened club. 'At the back there?'

'Yes. I know that woman.'

'I'm not surprised. She's probably here every day.'

Isla shook her head, blonde tresses waving like a flag in the breeze. 'No, she is not. Not for some time.'

'I don't understand.'

'I do not understand, either. Her hair is wrong. The woman is much younger. She once worked here. She danced. Then, she was taken to go with men.'

Lexi knew the girl was mistaken. No-one would return as a cleaner. Not after what they'd done, what they'd earned. Isla was wrong, Lexi was certain.

Until Isla spoke again.

'Her name is Madonna.'

Lexi saw the escort walk through the exit, but not before she noticed her footwear.

Madonna wore a pair of old white trainers.

**

Stephen Danskin held court. 'Breaking news, guys. I don't know what to make of it yet but I do know it's significant.'

Ryan, Lyall Parker, Todd Robson and Sue Nairn gathered around. Treblecock, on his way out, turned on his heel and joined the group.

'Latest from Graves. She's grabbed a screenshot of the guys Chamley interviewed for the security jobs. O'Hara's running through the list as we speak. You never know, there might be a lead in there somewhere.'

'Anything else?'

'Oh aye, is there not. That's just the hors d'oeuvres. You'll never guess what: she's found Madonna.'

The group shared their spontaneous disbelief.

'What?'

'Get in there, lass.'

'No way. Brilliant.'

'Where was she?'

Ryan was last to react. 'Dead or alive?'

'Well and truly alive. And, would you believe, she found her at the club.'

Todd Robson voiced his dissent. 'I don't buy that, guv. We know the others were taken by force, against their will. If the same happened to Madonna, how the hell's she managed to get away? More to the point, if she wasn't snatched and left her own free will, why the hell would she choose to come back?'

'That's the million-dollar question. But get this: she was there in disguise. Ilona recognised her, and Graves says she spotted her trying to break into the club's safe.' For Ryan's benefit, he kept details of the office escapade to a minimum.

Sue Nairn shook her head. 'As a woman, I can't imagine why she'd put herself in that predicament. I'm with Todd. Once she'd escaped the clutches of the Mayan, there's no way she'd want to go back.'

'I can think of a couple of reasons,' Ryan said. 'Firstly, that she didn't go back willingly. Remember Hadley Kutz's formula? The forty-seven percent controlled by gangmasters? What if someone ordered her back? Someone intent on revenge, for whatever reason? If Madonna was forced into prostitution, it wouldn't take much for her to be persuaded into breaking-and-entering. It'd come as a blessed relief after everything else she'd been ordered to do.'

Danskin considered the possibility. 'Flag that on the board, Jarrod. We could be looking at a territorial dispute here. What if we've two gangs competing for business, and Madonna's now been coerced into working for the other side?'

'Could explain what she was doing trying to break into the safe. Get information out to the other party,' Parker offered.

'Nice one, Lyall. Are you getting this all down, Jarrod?'

'Yes, sir.'

'You said you could think of a couple of reasons. What's the other?'

The Girl on the Quay

Ryan pointed out the four names on the board. 'We've got Jade, Kayla, and Ebony. All either dead or missing. That leaves us with Madonna who, according to Ilona Popescu and backed up by Ravi's intelligence, was the first to disappear from Orchid Petals' register.'

'So?'

'Let's say Madonna's pissed off at the Mayan, so she does a runner. Goes into hiding somewhere. Then, she decides to get her own back on him. If she's so intent on bringing him down, she could be the one behind it all. Let's face it, we know diddley-squat about her.'

Treblecock shook his head. 'I don't think so. She wouldn't have the nouse to do all this. She'd need to get a van, be strong enough to throw Ebony off the staiths, and to dump Kayla in that lake. She wouldn't be capable of any of that, surely? Would she?'

'I wouldn't be so sure, Treblecock. I think you might be seeing what you expect to see.' The group turned towards Stephen Danskin, but the words weren't his.

When he realised what he'd just said, Todd Robson ended the conversation with a 'Jesus Christ.'

**

Hannah finished her break, returned the phone to her back pocket, and became Lexi again as she slipped into the club via the rear fire door.

A short squat man dressed all in black stood invisible in the darkness. A frown etched tramlines across his brow. He tapped a finger against a gold tooth before following her into the corridors of the Whipped Cream club.

The show had reached its interval and Isla and a girl who appeared to be dressed in a negligee struggled to serve a gaggle of customers jostling for service at the bar. Hannah quickly took up her station and switched to Lexi-mode as she flirted with a middle-aged guy whilst taking his order.

She caught Ilona's eye and gave a slight nod. She received a pursed lip smile of acknowledgement in return before all three girls were engulfed by still more customers.

The sound of Marek Geso's drums over the sound system put an end to the chaos at the bar. By the time his Poison bandmates joined in with Unskinny Bop, the throng had departed to witness a leather-clad Dionne massage the on-stage pole as if her life depended on it.

With the Mayan watching her performance on the office monitor screens, perhaps it did.

'I wasn't expecting you tonight,' Lou Chamley said.

The Mayan smiled. 'I like to make sure you are kept on your toes, Chamley.' He poured himself a cognac. 'I presume you've heard no more from Luuk?'

'No, sir. It's all very quiet.'

'Good. Long may it last. How many chaperones are watching over the Orchid Petals girls tonight?'

Chamley dipped his hands into the papers on the desktop. He raised a sheet to his eyes and peered over the top of his spectacles.

'All ten tonight, sir, including my new recruits.' An errant droplet of spit landed on the page. Chamley dried it with the tip of his thumb.

'Ten, for how many?'

'We have twenty-one girls working tonight. We've got nearly half covered.'

'Yes, thank you, Chamley. I can do basic arithmetic, you know.'

'Of course. Sorry.'

The Mayan's attention drifted to the bank of monitors. Dionne had dispensed with her leathers and was draped over a table. A punter tipped his glass and dribbled lager over her breasts.

The Mayan raised his own glass. His face twisted as he took a sip. 'I want tequila today.'

'Sorry. I'll get you one right away.'

The Girl on the Quay

'No. Leave it. What was it Samuel Pepys said? *'A dram in exchange for the pox is an ill bargain indeed,'* I believe it was.'

'I don't understand.'

'I mean, Chamley, I don't want you out of my sight. I'm losing my collateral hand over fist and I don't trust anyone.' He fixed Chamley with a shark-like stare. 'I need you focused on keeping my business – and my girls – safe, not bringing me drinks like a poodle fetches a toy.'

Chamley's incisors nibbled his lower lip like a rabbit. 'Understood. I am focused, I promise you.'

'I'm pleased to hear it. I have tent poles at the ready, remember.'

The office fell silent. The Mayan watched the bank of monitors, six in total, sited on one wall of the office. One screen remained blank ready to spring into life when the private booths opened after the next interval. Alongside it, another focused on the stage where a brunette had taken up position ready to start her performance.

Beneath these, another pair of monitors covered the audience. On one, Titus could be seen walking between and around tables to the left of the auditorium. The other displayed the right-hand side over which the new guy, Hugo, watched with the intensity of a Presidential bodyguard.

A fifth monitor showed a feed of the entire theatre from a camera situated high above the bar. The final screen, the one the Mayan fixated on, covered activity at the bar.

The Mayan moved closer until his face was inched from it. He tapped on the glass. 'Who's this?'

Chamley smiled. 'That's our new girl. Lexi, she's called. She's proving to be highly popular. I think I made a wise choice there.'

The Mayan's eyes never left the girl with make-up like the cover of Aladdin Sane. He watched her toss aside her long black hair aside as she served a patron. She winked at the man. The customer handed his change back to the girl called Lexi. She smiled, a dimple puckering her cheek.

'See what I mean?' Chamley snickered. 'They love her. I can see you do, too. You always DID have an excellent eye for a girl.'

'Indeed, I have. I've also got an excellent nose.'

The Mayan turned away from the screen.

'And, right now, it smells a rat.'

CHAPTER THIRTY-TWO

The day was half over before Hannah roused herself. It wasn't only the early morning finishes which did for her, it was the whole charade she put on for the creeps in front of the bar. It wore her into the ground.

At least she wasn't working today. Today, she could be more like herself. She swung her legs over the edge of the bed and looked around the room which had become her home.

It was sparsely furnished in comparison to the rest of the apartment, more shabby chic than outright opulence. The other bedroom, however, the one Radka had shared with Ilona, was more brazen.

Hannah knocked on the door and padded into a caricature boudoir. Ilona lay on a fur throw spread over a large, round bed surrounded by mirrors.

'Okay if I run a bath?'

'This is your home too. You need not ask.' Ilona's make up was smeared over her face and pillow. 'I shall follow you.'

'Thanks.' Hannah gazed around the room. 'Ilona, I've got to ask you this. Did Radka ever bring clients here? It's all a bit…well, you know.'

Ilona's pale eyes rested on Hannah. 'No.'

'Good. Only, if whoever's doing this has been to this place, if they know where Radka lived, you could be in danger, too. You are being honest with me, aren't you?'

Ilona looked away. 'There was one time. A man wanted to make a movie. He booked Radka and Sobena. You know she is Jade, yes? He filmed them here. In this room. In our bed.'

Hannah's heart skipped a beat. 'Who? Who filmed them?'

Ilona shrugged. 'I do not know. I was not here. I could not watch them.'

'When was this?'

'Not recently. A long time ago.'

'I have to report this. Two girls missing, both hired together. If we know who it was…'

'It is not important, I think. The men, the rich men, often book two girls. Sometimes, there is more. It is not unusual. You really do not understand this world, do you?'

Hannah shuddered. 'I'm beginning to learn.'

'You will never learn. Not properly. It is impossible for you.' Ilona sat up. 'Now, you take bath, yes?'

'Yes.'

**

Hannah lay up to her neck in aromatic bubbles. She'd lit a few of the candles spread throughout the room, helped herself to a glass of prosecco, and tried to cleanse herself.

It didn't work. She couldn't switch off.

She leant over the edge of the tub, water cascading onto the marble floor, and reached into her bag. She brought out her phone, held it high above the suds, and scrolled through the images she'd snapped in Chamley's office.

She looked at the list of interviewees. Went over the names three times. None of them resonated with her.

Hannah scrolled onto the next image. A list of girl's names appeared, some of them with crosses scrawled untidily alongside.

Storm   x
Portia   x x
Madison
Cleopatra x
Naomi   x x
Mai Tai

In total, there must have been around thirty girls on the list. Their names meant nothing to her. Hannah set her phone on the side of the bath, closed her eyes, and slid beneath the hot water.

The Girl on the Quay

Something alerted her. She opened her eyes. A hazy outline shimmered above the water. Someone was in the room with her.

Hannah sat bolt upright, spluttering and gasping, her eyes wide.

Ilona squatted on the loo.

'Jeez, man. You scared the life out of me.'

'I am sorry. I did not think. Radka and I, we do this all the time. I guess it means I am comfortable with you, yes?'

Hannah breathed out noisily. 'Knock next time, though, yeah?'

Ilona nodded. 'I am sorry.' She looked Hannah up and down. 'Your policeman is a very lucky man. I hope he appreciates what he has.'

The words were spoken as a matter of fact, but they still embarrassed Hannah enough for her to fold her arms across her chest and sink into the foam.

'I need your advice on something, Ilona. Have a look at my phone, please.'

Ilona finished her ablutions and opened the phone. The screen lit up on the page Hannah read.

'Do those names mean anything to you?'

'Of course.'

Ilona scratched the pock marks on her face. Her eyes dulled even more than usual. Eventually, she spoke again.

'I have seen Radka with a list like this many times. It is a...' she searched for the word, 'a schedule. It is the escorts who have clients arranged for the following night. Where did you get this?'

'Chamley's office. What are the crosses?'

'It is simple. The cross means the girl is booked.'

Hannah sat up, modesty forgotten. 'And the second cross?'

'I do not know. But I can guess.'

'Guess, please.'

Ilona stared at the list. Was sure she saw the name Kayla at the top. She felt tears sting her eyes. She closed them. When she opened them again, the name at the top of the list said Storm.

'Some of the girls have, what you say, protection. The other cross I would say means they have someone looking after them. From a distance, of course. You would call it a tail, would you not?'

Hannah inclined her head. 'And the other girls?'

Ilona shrugged. 'They do not have anyone protecting them. Not on nights without a cross. The Mayan does not have enough to watch all of the girls.'

The interview list made more sense now. 'So, he's not only recruiting security for Whipped Cream, he's also taking on muscle to protect his investment in the girls.'

'Perhaps that is so. Now, please, you do not work tonight but I do. I must bath now.'

'Of course.' Hannah stood, bubbles clinging to her. 'One last question. Does the order of the list mean anything?'

'Yes. I believe the most expensive girls are at the top of the list.'

Hannah pondered Ilona's words. 'I'm puzzled. If the Mayan knows his girls are in jeopardy, why doesn't he assign protection to the most popular ones, like this Storm at the head of tonight's list?'

Ilona laughed. 'It is clear. They are the most expensive girls, so their clients are the richest. Sometimes, this means they are very important men. The Mayan would not want to risk one of the bodyguards talking to newspapers. Sometimes, even the most expensive girls go alone.'

Hannah, naked as a new-born but no longer shy, beamed. 'I could hug you, do you know that? In fact, come here.' She held her arms out.

The Romanian girl welcomed the embrace but, in her surprise, let Hannah's phone slip from her fingers.

It disappeared into the foaming bathwater.

**

The Girl on the Quay

The bullpen had seen one of its more normal days. Most of Danskin's squad were on desk duties, processing information, exploring Ryan's theories, or 'running ideas up the flagpole and indulging in blue-sky thinking,' as Inspector Cliché said.

Hannah hadn't reported in, but no-one was concerned. They knew it was her day off and the lass deserved a break after what she'd been thrown into.

By early evening, most of the squad had drifted home. Sue Nairn remained behind with Ravi Sangar, but when Danskin slipped his coat over his shoulders, Ryan decided he'd call it a day, too.

Ryan didn't realise the DCI was only stepping out for a breath of air, but the early finish meant he might just catch half an hour or so with his grandmother to assuage some of the abandonment guilt he'd accumulated.

He clambered into the Fiat at the same moment his phone vibrated. He checked the caller ID and frowned.

'Ilona?'

The voice was hushed and garbled. Loud background music made it impossible to hear.

'Whoa, whoa. Slow down and speak up. I can hardly hear you.'

The voice came back as a hissed stage whisper. 'I cannot. I am working, no?'

'How's things?'

'I am worried. About Hannah. I think she is about to be stupid.'

Ryan forgot all about his grandmother. 'What do you mean?'

'She thinks she may know how the girls are going missing. She has found out some girls are not followed by the Mayan's men.'

'Ilona, you're not making any sense.'

'I have no time to explain. But you must listen to me. I am thinking she is going to follow one of the girls tonight. She thinks the girl may be next in line to be taken.'

'Who? Where?'

'I cannot be sure, Ryan, but I think the girl will be meeting a client somewhere by the river. It is where Radka and the others meet many of their men.'

'Whereabouts? And when?'

'I know no more. The girl she has interest in, she has an appointment tonight. I am guessing it will be by the river.'

'You've got to stop her. Ring her. Tell her DCI Danskin says she can't go.' It wasn't entirely untrue. That's what Danskin would say, if he knew.

'I cannot. I have broken her telephone.'

Ryan blinked twice. 'You've what?'

'I have to go. I wanted you to know.'

The line went dead. Ryan stared at the phone in his hand while his brain processed what Ilona had told him. She was acting on a hunch. She had no evidence, no specific information - which meant Ryan had nothing substantive with which to warrant mounting a full-scale operation. Superintendent Connor would never authorise it.

Another thing he couldn't do was warn Danskin. The DCI might hit the bottle. That would do nobody, not Hannah, Ryan, the investigation, nor Danskin himself, any good. But Ryan knew he couldn't ignore it. He'd never live with himself if anything happened.

There was only one thing he could do.

He'd spend the night patrolling the quayside.

**

Storm by name, stormy by nature. The girl was furious. Her date had gone AWOL. It was fine for the Mayan; he got his fee up-front. For her, it was a wasted night. She stomped away from the Airbnb unsure what to do with the rest of her evening.

The Girl on the Quay

Hannah stepped out the shadows and followed Storm from a safe distance. The woman was about Hannah's age, the same height, with hair styled similar to her Lexi persona, but she could never be mistaken for Lexi. The colouring was wrong.

Storm's iceberg blue hair swished like an angry cat's tail as she picked up pace. She'd decided where she was going. It had been a while, but it was one way of making the night worthwhile.

Ten minutes later, she was perched on a stool the same colour as her hair at Malmaison's Chez Mal bar. She toyed with the cherries in her Martini for a time, one leg on the crossbar of the stool, the other hanging free like a child's on a swing. Apart from herself, there were only two couples and three businessmen in the lounge.

She ogled the men, smiled at them, looked away, then looked back again. She twirled her hair between her fingers. Let a stiletto dangle from her foot, her heel exposed.

In time, one of the men, the oldest of the three, approached the bar. He stood next to her waiting for service. Storm brushed her hand against his leg, briefly at first. Then, her long fingernails ran up and down the man's outer thigh.

The man smiled at her. She returned it with interest. The man put his mouth against her ear and whispered into it.

'I'm sorry my dear,' he said, 'You're not my type.' The barman approached. 'On the other hand, you, sir, are absolutely princely.'

Storm slid off the stool and made her way to the ladies.

**

Ryan's first problem was he had no idea what time the hit would happen, or if there was a hit at all. He knew Radka Vosahlo was picked up around two-fifteen a.m. The others, he had no clue.

A check of his watch told him he could have six hours or more to fill. He walked the length of the quayside and back without catching any sight of Hannah. He did it twice more with the same outcome.

He slipped into the Slug and Lettuce, took a window seat, and sipped a Coke while he watched the world go by. The world, but not Hannah.

At the far end of the quay, he bought another Coke and sat in the beer garden of the Tyne Bar. Ryan drank more quickly. For one, there was a nip in the air but, more importantly, there was little passing trade. He felt removed from the action.

Half-way through his drink, a girl with long, blonde-blue hair passed by without attracting his attention. She was followed, at a discrete distance, by a girl with a similar hairstyle. She, too, went undisturbed.

Thereby lay Ryan's second problem: he was looking for Hannah, not Lexi.

**

Hannah checked her watch. Ten forty-five. Storm had been inside the hotel for almost an hour. The thought crossed her mind that she'd met a client inside. She could be upstairs, in a room, for the rest of the night.

Hannah sat on the plinth of the River God statue. It was cold, hard, and uncomfortable. She shifted her position, rubbed the small of her back, and saw Storm emerge from the hotel.

If anything, the woman walked even quicker now. Hannah had to half-jog to make up lost ground.

It was her run which Ryan recognised; the way she tipped her head back like the guy in Chariots of Fire. It had to be her. He sprinted to close the gap.

Ryan had spent the last few hours mulling what to do if he found her. If anyone saw him intercept her, he'd blow her cover. She'd be in even greater danger back at the Whipped Cream club. Just as importantly, she'd go ballistic with him. A ballistic Hannah was the last thing he wanted.

The Girl on the Quay

So, rather than intercept her, he closed the gap between them to less than a hundred metres before slowing to a walk.

He still hadn't identified her quarry but, by the time their procession reached the Quayside Seaside, he'd worked out it had to be the girl with the blue hair.

His heart thumped like the pistons of a steam train.

**

When Hannah saw the woman walk onto the block between King Street and Lombard Street, her heart rate increased, too. 'This is where Radka disappeared,' she told herself.

When she saw Storm stop at an alleyway between the buildings, she held her breath.

The grille of a vehicle nosed out.

Hannah broke into a sprint. Behind her, Ryan followed suit.

Storm waved to the driver, just as the CCTV footage showed Radka Vosahlo doing.

Storm crossed the alley and a green Range Rover turned left before driving away, past Storm, past Hannah, and straight by Ryan.

The latter two released a breath and slowed to a walk, distances resetablished.

**

Storm crossed the foot of Dean Street. It was noticeably quieter than usual. She put it down to the fact it was a Wednesday night; a school-night. A quiet night in the city equated to a quiet night for her. She decided to quit while she was behind.

The forbidding stairway of Dog Leap Stairs beckoned to her. It offered her a quick route up to the Central Station and her train to Hexham.

She lay a hand on the rail and a foot on the bottom stair and looked up. The passageway was dark and narrow, and twisted upwards like a creeper. Dog Leap Stairs seemed like a highway to hell, not a stairway to heaven.

The squeal of tyres distracted her. Storm turned her head and looked along the quayside, searching for the speeding vehicle.

Hannah heard the tyres, too. She also saw the vehicle which caused it. It was a white transit van.

Hannah broke into a sprint as the white van sped towards the foot of Dog Leap Stairs. The gap between Hannah and Storm was less than forty metres by the time the transit reached Storm. It didn't stop. It drove straight on as Storm disappeared up the stone staircase.

When the transit passed the foot of Dean Street, Hannah knew she could stop running. She bent forward, put her hands on her thighs and, between gasps of air, laughed at herself for her paranoia.

She stopped laughing when she heard the brakes squeal behind her.

The van's rear doors flew open. A figure dressed in black, head covered by a balaclava, leapt out. She felt him grab her long hair and yank her towards the yawning blackness of the van.

Hannah saw a momentary look of astonishment cross the man's face as her hair ripped off her scalp. Her extensions dangled from his fingers like roadkill.

She made a bolt for it the way she was facing, back along the quay. She'd traversed the length of the van when the driver's door flung open. Hannah ran headlong into it.

The world turned black, illuminated only by iridescent shooting stars.

Before unconsciousness claimed her, Hannah could have sworn the last thing she saw was Ryan Jarrod, head in hands, sinking to his knees.

CHAPTER THIRTY-THREE

All things considered, Ryan thought Danskin took the news pretty well.

He swore, yelled at Ryan, grabbed him by the throat, swept the contents of his desk onto the floor, and propelled his chair against the wall.

The DCI snapped every pen within reach, punched the coffee machine, and kicked his filing cabinet with the sole of his foot so it crashed to the floor.

Yes, Danskin took it better than Ryan expected.

Better, in fact, than Ryan himself. The young detective was a broken man. Guilt consumed him like a township in plague. Snot and drool smeared his cheeks. Tears streaked a pinched and drawn snow-white face. His voice was a hoarse and croaked whisper.

When Danskin's office carnage came to an end, the DCI stood stock still. His nostrils flared as he snorted air. Finally, a calm descended on him and he was able to speak rationally.

'Now, it's your turn. Let it out, bonny lad. We all need to have a clear head tonight.'

Ryan retrieved Danskin's precious Corsodyl from the floor and, with a roar, flung it towards the window. It exploded against the glass, the contents smearing the pane crimson like something out of a Saw movie.

'That's better,' Danskin said. 'Okay. Now, listen up. Lyall, Sue, and Robson are on their way. Before they get here, go over the whole thing again.'

Ryan recounted the story from the moment he received Ilona's call, right up to the second he saw Hannah tossed into the back of the transit as if she were a carpet roll.

Parker arrived in time to hear the last of it. His mouth formed a narrow line in a grey face. Ryan went over the story again for Sue and Todd's benefit when they landed, their reaction equally grim.

Danskin's phone rang from the floor in a distant corner of the room. They all jumped. When he hung up, he spoke with a quiet determination.

'I've two uniform units ready and mobilised. Sue, I want you to man the fort here. The rest of you are coming with me.'

'Where to?'

'The Whipped Cream club. Louis Chamley's about to wish his mother had kept her legs shut.'

**

An armada of squad cars lined the road outside the Whipped Cream club. Another blocked off the junction with Pilgrim Street while one more angled itself across the foot of Worswick Street.

By the time Ryan, Stephen Danskin, DI Parker and Todd Robson marched into the club, Bachman Turner Overdrive had been silenced and the theatre was ablaze in light.

Customers scuttled to corners of the room like the cockroaches they were. Sheepish patrons wound their way downstairs from the private areas, dancers covered their modesty with anything to hand, and Isla pretended to be as shocked as Champagne and the other duty barmaid.

Titus and Hugo were held back by a group of uniformed constables, and an apoplectic Lou Chamley raged at anyone within earshot.

Danskin brought order to the chaos. 'Listen, everyone. Listen up. Just so you know, none of you will be going home anytime soon. I'm sure your wives know where you all are, anyway.'

Most the clients dipped their heads towards the carpet.

'You may as well all take a seat. My men will go around table-by-table. They'll need names, addresses, phone numbers and proof of ID.'

'This is an outrage,' Chamley spluttered.

Danskin walked up to him. 'You ain't seen nothin' yet; b-b-baby, you just ain't seen nothin' yet.'

Todd Robson twisted the club owner's arm behind his back and frogmarched him into the office. Stephen Danskin and Ryan followed while Lyall Parker remained behind to supervise proceedings in the auditorium.

On his way to the office, Ryan's eyes slid towards the girl Chamley knew as Isla. It was the only thing he could do to acknowledge her help.

He hadn't a smile left in him.

**

Ryan walked into the golden office just I time to see Todd deposit Chamley into a chair.

'This is harassment of the highest order, Danskin. You know that, don't you? Have you any idea how much you're costing me?'

'Shut. The. Fuck. Up.'

Chamley's eyes widened. 'You'd better have a damn good reason for this.'

'I think you could say I have an extremely good reason.' Danskin's eyes shone. Chamley thought it was the look of barely contained fury. Ryan knew it was the effort of withholding tears.

'You should know I'll have the best legal team throw everything they have at you.' He mopped perspiration from his forehead and drool from his chin.

'That's a very wise move. Trust me, you're going to need them.'

Ryan began sifting through the clutter on the desk.

'Hey! You can't do that. Not without a warrant.'

'Oh, but I have got a warrant with me,' the DCI said.

Chamley shook his head. 'I don't believe you. Tell the kid to put the papers back until I've seen the warrant.'

Danskin smiled. 'You've already seen it.'

'No, I haven't.'

'I'm telling you, you have.' He clicked his fingers. Todd Robson moved forward.

'See, there he is. I told you you'd seen my warrant. Satisfied?'

Lou Chamley considered objecting, then thought better of it. Instead, he settled for, 'What's happened to cause all this?'

Ryan had pulled on a pair of gloves and continued to sort through the contents of the desk. He saw the list of names Hannah had photographed. Ryan forced back a vision of her standing at the exact same spot only yesterday, free-spirited and, well, free. He shut his eyes momentarily.

'I'll tell you what's happened,' Danskin said. 'Another girl's gone missing, that's what.'

'No. No, I don't believe you. It's not possible.'

'I don't care what you believe, chum, because I'm telling you it's happened. Five girls now. Five. All mixed up with your sordid little club and even more sordid whore-house.'

'That's slander. I want my solicitor. Now.'

Todd pulled the telephone line from the socket. 'Oh dear. It's broken. What a shame. Never mind.'

Chamley turned puce. 'I'll get you for this, I'm warning you.'

'Why don't you tell us about the Mayan? We know you're nowt but a pawn. I'm after the cheese not the mouse.'

The chinless man blinked rapidly. 'You keep talking about the Mayan. I've no idea what you mean.'

Danskin patrolled the room in silence. Chamley's eyes never left him, except when Danskin glanced at him. Then, his eyes fixated on a spot beneath the desk.

Finally, Danskin spoke. 'You haven't asked about the fifth girl yet. Don't you want to know who she is?

'No. Um, yes. I suppose. Sorry, I'm struggling to take this all in. Who is it?'

'Her name's Hannah.'

The club owner's face contorted in genuine concentration. 'I'm not sure she is one of mine, Detective Chief Inspector. I know my girl's well and I can assure you I don't have anyone called Hannah.' A fleeting expression of relief crossed his face. 'You're wrong about this. So very wrong.'

'I'm not wrong. You know her better as Lexi.'

'What? The new bar girl? Isla's friend?'

'Yes. The very same.' He brought his head up close to Chamley, forehead to forehead. 'You see, Mr Chamley, Lexi, or Hannah, is one of mine. Female Office Hannah Graves of the City and County CID.'

Chamley's eyelids slid down. A sigh, more of a moan, escaped his lips while Danskin continued speaking. 'I promise you I'll get her back. No matter what the hell I have to do to you, I'll get her back. So, you cretinous toad, you can start by telling me about the Mayan.'

Before Lou Chamley could speak, Ryan interjected. 'Sir, you need to see these.'

'Not now, Jarrod.'

'Yes. Now, Sir.'

Danskin straightened. Took the papers Ryan held in his hand. He looked at the stiff, block capitals drawn by felt-tip pen. He scanned the second sheet, then looked back at the first.

He rubbed his brow.

'You were going to tell me about these, when?'

Chamley looked at the ransom notes. His get out of jail free cards. 'I didn't know what to do for the best,' he said. 'The man who sent them, he's a violent and dangerous man. He'd hunt me down.'

'The Mayan?'

'Stop going on about this bloody Mayan. No, it's the Dutchman. Luuk Van Eyck, if that's his real name. He supplies me with my dancers.'

Stephen Danskin swore. 'You're coming down to the station. Now.'

'What? What for? Surely the notes prove I had nothing to do with all this.'

'For a lawyer yourself, you're pretty bloody clueless, aren't you? Obstruction. Withholding information. Perverting the course of justice. Possibly, modern slavery. They'll do for starters.'

The office door opened. A couple of uniformed officers entered. On Todd's say-so, they prepared to cuff Lou Chamley.

Lyall Parker followed behind them. 'Sir, I've just had a wee message from DS Nairn back at the station. You'll want to see what it says.' The Scotsman passed his phone to Danskin.

He read a message Sue Nairn had forwarded directly from her own in-box.

Hello Sue. Aaron Elliott reporting back for duty. I've found something interesting about your cadaver. I think I know how the Fentanyl entered her system. She has a puncture wound in the webbing between ring and middle finger of her right hand. Strange place to inject yourself, don't you think? What's more, our girl was right-handed. The odds on her using her non dominant hand must be greater than those against Newcastle winning a trophy in my lifetime. Kiss-kiss. Aaron.

Danskin looked Chamley in the eye. 'Well, well, well. The list keeps getting bigger and bigger. Looks like we can add accessory to murder to it.'

Chamley's jaw dropped like an elevator.

The DCI started to walk out the office. Over his shoulder, he spoke to Todd Robson.

'Book him, Dano.'

CHAPTER THIRTY-FOUR

Danskin ordered Ryan home. 'Get some rest. You're done in, son. I need my DCs fresh and alert.'

'You've been at it longer than me, sir,' he objected.

'True, but I've learnt to channel my adrenalin over the years. It'll come to you, too, in time. But, not yet. Now, home. I'll call you if I hear owt.'

Despite Ryan's protestations, Danskin man-handled him into a patrol car and instructed a copper to take him to Whickham. 'He's not fit to drive. Make sure he gets back safely.' It was an order, not a request.

At six a.m, Ryan stumbled into his bedroom. He collapsed onto the mattress and dissolved into tears of grief, pain and helplessness, the warmth of Spud by his side no solace.

Sleep was impossible. He swung his legs over the edge of the bed and felt an object under the sole of his foot. He bent to retrieve it.

It was a tiny vial, a perfume sampler; Hannah's perfume left from the night everything started to go wrong.

Ryan raised the vial to his nose, closed his eyes, and inhaled her scent. He unscrewed the top, tipped a drop onto his fingertip, and traced a cross over his heart.

He fell into a deep sleep as her fragrance consumed him.

**

In splendid irony, Hannah's brain chose that moment to regain consciousness.

She awoke to the mother of all hangovers. A dull ache pulsed through her cranium, a heaviness above her eyes, the taste of puke in her mouth. She forced open an eye - and discovered she was blind.

She jerked upright, the pain forcing a groan from her throat. Both eyes were open now but all she saw was a black void. The air around her was fetid and stale, and cold. So very cold.

She felt her hands rest against metal, the surface crusted and scarred. She scraped her hands across it. Flakes of something layered her palms.

As she roused herself, Hannah became aware of a faint glimmer of light, the outline of a rectangle, in the distance. She exhaled noisily. She could see.

Gradually, she made sense of her surroundings. She was in a metal box of some description. A container, perhaps, or a solid cage; the rectangular shaped light, she realised, was dawn breaking around the edge of its doors.

A wave of nausea came over her. She pinched her nose and winced in pain. Her nose was broken. She brought her hands close to her face. Yes, she could make out blood on her fingers. She noticed something else: her palms were orange. Rust from the floor, she deduced.

Hannah forced herself to her feet. She swayed, reached out to steady herself against the walls of her prison, and sat back down again.

'Sweet Jesus.'

She remembered.

**

Someone was playing an old '78 in the distance, the tune jaunty and vaguely familiar. Ryan, still asleep, buried his head under the pillow, but still the noise came.

He folded the edges of the pillow tight around his ears. Mercifully, before he fully woke, the noise stopped.

Ryan turned over, his breathing deep and regular as he drifted back asleep.

Until the bloody racket started up again.

'Fuck's sake.'

He shot bolt upright. He recognised the tune. The Blaydon Races. It wasn't a '78. It was his phone.

Alert, tense, and scared half to death, Ryan reached for his bedside cabinet. The phone slipped from his jittery fingers. It landed face down on the bed. Heart trampolining in his chest, he turned it over so he could see the display.

For a second, relief washed over him when he realised the caller display didn't show DANSKIN.

The relief didn't last long. He accepted the call.

'What's happened, Ilona?'

**

Hannah forced herself to remain calm. She needed to think. She needed a plan.

She didn't have one so, with reluctance, she settled for the girly thing. She screamed for help. And slumped to the ground as if she'd been tasered.

'What the fuck?' Her hands shot to her throat. There was something around it. A band of some description. A collar, perhaps.

When the pain subsided, she became aware of another sensation. A dull ache at the base of her neck, below the shock collar. She raised her hand to it and felt a slight lump beneath her fingers.

'Okay,' she thought. 'Broken nose, from the door.' She remembered that bit. She felt her neck again. It reminded her of something. 'Think, Hannah Graves, think.'

It came to her. She'd been on a picnic with her mum and Danskin. She'd have been about ten at the time. She'd felt something on the back of her neck, put her hand to it, and the wasp injected its venom into her.

Hannah realised she'd been injected with something. She'd been drugged. Drugged, but not dead. Not like Radka Vosahlo. At least, not yet.

They – whoever they were - wanted her alive. But for how long? She had no idea how long she'd already been captive. Minutes? Hours? Days?

She touched the front of her trousers. Dry. Conscious or unconscious, her bladder wouldn't have known the difference. It would have functioned normally. 'Right. Not days.'

A modicum of calm settled over her. If it hadn't been days, her stepfather would, right now, have every man-jack in the City and County police out looking for her. Except, he didn't know what had happened.

Hannah smiled. She realised he did know. Of course, he knew. He'd know because, she remembered,m Ryan had seen it all.

Ryan would have told him.

**

'Slow down, Ilona. I can't understand you. Say that again.'

'I should have seen it last night. I was so upset, so worried, and so tired. Please forgive me. I have wasted many hours.'

'Seen what last night?'

'It was inside the mailbox. If it had been on the floor, I am certain I would have seen it, but it was not. It was folded. It did not fall through.'

Ryan rubbed his eyes until they watered. 'You need to calm down. Now, what was stuck in the letterbox?'

'The note, Ryan. The note.'

He was instantly wide awake. 'What does the note say?'

'Hannah has been kidnapped. He wants money. Lots of money. He says she will die if I don't give him lots of money.'

Ryan was already stepping into his shoes. 'I have to call this in.'

'No! You cannot. The note says I must not involve the police.'

'Fuck the fucking note. I'm calling the DCI.'

'Please, no. I am telling you as her boyfriend not the police.'

Ryan swayed, light-headed. He realised he'd stopped breathing. He ran a hand through his hair. Pulled strands until he became alert.

'Ilona, put the note down. Don't touch it. I'm coming over.' He went to pick up his car keys, then remembered. 'Shit.' His car was at the station.

'Stay calm. I'll be there as soon as I can.'

He dashed to the front door, lifted the keys to his dad's old Astra and, within moments, was screeching along Front Street as if he'd activated its flux capacitor.

Despite the warning, he knew he had to report it to Danskin. 'Sir,' he said as he careened down Lobley Hill Bank, 'There's been another ransom note. For Hannah. It means she's still alive.'

He quickly recounted the tale as he drove. 'I'm on my way but you'll be able to get a unit there quicker, sir.'

'No. You said the note said no police involvement. We have to assume the kidnapper's watching. Have you anything in your dad's car with you?'

'What do you mean?' A horn blared as he jumped a red light.

'A package? A bag? Anything that would make it look like you're calling to deliver something?'

Ryan scanned the floor. Glanced over his shoulder. 'There's an old holdall on the back seat.'

'That'll do. Take it in with you. If there's anyone keeping watch, you might just pass as a repair man of some description.'

Despite the circumstances, Ryan couldn't fail to admire his DCI's cool professionalism. 'How are you so calm?'

A laugh snapped back at him. 'I'm not calm. I'm shitting myself here, man. But that'll do neebody any good, least of all Hannah.'

Ryan fell silent as he neared his destination. He tried to clear his mind, to force a calm into it the way Danskin had. 'Why Hannah?'

'Don't let your mind go there, son. But we'll find out. And, when we do, we'll find her. We've got to find her.'

Ryan heard Danskin's voice break as he finished the sentence. The Astra veered into Radka Vosahlo's estate. A few minutes, and he'd be there.

'This has suddenly got real, sir, hasn't it?'

There was a sad determination in the reply. 'It has. Very real. The best thing we can do is never forget just how real.'

'I'm pulling up outside now.'

'Good. Now, remember the holdall. Get in there, talk to Ilona, and get that note back to the station bloody quick.'

After a pause, Danskin concluded, 'The squad's right with you, Ryan. They're all here. They want Hannah back as much as we do.'

Ryan doubted they did; he doubted it very much indeed.

CHAPTER THIRTY-FIVE

£50,000 CASH
TONIGHT AT MIDNIGHT
GREENHEART
DO NOT INVOLVE POLICE
BE ALONE OR LEXI DIES.

   The note lay face up on a glass-topped table. One edge was ragged and torn where Ilona pulled it from the jaws of the letterbox.

   Ryan stared at the ink until he saw it ripple through his tears. He sniffed them back and ran the back of his hand across his eyes. 'You touched this much?'

   'Of course, I have. I removed it from the door. I smoothed it out. I held it in my hands as I read it.'

   The words came out as a monotonous drone. Ryan thought she sounded different, detached, remote. Or was it something else? Resignation? Acceptance?

   'I make tea,' Ilona said. Tea was the last thing Ryan needed, but it brought a moment of everyday normality to proceedings.

   Whilst Ilona busied herself in the kitchen, Ryan fumbled in his pockets until he found what he was looking for: a rolled-up plastic evidence bag.

   Gingerly holding the note between pinched fingers, he dropped it into it the transparent bag and shook until the note fit snugly. He adhered the chain of custody seal as Ilona returned. She set the cups on the table. Ryan noticed her hands were steady, not like his own fumblings with the evidence bag.

   'What is it you are doing?' she asked.

'Evidence. Can't have too many fingerprints on it.' He knew it was probably too late anyway, the way Ilona described how she'd handled it.

'You must not show it. You can see what the kidnapper says. He says do not inform police. You have to do this alone. If you keep evidence, if you show it to anyone, he will know. He will kill Hannah. YOU will kill Hannah.'

Ryan sat back. 'Why did you tell me, Ilona?'

'You ask, why. It is clear, is it not? You are her boyfriend. I tell you because of who you are, not WHAT you are.'

'If I had been her dad, would you have told me?'

'I do not know. I think, yes. But I would tell you as her father not because you are a policeman.'

Ryan took Ilona's hands in his. 'Then let me tell her dad. He has a right to know.'

Ilona dipped her head several times, short, sharp movements.

'Good. One thing, promise me you won't tell anyone what you're about to overhear.'

She nodded again.

Ryan used speed dial to make the call. 'Sir, I'm coming in. I've got the note.'

Anger darkened Ilona's face. She stood. Prepared to rage at him for his betrayal. Then, in her pale, dull eyes, a light came on. Ilona put her hand to her mouth.

'Vai Doamne.'

Oh my God.

**

Ravi Sangar magnified the image fifty times and displayed it on the screen in the bullpen.

Danskin, looking twenty years older, sipped water. 'First impressions?' he asked.

'Doesn't mess about. No superfluous information,' Gavin O'Hara offered.

Danskin nodded. 'What does that tell us?'

'Kidnapper doesn't want to give away too much information,' Gavin continued.

'There's no grammar. No sentence structure. It's just words. What if English isn't his first language?' Sue Nairn offered.

The DCI scratched his jaw so fiercely Ryan thought he saw sparks. 'What about the handwriting?'

'Capitals, as you'd expect. Thick, blunt-tipped marker pen so we can't make out style or fineries. The letters are uniform in size. I'd guess he's used a stencil,' was Treblecock's sage offering.

'Aye,' Danskin agreed. 'It's professional, isn't it?'

'There's something else,' Lyall Parker said. 'It disnae look like he's applied any undue pressure. It's all even. Now, I'm nae expert, but if I was scribbling something together, with a hostage in the back o' ma van, I don't think my writing would so uniform, stencil or nae stencil.'

'What does that tell us?'

'Och, I'd say the note was drawn up before he took Hannah. Which means, he's made a deal of preparation. This bloke knows what he's doing.'

Ravi Sangar reduced the image size and displayed the two notes lifted from Chamley's office for comparison purposes. 'Probably, because he's done it before. See, I don't think there's any doubt we're looking at the same suspect, here.'

Silence hung heavy over the bullpen, each of the detective's lost within their own theory and counter-theory.

'Bring Hannah's note back up. Let's go through line-by-line. See if we get anything from that,' Ryan said.

'Good idea, Jarrod. Sangar – let's do it.'

£50,000 CASH

'Has Ilona got that sort of money?' Danskin asked.

'I doubt it. She was on the streets not long ago, wasn't she?' Nigel Trebilcock commented.

'Then, the note's meaningless. Surely the kidnapper must know she hasn't that sort of money.'

'Not necessarily,' Ryan said. 'What if he knows her very well? Like, well enough to know she'd have access to Radka Vosahlo's money? A high-class hooker could well have that much. The apartmen't not cheap, that's for sure.'

TONIGHT AT MIDNIGHT

'You could be right, Jarrod. 'Tonight at midnight' gives her no time to sort anything if she hasn't already got access to it.'

GREENHEART

'What the hell does Greenheart mean?'

They were stumped.

'Okay, let's move on. We'll come back to it.'

'Wait. It rings a bell.' They looked at Ryan. 'It's the drop-off point, and I know where it is.'

'Howay, man. We haven't time to arse about.'

Ryan began to doubt himself. He couldn't afford to be wrong about this. 'There's a country park near where I live. It's built on an old colliery site. It's been reclaimed and transformed into a nature park and trail. There's art installations dotted around. One, I'm sure, is called Greenheart.'

'Brilliant, Jarrod. Now we're getting somewhere.' For the first time, a hint of a smile appeared on the DCI's face.

'Let's not get ahead of ourselves, Ry,' Ravi said. 'Look at this.'

He imposed a webpage on the screen. When he read it, Ryan's heart sank.

'Greenheart is one of five sculptures commissioned by the Great North Forest. Artist William Pym was selected to design a scheme which linked the five sites through art. The sites - Watergate, Monkton, Herrington, Rainton Meadows and Hetton Lyons – were already linked by their shared past as landscapes entrenched in a history of mining and industry. They now share a future as accessible green spaces from reclaimed industrial waste.'

'Shit. There's five of the buggers.'

They all took time to read it again. They still all said, 'Shit.'

The Girl on the Quay

A nerve pulsed in Danskin's cheek. 'We can't cover all of these. Not in the time we've got.'

Ryan saw light at the end of the tunnel. 'We don't need to, sir. Not necessarily. Look at the others: they're all further south of the Tyne. All except Watergate and Monkton are well into Durham. I'm not a gambler but, if I was, I'd lay money on it being Watergate. It's the one closest to the Toon, where all the girls were taken.'

Lyall whistled. 'I think you've just become a gambler, son. With very high stakes.'

They mulled it over, before Danskin ordered them to move on.

DO NOT INVOLVE POLICE

Stephen Danskin pointed to the screen. 'I think we can take comfort from this one. I take it to mean he hasn't got a clue she's one of us.'

'Sorry, sir,' Treblecock interjected. 'It could just as easily mean he knows she is, which is why he's adamant about not involving us.'

'I disagree. Look at the last bit.'

BE ALONE OR LEXI DIES.

'Lexi dies. Not Hannah, but Lexi,' he emphasised.

Danskin looked at them individually.

'He hasn't a scooby who he's messing with.'

**

They grabbed a coffee and a sandwich and reconvened in a matter of minutes. Danskin had used the time to formulate a plan. It was a crap plan, one fraught with risk, but it was the best they had.

'Unless we can find an Ilona Popescu doppelganger, she's going to have to make the drop.'

'Hadawayandshit.'

'Never. She's not trained.'

'Och, it cannae be done. We'd be sending her to face a killer, in pitch dark.'

'I'd better get her ready, sir,' Ryan said.

**

The logistics proved complex. Ilona couldn't be seen waltzing into the Forth Street station for a briefing. They finally decided Ryan was the man for the job. Having already visited her in his repairman guise, he was the only one who could get in without arousing suspicion.

While Ryan made his return trip to Ilona's, Danskin ran interference with Superintendent Connor. Using a civilian as bait would go down with the top brass like a Christmas tree in Kingdom Hall. He needed all the skills of a seasoned diplomat to get this one through. Danskin didn't care; he was prepared to do it with or without back-up. Just, back-up would be easier.

He needn't have worried. Connor agreed to take the bullet if it went belly up. What's more, the Super mobilised armed response for the operation and organised Air Support to remain at a discrete distance. Connor hadn't always been as supportive, not by a long chalk, but Danskin appreciated him coming up tumps when it mattered.

Superintendent Connor even consented to Danskin's request for Ryan to lead the operation alongside him. Local knowledge, the Super, agreed, was imperative.

Danskin only hoped Ryan was up to it. The whole thing was a balancing act, like crossing Niagara Falls on a tightrope.

If they did nothing, Hannah dies.

If they spooked the kidnapper, he would flee and Hannah dies.

If Ryan blew it and his local knowledge let them down, the hostage taker would find an escape route with a bag of cash. When he discovered the cash was fake, Hannah would die.

If the kidnapper, this Luuk bloke Chamley had wittered on about, or whoever else it may be, wasn't acting alone, Hannah would die.

The Girl on the Quay

The only hope was to pray it was a one-man band, catch him in the act, and squeeze him until he revealed where Hannah was.

It was a long shot. An impossibly long shot.

It was the only shot they had.

CHAPTER THIRTY-SIX

Ryan was astonished how quickly and meticulously Danskin planned the operation. He'd put so much together in such a short space of time, Ryan feared something must have been missed. The fact he couldn't figure it provided him with reassurance, if not guarantees.

While Danskin put the rest of the jigsaw together in HQ, Ryan fully briefed Ilona in her apartment. When he was sure she'd taken it all in, he despatched her to her bank, following at a safe distance, where Gavin O'Hara had been planted.

O'Hara welcomed Ilona into a side office where he handed her a case brimful with unmarked twenty-pound notes. Her eyes widened at the sight of the cash. Ryan and O'Hara had chosen not to tell her the notes were fake, and it was clear she hadn't twigged. They also kept from her the fact the case had been fitted with a GPS tracking device; O'Hara because he didn't know, Ryan because Danskin had asked him not to reveal it.

Ryan returned to the station for his final briefing and a verbal rehearsal. Lyall Parker would remain at the station with Ravi Sangar, monitoring operations via radio.

Lyall also set to work completing the paperwork which would see Chamley's stay in custody extended, while Ravi prepared the finishing touches to a court order request for access to Orchid Petals client database. Nigel Trebilcock, meanwhile, was tasked with uncovering whatever he could on the mysterious Dutchman, Luuk Van Eyck.

At precisely eleven p.m, an unmarked squad car fitted with fake taxi plates was despatched to collect Ilona Popescu and bring her to Watergate Forest Park.

**

Ryan and Danskin travelled in one car, Sue Nairn, Gavin O'Hara and Todd Robson in another.

Ryan and Danskin undertook a recce of the main car park off Whickham Highway. Greenheart, the drop-off point, was at the westernmost fringe of the woodland trail, flush against Washingwell Woods. The kidnapper would have a two-mile hike over rough and wooded terrain to make it back to the main car park, so Ryan and his DCI weren't surprised to find it deserted.

This would be their base.

The second vehicle continued straight on, up Streetgate in the direction of Sunniside. Nairn would circumnavigate the area, covering Sunniside, looping round the southern fringe of Whickham, down Broom Lane and back along the Highway. On her first circuit, Robson and O'Hara leapt from the car at strategic points and took up position amongst the trees and woodland of the Forest park, supplementing armed officers already deep in the woods.

The armed response unit vehicles, easily identifiable by the large asterisk on their roof, were parked out-of-sight in the grounds of the nearby Emmanuel College, while the dog handlers used the car park of the Highwayman pub.

Danskin had the Air Support Unit on standby, circling the skies around Washington. This put them out of earshot but close enough to respond within six minutes. What Danskin hadn't told Ryan was it also meant they were a similar range from Monkton, Herrington and the other Greenheart artworks.

Danskin wanted belt and braces for this operation just in case Ryan was wrong about the location.

At eleven eighteen, Ilona's taxi pulled up alongside Ryan and Danskin. They stared at her. She looked as nervous as a bride in her carriage and as mournful as widow following the hearse.

Ryan introduced her to Danskin. She looked at the DCI with empathy showing in her usually lifeless eyes.

'You okay?' Ryan asked.

'No, I am not. I am frightened.'

'You're bound to be,' Danskin said, 'But we've men in the trees all around. You won't see them, but they're there. We've dogs, as well.'

'Will the dogs not bark? If they do, the kidnapper will hear.'

'True, but this is a popular spot for dog walkers. It won't alarm the basta…kidnapper.'

'It is midnight. People would not walk their dogs in a forest at night.'

She was right, of course, but it was a chance Danskin had to take. He ignored her remark.

Ryan and Danskin ushered her back into the fake cab. They sat either side of her. Ryan produced a map, Danskin a pen-torch. As Ryan was familiar with the park, he took the lead.

'Okay. There's two main walking trails through the park. There's also a cycle route. You'll be using that one because it's not as secluded as the others. As soon as you enter the park through the gates there,' he pointed into the darkness, 'The path splits in two directions. You'll take the one to your right. Continue straight ahead until you come to a stream, and then a lake. It will take a while for you to get there.'

Ryan paused to make sure the woman was following him. 'Now, this is important. The path splits again at this point. You must take the path to your right, away from the lake. Remember, take the route to your right, yeah?'

Ilona nodded. 'I go right then right again.'

Ryan exhaled. 'Good. You got it.' He didn't want to have to point out that both Ebony and Kayla were found in water. Water wasn't good. Fortunately, Ilona understood.

'This path will snake in an S-shape. You may think you've doubled back on yourself. You haven't, okay?'

She nodded.

'When you get to this point, you'll be in thicker woodland, with a forest just beyond the park's boundaries. It'll be dark in there. Very dark. But, remember, we'll have people all around you.'

'There is so much. I do not think I can do this.' Ilona trembled like a sapling in a gale. She reached for the door handle.

'Ilona,' Ryan said. 'Look at me. Look at me, Ilona. That's right – look at me. See, I'm here for you. We all are. And remember, you're doing this for Hannah.'

Ilona closed her eyes. Took a deep breath. 'And Radka.'

'Yes, that's right. You're doing it for Radka.'

When he was sure Ilona was back with him, he continued. 'When you get to the boundary fence between the trail and the forest, you're nearly there. One last loop and the trees open out.' He traced the route on the map with his finger.

'Right in front of you, you'll see Greenheart. You can't miss it. It's a metal arch over the pathway. It looks like, I dunno, a ribcage, I guess. It'll be right in front of you, and we'll be all around you.'

Ryan and Danskin stared intently at Ilona. They watched fear, doubt, and indecision pass over her features like light and shade. Finally, her jaw stiffened, and her lifeless eyes shone with a determination Ryan had never seen in them.

'Now, have you any questions?'

'I have one.'

'Fire away.'

'Can I please go get the bastard now?'

**

'She's a plucky bird,' Danskin commented as Ilona disappeared from their view into the grounds of Watergate Forest Park.

Ryan agreed. 'She's hardened to it, poor lass. God knows what sort of life she had in Romania, but to enter the UK the way she did, end up taking beatings off that Charlie

Charlton bloke, then live on the streets, could her life have been any worse over there?'

'Aye, you're right. Same goes for all Chamley's girls. Why whore over here when they could just as easily whore where they were?'

''Cos they didn't have a choice, sir. They were trafficked here, remember. At least Ilona came of her own volition.'

Stephen Danskin opened the car door. 'Howay, let's get some air.'

They stood beneath English oak and horse chestnut trees, shielding them from a moon which played peek-a-boo behind an array of threatening clouds.

Ryan and Danskin buttoned their jackets against the chill spring air. From deep within the woodland, an owl called to its mate. Ryan glanced at the DCI.

'Divvent worry, Ryan. It's just an owl. You've been watching too many cowboy and Indian films.'

Danskin was right, of course. It was just an owl.

Wasn't it?

**

Ilona heard the owl, too. Gooseflesh rose on her arms, downy hair at the nape of her neck stood to attention.

'I am frightened,' she whispered into the hidden dot of a microphone attached to her collar.

'You're fine,' Ryan comforted. 'Just keep following the path to your right.'

She did. She came to a fork in the path. Right again, she remembered Ryan's instructions. She veered onto it.

The path narrowed; the surface uneven. Dense foliage closed in around her like night. She grasped the case tight in her fist, her fingers numbing with the exertion.

She sensed something cross her path. She hesitated, whimpered, then screamed as a single, klaxon-like honk shattered the silence of Watergate Park.

The duck waddled across her path and disappeared into the bushes.

Ilona heard her breathing loop from her microphone to her earpiece as if Darth Vader stood alongside her. 'I have come wrong way. This is not as it should be.'

'What do you mean?'

'You said the pathway was open. This is not.'

Ryan exhaled. 'Wait a minute.' He unfurled the map as Danskin held the torch up against it.

'Okay. I see now. You turned off the path too early. There's a nature walk heading off to the right before the turn you need. Turn around and retrace your steps.'

'I am sorry.'

'Don't worry,' Ryan reassured her. 'That was my fault. Remember, you take the path to the right only when you come to the stream. If you don't see water, you'll hear it. Ignore any other turn-off you come across before then.'

He switched off his mic. 'This is harder than it looks,' he said to Danskin.

The DCI had no words.

Ryan flicked on the mic once more. 'Okay. Once you're back on the cycle path, continue straight ahead. Remember, you're looking or listening for water. You may hear a waterfall. There's an ornamental one nearby.'

A memory of dragging Ebony out of the mudflats of the Tyne and Radka Vosahlo from Northumberlandia's shallow lake came to him. 'Just trust us,' he said. We've eyes on you.'

As Ryan muted his mic, Danskin whispered into his.

'Air Support, where are you?'

The reply came back amid a burst of static and cacophonous motor-roar. 'We can be there in three.'

'Good. Ready thermal imaging. I want to know any heat signatures you pick up in the park. We've men in there but I need you to tell me everything you pick up bigger than a mouse.'

He flicked his mic off, then instantly switched it back on. 'Make that a rat.'

**

Ilona's imagination ran riot. She saw and heard things all around her; things that weren't real, ghostly things. Murderous things.

She came to a fork in the route. Was this the correct turn? She cocked her head to one side. Strained to hear. There it was. A tinkle like a wind chime. The sound of a running stream. Imbued by confidence, Ilona veered right.

A rickety wooden bridge stood astride the stream like a hump-backed dowager. 'Do I cross the bridge?'

Ryan checked the map. 'Excellent. You're on the right path. Yes, cross the bridge, then continue straight on. You'll come to another crossroads. Ignore it. Repeat, ignore the next crossroads. Just keep going. You haven't too far to go now. You're doing really well, Ilona.'

Danskin flicked the torch onto his watch.

Twelve-oh-five.

'We're running late. How much longer?'

In this light, I'd say maybe ten minutes, max.'

Danskin let out a long, impatient breath.

**

Ilona stopped stock-still. She'd imagined every bush rustle, every twig snap on her route. This time, though, it was real. She knew it. She sensed it.

She took another few steps. The bracken moved with her. She wasn't mistaken. She was being stalked.

Ilona moved off again, slowly, one step at a time. The branches swayed with her. She struggled to retain her composure.

Quickly, she swung her head to her right. A shadow dropped to the ground.

Ilona carefully raised her hand to her collar. She twisted her neck to bring her head as close to it as she could.

When she spoke, her voice was tremulous, less than a whisper.

'It is him. He is watching me.'

CHAPTER THIRTY-SEVEN

'Where are you, Ilona?'

'I do not know.'

'Describe it to me. You're across the water, I know. Now, what's the vegetation like.'

'I do not know what you mean. Ask me again, please, then help me.'

Ryan could hear the panic in her voice. 'Calm down. Is the man to your right or left?'

Nothing.

'Ilona, is the man on your left-hand side or your right? What side of the path is he on?'

Silence, apart from her breathing. Raspy, urgent, terrified.

Danskin put his mouth close to Ryan's mic. 'If you're not able or are frightened to speak, tap your mic once.'

A thunderous echo came into their earpieces.

'Understood. If the man is to your left, tap once. If he's on your right, tap twice.

Thump. Thump.

Ryan nodded his understanding to Danskin and asked the next question while looking at the map.

'Ilona, it's Ryan. Use the same code to answer. Are the bushes and trees closer to your left or your right?'

Thump. Thump.

He traced a finger over the map. 'Final question. Are the trees taller here than most of the ones you've passed? Once for yes, twice for no.'

There was a pause. Ryan pictured her trying to decide.

Thump.

Ryan's finger moved back half an inch. 'She's there.'

'All units. Do we have anyone in the trees west of her position?'

Ryan jumped in. 'It's just beyond the trail heading towards the Whickham exit.'

Danskin was ready to go. Ryan was ready to go. All units were ready to go. All it needed was Dankin's word.

'Repeat, do we have personnel in the trees?'

A burst of static.

Then, 'Aye, sir. It's me.'

Ryan and Danskin's bodies relaxed.

'Stand down. It's fucking Robson.'

**

Ryan tried to make light of it. 'It's all good, Ilona. See, I told you we had men watching over you. Everything's cool.'

'Cool, my arse,' Danskin retorted. 'I'm wired like a power station here. Jesus Christ. I thought we had him. Shit.'

Ryan picked up where he'd left off. 'Okay, Ilona. Try to relax. You're nearly there. I want you to keep on walking. This is where the path meanders a bit.'

'Sorry, I do not understand.'

'It's not a straight line. Like, a piece of spaghetti.'

Danskin looked at him. 'Really?'

Ryan shrugged and continued. 'You'll go through some really dense trees. The path takes you through the centre of them, and Washingwell Woods will be on your right. Ignore them. You're not going into the woods.'

They listened to Ilona's breathing. Rapid, shallow, noisy.

Danskin checked his watch.

Twelve-twenty three.

'Robson's set us back. What if he's given up?'

'Sir, calm doon. He won't give up that quick. Not with fifty grand at stake.'

'There's more than bloody money at stake here.'

'Don't you think I don't know that?' Then, 'Shit.'

They'd left their mics open. The last thing they needed was to spook Ilona with their squabbling.

Fortunately, Ilona was otherwise engaged.

'I think I can see it.'

'Describe it to me.'

'It is as you say. Like ribs. There is a seat either side of it. They are, um… benches, yes?'

'Yes. That's it. Any sign of the kidnapper?'

Ilona screwed her eyes up. Squinted into the darkness. Hoped for the moon to reveal itself and, with it, the kidnapper, too.

'I do not see him.'

Danskin felt his jaw clench. His teeth ached from the pressure put on them. 'I need me Corsodyl. Trust you to bloody smash it,' he said.

Ryan's grim smile went unseen. 'Okay, Ilona. Walk up to the bench. Sit down. Wait for him.'

She walked slowly up to Greenheart, a series of half-arches constructed out of weathering steel linked by metal rails. It bore no resemblance to the heart which hammered to escape her chest.

'What is behind here?'

'Nothing. The path turns left and runs through the rest of Watergate Park. You've Washingwell Woods over the fence.'

'I have also a car.'

The detectives looked at each other. 'What?' they asked in unison.

'There is a car. I saw it when the moon shone. It is silver, just like the moon.'

Danskin screamed into his mic.

'All units are go. GO, GO, GO.'

**

Todd Robson was closest. He sprang from the bushes feet from Ilona, sending her tumbling backwards in shock.

The roar of the Eurocopter's engine, the metronomic whup-whup of its rotor blades, wrapped itself around Ilona as it swooped down clear of the trees. The chopper's floodlights switched on. Three slivers of iridescent light, like a scene from Close Encounters, bathed the area. One beam zoomed in on the silver car, the other two roamed the surrounding landscape.

From nowhere, a posse of heavily armoured firearms officers descended. They raced, half-crouched, towards the car. Todd Robson sprinted behind them. Gavin O'Hara emerged and tended to the shell-shocked Ilona.

The lights were blindingly white. Robson squinted through half-closed eyes towards the car. He signalled for three armed men, rifles raised, to take one side of the car. Another two took the left.

They inched forward from the vehicle's rear. Todd reached for the car door. Nodded to the gunmen and tore open the door as he moved out the way.

Shouts rent the air.

'Freeze!'

'Freeze!'

'Armed police!'

'Do not move!'

Over the radio, Danskin's urgent voice pressed for information.

'For God's sake, what's happening? Have you got him?'

The silence lasted less than three seconds, but it was too long for Danskin.

'Repeat: have we apprehended the suspect?'

Todd Robson's voice came back over their earpieces.

'Negative. All units, fall back. It's not our man.'

Inside the vehicle, the red-faced woman occupant, her dress hunched up to her hips, rolled off a man desperately fumbling with his trousers and his erection.

**

By the time Ryan and Danskin made it to Greenheart, Ilona was seated between a female officer and O'Hara. She quivered like a timid mouse. O'Hara took off his coat and wrapped it around her shoulders.

'Anything?' Danskin's voice was flat. Monotone. Defeated.

The Girl on the Quay

Todd Robson shook his head. 'Nothing, sir. Kidnapper will be long gone.'

Danskin sighed, eyes cast downwards. 'What about DS Nairn? Did she get owt?'

'Negative, sir. I've checked with her. She saw nothing suspicious and she must have circled the area umpteen times.'

Ryan tipped his head to the heavens. Gulped in air like a fish out of water. 'Do you think he ever was here?'

'What do you mean?'

'I don't know. Just wondering. I mean, the Mayan never coughed up for any of the others. Why would he expect this to be any different?'

Slowly, Danskin raised his head. Ryan thought he saw a glimmer of a smile on his lips but knew he must be mistaken.

'You know what, Jarrod, this one was different. Why didn't we think of it before? The others, they were all Luuk's women. Whatever went on between the Mayan and Luuk Van Eyck was all about the sex trade. High-class hookers worth a fortune, to the Mayan in clients and to Van Eyck as cattle.'

Ryan began to see Danskin's logic.

The DCI continued. 'Hannah wasn't in the same league. Hannah, or Lexi, was just a bloody barmaid.' His voice choked. He cleared it with a cough. 'Why the fuck would he be interested in a barmaid?'

'Could just be a change of tack, sir,' O'Hara reasoned. 'I mean, he'd had no luck with the Mayan. If he knew Isla, as he'd know her, had access Kayla's money, why not take her new BFF? It makes sense.' He saw the DCIs disbelieving look. 'Doesn't it?'

'No, O'Hara, it doesn't. It doesn't make the least bit sense. You see, if Luuk Van Eyck is in Holland or somewhere else in Europe, he wouldn't even know Ilona or Hannah existed.'

Danskin was already marching back towards the exit. 'Let's get back to the station. See if Treblecock's got anything on the Dutchman, and hope Parker's still got Chamley on ice.'

Ryan scuttled after him, Todd Robson, too, while Gavin remained behind to tend to Ilona until Sue Nairn reached the scene. Nairn would lead on Ilona's debrief.

The DCIs mind was ablaze with ideas, theories, and options. He spouted forth with them all the way back to the car. Most of them were gobbledegook, all of them a product of a desperate and exhausted man.

Ryan caught his arm. 'Slow down, sir. You'll have a coronary.'

'I can't rest, son. Not until I've got Hannah back. I don't care what happens to the bastard who took her any longer, all I want is Hannah. The kidnapper can rot in hell or take the throne of England. As long as I get Hannah back, I don't care about him,' he repeated.

'Sir, man, you're knackered,' Robson said breathlessly. 'You've never stopped.'

'I'm fine. Don't try telling me I'm not, Robson.'

'In that case,' Ryan said, 'I'll be the one to tell you. Stop. Go home. Even if you don't sleep, get some rest. You can't keep going. It'll be seventy-two hours without sleep by the time tonight comes round.'

Danskin rounded on him. 'Shut it. You don't know how I'm feeling.'

'With respect, sir, I think I do.'

Danskin stopped dead. Glowered at Ryan. Muscles twitched all over his face. Finally, his face relaxed. 'Yeah, I guess you do.'

The DCIs shoulders heaved, his bottom lip trembled. Tears filled his eyes, spilled over, cascaded down his cheeks. A bubble inflated at the tip of his nose. He sniffed it back.

Robson looked at the ground, embarrassed.

The Girl on the Quay

Ryan held the DCI. Cradled his head into his shoulder. Felt it grow wet with Danskin's tears.

After a while, Ryan released him. 'Go home. Promise me. In the morning, Parker will make sure Chamley's there for you to question. Treblecock might have some news on Luuk. Ravi should be into the agency client database. Most importantly, you'll be fresh and ready to go, yeah?'

Danskin heaved a sorrowful lament. He looked at Ryan. Dipped his head. 'I guess you're right.'

'I am right. You know I am. One more thing. Corsodyl only, promise?'

Danskin managed a smile. 'It's all I've got in.'

As he headed towards his car, he turned to face Ryan. 'You'll make a great son-in-law, one day,' he said.

As he drove off, Todd let out a whistle. 'Foreskin's completely lost it, poor bugger. On top of all the bubbling like a bairn, the saying's *'you'll make a great husband'* isn't it?'

Ryan smiled mournfully. 'I know what he meant.'

Danskin's car disappeared from view.

CHAPTER THIRTY-EIGHT

'...the park behind me remains closed to the public this morning,' the elfin-faced reporter said to camera, 'But, as for what really went on in there last night, no-one really knows. The police and emergency services remain tight-lipped, prompting some local residents to dub it the Geordie Roswell. It certainly isn't that but, for now, whatever events did occur in these woods must remain a mystery.'

The reporter smiled into the lens. She flicked back strands of wind-blown hair. 'Back to you, Naga and Charlie.'

The Asian woman in the studio rolled her eyes. 'The truth is out there,' she joked. 'We'll keep you up to date with that story as it develops. Megan Wolfe there, reporting from Watergate Country Park, near Gateshead. Right, time for the weather. Here's Carole...'

Lyall Parker switched off the newsfeed.

'Bloody hell,' Todd Robson swore, 'When did Wolfe get a job with the Beeb? The she-devil's had a bit of a promotion from the local rag, hasn't she?'

'Shit still stinks of shit, wherever it lands.' Stephen Danskin stood in the doorway, haggard and unshaven.

'Sir, how are you?' Parker enquired.

'Better than yesterday. Because, today, I'm going to find Hannah Graves.'

Haggard and unshaven he may have been, but Ryan was comforted by the glint of steely determination in his DCI's eyes.

**

Someone else had steel in their eyes. Steel of a different kind.

Hannah stared at the four metal walls around her and sank to the floor. She brought her knees to her face, wrapped her arms around her shins, and wept.

The confidence of yesterday was long gone. She struggled to think. Was it yesterday? Or last week? Or, could it have been earlier today? She had no way of knowing. For the first time, it dawned on her what imprisonment was like. All those she'd arrested, given evidence against; all those she'd helped send to jail, they all felt like she did right now.

Except, they weren't all in solitary.

Neither were they on death row.

Hannah had explored every inch of her cell. She'd checked every bolt, every rivet, every nut and screw for weakness. There wasn't one. There was no way out.

She'd hammered on the walls but received no reply apart from bruises and scrapes on her knuckles. She'd screamed for help, twice; her only reward an agonizing jolt of electricity and a paralyzed voice box.

All of that, she'd learnt to live with. Now, as she squatted in a corner of her prison and strained to urinate, reality hit home. She barely squeezed out enough to fill a test-tube. And it was the colour of the rust on the walls of her cell.

If she didn't get something to drink soon, she'd dehydrate.

If Ryan didn't reach her soon, she'd die.

How could Ryan reach her? Even she didn't know where she was - she didn't even know which country - so, she asked herself again, how could Ryan find her?

Of course, she'd die.

**

Stephen Danskin wasn't going to let her die. He held audience with his squad.

'Right, you lot,' he said, 'It goes without saying our working assumption is that DC Graves remains alive. We know whoever is doing this kept Radka Vosahlo for several days. We work on the theory he's doing the same with Hannah, too.'

Ryan was sure he wasn't the only one thinking that Jade, Kayla, or Ebony hadn't set a failed trap for the kidnapper, but he forced his worry back beneath the stone it crept out from.

Danskin continued. 'We never, ever rule anything out, but let's run through what we believe. The Mayan wouldn't blackmail himself. No matter what he does or who he is, that's one thing he wouldn't do. What we do know, though, is that he's the key. Lyall, I want Chamley in the interview suite in fifteen minutes. Preferably, without his brief but that's unlikely. I want him grilled until we know everything there is to know about the Mayan. He'll deny he exists. I don't care. Find out.'

Ryan studied Stephen Danskin as he spoke. On the surface, the DCI seemed in control, more like himself, but Ryan saw the tightness around his mouth, tension in his eyes, and nerves in the way he rubbed thumb against index finger as he spoke.

'Another theory we need pursue is that the perp is a disaffected client, a nutty client, or a perverted client. Ravi, where are we on the court order for access to Orchid Petals client database?'

'It's being heard at nine-thirty, sir. Should be a formality.'

'Depends who we've got. Do we know who's sitting?'

'Not yet.'

'Okay. Lyall, I want you to head up that side of things. Make sure we get it passed, then work your way through the buggers on it with Ravi and Todd. I want red flags on anybody and everything that looks odd.'

'Sir.'

'Our other possible lead is the Dutchman, this Luuk Van Eyck. Chamley's pretty sure he's in it up to his neck. We're agreed one possibility is a turf war between him and the Mayan, yeah?'

He waited until he received murmured consent.

'DS Nairn, you're leading on the Luuk Van Eyck trail. You've got O'Hara and Treblecock.'

'What about me, sir?' Ryan asked.

'You're with me, Jarrod. I'll be overseeing both strands. Make sure the guys are making progress, that the enquiries run in tandem. We'll take a helicopter view.'

Ryan had a flashback to last night. To a helicopter beam illuminating Watergate Country Park, trees bowing in deference to the downdraught like palms in a hurricane, to Ilona Popescu shivering on a wooden bench in an open glade beneath the Greenheart structure, and to a broken Stephen Danskin finding comfort in his arms.

Stephen Danskin was broken no more. He was steely, determined, and managing his emotions as successfully as the operation.

Ryan and Danskin held a shared belief they'd find Hannah, alive and well. How long they'd remain confident was anyone's guess.

**

The debrief to Superintendent Connor was long and difficult. The Super was not a happy man. Besides the fact he had a valuable officer missing and endangered, he was fighting off the press with one hand and crazy UFOlogist conspiracy theorists with the other.

By the time Ryan and Danskin emerged from Connor's office, the DCI's mood sped downhill faster than a runaway train.

Parker informed him they still hadn't received clearance to interrogate the agency's database. Chamley's brief had raised an objection based on some obscure GDPR exception.

'Bollocks.'

Not only that, the brief attended Lou Chamley's interview and had clearly advised his client to adopt a strict 'no comment' approach. Thirty minutes questioning led nowhere.

'Bugger. Sue, tell me there's some good news on the Van Eyck front, for pity's sake.'

O'Hara answered for her. 'I've tracked down the officer heading-up a Dutch investigation. I'm about to call him.'

'Do it; do it now.'

Gavin checked the number on his monitor screen and dialled it meticulously. The odd, elongated ring tone indicated the call was being routed to foreign shores. O'Hara cleared his throat and spoke slowly and deliberately.

'Hello. My name is Detective Constable Gavin O'Hara. I am a member of the City and County CID in Newcastle. That's in England. I am calling about an ongoing investigation into a Luuk Van Eyck.'

O'Hara waited for a response. When none came, he asked, 'Do. You. Speak. English?'

After another pause, the reply came.

'Why aye, bonny lad. 'Course I do, man.'

**

DI John Craggs was sitting at Henrik Kramer's desk in the Politiebureau Ijmuiden when the phone rang.

He was lost in thought, gazing into space as a tram cut a swathe through the plaza outside the station. Automatically, he picked up the receiver before realising the only words of Dutch he knew were 'Ja' and 'Johann Cruyff.'

It was a relief, not to say a shock, when he heard O'Hara's Geordie accent. From the silence down the line, it was clear a Mackem in Ijmuiden came as an even greater surprise to the caller.

'Less of the Mackem, if you please, DC O'Hara. I'm a Durham lad. I'm Detective Inspector John Craggs from Prince Bishop force.'

'Whether you're a Mackem or not, what the hell are you doing ower there?'

When he heard that, Danskin stopped what he was doing and ordered O'Hara to put the call on speaker.

'Would you believe, I'm investigating Luuk Van Eyck. Not very joined up, are we?' he laughed. 'Tell me what your interest is in him.'

'One of our guy's has gone missing. She was working undercover at a strip joint run by a creep named Louis Chamley. Mean anything?'

'Nope. Carry on.'

'From what we gather, Chamley's a front man for someone who goes under the name of the Mayan. Chamley and this Mayan character also run an escort agency. This is where it gets interesting. The hookers, the best ones, have been disappearing. We thought four, but one's been sighted. At least two of the other three are dead.'

Ryan interrupted the conversation. 'DI Craggs, my name's DC Ryan Jarrod. We've got you on speaker phone. We mounted an exercise to catch the killer-stroke-kidnapper yesterday. It went pear-shaped. We don't want our officer to go the way of the others.'

They could almost hear Craggs thought processes. 'Where does Van Eyck fit in?'

Gavin O'Hara was relegated to the subs bench as Danskin spoke next.

'This is Detective Chief Inspector Stephen Danskin speaking now. Our information is that Luuk Van Eyck may be behind the kidnappings. One of the theories we're working on is that it's some kind of gang war; that the Mayan and Van Eyck are in competition. What's your thoughts - and why the hell are you out there investigating him?'

Craggs rubbed both temples with the index finger of each hand as he digested the information.

'Long story cut short, I'm here because someone working for Van Eyck wanted rid of me. He thought I was one of the Mayan's men.'

'Why the fuck would he think that? Okay, Craggs. From the beginning.'

Craggs was taken aback. The fact Danskin, a DCI but a DCI out of Craggs's jurisdiction, referred to him by surname irked him. Nevertheless, he let it pass.

'I was called out to a trawler anchored off the Durham coast, south of Seaham. It was Dutch. The Stellendam if you want the fine details.'

'Not yet, Craggs. I just want the damn story.'

'Okay. The Stellendam was skippered by a bloke called Remi Theijs. Theijs was under the thumb of Van Eyck. The trawler was abandoned like the Marie Celeste but, get this, there was evidence Theijs and the rest of the crew were slaughtered. What's more, the hold was full of stuff belonging to lasses.'

'That figures. One of the threads we're following is that we're looking at a people-trafficking ring here. Looks like we have evidence now to back that up.'

'Oh aye, not half. The Dutch authorities have been after Van Eyck for years. Seems he brings over the lasses from aal ower the world, grooms them into prostitution, then sells them on.'

Danskin snapped his fingers. 'Bingo.'

Sue Nairn piped up. 'Who are his contacts, do we know?'

'Nah, not sure. At least, we don't know any of the big players.'

'What do we know about his background? Anything that confirms he's capable of kidnap, as a revenge motive rather than for profit?'

'He's a ghost, but I know from personal experience his crew had a confrontation with a Russell Morton. He's local and was one of the guys who transferred the last batch of lasses ashore. He picked them up off Blackhall Rocks. Seems he was one of three working for the Mayan.'

Danskin double-checked the call-record facility was active. He didn't want to lose any of this.

'Did you get owt from this Morton bloke?'

'Well, he thinks Van Eyck's done for the other two in retaliation for the way they wiped out the Stellendam crew. Morton's sure it's only a matter of time before they come looking for him. He's living like a hermit in a place called

Pirate's Cave, though you might find him in a boat moored offshore. I'd love it if you brought him in.'

He looked down at his bandaged feet and a crutch propped alongside him. 'I've got a score or two to settle.'

Craggs heard the sound of a chair scraping along the floor. 'On it already,' a voice said. Nigel Trebilcock, though Craggs didn't know it.

'Owt else?' Danskin asked.

'Not a lot yet. He's got himself a lass, apparently. One of his hookers. DI Kramer, who's fronting things over here, is searching for her. He's adamant he can get her to talk. Trouble is, she's done a runner.'

'Can't say I blame her, by the sounds of it.'

'Aye. For what it's worth, she goes by the name of Madonna.'

CHAPTER THIRTY-NINE

For the first time in days, Danskin saw light at the end of the tunnel. Only a pin-prick, but it was there.

Everything pointed to the Dutchman.

'Lyall, get Chamley back into the interview suite. If he won't talk about the Mayan, let's see what he knows about Van Eyck.'

Parker was already on the phone arranging it.

'Treblecock's checking the form on this Morton guy. When he gets back, I want you, O'Hara, to gan with him down to this Pirate's Cave place.'

'Sounds like a frigging Disney ride', Todd Robson commented.

'For that, you can go with them. The Johns on the Agency's list can wait, if we ever get access to it. Ravi, where are we on that?'

Ryan didn't hear the retort. He was answering his phone. The call didn't last long, less than a minute. He spent longer slumped in his chair, going over what he'd just heard.

When there was a break in Danskin's orders, he spoke.

'Sir, can I raise a point?'

He didn't quite know what his point would be so, when Danskin said, 'Go ahead,' he didn't. Not straight away.

'Jarrod? What you thinking?'

'This'll sound odd, but bear with me.' He desperately tried to unscramble his brain. 'We know Hannah's disappearance differs from the others. There's the note going to Ilona, not the club. The request for a drop off while the others just demanded payment, presumably in the knowledge that the Mayan knew how to get funds to Van Eyck.'

'Get to the point, man.'

'What if there's two separate things going on here? The turf war between the Mayan and Van Eyck, and a separate reason for snatching Hannah?'

'Why would anyone do that?'

Ryan stared into space. The eyes of the squad all focused on him. 'What if someone has a grudge? Against one of us, like.'

'Who?'

'How about, me?'

Danskin tutted. 'What the hell makes you think that?'

Ryan pushed his arms into his coat as he stood. 'Because, that was me gran's care home. She's gone missing.'

**

Ryan arrived at the care home to see his father ranting and raving about duty of care and other stuff he had no idea about.

Angela Doyle tried her best to placate him. She looked to James Jarrod for support, but Ryan's brother paced the reception room like a caged tiger.

When she saw Ryan at the door, the relief on her face was palpable as she buzzed him through. The look of relief didn't last. Four uniformed police followed Ryan into the reception area.

'Is there any need for all this?' Angela said, thinking of reputation-management.

Norman Jarrod pounced on his son immediately. 'Arrest her, will you? Gross negligence, that's what this is. They take a fortune off us and for what?'

'Calm doon, faatha, man. Let me handle this. Is there somewhere we can talk?'

'Yes. Yes, of course.' She led Ryan and his entourage into the office. 'I'm terribly sorry about all this. We really do try our best, you know. Our doors are always secure. No-one can just walk in-and-out.'

'Angela, I'm sorry to say I'm here in a dual capacity. You see, there's a possibility gran didn't leave of her own volition. We've reason to believe she may have been taken.'

'Good heavens.' She reached for the chair. Sat down slowly. 'Why would anyone do that?'

'I'm not at liberty to say, I'm afraid.'

Ryan saw his dad's face pressed against the glass of the office, his nose squashed like Spud's. Ryan shooed him away and closed the blinds.

'Do we know when gran disappeared?'

'She was here when the meds trolley did the rounds but, when we called our residents for lunch, I'm afraid Doris didn't show. We assumed she was still in her room. One of the girls went to her room and found it empty. That's when we knew.'

'When did the trolley do the rounds?'

'I'm not sure. We had an agency girl do it. It was later than usual, perhaps half an hour before lunch.'

'I take it the doors are monitored by CCTV?'

Angela nodded.

'Can I see it, please?'

They waited until someone with the technical skills to retrieve it showed up. Norman Jarrod asked what the hell was going on, Ryan told him he'd explain later. James continued to wear a furrow in the carpet.

Finally, the CCTV footage was loaded and ready to roll. Ryan and Angela Doyle scrutinised it. For a while, nothing showed. A couple of visitors arrived, a red-clad postman delivered the mail, mundane things.

Ryan checked the time display on the screen. 'Ten minutes to lunch, yeah, and still no sign?'

'That's right. The staff will be in the dining room now, setting places and readying things for lunch.'

A figure walked into view. Not Doris Jarrod, too young. The woman – or, Ryan reminded himself, a man dressed as a woman – had their head down, scrolling through phone messages.

The person still had their head down as they approached the door. Still played with their phone as they pressed the door release button. Wind ruffled the posters on the wall of the hallway as the person opened the door. And continued to hold it open.

Another figure shuffled into view, hunched and shambling.

Doris Jarrod took the door and wandered out.

Ryan sat back and watched the last few frames again, wondering if it was the last time he'd ever see his grandmother.

He put his sensible head back on.

'Okay. Question is, was the first person simply distracted and didn't realise she was letting a resident out, or was it a ploy?'

'I'm sure it was an accident.'

'Really? They didn't sign out, did they?'

He had a point.

'Let's have a look at the book.'

Angela and Ryan hurried to the hallway where the visitor's book lay. Ryan took photographs of the entries, made lists.

A carer hurried to join them.

'We've found her.'

Angela closed her eyes in relief.

Ryan asked, 'Alive?'

The carer looked stunned. 'Yes, of course she's alive.'

This time, Ryan allowed his eyes to show relief. 'Where?' he asked.

'On the grass outside Southfield Terrace. One of your Community Police officers found her. She told her she was lost.'

'Thank fu…thank goodness,' Angela said.

Ryan smiled. 'She's been trying to get home. The Drive's up that way.'

'I'd better go tell your dad.'

'That'll be an idea, before he spontaneously combusts.'

Ryan raised his eyes from the guest book. They settled on the portrait. He didn't know why, but he asked, 'Do you see much of Max Bonhomme?'

Angela followed his gaze to the picture of the opening ceremony. 'No. Hardly ever. Of course, he doesn't own the place now so there's no reason why he should.'

'He doesn't?'

'No. Sold it a while back. This one, and a couple of others. Don't know why.'

Ryan didn't know why his heart was racing.

'Did you ever meet his wife?'

Angela didn't need time to think about the reply. A sardonic smile crossed her face. 'Yeah. The only other time I met him was when he came to sell the place. She came with him.'

'Why the smile?'

'Well, they were an odd couple, weren't they? But they say money talks, don't they?'

Ryan brought out his phone. Opened the picture gallery. 'Is this her?'

He held up the phone so the photograph of Jade was visible.

'No, that's not her.'

'Sure you don't want to look again?'

She smiled again. 'I'm quite sure. You see, the woman he was with was black.'

**

'Sir, I want units to Darras Hall. Now. I think I've cracked it. It's not the Mayan. It's not Van Eyck. I'm pretty sure it's Max Bonhomme.'

'Okay, I'm scrambling a team now.' He gestured to Parker. 'I need to know what I'm committing to, though.'

Ryan was already on the A1 heading north towards Ponteland. 'Bonhomme's connection to Jade is well known. He reported her missing. I now think that was guilt.'

'Go on.'

'Ilona told me Jade and Radka, in her Kayla guise, occasionally played tag-team. I think the two of them might have worked together on Bonhomme. Now, if we can prove that link, we've a helluva good case.'

Danskin checked his watch. 'Our plea for access to the Orchid Petals data is being heard as we speak. Assuming we get the go-ahead, I'll have Ravi check out the bookings. That'll give us proof.

'That's not all. He's also attended events with a tall black woman with short cropped hair. Sound familiar?'

'Ebony!'

'Give that man a coconut.'

'Fan-bloody-tastic. I'm on my way. I'll meet you there.'

**

Both ends of the leafy avenue were already cordoned off when Ryan arrived. No sooner had he parked up, Danskin's car rolled into view. The DCI's face was flushed with anticipation, verve, and Corsodyl.

'You realise this doesn't answer all our questions, don't you? But it's the best lead we've ever had, Jarrod. Well done.'

DS Nairn was with Danskin, hence the DCI's formality. 'Ravi's trawling Orchid Petals as we speak,' she said. 'We've just received the go-ahead. He's concentrating all his initial efforts on Bonhomme. He'll keep in touch.'

They watched as a group of officers in protective gear, visors, the works, edged their way towards Bonhomme's mansion from either end of the road.

'We've got men heading out the back, too,' Danskin reassured him.

'Do they know about the dog? He's got a bleedin' werewolf round the back.'

Danskin opened the radio. 'We got wildlife. Watch out for the dog.'

'Roger.'

The men were either side of the double-fronted door now, waiting for the word.

'Care to join me on this one, DC Jarrod?'

'You bet your life I would, DCI Danskin.'

'Sorry, Sue. You're the wallflower on this occasion.'

'Sigh. Story of my life,' she joked, putting the back of her hand against her brow.

Danskin and Ryan joined the men at the door, each taking up position on opposite sides.

Danskin addressed the officers. 'Do we have our Big Red Key ready?'

'Sir.'

Two officers moved in front of the door, Enforcer battering rams in hand.

'On three.' Calmly, Danskin counted down. 'One. Two. Thr…'

He didn't even finish the count. The Enforcers pounded against the door, one by the lock, the other centre-stage. The door splintered on the third attempt. Big feet encased in heavy boots completed the entry.

'Police!'

'Stay where you are!'

'Nobody move!'

'Get down!'

The orders were screamed, garbled, sometimes contradictory. It didn't matter. The only purpose was to scare the shit out of whoever was inside.

A hound hared from the kitchen, lips withdrawn, fangs bared, spittle hanging from incisors. It leapt towards the first man through the door

The second officer brought it down, mid-air, with a taser.

The officers spread throughout the house, room-by-room. All empty.

The Girl on the Quay

They edged up the staircase, pausing at each bend.

All quiet.

They flung open the first bedroom door. Soft toys littered the floor. No people.

The second bedroom yielded similar results. More toys. No occupants.

The bathroom was deserted.

Only an office and the master bedroom remained unsearched.

Two men waited for the order to break down the office door, while another pair crouched low and swept into the master bedroom.

It was there they found Cassie Bonhomme lying on the bed, forehead soaked in sweat, eyes wide with terror, face contorted in pain.

'Where is he?'

Cassie Bonhomme raised her head. 'I wish I knew.' Her voice strained through clenched teeth. 'I'm home alone. The kids are at my mothers, he's not here, and he's taken my phone.'

The officers looked at each other, waiting for instructions.

Danskin stepped into the room, Ryan behind him. 'Where do you think he might be?'

'Right now, I don't give a toss.' Cassie Bonhomme let out a scream. 'Because, right now, I'm having his baby. I mean, I'm having his baby NOW. Right. Fucking. NOOOWW!'

The final word came out like the howl of a wolf.

CHAPTER FORTY

Back at Forth Street, they all took a moment to reflect. They knew their man. They just had to locate him, that's all.

Ravi Sangar updated them all on Bonhomme's activities. 'The bloke's a perv. I mean, a prolific perv.'

He brought up a spreadsheet and displayed it on the big screen. Page-upon-page of times, dates, and names; some of which were well known to Danskin's watch.

Unsurprisingly, Jade took centre-stage. Bonhomme had been right when he said he met up with her every ten days or so. But, since she went missing, a litany of other names appeared.

Ebony was on there, both before and after Jade's disappearance. There was a Savannah, a Zoe, Mai Tai featured along with a Priti and a Co-Co.

Ravi's research showed Bonhomme had indeed hooked up with Jade and Kayla together - on more than one occasion. Three times, to be exact.

Todd whistled. 'Must cost him an absolute mint for all of this. I mean, the Agency fees alone could keep me in ale for a year, and that's before his little extras. God knows how much they run up to.'

A thought crossed Ryan's mind. 'What's his finances like? Has anyone looked into them? Sure, he lives in a mansion - but it's got to have a mortgage bigger than Bolivian natural debt and it'll cost a bob or two run as well. He's got two kids...'

'Three,' Sue corrected.

'Aye, three kids. What I'm thinking is, when I was looking for my grandmother, the manager of the care home mentioned Bonhomme had sold a few of his homes. Did he use the capital from that to fund his habit, or did he sell them because he was going bust?'

Danskin sat back in his chair. 'We've been working on the basis he's a twisted perv. What I've he's a bankrupt twisted perv? That gives him extra motive.'

'I'll check it out, sir' Ravi said.

Danskin saw the pensive expression on Ryan's face. 'What's the matter, Jarrod? You look unsure about something.' Danskin barely got the words out through his elongated yawn and stretch. 'I'm knackered,' he said.

Ryan was on his feet, reading the crime board. He shook his head. 'It's probably nothing but - why Hannah? Why her? I mean, it's the other end of the spectrum, isn't it?'

'I see where you're coming from, but he had nee luck blackmailing the Mayan, had he? If he knew Radka well, he'd know she was with Ilona. If he's been watching her, we can assume he knows she's got a new buddy. Perhaps he thought Hannah was her new bed-mate. If Ilona had Radka's money, he could be thinking she was easy pickings.'

'I suppose.' Ryan wandered to the window. He watched an ancient Pacer train shudder its way into the station. 'We need to find him, though. Chances are, wherever he is, so's Hannah.'

He swallowed. The others fell silent. For a moment, even Danskin had forgotten what the stakes were.

'Where would he go?' Ryan asked.

The silence hung over the bullpen like Madame Guillotine, finally broken by Lyall Parker.

'Sir, I know you're not a great fan, but would a profiler help?'

Danskin vibrated his cheeks. 'Hadawayandshite. Look at the last time we used one. What was her name? Connor's mate, man.'

'Imogen Markham, sir.'

'Aye, that's her. No thanks. I'd rather throw a dart at a map. See where it ends up.'

Lyall Parker tried again. 'I just thought it might give us a new perspective. A fresh pair of eyes cannae do nae harm.'

'That mightn't be necessary,' Ravi Sangar suggested. 'Ryan might be a bit of a young pup when it comes to this game, but he knows his stuff. See what you all make of this.'

On the big screen, he brought up Max Bonhomme's bank account details.

Danskin frowned. 'Is this legal, Sangar?'

'Um, well, let's just say we'll apply for retrospective permission, then go in as if we'd never seen it before.'

Danskin snickered. The laugh became lost in a whistle when he saw the statement on the screen.

'Will you look at that? I take it it's not in red because that's your favourite colour, Sangar, is it?'

'Nope sir, it certainly isn't. Bonhomme might have the trappings of wealth but he hasn't got a pot to piss in. In fact, looking at this, he hasn't even got much piss left, either. Orchid Petals signature is all over his account. He's whored away every penny he's ever had.'

Danskin rubbed his palms together. 'Yesss! What about credit card? Maxed out, I'd guess.'

Ravi made a few clicks. 'I've got me hands on it but I haven't checked it out yet. It's about to get its premiere, right about…now.'

He clicked once more and the statement appeared.

Stephen Danskin picked up a mug and crashed it against the floor.

'Fuck!'

'Sir?' Lyall Parker asked.

'It's not Bonhomme. It can't be him. At least, not directly it's not.'

'How do you mean?'

'Look at the most recent entries, man. He used his credit card the day Hannah disappeared. Twice, in fact: morning and afternoon. And, first thing the next day, too.'

The others followed Danskin's train of thought.

'Look where he used it. A petrol station in King's Lynn. Sainsbury's, in Norwich. And the Bell Inn - Norwich, again. He's been in bastarding East Anglia for days.'

Even as they looked at the live statement, another charge pinged its way onto Max Bonhomme's account.

Hands of an Angel Personal Services. Lowestoft.

'Frigging hell. He's shagging a Tractor Girl as we speak.'

He sank back into his chair, hand to forehead.

'We're back to square one.'

**

A stunned silence, like that following news of a sudden bereavement, settled over the bullpen.

Todd Robson chewed his bottom lip. Ravi sat frozen in time, fingers hovering above his keyboard. Sue's eyes glazed, Gavin shook his head, and Stephen Danskin seemed to shrivel like a week-old party balloon.

Lyall Parker stepped up to the plate. 'Nae bother, boys – we'll just get oor heads up and go back to our previous leads.'

His words roused the group out of their inertia.

Ravi responded first. 'Okay. I'll get back to the rest of the John's on the agency books. The good news is, it looks like we can rule one out. That's progress.'

'Good. Gavin, you and Treblecock get yourselves off to the cave place, as planned. At the very least, talk to the Bishops. See if they've got owt on this Morton character.'

Lyall looked towards Danskin. Saw a semblance of spirit lift within him. 'Does this change your mind about bringing in a profiler, sir?'

Danskin shook his head. 'No, it doesn't. Not in the slightest. I've got the best team a man could wish for. We'll solve this. We've got to, man.'

Ryan raised his eyes from the floor. He tried to gather strength as he sought inspiration from somewhere, anywhere. His eyes settled on the crime board. Alongside it, a hasty sketch of a triangle.

He stood. 'Sir, I'm going to try something. I know someone who might be able to help. Not a profiler, exactly, but someone who'll understand the psyche of folk involved in vice.'

He rose to his feet. 'I've a call to make.'

**

In the lift lobby, away from eavesdroppers who might identify his informant from the conversation, Ryan made the most important call of his, Stephen Danskin's, and Hannah's life.

'Olivia, this is Detective Constable Ryan Jarrod.'

After a moment's thought, the name registered with Hadley Kutz's secretary. 'Hello, Ryan. How are you? I hav…'

'Sorry to interrupt, but this is vitally important. It really is a matter of life and death.'

'Oh, are things that bad? I'm so sorry, Ryan. Please, don't do anything silly. I can give you a few numbers to call…'

'No, man. You don't understand. I need to speak to Dr Kutz. He's my last hope.'

'He's on holiday, Ryan. I told you.'

'Get a message to him.'

He heard the tone in Olivia's voice. 'I will do no such thing. Not given his family circumstance. No, I won't.'

Ryan took a deep breath. He'd have to tell her. 'Look, this is police business. I'm ringing in my official capacity. I need to pick his brains. Urgently.'

'I'll get him to ring you as soon as he gets back. I promise. The first thing I'll do is make sure it's the first thing he does. I can't do any more than that.'

'Shut up and listen.' He heard the intake of breath at the other end. 'I said it's a matter of life and death, and it is. I can't say more except it's Hannah's life I'm talking about. She's in danger.'

He heard Olivia gasp.

The Girl on the Quay

'So, you see, it can't wait until Dr Kutz gets back from Germany.'

There was no reply.

'Olivia?'

'I don't understand. Dr Kutz isn't in Germany. What makes you think that?'

Ryan sucked air between his teeth. 'You told me he was visiting family. His mother. At death's door, you said.'

'She is, but not in Germany.'

'Kutz is a German name, isn't it?'

Olivia knew where Ryan was coming from now.

'Oh, I see. Yes, it is, I believe. But Dr Kutz takes his name from the original Kutz line, going back centuries.'

'Listen, just get a message to him, wherever the hell he is. Please.'

'Seeing it's you, I'll try. But not yet. It's the middle of the night over there.'

He knew he shouldn't ask. Knew he'd extend the conversation interminably. But it was too late. The words were out his mouth and he couldn't force them back. 'Where the hell is he, like?'

'Dr Kutz is in Mexico, the land of his ancestors. He's Mayan. Didn't you know?'

CHAPTER FORTY-ONE

Ryan shuffled back to the bullpen like an escapee from a Zombie apocalypse.

He was aware of activity going on around him, conscious people were talking, but they may as well have been naked and speaking in tongues for all the notice he took.

He felt his way onto his seat like an octogenarian. Stared into space. His eyes roamed the room, focusing on nothing, until they came to rest on a sheet of flipchart blu-tacked to the wall.

'Sir,' he said quietly. 'Can I have a word?'

Once inside Danskin's office, the DCI waited patiently. 'I take it you didn't come in here for a break, did you?'

'Hmmm? Oh, no.'

'What is it?'

'I know who the Mayan is.'

Danskin jumped to his feet. 'What?'

'It's someone I know. Well, sort of.'

You know him? Who, man, who?'

Their eyes met. 'Hadley Kutz.'

The name didn't register. Not at first. Danskin furrowed his forehead. Raised an eyebrow. 'Name rings a bell.'

'It should do, sir. He's a clinical psychologist. A sex therapist, to be exact. And, he's the man who gave me the information on the sex trade in the first place.'

'Your 'triangle man'? The bloke who knows all there is to know about prostitution? The man who knows every statistic going about its demographics? The one who knows where they originate from?'

'That's him, sir.'

'Don't just sit there, man. Where do we find him?'

Ryan remained seated. Shook his head. 'That's just it, sir. We don't. He's in Mexico.'

**

Squad cars and forensics swarmed into the grounds of Dr Hadley Kutz's practice in Low Fell like flies to a dog turd. They removed every piece of equipment, every morsel of IT, every file in the building. They even took Olivia who, for the first time in her life, was rendered speechless.

Chamley was hauled in for another interview. This time, he was more forthcoming. With his nemesis identified, out the country, and with every port and airport in the land primed for his return, he 'Sang like the proverbial canary,' as Lyall Parker described it.

'The weight of the world's off the man's shoulders,' Lyall added. 'He knows he'll go down for the charges levelled against him, but his brief also knows they'll mount a strong defence based on threat to life. Plus, Chamley's now assisting us fully. The brief's banking on leniency.'

'Bastard doesn't deserve it. He's in it so deep he'll need snorkel and flippers. Any judge worth his salt will recognise that.'

He put his head in hands, mirroring the pose of Ryan Jarrod next to him.

'We've lost her haven't we sir?' Ryan sobbed.

For the first time, Danskin acknowledged it as fact. 'Aye. We've lost her, son.'

**

Parker ordered Ryan home. Danskin, too. The rest of the team would tie up the loose ends. Kutz, obviously, must have seen Hannah behind the bar of the Whipped Cream club. He'd made the connection between her and Ryan. He knew Ryan was CID so, by Hannah was, too.

Running scared in the knowledge the police were closing in on his cartel, the Mayan arranged for Hannah's kidnap. Probably killed her there-and-then, but made it look like a hostage situation. Made it look just like the others.

The others. Parker found their demise a problem. Why would the Mayan, Hadley Kutz, get rid of his greatest assets?

Lou Chamley provided the key. More mitigation for the judge to consider. Chamley revealed Van Eyck was coercing the women into returning to him. It was all set up. Ferry tickets, the works. Rather than lose the girls to Van Eyck, Kutz had them killed. Simple as. And, it served as a warning to any other girl who thought about treading the same path.

Wearily, Lyall Parker filed the papers away. Case closed.

All that remained was to locate the body of Hannah Graves.

**

Ryan tossed and turned in his bed. The night dragged on forever. He checked his bedside clock. The green glow told him it was not yet two forty-five.

He pulled the bedclothes over his head.

Five minutes later, he threw them aside.

In the glow of the clock, a small object stood on his bedside cabinet. He reached for it and cradled Hannah's perfume against his cheek.

Ten minutes later, with sleep finally threatening to overcome him, the Blaydon Races ended all hope of it.

'Have you any idea what time it is, man?' he groaned almost before the phone reached his lips.

'I do. It's nine p.m.'

Ryan rubbed his eyes. 'What? Who is this?'

'Hadley Kutz.'

Electricity shot though his body and jerked him wide awake.

'Where is she?'

'I don't know, Ryan. I really don't.'

'Don't mess with me, Kutz. Not now. Not after everything. Of course you know where she is. You had her snatched. You killed her.'

The silence deafened Ryan. Finally, he thought he heard a sigh.

'I promise you, I don't know where she is. I didn't take her. I didn't take any of them. I'm not an evil man, you know. Not really. I help people. People like you, Ryan. You know I tried to help you and your girl.'

'You are the most evil bastard I know,' he hissed. 'Hannah never hurt anyone. She didn't deserve this.'

'I know. That's why I'm calling you. Even now, I'm here to help you.'

'You're bloody mad, do you know that?'

'On the contrary. I'm perfectly sane.'

'Then, why did you take her?'

This time, he was sure he did hear a sigh. It sounded beyond sad. Remorseful, even.

'I feel responsible, but I didn't take her. That's why I'm calling you. As soon as I got Olivia's message, I understood everything. It was obvious. It was clear as day.'

'Cut the crap and tell me where she is!'

'I genuinely can't. But, I know someone who might.'

None of this made any sense. Ryan shook his head. Tried to disperse the fug inside. Impatient as he was, he knew Kutz pulled the strings of the conversation. All he could do was listen to what the Mayan had to say. Then, he would fly to Mexico himself, if necessary, and hunt the bastard down.

As if reading his mind, Kutz said, 'Listen carefully, Ryan Jarrod, because this is the last you'll ever hear from me. Tomorrow, I shall be in Venezuela. I'm sure you know there's no extradition treaty between the UK and Venezuela. This is our last chance to find your lady friend, alive or dead. Are you ready?'

Ryan had made it to his bedroom door. 'I don't want to rely on memory. I need a pen and paper. Can I put you on hold? Please, don't hang up. I won't be a minute.'

'Don't worry, Ryan. I'm not going anywhere. I've all the time in the world…'

Ryan reached for the mute button. Before he hit it, Kutz finished his sentence.

'...unfortunately, I think that's one thing Hannah hasn't.'

**

Ryan had no intention of fetching a pen and paper. Instead, with Hadley Kutz on mute, he made straight for the landline.

Stephen Danskin picked up on the second ring.

'Sir, don't say a word. Just listen. Hadley Kutz is on my mobile. He says he didn't take Hannah. I don't know if I believe him, but he's about to talk. I'm going to put him on speaker phone. I'm going to leave this line open, too. Set your mobile to record. Whatever he says will be the best, possibly the only, evidence we get.'

Danskin hadn't spoken but Ryan could tell he'd understood by the urgent breathing.

'Sir, I'm coming off mute now.'

He lay the landline handset on the table next to his mobile.

'Okay. I'm ready. Please, be quick. Remember what you said: Hannah doesn't have long.' In his heart of hearts, he already felt they were too late.

'It will take as long as it takes, young man. I want to tell you something about myself first. Something that will make you see that I was correct when I said I'm not a bad man.'

Ryan beat down the urge to tell the Mayan to cut to the chase. He couldn't afford Kutz to hang up on him. Not now.

'When I was about your age, I moved to Miami. It was a whole new world for a small-town Hispanic boy from Yucatan. Miami was free. Liberal. It drew me in. I developed an addiction. Not drugs. I never did drugs. It was an addiction called satyriasis. Have you heard of it?'

'No.'

'Put simply, I was a male nymphomaniac. I slept with any woman who moved. It cost me the love of my life. When Carmel left me, I knew I had to do something about it. I saw someone. The way you saw me.'

Ryan closed his eyes. He didn't want Danskin to know about his little professional sessions. So, he asked, 'What happened?'

'I was cured. That's what happened. I was also fascinated by the therapy; how I could be cured just through talking. I looked into the subject. I thought, 'I can do that.' So, I did. I came to England, qualified, and you know the rest.'

'Can we talk about Hannah now?'

'All in good time. I'm getting there. Very soon, I realised there were many others out there with the same issues I once had. Men with urges. Uncontrollable urges. I realised what sex, any kind of sex, meant to so many. They didn't want love – not like you and Hannah – they just wanted sex.'

The Mayan stopped talking, as if he'd been transported to a different realm. Just as Ryan feared the call had been disconnected, Kutz spoke again.

'Women would make appointments with me, too. Some were ex-prostitutes wanting to go straight. They'd found the 'love of their life', or so they thought, and realised they must change. Some of their stories were horrific. Beatings, rape, forced abortions if they fell pregnant. Really, really horrific abuse.'

Ryan couldn't stop himself. 'Yet not horrific enough to prevent you from following suit.'

Kutz tutted down the line. 'You are absolutely wrong about that. You see, I found out many of these women had been lifted from their homes across Europe with promises of a steady job. They were promised the earth. What they got, was hell.'

'So why capitalise on their misery?'

'You still don't understand, do you? Yes, I spotted an opportunity. An opportunity to become rich. I already knew men would stop at nothing to get what they wanted. They'd pay anything to feed their addiction. So, I provided them with it.'

'Exactly.'

'Ah, but it was all about the girls' welfare. I did it all for them. I emancipated them.'

Ryan's laugh was one of incredulity.

'Don't mock, Ryan. You see, I bought the girls from squalor, filth, and slavery. I set them free. I brought them to a new land. With Orchid Petals, I didn't take their earnings. They kept every penny for themselves. They lived a life of luxury, far removed from the pimps and addicts and thugs they'd been used to. That's why they stay with me.'

'Except they didn't stay with you. They disappeared.'

'That was my greed. Greed, and Luuk Van Eyck.'

'Tell me about Van Eyck.'

'He supplied me with the girls. He identified them from brothels in Amsterdam. Some, Berlin, but mainly Amsterdam. I paid him, he shipped them to me. Except, I got greedy. I tried to fleece him. I stopped paying the going rate.'

'And he took back his girls, demanded you paid a ransom and, when you didn't, he killed them.'

Kutz laughed. Ryan thought he'd never stop laughing. Eventually, he did.

'That's what I thought. I told Olivia I was going home to see my mother.'

'You never went, did you? I thought she was sick.'

'She's certainly not very well. In fact, she's so unwell she's been dead eleven years.' He laughed again.

'No, I wanted to see for myself what Van Eyck was up to, without the distraction of my practice. I took a more hands-on approach, which is how I came to find the ransom notes. I was determined to ignore them. There's no way I was going to bow to the Dutchman.'

'I need to know about Hannah. Time's running out.'

'Ah yes, Hannah. You see, I knew you and your colleagues had been sniffing around; that you'd caught the scent. When I saw Hannah in the club, I knew it was serious. That's when

I knew my little enterprise had run its course. That's when I did return to Mexico.'

Ryan rubbed his brow. 'I still don't get it.'

'You're not stupid, Ryan, and neither's your girl. I'm sure between the pair of you, you must have worked it out.'

Silence told the Mayan he hadn't.

'I'll spell it out for you, shall I? When Olivia told me you wanted to talk, and that Hannah had gone missing, it was as if a light came on. The blackmailer knew who Hannah was. He knew I wasn't going to pay for the release of my girls, not to Van Eyck. So, he tried someone else. He tried Hannah, and he tried you.'

'You say 'he'. Who's he?'

'The one man I revealed Hannah's identity to. The one man with a chip on his shoulder. The one man who believes he's worth more than he earns. The one man who thinks he's better than the cockroach he is.'

Ryan knew who he was going to stay before Kutz named him.

'Lou Chamley,' Ryan said.

'You're a clever young man, Ryan Jarrod. I'm sure your lady friend is equally bright. With whatever Hannah discovered at my club, and your very capable brain, you'll find enough evidence to nail the buck-toothed snake.'

Ryan's brain swam. He'd solved the case, but he was no closer to finding Hannah.

'So, you see, Ryan Jarrod, I really am not a bad man. I truly hope you find your lady friend and, if you do, I shall raise a tequila in your honour.'

Seconds before the line went dead, Hadley Kutz spoke to Ryan for the final time.

'Goodbye, Mr Jarrod. I wish you well.'

CHAPTER FORTY-TWO

An army of uniform cops descended on Lou Chamley's Lamesley home, prepared to dismantle it brick-by-brick if necessary. Sniffer dogs patrolled the grounds, while mechanical diggers stood by, patient as vultures, should excavation be required.

Lou Chamley himself was cuffed and bundled unceremoniously into the back of a car, the cop with the cuffs ensuring he smashed his head against the roof as he entered. Todd Robson would have been proud.

As soon as they got the call, Robson himself, O'Hara, and Nigel Trebilcock raced to Forth Street. Alerted by Craggs, the lads from the Prince Bishop force had already searched Russ Morton's cave, found no sign of the man, so they'd despatched a coastguard helicopter with instructions to locate his launch but not intervene.

A mile out from Seaton Carew the chopper crew spotted it adrift and, presumably, out of fuel. They had a clear view into the Pescador. Morton wasn't aboard. The working assumption was he'd made a swim for it and perished at sea. As he was no longer a person of specific interest, Danskin's men left the search for his body to the Prince Bishops.

The minute they arrived back at the station, Robson and Treblecock worked alongside Ravi Sangar in a review of potential locations where Chamley may have held his hostages.

Gavin O'Hara and Sue Nairn, meanwhile, sifted through evidence as they prepared the case against him.

Stephen Danskin and Lyall Parker took to the custody suite in the bowels of the station to interview Chamley while Ryan Jarrod sat powerless and impotent, tapping the surface of a desk like a drum majorette on Whizz.

One hour passed without an update from Danskin and Parker. One hour became two. Two segued into three. Still the interview rumbled on. Ryan's stomach felt gripped by a vice. Every muscle, every sinew, ached from the tension.

Thirty minutes later, Danskin walked into the bullpen. He looked like death. Lyall supported him by the elbow.

'Anything?' Sue asked.

Danskin shook his head. Parker provided an update to say there was no update.

'He's barely whispered a word. The bastard's sticking to the 'No comment' line. His lawyer's got his lips stuck up with superglue.'

'You've had him nearly four hours, man. He's got to have said something.' Ryan's plea was desperate. Agonizing.

Lyall Parker shook his head. 'He spoke only once. We played him the recording of your conversation with Kutz. He looked like he'd been hit by a ton of bricks. You could tell he knew, then, that we had him. His brief asked for an adjournment. We refused, of course. It was the only time he veered from *nae comment*.'

Lyall looked at his notes. 'His exact words were, 'You're taking the word of a self-confessed gangmaster over me? You'd better find her body before you accuse me of such things.'

Ryan saw Danskin wince before Lyall continued.

'His lawyer had a stern word and reminded him no' to comment. Just as well. The guv'nor was aboot to disembowel him if he said anything else.'

Lyall shepherded Stephen towards the coffee machine. Sue Nairn and Treblecock shared an empathetic look, while the others returned to their research with renewed determination.

Ryan had to do something. The Mayan's words played on a loop inside his brain. *'With whatever Hannah discovered at my club, and your very capable brain, you'll find enough evidence to nail the buck-toothed snake.'*

He called up Hannah's reports on a PC, and it smacked him right in the face.

The names had been there all along. They just hadn't meant anything. Five minutes of rudimentary research and a cross-check with John Craggs's report from Ijmuiden confirmed it.

'Sir, I think I've cracked it.'

**

'What are we looking at, Jarrod?' Danskin was at his shoulder in a flash.

'It's one of the images Hannah snapped from the office of the Whipped Cream club.'

'And?'

They were all around him now, eager to discover what Ryan had unearthed.

'These are the pukka employees of the club, not the pseudo 'volunteers.' Specifically, it's a list of the security personnel at the club, and the chaperones for the agency girls.'

'What's the significance?'

'Here.' He highlighted two names. 'Among the chaperones, we have two blokes, Anthony and Aidan, who have the same surname. They're Anthony and Aidan Haines.'

'Brothers?'

'Yep. And they have a third brother by the name of Adam. Ring any bells?'

The squad shook their heads as one, so Ryan continued.

'Our man in Ijmuiden, Craggs, investigated the boat the Mayan sent to rendezvous with the Stellendam. It was crewed by Russ Morton, John Manville, and…'

'…Adam Haines,' Danskin finished.

'Precisely. Chamley recruited them all. They worked for him, not the Mayan. What if Chamley used the Haines brothers to target the very girls the Mayan expected them to protect?'

'Bloody hell, man. This could be it. Everybody, I want everything you have on the Haines family.'

It didn't take Ravi long.

'Sir. I might know where he kept them.'

They crowded Sangar the way they had Ryan.

'Anthony Haines owns a storage facility. I've got it on Google maps. It's in North Shields.'

The satellite view showed row upon row of shipping containers stacked on reclaimed industrial wasteland, bounded by twelve foot high barbed-wire fence and protected by sturdy metal gates.

'It's certainly a possibility, and it's roughly the direction of travel the van took with Radka.' For the first time in days, Danskin sounded upbeat.

'It's more than that, sir,' Ryan added. 'Look at the location again. It's less than half a mile from where the shift worker reported a white van wiping out the wing mirrors of a line of parked cars.'

Ryan and Danskin locked eyes.

'Let's go get her, Jarrod.'

**

Vans of a different white hue, these emblazoned with the yellow and blue checks of police vehicles, raced along the quayside; vans with sirens blaring and lights ablaze.

A fleet of cars followed, whilst Danskin's own vehicle preceded the caravan. Danskin had already scrambled the police Eurocopter, and one of the two Tactical Flight Officer's aboard radioed in to say it was on its approach.

'Deploy thermal imaging,' Danskin ordered into the radio. 'We haven't time to search every container. Report any hot spots immediately.'

Ryan, sitting alongside Danskin with Lyall and Todd in the rear, pointed skywards. 'There's the chopper, sir.'

Danskin ducked his head so he could see the Eurocopter as it circled the site. He saw it tilt as it swooped lower and veered left.

'Do you have anything? Check the containers. Check every one of 'em. Check the bushes. Check every bloody thing there. We'll be with you in two.'

Danskin's car took a bend on two wheels and skidded to a halt in a hail of gravel. The gates were locked and bolted.

'The MoE guys are in the first van, sir,' Parker reassured him. 'They'll mobilise the cutting gear as soon as they get here.'

The Eurocopter stopped circling. It hovered in situ, vacillating unsteadily in the wind.

'You got something?' Danskin asked.

Despite the engine noise, the pilot's reply came through clear and unequivocal.

'Yes, sir. We've got a hotspot. If it's her, she's in an orange container fourth row in, three down. First two are blue. She's in the next. Repeat, it's orange.'

Danskin and Ryan yelled in triumph.

The pilot spoke again. 'She's not moving, sir. The thermal's cooler than I'd expect to see. She's in trouble.'

Danskin reversed the car, floored the accelerator and, in a screech of wheelspin and cloud of dirt, drove straight at the wire fence.

The fence buckled and gave away. The vehicle's offside tyres exploded as barbed threads wrapped themselves around the rubber but Danskin sped on, sparks flying as metal hubs scarred the surface.

Two vans and an ambulance careened through the gap they'd created, the rest of the fleet closing in on them.

Ryan was out the car before Danskin applied the brakes. By the time the car drew to a halt, he was banging on the container walls. 'Hannah, it's Ryan. I've come for you. We're all here.'

Danskin and Todd joined him. 'Hannah,' Danskin screamed. 'Hang in there. We're coming for you now.'

The Method of Entry crew started unloading their kit, cutters and blowtorches.

The Girl on the Quay

'We haven't time, man. Hurry up,' Danskin implored.

Ryan looked up at the chopper. He could see the TFOs in the cockpit, their faces as taught as his own. He opened comms with the chopper. 'Where is she?'

'Right hand rear corner.'

Ryan turned to Danskin. 'Sir, authorise ballistic entry.'

'What? No way.'

'Listen, you heard them: she's running out of time. It's the only way. Hannah's in the rear corner. As far from the doors as she can get. The cutters won't get through in time.'

Danskin dithered. Caught between a rock and a hard place, he was paralysed. Ryan made the decision for him and radioed the nearest van.

'MoE team, we're going for a ballistic entry. Repeat, ballistic entry.'

Stephen Danskin stood motionless, the only part of his body to move were his eyes which blinked rapidly.

Parker comforted him.

Todd Robson whispered to Ryan. 'That was some call, kiddo.'

'It was the only call.'

The MoE team busied themselves. In minutes, they'd primed a small device just sufficient to deliver a controlled explosion. Just enough.

The sound was cacophonous. Ryan though his ear drums had imploded. All he could hear afterwards was a ringing as if he had his head against a fire alarm.

But, it worked. He saw the door vibrate and shudder then, as dust settled around it, the door fell inwards.

Ryan gave a victorious roar.

The left-hand wall fell outwards. Then, like the house in Buster Keaton's Steamboat Bill, the right-hand wall followed. With nothing to hold it up, the metal roof of the shipping container plummeted downwards, down towards the stricken Hannah Graves.

Ryan saw it all in slow motion. He ran towards the container and was inside the ruined shell almost before the roof hit the deck.

Amidst the dust and dirt and metal shrapnel, Ryan's eyes sought Hannah. The roof had fallen at an angle. There was a gap between floor and ceiling of no more than a foot.

Ryan saw Hannah lying in the gap, only her head visible.

Slow motion became fast forward. He slid across the surface, prostrated himself alongside Hannah. He couldn't get in beside her. He couldn't reach her chest to check for a heartbeat. Couldn't reach her wrist to feel for a pulse.

All he could do was put his ear to her lips to check she was breathing.

'You were only supposed to blow the bloody doors off,' she whispered.

**

The paramedics hauled Hannah out of the rubble. They attached a saline drip, had another two on stand-by, and checked her over.

She was bloodied and bruised and weak as a baby, but dehydration was her only enemy. With the drip attached, it was an enemy soon to be defeated.

Hannah refused a stretcher. The ambulance was only yards away. She'd make it. Ryan took her arm to escort her.

'I'll take her now, sir,' the paramedic insisted.

'Leave them,' Danskin said. 'Let him do it. They need it.'

The paramedic stood aside.

Ryan helped her to the doors of the ambulance. They turned to face each other; hands clasped. She tilted her head. Lips dry and cracked as an old ceiling sought his.

Hannah pulled away. Smiled up to him.

Ryan kissed her again. Their lips locked. He lifted her off her feet. Swung her round. She ran her hands through his hair.

'For Christ's sake, you two,' Todd Robson joked, 'Get a room, will you?'

Ryan broke away from Hannah's embrace.

'You know what, Todd, as soon as they've checked her over, that's exactly what we're going to do.'

****

Author's note:

Thank you for taking the time to read *The Girl On The Quay* - it means a lot to me.

If you did enjoy it, please tell your family, friends, and colleagues. Word of mouth is an author's best friend so the more people who know, the greater my appreciation.

I love seeing your feedback so please leave a review of your experience reading the second Ryan Jarrod novel.

If you'd like news of the next book in the series, you can follow me on:

Twitter - @seewhy59
Facebook - @colin.youngman.author

Thanks again.
Colin

****

About the author:

Colin had his first written work published at the age of 9 when a contribution to children's comic *Sparky* brought him the rich rewards of a 10/- Postal Order and a transistor radio.

He was smitten by the writing bug and has gone on to have his work feature in publications for young adults, sports magazines, national newspapers and travel guides before he moved to his first love: fiction.

Colin previously worked as a senior executive in the public sector. He lives in Northumberland, north-east England, and is an avid supporter of Newcastle United (don't laugh), a keen follower of Durham County Cricket Club, and has a family interest in the City of Newcastle Gymnastics Academy.

You can read more of his work (e-book and paperback) exclusive to Amazon:

The Angel Falls *(Ryan Jarrod Book One)*
The Doom Brae Witch
Alley Rat
DEAD Heat
Twists*

(*An anthology)

****

Printed in Great Britain
by Amazon